HOLDING PATTERN

HOLDING PATTERN

by

MAGGIE FRIEDENBERG

Philadelphia, PA

This is a work of fiction. All of the characters, organizations, publications, and events portrayed or mentioned in this novel are either products of the author's imagination or are used fictitiously.

First edition: 2022

For information, contact Sandy Toes Press,
PO Box 11515, Philadelphia, PA 19116

Cover designed by MiblArt
Author photo by Elizabeth Friedenberg

Library of Congress Cataloging In-Publication Data

Names: Friedenberg, Maggie 1974– author

Title: Holding Pattern: Novel / Maggie Friedenberg

Description: First edition / Philadelphia: Sandy Toes Press, 2022

Identifiers: LCCN 2022904176 / ISBN 979-8-9857545-0-6 (paperback) / ISBN 979-8-9857545-1-3 (ebook)

Subjects: Realistic – Fiction / Contemporary – Fiction / Romance – Fiction / Infertility – Fiction / Miscarriage – Fiction / Divorce – Fiction / Addiction – Fiction / Cancer – Fiction

for Jimmy... finally

A NOTE FROM THE AUTHOR

Content warning: this story contains a scene
in which one of the characters experiences
a pregnancy loss (miscarriage). I understand this
content may be emotionally distressing for some
readers. If this applies to you, please know I am
deeply sorry for the grief you've experienced,
and I've done my best to deal with the subject
with sensitivity and respect. Other sensitive
issues addressed within the story include drug
and alcohol addiction and recovery, infertility,
infidelity, divorce, illness, and death.

As a lifelong reader, I've always processed difficult
emotions best through stories, and hope my stories
might provide the same opportunity to others.

SPRING 2005

It was nine o'clock. The house was quiet. Logan tiptoed through the living room where, only hours before, dozens of party guests had gathered to celebrate his eighth birthday. Now the guests had gone, his parents were in their bedroom watching TV, and Logan was about to embark on a secret mission.

Search and rescue.

He tiptoed through the kitchen and out the back door. Once outside, he slid his feet into the sneakers he'd carried with him, wanting to stay as quiet as possible. Cool night air danced upon his skin as he moved through the shadows.

At the end of his block, Logan froze as a passing car threw its light upon him. His heart pounded. Should he turn back? Was it too dangerous out here, alone, no grown-ups in sight?

Logan shook off the fear and continued. The mission was too important, the subject of his search too precious to let anything stand in his way. He sped along, focused on the task at hand, until finally he reached the edge of the park.

Earlier today, his mom and grandma had brought him and his friends to this park to play, while the other guests stayed behind at the house, doing whatever boring things grown-ups did. The children played games until his mom and grandma were exhausted and let them run wild. That's when it happened.

Logan had been playing with his new red remote controlled airplane, a gift from his parents that very morning. It soared on broad shiny wings, higher and higher, until it crashed into the branches of a tree, far above his head.

He'd glanced around to make sure nobody else had seen his blunder. Logan considered climbing the tree right then, but he heard his mom calling out that it was time to go. He couldn't let her know what he'd done. He stashed the remote in a nearby bush, promising himself he'd return as soon as he had a chance to retrieve the airplane.

Now it was time to get it back.

-1-

Richard walked through the park, hands in his pockets, lost in thought. Thin fog settled in among the bushes and trees. His breathing became labored as the path began to incline toward the tree-lined area of the trail that would lead him towards home. He made another silent commitment to return to the gym, one of a thousand promises he'd made to himself since Melinda divorced him over two years ago. The woman's face appeared in his mind, her slim features and pale gray eyes. As he began to relive their separation, his thoughts turned from tender to tormented.

He was in the middle of the incline when he heard the noise.

Richard was sure it came from right beside him. A muffled sob, the faintest sound of distress. He stopped and looked around, wondering what manner of thing made such a noise. His heartbeat quickening, he began walking again.

To his right stood a large grove of trees, a mixture of ash and elm, some as high as the older houses in the surrounding neighborhood. As he hurried past, he heard the sound yet again. This time, a timid plea followed.

"Hello?" the small voice ventured. Richard froze. The area surrounding the park was relatively safe. It wasn't fear that held him in place, but the overwhelming sense that he had just heard a child's voice.

"I need help. I'm stuck in the tree." Certain now that it was a child, he walked to the edge of the grove, looking around. The fog had settled on the hillside, mixing with the dark of the night.

Richard's question was as tentative as the small voice. "What...uh, what tree are you in?" He looked up, unable to see where the foliage ended and the night sky began. He rested his hand against the smooth hard bark of a massive ash.

"I'm over here," the voice said. Richard turned, walking to his right.

"No! The other way."

"This way?" Richard asked, pointing. If he turned left, he'd be facing back the way he had come, and there were no trees there.

"Behind you. By the bench?" Richard turned around. Sure enough, a wooden park bench sat just below the low limbs of an ancient elm.

He looked up to see a pair of small feet dangling from one of the branches, about five feet above his head. This was a young kid, probably less than ten years old. What the hell was he doing out this late at night? Where were his parents?

"You'll have to climb down. I'll be right below you."

"I can't," the child replied.

"Sure you can. You got yourself up there, right? Just turn around and come down backwards."

The kid didn't answer. Instead, he began crying again.

Richard sighed. How was he going to get this kid down?

Natalie opened the front door of her sister's house, hoping to slip out without her family's traditional long goodbye. "Goodnight," she called, putting one foot out the door.

"Natalie! Don't go yet," her sister Christine called back from the dining room. She got up from the table and went into the kitchen. Natalie's parents and brother-in-law met her at the door, giving goodbye hugs and kisses, wishing her *happy birthday* yet again.

Christine emerged with a grocery bag full of leftovers. "Here you go," she said, handing it to Natalie and giving her a hug.

Right, because I can't even manage to feed myself. "Thanks," Natalie said, forcing a smile.

As the rest of them drifted back to the dining room, Natalie's mother, Kathy, took a step forward.

"Here. Just think about it." She handed Natalie a business card.

Natalie glanced at it. "What is this?"

"It's a couples therapist. I was talking with one of the other teachers—"

"Mom." Natalie tried not to roll her eyes. "I wish you weren't out there talking about me to complete strangers."

"She's not a complete stranger. I told you, she's someone I work with. I mentioned you and Ben were having some problems—"

"Mom, we're separated."

"Well, that's a pretty big problem."

Natalie stared at her mother, unsure whether to laugh, cry, or tell her off.

"I'm just so worried about you. And Ben."

"Hey, Mom, how about next time you guys invite Ben to Sunday dinner, instead of me?"

Natalie walked out the door and got into her car, crumpling the card in her fist. She shook her head

and groaned before turning the key to start the engine. Driving away from her sister's house was a relief.

When she'd first left Ben, her family was convinced she was having some sort of mental breakdown. Or maybe a long overdue teenage rebellion. Natalie was always the good little sister, always doing what everyone expected of her. She and Ben had been together since high school. She wouldn't wake up one day and decide to leave him. And yet she had, or at least that was how things appeared to them.

Now, more than three months later, her sisters both avoided the subject, pretending everything was okay. But her mother was certain the next self-help book or exercise class or antidepressant she recommended would be just the thing to cure Natalie of thinking she was better off alone.

She would skip these family dinners altogether if not for her nieces and nephews. *My favorite people,* she thought. The kids were still happy to see her. They piled into her lap and smothered her with hugs. Gave her a reason to go on breathing.

As she turned her car down the street that would take her to the interstate, she noticed a man standing beneath a tree at the edge of a small park, staring into the canopy overhead. He turned in her direction, raising his hand as if to flag her down.

Natalie slowed the car to a crawl. Taking a closer look, she glimpsed a small, sneaker-clad foot dangling from one of the branches. In her own neighborhood, in the city, she would have kept driving past. But here in her sister's suburban town, it was rare to see someone out at this hour, let alone anything as strange as a small person in a tree. She stopped the car and lowered the window.

"You guys okay?"

The man took a step in her direction. "There's a little kid stuck up here. He's scared and won't come down." He tossed up his hands, exasperated. "I'm not sure what to do."

Common sense told her to keep driving. After all, this could be a scheme to lure women drivers away from their vehicles. But she was compelled to help the little boy. *I must have a death wish*, she thought as she exited the car.

She approached the tree. The boy's crying reached her ears before she saw his face. He was perched on a wide branch several feet above her head.

"What happened?" she asked the man. He was a bit older than she was, maybe mid-forties, with dark hair and eyes, his mustache and goatee flecked with gray. He stood a few inches taller than Natalie. Not bad-looking, for an older guy.

"I was walking past and found him here, about two minutes before you pulled up. I tried to tell him how to get down, but he just started crying." His voice was deep and resonant, with more than a hint of Southern drawl.

Natalie called to the boy, "What are you doing up there?"

"I lost my airplane. I came up here to get it, and now I can't get down."

"Where are your parents?"

"At home. In bed. I snuck out." His voice cracked as he tried to hold back a sob.

"It's going to be all right. We'll get you down. Okay?"

The boy nodded.

Natalie eyed the park bench, wondering how sturdy it was. "My name's Natalie. What's yours?" she asked, taking a step up.

"Logan."

"What grade are you in?"

"Second."

"Second grade! So you're, hm, seven? Or eight?"

"Eight. It's my birthday."

"Oh, happy birthday!" She pointed to the airplane. "Was this your present?"

He sniffled. "Yes."

"I had a birthday, too. Last week." She pulled down on the thick limb below Logan's, testing its stability. It didn't budge. She hoped it was strong enough to step onto without breaking it.

"How old are you?"

"A lot older than eight." She grinned at Logan, and he smiled back. Lifting her right foot, she began to pull herself up into the tree.

"Um, is that a good idea?" the man asked from behind her. "That branch doesn't look very strong."

She turned her head, narrowing her eyes at him. "Is that a comment about my weight?"

"Oh, no… I mean…" he stammered. "Maybe we should call the fire department or something."

"I'm perfectly capable of helping this boy down."

"Well, he got up there himself, I think he could probably get himself down if we tell him how."

"He's terrified. He'll never come down alone."

"I just don't want to have to climb up there and get both of y'all down."

"You know what? I don't think Logan needs *your* help. Why don't you just go?" She made a dismissive motion with her hand.

To her surprise, instead of firing back, he laughed. "Okay, Miss Natalie. If you're so sure, I'd like to see you do it." She turned away again. "I'm Richard, by the way… Richard Rung."

Natalie finished pulling her body up onto the lowest limb and crept forward until she reached the tree's trunk. She stood, one hand on the trunk for support, and turned back in Richard's direction.

"Pleased ta meetcha," she replied in an exaggerated imitation of his Southern drawl. She turned towards the boy. "Logan? I need you to trust me, okay?"

Richard couldn't take his eyes away from the soft curves of Natalie's body as she climbed into the tree to rescue the boy, who was still sniffling, arms tight around his treasured toy. He stepped back from the tree and lit a cigarette, taking a deep inhale, blowing smoke towards the sky. Somehow, Natalie managed to perch herself right below the boy in the tree as he watched.

Richard marveled that the bough hadn't snapped—she was a big girl, not that it bothered him. He'd always had an appreciation for the ample beauty of curvaceous women. Hell, he had an appreciation for all women. But Natalie was quite lovely. Honey-blond hair rippled down her back in shiny waves. Her cheekbones were high, her blue eyes warm and tender, especially when she talked to the boy, as she was doing now. Richard couldn't make out what she was saying, but he could see the boy's body relax.

After a few minutes, she spoke to him. "Richard?" He liked hearing her say his name. "Can you hold on to Logan's plane while we climb down?"

"Sure." He reached towards Natalie, who lowered the plane into his hands. "Careful now," he said, standing beneath them.

Natalie put her hand out for Logan, who took it and slid down onto the branch where she stood. Together, they inched their way down, Logan holding tight to her hand. Richard would have loved to know what she'd said to him to get him to stop being afraid and follow her, but he had a feeling any member of the male species would follow after Natalie without a second thought.

Natalie eased her way onto the park bench while Logan sat on the branch above her. "Hang on, Logan." She steadied herself with her hands and stepped down to the ground. "Now, come down slowly," she told him, motioning for him to lower himself into her arms.

"Here, I'll get him." Richard moved toward the spot where she stood. He took one last drag and dropped his cigarette to the ground, stepping on it to put it out.

"I can do it," she replied.

"He's a big kid."

She glared at him. "I don't need your help... Dick, was it?"

Richard chuckled again. "Suit yourself." He backed away, sensing this wasn't going to go as smoothly as Natalie planned.

Logan shifted his gaze from one to the other of them, his forehead tense. Natalie lifted her arms, and he slid down until his legs dangled by her head. She put a hand on each leg to steady him, and he lowered himself with his arms. But then his foot jerked back, the toe of his sneaker striking Natalie in the center of her chest, catching the neckline of her shirt as the two of them tumbled to the ground.

Richard suppressed a laugh. Logan jumped up, rubbing his knee where it had hit the ground,

but Natalie lay still, eyes unblinking. His chest tightened. She'd hit her head. Hard.

"Natalie, are you okay?" He knelt beside her, trying not to stare at the skin Logan's shoe had exposed.

"Ouch," she whispered. Lifting her head, she touched the back of it, wincing. She looked at Richard, following his gaze to her chest. Logan's shoe had ripped her shirt almost all the way down to her waist. "Shit," she muttered, sitting up, trying to pull the shirt closed.

"Here." Richard unzipped his hooded sweatshirt and handed it to her. Underneath he wore only a short-sleeved t-shirt, and the sudden coolness brought up goose bumps on his skin.

"Thanks." She pulled the sweatshirt on and zipped it up to her neck. Richard stood, extending his hand to her. Hers was warm and smooth. The fabric of his sweatshirt hugged her curves. The touch of her hand and the sight of her wearing his shirt sent a small thrill through his body.

"How's your head?" He reached for it, but she pushed his hand away.

"Don't."

"We need to get you some ice." He turned to find Logan, who sat cross-legged on the bench, airplane in his lap, eyes on the two adults, a curious look on his face. "How far away is your house?"

-2-

Twenty minutes later, Natalie sat on the couch in Logan's living room, an ice pack pressed to the back of her head as Richard regaled the boy's parents with the tale of the heroic rescue.

Logan's mother, Donna, handed Richard a mug of coffee. "Are you sure I can't get you anything, Natalie?"

Natalie gave her a weak smile. "No, thanks." Her head throbbed. All she really wanted was to go home and lie down.

Richard had taken the keys to her car and driven her and Logan the short two blocks to the house, knocked on the door, and explained what happened. His parents, visibly upset, sent him to his room, promising they would talk more in the morning. Donna got Natalie the ice pack and invited them in for coffee. Natalie would have preferred to decline, but before she could object, Richard led her inside to the couch.

"I can't thank you two enough for bringing Logan home safely," Donna said for the third or fourth time.

"It's no trouble at all," Richard replied. His Southern drawl seemed more exaggerated than it had been outside, beneath the tree. "I have two kids of my own... I'd hope anyone else would do the same for them." He sipped the coffee.

"He's obsessed with airplanes."

"Oh, really?" Richard fished a business card out of his wallet. "Give me a call sometime... I'll give him a behind the scenes tour of the airport."

"Wow, thank you." Donna took the card. "He'd love that. I still can't believe he snuck out of the house." She looked at Natalie, then back at Richard. "My god, what if you two hadn't driven past?"

Richard corrected her. "Actually, I was walking through the park. Natalie stopped to help when she saw me standing there, talking up into a tree. I'm surprised she didn't assume I was an escaped mental patient."

"I did," Natalie mumbled.

Donna laughed. "I just thought you were... together, I guess."

"No, we both happened to be there at the same time. Just lucky."

Richard looked at Natalie. She tried to glare at him, but pain shot through her temple, forcing her to shut her eyes.

"Well, thank goodness you were," Donna said. "I hope you don't mind me saying so, but you have a great accent. Where are you from?"

"Thank you, I don't mind at all. Atlanta, Georgia, mostly, but I've lived all over the South. Tennessee, Florida, West Virginia. Been in the Atlanta area for most of the last twenty years. But I've been in Philly since the beginning of February."

Donna seemed fascinated. "Wow, that's really interesting."

Logan's father cleared his throat at his wife's flirtatious tone. Natalie stifled a giggle. Donna blushed.

Richard never faltered. "Well, it's getting late. I suppose I'd better get Miss Natalie home." He gulped down the rest of the coffee and stood, setting the empty mug on the table.

Greg offered him his hand. "Thanks again for bringing Logan home safely."

Natalie rose from the couch. She took a step forward, but the room tilted. As her knees began to buckle, Richard caught her from behind.

"Whoa, careful." His voice was tender, and his arms strong and steady.

"I think you'd better take her to the hospital," Greg said.

"No, I don't want to go to the hospital," Natalie whimpered.

Donna insisted. "You could have a concussion, hon. Better to go and get it checked out."

"I'll take her," Richard assured them.

She opened her mouth to argue, but another wave of dizziness threatened. She turned her face towards Richard's. His eyes met hers.

"It's okay. I've got you," he said. His voice was gentle. She felt her body relax into his arms.

"Okay. I'll go."

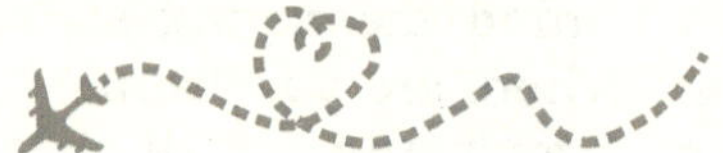

Richard paced the floor outside the emergency room cubicle where Natalie lay on a gurney, waiting to be seen by the doctor. He was supposed to sit next to her and keep her from falling asleep, but he was more than a little annoyed that she hadn't been seen yet. Not to mention the fact he was exhausted, and in desperate need of a cigarette.

On the short ride to the hospital in Natalie's car, he'd asked her if she wanted him to call anyone. "You must have a...boyfriend? Roommate?"

"No."

"Are you sure? There must be somebody."

"I'm all alone," she said, overdramatizing. She laughed, then winced. "I'd rather not bother anyone this late at night. It's not worth it. I'm fine." She closed her eyes again.

"Don't go to sleep, okay Natalie? Stay with me, baby girl."

The term of endearment made her groan, her eyes narrowing at him again. He laughed.

Richard walked back into the tiny space, sitting on the chair next to Natalie's bed. She lay on her side, an ice pack propped on the pillow behind her head. She'd balked when the nurse handed her a hospital gown, but conceded and put it on, keeping her own clothes on from the waist down. A small television set droned beside the bed, neither of them watching.

She took the ice off her head and turned, meeting Richard's eyes. "I should have just taken the plane from him and let him climb down himself."

"That's all I was trying to tell you," he said, chuckling.

"Richard... You don't have to stay. You can go ahead home if you need to."

"No, it's okay."

"I'm sure you have better things to do than sit around here with someone you don't even know."

"You shouldn't be alone." She shouldn't drive herself home, either, but he'd argue that point when the time came.

The doctor showed up. She was young and pretty, with smooth, light brown skin and glossy black hair.

"Hi, I'm Dr. Gold." She shook Natalie's hand and then Richard's. "Sorry for the wait."

"Busy night?" Richard asked.

"Always." The doctor's smile was tired. She turned her attention to Natalie. "You had a fall?"

Natalie nodded.

"And then she fainted," Richard said.

"I didn't faint," Natalie corrected him. "I lost my balance or something."

"Well, let's take a look." The doctor shone a light in Natalie's eyes, checked her reflexes, and examined the bump on the back of her head. She asked her name, birthday, and if Natalie knew what day it was.

"How much pain are you having? Scale of zero to ten, where zero is no pain at all and ten is the worst pain you've ever experienced."

"I don't know... six or seven. There's a constant ache, but every so often I get this wave of pain that comes from the back and shoots through my skull into my eye sockets."

"Sounds pretty painful. Any nausea or vomiting?"

"Nope."

"Dizziness?"

"When I stand up."

"Can you remember what happened before you fell?"

"A kid had climbed up into a tree and got stuck." She glanced at Richard. "I was trying to help him down, and I guess he was heavier than I'd thought, and I fell backwards."

"You fell out of a tree?"

"No, I was already back on the ground when I fell."

"You have a large bump on the back of your head. That's actually a good thing, because we want the swelling to go out, not in, which would put pressure on the brain. Otherwise, you seem okay. We're just going to take you for a quick scan to make sure you don't have any serious injuries."

"And if she does have one?" Richard asked.

"We'll see what the scan shows but it's not likely to be severe, considering her responsiveness." She turned back to Natalie. "If you have a concussion, you'll just lay low for a few days. Take a day or two off work... You might want to do that anyhow. And you'll probably have a nasty headache for a while."

"I've already got that."

"Any chance of pregnancy?"

Natalie's expression darkened. "No."

The doctor patted her knee. "Someone will be here in a few minutes to take you for the test, okay?"

Richard thanked the doctor as she left the room.

"You flirt with everyone, don't you?" Natalie asked.

"Was I flirting with the doctor?"

"And the triage nurse. And Logan's mother."

"People are a little friendlier to each other where I'm from."

"There's friendly, and then there's 'I'd like to see you naked'." She imitated his voice.

"Jealous?"

She gave him a death stare. "You're hilarious."

He laughed, getting up from the chair. "I'm gonna take a peek at the vending machines out in the waiting room. Can I get you anything?"

She thought for a minute. "A Coke."

"What kind of Coke?"

"Is that another comment about my weight?"

Richard blinked. "What?"

"I'm fat, so I must drink *diet* Coke, right?"

"I—no! I was just asking—"

"A *regular* Coke, okay?"

He put his hands up. "That's all I wanted to know." He left, pulling the curtain behind him.

Christ, she's sensitive about her weight. Doesn't she know she's gorgeous? How did he manage to keep lighting her fuse? He had forgotten that in the North, Coke meant regular Coca-cola, not any variety of carbonated beverage as it did where he was from.

In the vending area, he pulled a few dollars out of his wallet and bought two *regular* Cokes and a small bag of pretzels. He was dying for a cigarette, but he didn't want to be gone too long in case they came to take Natalie for her test.

Back in the narrow cubicle, Richard handed Natalie the Coke and offered her a pretzel, which she declined.

She opened the bottle and took a sip. "Look, you don't have to stick around and wait for me to have the test. I'll be fine. Why don't you call a cab? I'll pay for it. I'm sure you have somewhere else to be." She reached for her purse and pulled out a twenty, offering it to him.

"It's almost midnight, Natalie. The only place I need to be is in bed."

"Well, *go,* then! I'm sure your wife is worried about you."

He held up his bare left hand. "No wife. I'm all alone," he said, mimicking her tone from earlier.

Her face softened. "Divorced?"

"Yeah."

"Me too. On my way, anyhow."

"You're too young to be divorced!" he blurted.

"Yeah, I know. Everyone thought I was too young to get married. Now they think I'm stupid for leaving."

He could hear the rawness beneath her casual tone, the tender pain that was still fresh. It jabbed at the scars on his own heart. He had an

overwhelming urge to reach for her and hold her close. *Jesus, I must be tired.*

"It gets easier," he said in a gentle voice, not believing the words he was saying, but wanting to comfort her in some small way.

She twisted the corner of the blanket in her hand. "I sure hope so." Her eyes flicked back in his direction. "How long?"

"Until it gets easier? Hard to say."

"No." One corner of her mouth curled upwards, revealing a dimple in her left cheek. "How long have you been divorced?"

"Two years. My fault. Alcohol and drugs. I'm sober now, but..." He shrugged. "She's already remarried."

"Oh," she said. "I'm sorry."

He tried to think of something to say to lighten the mood, but she beat him to it.

"Really, you don't have to stay. I'll be fine. I'm not a damsel in distress. I don't need you to rescue me. Besides, I live all the way up in the city. You don't want to drive me home." She held the money out again, but he waved it away.

"How will you get home?"

"I'll call my sister. She lives pretty close." She tucked the money back into her purse.

So she had people who cared about her after all. That was heartening, at least. She wasn't a lost soul wandering the planet alone, like him. "I'll just stay until you're sure—"

"Just go!"

Her forcefulness surprised him, but he wasn't going to stay where he wasn't wanted. He still had a smidgen of pride. He stood up. "Okay then, Miss Natalie. Good luck to you."

"Oh, God. I'm sorry." She put her head in her hands. "I hate hospitals. I've never gotten any good

news in the emergency room." Her voice shook. Richard stood frozen in the doorway, looking at her, unable to tear himself away.

The nurse appeared, along with a young man pushing an empty wheelchair. "Ready, Natalie? We're going to take you for your CT scan now."

"Okay." She stood.

Richard hesitated as Natalie settled herself into the wheelchair.

The nurse looked at him as she tucked a blanket around Natalie's legs. "I'll need you to stay in the waiting room, sir. We'll let you know as soon as she gets back."

"Oh, well, I was just going to head out."

Natalie turned to him, her eyes full of fear. "Wait, Richard..." She swallowed. "Will you stay?"

"I'll wait for you." He reached out and squeezed her hand.

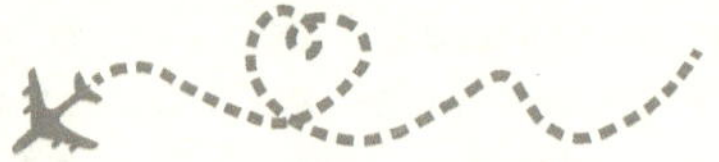

It was almost two in the morning when Richard pulled Natalie's red Focus up to the curb. She lived in the second floor apartment of a converted row house, only a few blocks from the highway. The pain medicine had kicked in and she had dozed on and off in between giving him directions to her place.

The doctor said she didn't have a concussion. She'd be sore for a few days, but would be fine. They'd given her a prescription and sent her on her way. She chatted with Richard for a few minutes on the ride, but she'd grown sleepy as they drove.

Now Richard needed to get her up the steps and into bed. *Not* into *bed, dirty old man*, he told himself.

"Natalie." He patted her arm. "Natalie. Wake up, baby girl."

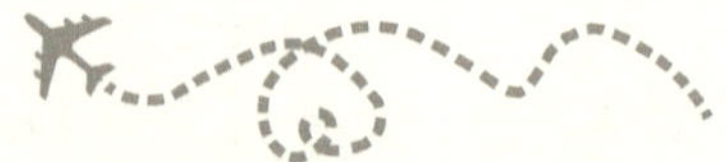

"Mmm?" She opened her eyes. "Oh, sorry. I didn't mean to fall asleep."

"Let me help you inside, okay?"

"Okay," she whispered, closing her eyes again.

Richard laughed. "Natalie."

Her eyes popped open. "I'm awake."

"I'm gonna come around and open your door, okay? I need you to walk up the steps."

Richard got out and walked to the passenger side, opening the door. He put an arm around her waist. "Come on, darlin'...that's it...one foot in front of the other."

They made their way up the steps to her apartment. Richard used her keys to unlock the door. A soft black and white cat rubbed up against his left leg, meowing. He bent to scratch it under the chin. "Hey there, fella."

"She's a girl."

"My mistake. What's her name?"

"Sushi."

"Sushi?"

"Because her little pink nose looks like a piece of salmon in the middle of a sushi roll," she explained.

"Let's get you to bed." He spotted the door to the bedroom and led her to it, his hand on the small of her back. He pulled her covers back, sat her down, and eased her shoes off.

"Lie down," he said. She curled onto her side.

"Thank you," she whispered, closing her eyes.

He pulled the covers up, staring at her face. He hated to leave her alone, but he couldn't stay. He reached for his wallet and pulled out one of his business cards, scribbling his cell phone number onto the back.

He took one last look at Natalie before turning off the light.

-3-

When she woke up Monday morning, Natalie wondered if she'd dreamed the whole thing—Logan, the tree, the hospital. The pain when she touched her head jolted her back to reality.

But what had become of Richard? He'd tucked her into bed and disappeared into the night. She was still wearing his sweatshirt when she woke up, *University of Tennessee* embroidered on the left side. His business card was on her nightstand, a handwritten note scribbled on the back. *Call me if you need anything – R.* She smiled, still a bit unable to believe how kind he'd been. He must have spent a fortune on the cab ride back to the suburbs.

Against her better judgment, she called her mother, to tell her she'd been in the ER. As expected, Kathy overreacted.

"What? Why didn't you call us?"

"Mom, I'm okay. It wasn't that big of a deal, I just wanted to get it checked out."

"I wish you'd called us, honey. Now that you're living alone, I worry about you all the time." More criticism about the separation.

But later that morning, it was her mother who got her prescription filled and brought her some lunch. She shook her head when she heard the story about Richard.

"God sent your guardian angel, huh?"

"*Mom.*" Natalie rolled her eyes.

Along with the separation, her mother refused to accept that Natalie had stopped attending church, or even believing in divine intervention. Despite following what she'd been taught and trying to do the right thing, whatever god existed seemed to have decided Natalie's prayers weren't worth answering.

Now it was Wednesday, and Natalie sat at the large desk in her classroom, combing through the pile of assignments the substitute teacher had left after her two-day absence. She debated throwing them all into the trash. Couldn't the sub have let them watch movies and play games, instead of assigning sentences and math problems? She closed her eyes, pressing her fingers against her temples.

She hadn't called Richard. She knew she should at least thank him for all he'd done for her. And offer to return his sweatshirt. Yet, she was hesitant.

Her students would be back from recess soon. Maybe she should wait until later. *No, I should do this.* She took a deep breath and started to dial his office phone number.

"Richard Rung," he answered.

"Hi, Richard. It's Natalie Kelly."

"Natalie," he said, sounding like he'd been waiting for her call. "How's the head?"

"Better, thanks."

"I'm glad. I was worried about you after I left."

"You were?"

"It's not every day I take a young lady to the emergency room in the middle of the night."

"Well, next time you need to go to the emergency room in the middle of the night, I'm your girl."

"I'll be sure and take you up on that sometime."

"Deal." He was easier to talk to than she remembered.

"I'm glad to hear from you. I have a problem I need your help with."

"Oh?"

"Yup. You remember Donna. Logan's mother? She called me," he said, chuckling. "She wanted to bring Logan to the airport, like I offered. So she brought him yesterday after school and I showed the two of them around. And she kept mentioning how she wants to thank me for helping out the other night."

"Oh?" She wondered what that had to do with her.

Richard lowered his voice. "I mean, I get the feeling she wants to really *thank* me. You know what I'm saying?"

Natalie giggled, her cheeks flushing. "So what did you say?"

"Well, I had to find a way to deflect her, so I kept telling her you were, of course, the real hero of the story, having climbed up into the tree and all that. I mean, damn. I'm still impressed. How did you know the right thing to say to the kid to get him to follow you down? That was amazing."

"I've got a nephew that age."

"You're good with kids."

"I'm a teacher."

"I didn't know that."

"Yeah, and I have about three minutes until they come back from recess," she said, trying to speed the conversation along. "So, what did she say?"

"Right. Well, eventually I got her to agree that she—and her husband, of course—should take the two of us out for dinner this weekend, instead. What do you think?"

"Oh! Umm, well..."

"Look at it this way. You'd really be helping me out, plus you'd get dinner out of it."

"When is this?"

"Saturday night?"

Natalie was quiet for a minute.

"You do owe me a favor," he teased.

"Okay, I'll go."

"You will?"

"Sure, why not."

"Okay! Great. So…should I pick you up?"

"You don't have to."

"No, I want to. Around seven?"

"Okay…"

"Is that okay? I could meet you at the restaurant if it's not."

Uneasiness settled into her stomach. It wasn't that she didn't want him to pick her up, it was that his picking her up made it seem more like a date than a simple favor. She didn't want to give him the wrong idea.

"Natalie? Are you still there?"

"It's okay. Saturday at seven."

"I'm looking forward to it. Call me if anything changes."

"I will."

Natalie sat staring at her phone after she hung up. *What did I just agree to?*

At lunchtime, her friend Lauren came into her classroom to eat with her. Lauren taught art down the hall from Natalie, and was eager to hear about her injury and the story surrounding it. Natalie's description of Richard intrigued her.

"So this guy you'd never met before scooped you up, took you to the ER, and stayed with you

the whole time? Then took you home, tucked you in, and disappeared?" Lauren asked, unwrapping a sandwich.

"I know. It's weird, right? Who does these things?"

"I don't know, Nat...your guardian angel?"

"You and my mother." She rolled her eyes. "He seemed like a genuinely nice guy. He's not from Philly, so maybe that's it. He just moved here, from Georgia, I think."

"Does he have a Southern accent? Well, howdy there, little missy, I reckon we oughta git you to the hospital," she drawled, laughing.

"Less John Wayne, more...Rhett Butler."

"Rhett Butler? Oh." Lauren fluttered her eyelashes and pretended to fan herself. "A Southern gentleman. Is he dashing and irresistible?"

"He's older."

Lauren raised her eyebrow. "How much older?"

"I didn't ask him how old he was," she said, laughing. "Not too much older. But he has a little gray hair."

"Huh." Lauren took a bite of her sandwich.

"Anyway, he helped me out, and I said I would go with him to this dinner, to thank him or whatever. But I got the feeling he thinks this is kind of a date."

Lauren considered that. "So you think he likes you."

"Maybe."

"Do you like him?"

Natalie blushed and looked away.

"You do!" Lauren grinned.

"No. I don't know. Maybe," she said, trying not to smile back.

"Well, is that so bad?"

"I'm still married."

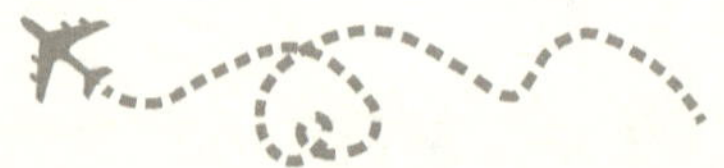

Lauren shrugged. "You're separated."

"Yeah, I know." *But I never intended to date anyone.*

"Look, you're separated, not dead. Don't you deserve to go out and have some fun?"

"I guess."

"So what's the harm in one dinner? Obviously he's a nice guy. He's not ugly, right?"

"No. He's not ugly. He's a total flirt. A little pushy."

"Aren't they all?"

"And he smokes." She made a gagging noise.

"So he has one flaw. Go for it, Nat. You deserve to have a good time. You've been hiding out in that apartment for months."

"I think I'm entitled to hide out."

"For a while, sure. But, Nat. You're young, you're gorgeous. Relax. Have fun. Life is short. Live in the moment."

"Please. I'm far from gorgeous." She pointed at her rounded belly.

Lauren rolled her eyes. "I don't think you've seen the way guys look at you. Maybe you're a little chunky—so what? You have great boobs, your face is beautiful, and I'd kill for your hair."

Lauren was five years younger than Natalie, tall and lean, with long, dark curls she complained needed way too much maintenance. Natalie often found herself envious of Lauren's carefree independence. If she hadn't been so focused on marriage and babies, maybe she would have been able to enjoy her own twenties a bit more.

"This guy likes you. Let him take you out. Trust me. You need this. It'll do wonders for your self confidence." She grinned. "Sometimes going out with someone can just be fun, it doesn't have to mean anything." She paused. "There is one problem, though."

"What?"

"I've been begging you to come out with me every weekend now for months, and you always find some excuse not to go. Now this guy you barely know comes along and you agree to a date right away? I'm hurt. I'm deeply offended."

"You're right. I suck."

"You owe me a girls' night."

Her friend was right. She'd become a recluse since she and Ben had separated. It was easier to be alone, or at least she kept telling herself that.

For the first few weeks, it had been bliss. Natalie enjoyed the quiet, the solitude. She took a long bubble bath every night. She ate cereal for dinner. Her daily life took on a predictable routine she found comforting. Weekends were for laundry and lesson plans, or the occasional Sunday dinner at her mom's or sister Christine's house. She appreciated the sparseness of her life, the lack of drama, and the abundance of time.

At first, Ben had begged her to come home, but she refused. He sold their house and put their furniture into storage, and Natalie kept the cat. Ben moved in with his older brother Jason and his family, sleeping in one end of their basement.

He still called every few days, and sometimes he came by to check on her and the cat. He tried sometimes to plead his case, but Natalie was quick to shut him down. She guessed he wasn't dating anyone, though he probably wouldn't tell her if he was. But she hadn't thought about anyone else, either. Until now.

Her first impression of Richard hadn't been good. He'd had no patience with the boy in the tree, or faith in her ability to get him down safely. But when he stayed by her side at the hospital, took her home, and tucked her into bed, she had to rethink her opinion.

A night out would be an interesting change of pace, if nothing else. She was looking forward to seeing him again.

-4-

Richard couldn't stop thinking about Natalie. Not since he'd left her apartment early Sunday morning. Her hair, her eyes, her body. But something beyond the physical attracted him, too. Her fiery temper, her guardedness, her stubborn refusal to accept help, covering up something raw and wounded that lurked behind her eyes. She reminded him of a younger version of himself, trying anything to deaden the pain. What—or who—had caused her so much heartache at such a young age?

He knew the chance that Natalie would be interested in him was small. Hell, he was almost old enough to be her father, at least in theory. He'd heard her give her date of birth at the hospital. She was only thirty-one, making him a full fifteen years older. He hoped she'd be able to see past his age, past the differences between the two of them, and consider him simply as a man who wanted to get to know her better. But God help him, he was only a man, and he'd already imagined taking her to bed more than once. Her soft curves pressed against him, her warm flesh giving way beneath his fingertips... *Okay, enough.*

He hadn't been this eager to go out with someone in a long time. There had been a handful of women since his divorce from Melinda, but they were only dates. Encounters. Fun, but lacking significance.

But, Natalie... He had a feeling she was worth more than one night of casual fun. When she'd flashed her eyes at him, he was done for.

Ridiculous, he thought. *I'm too old for her, and I have too much baggage.*

His thoughts turned to his daughters, his eyes resting upon the framed photograph on his desk. Hannah was sixteen, Bella was twelve. They'd witnessed his descent into addiction and, like their mother, were still skeptical of his sobriety.

Not long after he and Melinda worked out an every-other-weekend arrangement, the airline offered him a promotion that included a temporary relocation to Philadelphia. He took it without a second thought, wanting some distance from Melinda and her new husband, as well as the constant reminders of his past mistakes. But what began as an exciting adventure in a new city had now become an experiment in seeing how much loneliness he could endure.

Outside of work, he didn't know anyone. He tried a few times to connect with neighbors in his small townhome community, but many were transients like him, uninterested in forging friendships. And while his recovery had led him to rely on a higher power, he wasn't exactly the type to go sit in a pew on Sunday morning. Lately he'd resorted to going to the local coffee shop several times a week just to have a chance to chat with the barista as he ordered.

It was harder than he'd thought it would be knowing his daughters were almost a thousand miles away. They'd come to stay with him for a few days in late February during a school break. He thought they would be excited to visit a new place, but they complained about the cold and missing their friends.

He'd rented a townhouse, rather than one of the extended stay hotel suites he usually stayed in, so the girls had their own space. He decorated a bedroom for them with the hope that they would want to come to see him often. Bella was more easygoing during their visit, but Hannah was sullen. It took until the night before they were supposed to fly home for her to say more than a few words to him.

They ordered pizza and watched movies on TV until his eyeballs burned in their sockets. Bella fell asleep in the recliner, and Hannah went to take a shower. She came back to the living room in red pajama pants and a baggy black t-shirt. Richard patted the couch next to him and she surprised him by curling up next to him and putting her head on his chest. Her brown hair was still damp and smelled of fruity shampoo. He smoothed it back and kissed her forehead.

"How about some coffee?"

She looked up at him and nodded. Like her daddy, Hannah had been a coffee fiend from childhood, always asking for a sip from his cup, and at age twelve had begun pouring herself a mug from the coffee maker in the kitchen. Melinda hated it, blaming Richard for being a bad influence. He was unable to see the harm. She was allowed to drink Coke, and sweet tea. Was coffee all that different?

In the kitchen, he poured them each a mug of coffee, setting them on the table. Hannah scooped a spoonful of sugar into her cup and topped it off with cream.

She blew across the top of her mug, took a sip and grinned. "Mom still hates when I drink coffee."

"I won't tell her." He grinned back, holding up his pinky finger. She wrapped her pinky around his and shook on it. "I've missed you, Princess."

Without warning, her eyes filled with tears. "I miss you, too, Dad."

"Hey, now."

"I'm sorry. It's just hard. Things were finally getting good with us and then you moved away."

"I'm so sorry, Hannah. You're right."

"Why did you leave?"

He looked down at his coffee. "I guess I didn't think about how it would make you feel. That was stupid." He sighed. "I was still hurt and feeling sorry for myself over what happened with me and your mom."

"You weren't there all the time when I was little, but at least we were a family. Now you're gone and she just wants to be alone with Neil. She couldn't wait to get us out the door and onto the airplane to go see you." The tears spilled over, down her cheeks.

He grabbed a napkin and patted her cheeks. "Listen to me. You know your momma loves you. She and Neil are still newlyweds. They need some time to themselves every once in a while." He tried not to picture what that time might look like.

"It's so different now."

"I know it is. But that's life, Princess. You'll see." He cupped her chin in his palm. "It's not fair to you that we split up, I know that. I really do. But it's good your mom has someone to love, isn't it?"

"I guess. But I hate that you're all alone here in a strange place. And I miss you."

"I miss you, too. Now smile for me." She sniffled and looked up at him, but she couldn't manage a smile yet. He made faces at her until she giggled.

Once they left for home, the house felt bigger and emptier than it had before their visit. He wandered through the rooms, unsure what to do with himself. That was when he'd begun his walks around the neighborhood. He'd walk for hours, sometimes up

and down the different streets, sometimes through the park. Until the night he met Natalie.

He shook off his melancholy and focused his thoughts again on the woman who'd staked a claim on him the other night. He hoped this dinner with Logan's parents would provide him the opportunity to see her again. And again.

-5-

Late Saturday afternoon, Natalie stood in her bedroom in front of the open closet door. She'd been trying all day to decide what to wear, and she still had no clue. She had a few nice outfits, but they all looked like teacher clothes. Khakis, cardigans, sensible shoes.

She held up different combinations, shaking her head. Nothing looked right. Sushi rubbed against her legs, meowing. "I know," Natalie said. "I'm ridiculous."

She peered into her closet one more time, spotting a black and white, knee-length sundress. She would need to wear a cardigan with it, but what the hell—when was the last time she'd had a chance to dress up?

She glanced at the clock. *Shit.* Almost six o'clock and she still had to shower. She hung the dress on a hook outside her closet and headed for the bathroom.

She rushed through washing her hair, wondering for the hundredth time whether Richard wanted this to be a date. Or if *she* did. She wondered if she knew what a date was, or how it was supposed to go. She hadn't been on one since high school, and grown-up dates were probably somewhat different.

Maybe Richard was lonely in a new city and wanted a friend. That wouldn't be too bad. Anything more than friendship, well, she wasn't capable of that. Or maybe... No.

She took a deep breath, thinking about what Lauren had said. *Have fun. Live in the moment.* But she wasn't sure she knew how. After all that had happened between her and Ben, she wondered if she could have fun with a guy again.

Richard drove towards Natalie's apartment, his stomach in knots, trying hard not to sweat. He had the air conditioner on full-blast, although it wasn't very warm out.

He wished he could have Natalie all to himself this evening, but he was sure she wouldn't have agreed to see him without the other couple in attendance. He debated all day whether or not to bring her flowers, deciding at the last minute to go ahead and do it. A simple bouquet sat next to him in the front seat of his truck. He hoped she wouldn't think it was too forward. If nothing else, it would be nice to have a friend.

He knew she'd been hurt. Nobody made it out of a marriage unscathed. And the fear he'd glimpsed when she asked him to stay hadn't come out of nowhere. He would have to take his time with her. It wouldn't be easy convincing her to let him into her heart. If it was even possible.

He parked his truck out front of her house right at seven o'clock. He didn't know yet whether she was a stickler for punctuality, or if she tended to run late. Better to show up right on time.

His heart did cartwheels in his chest as he rang the doorbell. *Settle down. Breathe.*

After a moment, the door opened. Natalie was barefoot, her hair still damp, but damn, she looked

good. A smile turned up the corners of her lips, and as her eyes found the flowers he held in his hand, she broke into a grin.

"Hey." She took a step backwards from the door and motioned for him to follow her into the foyer.

"Hi." He grinned back, stepping inside. "These are for you." He held out the flowers. "A belated get well soon." *Ugh, I'm an idiot.*

Natalie took them from his hand. "That's so sweet. Thank you." She looked at him for a second before opening her arms and leaning in to give him a hug.

It was awkward and lasted only a second or two, but he felt his face flush, the touch of her hands having caused every nerve in his body to awaken.

"Is it better? Your head, I mean?"

"Yeah, I'm fine. I got to take a mini vacation from work, so it's all good."

"Good."

"Let me go put these in some water, and find my shoes... You want to come up for a minute?"

It was tempting, but he worried he'd make a bigger idiot of himself if he went up to her apartment. "I think I'll stand out here on your porch and grab a smoke, if that's okay."

"Sure. I'll be down in five, okay?"

"You bet."

Natalie hurried up the stairs and into her kitchen, grinning, hoping Richard hadn't seen how happy the flowers made her. She was like a little girl with a crush. She'd forgotten the combination of awkwardness and exhilaration that came from

seeing the person you liked. Pausing to inhale the scent of the flowers first, she set them down next to the sink.

She found a vase in the back of a cabinet and filled it halfway with water. Sushi jumped up on the counter to inspect the flowers. Natalie laughed and scratched the cat's head before setting her back down on the floor. "You'd better not eat these while I'm gone, you naughty thing."

She arranged the flowers in the vase and set it on the kitchen table. They were lovely, and it was obvious this wasn't a cheap supermarket bouquet. Her stomach fluttered. *This is crazy. I'm not ready for this.* But Lauren's voice echoed in her mind again. *Have fun.*

Natalie slid her feet into her shoes and picked up her purse before heading down the stairs again. She had a gift bag to give to Logan's parents, something small she'd picked up for him. She wished he was coming along tonight. It was easier to talk to kids than other grown-ups.

She grabbed a jacket from the hook behind the door, in case it got chilly later. Spring weather in Philadelphia was fickle, and though the temperature had been in the sixties today, it was sure to plummet once the sun went down.

Natalie opened the door. Her landlord, Jean, was on the porch smoking a cigarette with Richard, laughing at something he'd said.

"Hey. I was just getting to know your friend," Jean said. She was tall and thin with long, straight, brown hair, and had a deep, raspy voice with a thick Philadelphia accent.

"And? What's the verdict? Am I allowed to go to dinner with him?"

"I guess he's harmless."

"I'll have her home by curfew," Richard chimed in.

"You'd better."

Richard turned to Natalie. "Ready to go?"

"I'm ready." She hugged Jean. "See you later."

"I like him," Jean whispered in her ear. "But be careful."

Jean's words warmed her heart. "I will."

Richard extinguished his cigarette in Jean's ashtray. "A pleasure meeting you, Jean."

"Same here," Jean answered, going back inside..

Richard walked a few steps towards the black Ford Ranger that was parked at the curb.

Natalie looked at the truck. "This is you?" She'd have to tell Lauren; maybe he was a little bit John Wayne after all.

He opened the passenger door for her. "Yes, ma'am."

She climbed in and he shut the door behind her.

They drove towards the interstate. "Where are we going?" she asked.

"Logan's parents made the reservation. Someplace in South Philly. I think it's Italian." He mentioned the name of the restaurant. She'd heard of it.

Natalie motioned towards the radio, which Richard had set to a country music station. "May I?"

"You don't like country?" he asked. Natalie made a face. "What kind of music do you like?"

"A little of everything," she said.

"Who's your favorite?"

"David Bowie."

"Bowie. I saw him in concert once. Sometime in the mid-eighties."

"In the mid-eighties I was still in elementary school."

Richard laughed. "Ouch. Okay, I'm old. Go ahead." He motioned towards the radio.

She fiddled with the buttons until she found a station she liked. "Is this okay?" The song was a popular one.

"Hmm…" He frowned, and she shook her head, laughing.

She changed the station a few more times. "How's this?"

"Elvis? Really?"

"Yeah. I like Elvis."

"Me too." He grinned at her again. Her cheeks grew warm as The King belted out *Suspicious Minds*.

They parked the car and walked into the restaurant. Richard stepped in front of her to open the door. "Thanks," she said, surprised by the gesture.

The restaurant was busy, and although Greg had made a reservation, they had to wait to be seated. Donna greeted each of them with a hug, and Natalie handed her the gift bag. "For Logan. A remote control truck. I figured it would keep him closer to the ground."

They all laughed. "That's sweet, thank you," Donna said. "Want to go have a drink while we wait?"

She glanced at Richard, hoping he wouldn't be put off by her having a drink.

He winked at her. "It's okay. I'm gonna go grab a smoke."

Natalie followed Donna to the bar. They each ordered a glass of wine.

"So, how is Logan?" Natalie asked.

"He's fine. I'm still a wreck." Donna shook her head. "I get up and check on him every fifteen minutes during the night. I still don't think he gets how dangerous it was, what he did. Kids!" She made a sound of exasperation.

Natalie frowned, taking a sip of her wine. "I'm just glad he wasn't hurt."

"How's your head?"

"Better. No permanent damage."

A group of noisy young guys gathered next to where they stood at the bar, talking and laughing. One of them bumped into Natalie's elbow, spilling a few drops of her wine onto the floor.

"I'm so sorry," he said, handing her a napkin before looking at her face. "Wow, hi."

Natalie gave a half-hearted wave and turned away, rolling her eyes.

Donna shook her head. "Like I said. Kids."

Natalie snickered.

Donna looked over her shoulder. "Richard seems like a good guy, though."

"Yeah, I don't know him all that well."

"You should. I mean, get to know him. He's handsome, successful..." She looked in his direction again. "And he obviously has a thing for you."

Natalie wondered if Donna was encouraging her or if she was being sized up as competition for Richard's affection. She decided to play along. "You think so?"

"Oh my god, yes. You should have heard him on the phone, all he could talk about was how great you are."

"Huh." Natalie sipped her wine.

"So?" Donna asked.

"Something to think about, I guess."

Donna gave her a peculiar look, and Natalie shrugged. Greg waved to them, signaling that their table was ready. *Thank God.* Donna handed some money to the bartender and they carried their glasses to the table. Richard pulled Natalie's chair

out for her and waited for her to sit down before taking his own seat. She'd have to get used to this Southern gentleman thing.

The restaurant was crowded and the service was slow. Donna went back to the bar for another glass of wine while they waited for their server. They were all running thin on patience by the time he came over, giving an unconvincing apology for the long wait as he set a bread basket on the table. They each placed their orders. Greg looked at the wine list and selected a bottle for the table, then excused himself to the men's room. Donna turned her full attention on Richard, who looked embarrassed. Natalie took a slice of bread from the basket. It was going to be a long night.

"So, Richard, I wanted to ask you the other night, but I never got a chance. What brought you to Philly?" Donna's tone was flirtatious. Richard glanced at Natalie, who smirked.

"The airline I work for just swallowed up two other, smaller airlines that both had pretty decent-sized operations here at Philadelphia International. There's a lot of administrative stuff to work out, so they offered me a chance to oversee the transition for the first few months."

"Oh, that must be interesting," she said, her eyes wide.

"A lot of paperwork."

"So you're just here temporarily?"

"That's the plan." He glanced at Natalie.

Greg returned to the table as the waiter brought the bottle of wine. He started to pour everyone a glass, but Richard held his hand over the rim. "None for me, thanks. I'm driving."

"Oh, a little won't hurt. Pour him half a glass," Greg told the waiter.

"Really, no thanks. I'm high on life." Richard's smile remained on his lips, but Natalie noticed the warmth in his eyes had disappeared.

"What, you don't drink at all?" Greg seemed to take offense at Richard's refusal.

"Why don't you let him be?" Natalie said.

They all looked at her. Richard gave a slight shake of his head, as if to discourage her. Greg scoffed and looked at his wife. Richard pretended not to notice.

Damned Southern manners. Her cheeks flamed. She stood and excused herself to the ladies' room. She took her time washing her hands and checking her makeup in the mirror, dreading her return to the table.

On her way back, she spied Richard outside the front door, smoking again. She stepped outside and stood next to him.

He exhaled and smiled at her. "Have I told you how pretty you look tonight? Damn. Just...damn. Stunning. I like that dress." His eyes lingered on her legs long enough to make her blush.

"Richard, why didn't you–"

"Listen," he interrupted, holding up his hand. "I know, I told you I'm a recovering alcoholic and addict. It destroyed my marriage and broke up my kids' family. But I don't need to divulge all that this evening, not to them. I've been sober for over two years now, and it's my business to tell or not tell as I see fit. I don't feel like getting personal with these people." He nodded in the direction of their table and made a face to indicate his dislike for Donna and Greg. "Honestly, the only reason I wanted this dinner to happen was so I'd have an excuse to see you again. I was worried you'd say no if it was just me asking you out." He took a last drag on his cigarette and ground it out in the ashtray. His eyes twinkled as he looked at her.

"You could have asked."

"Would you have said yes?"

She hesitated. Richard chuckled.

"Do you want to go back in?" he asked her.

She laughed. "No. Do you?"

"No."

"Let's get out of here," she said.

He glanced at the door. "We can't just leave."

"Can't we?" She grinned. "Come on. We'll go have a slice of pizza."

"I'm sure I'll regret not saying yes, but let's try and make it through this."

"You're the boss," she said, as he opened the door for her.

-6-

Quiet disappointment hung in the air as Richard drove Natalie home. The evening hadn't improved after they'd gone back inside. Natalie had sat in silence, picking at her food. Donna's attempts to flirt with Richard got more obvious with each successive glass of wine. Richard tried to deflect her without being impolite. Greg was embarrassed. The food was excellent, but nobody was able to appreciate it. Natalie took most of her dinner home in a box. It was a relief to say goodbye.

Every so often, Richard would glance at Natalie as he drove. Or he would see her looking at him out of the corner of his eye. But neither seemed capable of speech at the moment.

Richard pulled up in front of Natalie's place and cut the engine. "Well," he said, staring straight ahead. "You were right."

"I was?"

"You said I would regret not getting the hell out of there when we had the chance."

"Did I say that?"

"Well, you thought it."

Natalie gave a short laugh. "Yeah."

"I'm sorry this evening sucked."

"It's not your fault it sucked."

"Yeah, but I asked you to come along. Can you ever forgive me?"

She gave him the dimpled half-smile he was beginning to find irresistible. "I'll consider it."

He got out of the truck, opened the passenger side door for Natalie, and walked her to her front door.

"Well, goodnight, I guess." She turned towards the screen door. Richard reached past her, opening it for her. She pulled her keys from her purse and unlocked the inner door.

"I'd like to see you again," he said. "For real this time. Let's go out, just you and me."

She turned to look at him. "I don't know, Richard..."

"Listen. Let's go someplace fun. I've been living here for two months and I still don't know this city at all. You pick the place. Tell me where we should go."

"Well..."

"Let me make it up to you. Saturday after next? Please."

She shook her head, but smiled. "Okay."

"I'll pick you up at seven?"

"I'll be ready."

"Goodnight, Natalie." He put out his arms, and she hugged him. Her hair smelled sweet, like honey. He could have held her for hours, but she drew away.

"Goodnight." She turned away, closing the door behind her.

Richard let out a heavy sigh as he got back into the truck. What a mistake this evening had turned out to be. Next time had to be perfect—he would make sure of it.

-7-

The second date was almost as much of a disaster as the first.

Richard had said to pick someplace fun, but Natalie didn't have a clue. She asked Lauren for a few ideas, but most of her suggestions were bars. Given Richard's history, she didn't think a bar would be appropriate.

She decided on an Asian Fusion restaurant she'd been to a few times. But when they arrived, the place was crowded, with loud music blaring, making it almost impossible to talk. Their table was only a few feet from the front door, and the night air was chilly, which made their food cold.

But the highlight of the evening came when Natalie caught sight of a woman who worked with her husband. She turned and saw Natalie looking at her, and whispered in her friend's ear.

"What's wrong?" Richard asked.

Natalie frowned and shook her head, her heart racing.

The woman approached their table, a fake smile plastered on her face. "Hi, it's Natalie, right?"

"Hi Jeanette, how are you?"

"I'm great, how are you?"

"I'm okay, thanks." She willed the fake smile to stay on her lips.

"Good." Jeanette gave a smile right back. She looked at Richard. "Oh, is this your dad?"

Richard seemed ready to choke on his mouthful of rice noodles.

Right, because I have nothing better to do on a Saturday night than go out to eat with my dad. She clenched her fists. "My friend, Richard."

"Hi," Jeanette said. "Nice to meet you." She gave him the same fake smile.

Richard wiped his mouth with his napkin. "Evening."

"Well, good to see you, Nat."

Natalie forced another smile. "Yep. Take care." As soon as Jeanette was out of earshot, she added, "Bitch."

"Well, that was pleasant," Richard said.

Natalie rolled her eyes.

"How do you know her?"

"She works with Ben." She cleared her throat. "My husband. Ex-husband, I guess." She hadn't said it like that before. It sounded strange.

"So he'll get an earful Monday morning?"

She set her chopsticks down. "I'm sure."

"What kind of work does he do?" Richard asked, using his chopsticks to pick up more noodles.

"He's in accounting." She appreciated his attempt to shift back to small talk, but it wasn't going to work. She stood and grabbed her bag.

Richard looked worried. "Are you leaving?"

"Ladies' room. I just need a minute." Her heart pounded as she hurried away from the table towards the bathroom. She couldn't breathe. She locked herself inside a stall and squeezed her eyes shut. *Don't cry. Don't cry.* She forced air into her lungs and exhaled, slow and steady.

Shit.

"I'm sorry," she said on the ride home. "Another shitty evening."

Richard was quiet.

"I mean, did you see the way she looked at me?" she fumed. "And now she's talking shit about me with her little friend..."

They stopped at a red light and Richard looked over at her. "You and that temper, Miss Natalie. Did it ever occur to you that maybe she was jealous?"

"Jealous of?"

"Of you, darlin'. Look at you. You're gorgeous."

Natalie groaned.

"So she wants to gossip about you, so what? 'She left her husband, now she's out with another man, blah blah blah'," he mocked in a nasal falsetto. "People will always judge one another. I say, fuck them. If their lives are so empty they have to entertain themselves by sitting around talking about me, they can go ahead. I won't get angry."

She laughed, feeling her face soften. "I don't think I know how to not get angry."

"The real trick is knowing how to not let the anger get *you*."

She stared out the window. Anger was the only emotion she allowed herself these days. She had grown weary of sadness.

He stopped at the next red light and turned to look at her. "Tell me something, honestly." His face was serious.

"Okay."

"Do you think I look old enough to be your dad?" He laughed.

"No. My dad is in his sixties."

"And how old am I, in your estimation?"

"Oh, I don't know. Not that old." She looked him over, not wanting to offend him by guessing wrong. "Forty, forty-five-ish?"

"Forty-six."

"Okay."

"Does that bother you?"

"No."

He turned his eyes back to the road as the light turned green. "Good."

When they arrived at her house, Richard walked Natalie to her front door once again. He took her hand, lacing his fingers with hers. "I'll be out of town next weekend, to see my kids. What are you doing the following weekend?"

"I don't know."

"Let's try again. Just one more time. And if disaster strikes, we'll take it as a sign."

"Richard..."

"Don't say no. You haven't even heard what I'm asking yet."

She pulled her hand from his and crossed her arms over her chest. "I'm listening."

"What if we go someplace quiet, where there's no chance of running into anyone you know?"

"Like where? Canada?"

He laughed. "I don't know yet. But say yes. If it doesn't go well, you can tell me to hit the road."

She took a deep breath. "Okay. What should I wear?"

"Totally casual. Just be yourself."

"I can't believe I'm agreeing to do this again."

"Admit it, Miss Natalie, despite these two horrifically unsuccessful dinners, you like me a little bit." He opened his arms for a hug, and she

surrendered. "I'll call you when I get back. And I'll see you Saturday after next."

Natalie walked inside, wondering what it was that made her keep saying yes.

On Monday night, Ben stopped by Natalie's apartment unannounced. He smiled when she opened the door.

"Hey, beautiful."

She stood back and crossed her arms over her chest, waiting for an interrogation. "What's up?"

"I brought you something." He held out a white bakery box.

"What is it?"

"Cupcakes."

"Chocolate?"

"Of course. Can I come in?"

"Sure."

He followed her upstairs, bending to pet the cat before taking a seat on the couch. "It's the Sushi Monster," he said as she hopped into his lap, nudging him to continue petting her.

Natalie opened the box. Six chocolate cupcakes, with thick chocolate icing and colorful sprinkles. They smelled delicious. "Do you want one?" she asked Ben.

"Sure."

She handed one to Ben, along with a napkin, and sat at the opposite end of the couch with her own. He waited a few minutes before asking the question she was dreading.

"So, who's this guy you were out with?"

"What did Jeanette tell you?"

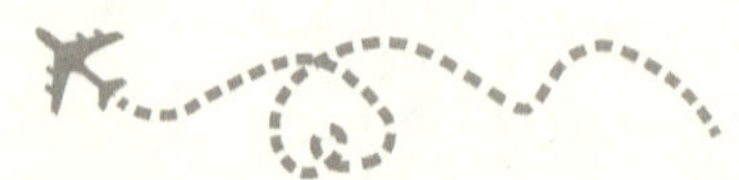

Ben shrugged, playing it cool. "Just that he was older."

Natalie smirked and took a bite of her cupcake.

"What's going on, Nat? Is this the real reason you left? You met someone else?"

"Ben, no. He's a friend."

"Just a friend?"

"Barely even that."

"Are you sure?"

She hesitated. "Yes."

"Well, who is he?"

"I met him a couple of weeks ago. I fell and hit my head. He was there when it happened and took me to the emergency room."

"What?" Ben sat up straight, almost dropping his cupcake. "You fell? What happened?"

"It's no big deal, I'm fine now."

"You should have called me, Nat, you know I would have taken you."

She swallowed, unable to stop herself from thinking about the last time Ben had taken her to the emergency room.

It was a perfect fall Sunday. They slept in, did the crossword puzzle together, and went out for ice cream after dinner. Natalie was finally able to enjoy food after the weeks of nausea that had plagued her. They curled up on the couch to watch TV together.

After a few minutes, Natalie felt it. A sharp cramp across her lower back, a rush of warm fluid, followed by a cold, sickening sensation in the pit of her stomach. At first, she ignored it. But another cramp came, and then another. She stood and walked upstairs to the bathroom without saying anything to Ben.

"You okay, kid?" he called up to her. She closed the bathroom door behind her, knowing if she opened her mouth she would start screaming.

Maybe it's nothing. I'm overreacting. *She took a deep breath, sat on the toilet and looked down. So much blood. It had already soaked through her underwear and her pants. Her stomach lurched.* "No," *she moaned.* "Please, no." *Her abdomen seized. She wrapped her arms across her chest, closing her eyes.* Not again. Not this baby, too. *A wave of nausea gripped her. She knelt in front of the toilet and expelled the contents of her stomach.*

She slumped against the side of the bathtub. Numbness washed over her. Maybe if she stayed here, quiet, she could just bleed to death. It didn't sound so bad.

After several minutes, Ben tapped on the bathroom door. "Nat? You okay?"

"I'm just feeling a little sick." *She couldn't tell him.* Not again.

"I'm coming in." *He opened the door.* "Oh, god, no. Natalie."

She sobbed. "I'm sorry."

The rest of the night passed in a blur. Ben cleaned her up and drove her to the hospital. She was hooked up to an IV and taken for an ultrasound scan, which confirmed the baby's heartbeat had stopped and she was miscarrying. Again. She saw the look on Ben's face, heard the sound he made as he tried to hold back tears.

She was put under anesthesia for a D&C, and she slept until morning, when the surgeon came into her room and told them how sorry he was for their loss.

"This is your fifth miscarriage. Maybe it's time to stop trying to get pregnant," *he said. He meant to be helpful, but his words shredded her heart.*

Natalie pushed the memory away and forced herself back into the present. Ben watched her, his eyes sad. She knew he could read her thoughts. He

was right there, reliving the whole thing along with her, though neither of them spoke a word about it.

He put his hand on hers. "I'm sorry I wasn't there. When you fell, I mean."

"No, it's okay." Ben's hand was warm. Her body ached to pull him closer, to feel his arms around her.

"You know I love you, Nattie."

She pulled her hand away. "I know."

"I thought this separation was because you wanted to be by yourself for a while. To sort things out. Not to start dating someone new."

"I told you. He's a friend."

"Then why were you out on a date with him?"

"It wasn't a date. Not really."

"Not really?"

"He just moved here, he doesn't know anyone in Philly. We were only having dinner." She saw the skepticism in his eyes.

"So you're not interested in him?"

She looked away.

"Natalie." He took her hand again, brushing his thumb over her wrist. "It's not too late for us, is it?"

She pulled her hand away again. "Ben..."

"I miss you so much." He slid closer to her, his hand on her thigh. She kept her eyes down, her body responding to his touch even as she willed it not to. He kissed the side of her face, his lips lingering by the tip of her earlobe, his breath warm on her neck.

She forced herself to move away from him. "Ben, please? I can't do this. It's not okay."

"I'm sorry, Natalie. I don't know what else I can do." Her heart wrenched inside her chest. Ben moved a few inches away on the couch, defeated. "Okay." He ate the last bite of his cupcake, grabbed

the remote and turned on the TV. He flipped the channels, settling on a rerun of *Friends*, laughing in all the appropriate places.

She'd always been impressed by his ability to switch gears with ease. For Natalie, it was difficult to pull herself out of any kind of bad mood. She didn't know how to move past what had happened. She didn't think she'd ever be able to.

She stayed in bed almost a week after the miscarriage, exhausted, sore, heartbroken. She knew everyone was concerned about her, but she couldn't seem to find the will to get out of bed, or take a shower. She didn't eat much.

One night, Ben sat down on the edge of the bed, smoothing out the sheet with his hand.

"Hey, kid."

She turned and looked at him, not answering.

"It's time to get out of bed," he said.

"I'm not ready."

"Natalie." His voice was soft, like a sigh.

She turned away.

"I hate seeing you like this." He lay down next to her on the bed and rubbed her shoulders. "What can I do, Natalie? I want to help."

"Let me be for a while."

"You've been in bed almost a week."

"I know." She turned on her side, pulling the comforter up to her face.

"I think maybe we should call the doctor, Nat. I don't think this is normal."

"No," she said. "It's okay. I'll get up."

"Why don't you get dressed and we'll go out to dinner? Nothing fancy, just some comfort food. How does that sound?"

She thought about it for a minute. She did feel hungry for once, and she wanted to take the concerned

look off Ben's face. She hated what she was doing to him. "Okay. I guess so."

He leaned in and kissed her on the lips. "I love you."

"I love you, too."

She managed to drag herself to the shower, put on clean sweats, and pull her hair into a ponytail. Ben took her to a diner near their house and ordered them both bacon cheeseburgers and apple pie for dessert.

She was still a little sore and tired, but she would be able to go back to work on Monday. She was actually looking forward to it. She looked at the treats in the bakery case while Ben paid the bill.

"You want something to take home?" he asked as he finished paying.

She shook her head. "Nah." She slipped her hand into his and they walked out the door. "I should probably work on taking some of this weight off now that I'm not—" Her voice caught in her throat.

Ben stopped walking. "Oh, Nattie." She buried her face in his shoulder, sobbing. Ben wrapped his arm around her waist and walked her to the car, opened her door for her and shut it gently after she got in.

"You okay?" He pulled the car out of the parking lot.

She shook her head and sniffled. "No."

"We can keep trying. What do they know? We'll keep trying until it happens."

"I don't think I can go through this again. I don't think I have it in me."

"Well, this isn't our only option, you know? We can look into adoption. Or a surrogate—what about asking one of your sisters?"

She pictured her sister Lisa, walking around, pregnant with their baby, while she sat at home, her own body an empty void. "I can't even think about that."

"I'm just saying, this isn't an unfixable problem."
But it didn't feel that way to her.

It still didn't feel that way.

Ben left after the episode of *Friends* was over, carrying her trash downstairs and setting the can at the curb for her, as she watched from the doorway. He came back to the front door to kiss her goodnight. She turned her face as his lips approached hers, like she always did, causing them to land on her cheek. She couldn't remember when she'd started dodging his kisses. Probably around the time when their intimate moments were decided by dates on a calendar. She wondered if Ben realized how long it had been since she'd been able to let down her guard with him.

"I love you," he said, holding her close.

"I know," she whispered, closing her eyes and inhaling his warm, familiar scent. *It would be so easy,* she thought. So easy to stay in his arms, to slip back into the life they had shared as if nothing had happened, to pretend it was possible to be happy when all their hopes and dreams for the future had burned to the ground. *But I can't...* She pulled herself away from his embrace. "Goodnight."

"Maybe I'll stop by again over the weekend."

She sighed.

"What?"

"Don't you think you're making this harder? Coming over here, hanging out like this?"

"What am I supposed to do, Nattie? We said for better or worse, remember? I want to make it better. I'm not ready to give up." He brushed his lips over her forehead and stepped out the door, not looking back.

She shut the door behind him and listened for the sound of him getting into his car. As he pulled

away, she collapsed against the door, her eyes burning. Half of her wanted to run after him and beg him to come back inside. The other half wished he would leave her the hell alone.

Jean's door opened. She spied Natalie leaning on the door, wiping her eyes with the back of her hand. "Uh-oh. What's wrong?"

Natalie shrugged.

"Ben was here," Jean said.

"Yeah."

"He heard about your date?"

She nodded.

"Are you okay?"

"I will be."

"Is he?"

She shook her head and covered her face with her hands.

"He'll get used to it."

Natalie sniffled.

"If you need anything." Jean pointed to her open door.

"Thanks."

She walked up the steps, grabbed her phone, and dialed Richard's number.

"Hey," he answered. "I was just thinking about you."

-9-

Atlanta was already hot and humid, although it was only the end of April. The jacket Richard had needed in the chilly Philadelphia morning was tossed upon the passenger seat next to him, and he lowered the car windows to breathe in the warm Southern air. The magnolias were in full bloom, and their rich, seductive sweetness filled the car as he drove south along the highway, towards the house he had once called his own. Turning the rental into the driveway, he killed the engine, hesitating for a moment before exiting the car. He pressed the button to engage the lock and walked to the house, his steps slow. Even after more than two years, it was strange to ring his own doorbell.

Bella answered. "Daddy!" She threw herself into his arms, and he wrapped them around her, grinning. "Hannah! Daddy's here," she called up the stairs. "Come in," she said, tugging on his arm.

"Oh, I don't know, Bella." He hadn't been inside the house in a long time. Only once since the day he was ordered out, when he'd come with his sponsor, Mike, to vouch for his sobriety and plead his case to be able to see the girls. He swallowed, remembering the desperation and shame of those days. Things were a little easier between him and Melinda now, but nowhere near friendly.

"It's okay," Bella said.

"Just for a second." He stepped into the foyer. *Home.* The sensation washed over him.

At the sound of Richard's voice, their chocolate lab, Nora, came bounding into the foyer to sniff him and demand love. "Nora!" He knelt to hug her, ruffling her fur. "Who's my good girl? Who's my good girl?"

Bella giggled. "She misses her daddy."

Richard stroked Nora behind the ears, letting her nuzzle his face. "Do you miss me, Nora? Huh? I miss you too. Yes I do. Yes I do." Bella giggled again. He looked up at her. "Where's your mom? I'm supposed to wait for you outside. I don't want to make her mad."

"It's okay, Richard." Melinda's slight form came into view. He stood, his heart leaping in his chest. She opened her arms and gave him a quick hug. Being hugged by her was new. Usually, both girls were ready to go when he arrived, his interaction with Melinda limited to a brief exchange of information in the driveway. "How are you?" Her sweet Southern drawl melted over him like warm honey. He'd always believed her voice was out of sync with her tiny frame. It belonged on someone taller, broader.

"Doing okay, and you?"

"I'm well, thank you. How's things in Philadelphia?" She drew the word out into five long syllables, unlike the clipped way it was pronounced by the city's natives.

"It's different, for sure," he said, stroking Nora's head. "I've learned to just stay out of people's way. How's work?"

"Oh, same old. People treat their bodies like garbage dumps, and we fix 'em up so they can keep on doing it."

He pretended her comment wasn't about him. "Neil okay?"

She nodded. "He should be home any minute."

Richard took a quick glance around the foyer. To the left was a narrow hallway leading to the garage, to the right, a shorter one that led to a half bath and the room that had been his den. His quiet place to work or read, watch football, or, more often than he'd rather admit, sneak a few drinks before bedtime. He wondered if Neil had taken over that room like he had the rest of the places and people Richard cherished.

Melinda crossed her arms over her chest, breaking through his self-pitying reverie. "Will you be up there for much longer?"

"Through the end of this year."

"That's a long time."

"It's not so bad."

She raised one eyebrow. "Making some new friends?"

He gave her a half-smile. "Maybe."

"Someone special." She said it as a statement, not a question.

"Someone I like."

Small talk with his ex-wife was strange enough, but her asking about his dating life was downright bizarre. He became very aware that Bella was still standing there, watching them, taking in everything they said. He blinked and turned towards her. "Where is your sister?"

"On the phone. I'll go get her." Bella scampered off.

Nora nuzzled his hand. He rubbed her head.

"Well, come on in and sit down if you want," Melinda offered. "You know your daughter's like you, never shuts up. She could be on that phone for another hour."

He followed her into the family room at the back of the house, which opened up into the kitchen. Nora trotted behind them. It was like stepping back in time. Everything looked and smelled the same. Only the dad in the family photos had changed.

"You want a glass of tea?"

"Sure. Thanks." He sat on the edge of the sofa and listened as the ice cubes clinked into the glasses. Nora plopped down at his feet.

They'd bought this house when Hannah was a baby. It was brand new construction then, a two story Colonial with four bedrooms, three and a half baths. They added a huge deck off the back of the house and a small balcony off the master suite. Of all the things he was proud of in his life, buying this house for Mel and his kids was at the top of his list. Having grown up dirt poor and always moving from one place to another, owning a home of his own was something of which he was exceptionally proud. Especially one this big and beautiful. It was the only place that had ever felt like home to him.

Melinda sat down next to him and handed him a glass. He took a long sip and put it down on the coffee table next to hers. The local news droned on the TV. Melinda crossed her legs, dangling her shoe from the tip of one toe.

"So the girls are doing okay?" he asked, unable to stand the awkward silence.

"They're okay. Grades are good. Hannah's getting ready for junior prom. I'm sure she'll tell you all about it this weekend."

"Prom?" He made a face.

"In two weeks."

"With a boy?"

Melinda laughed. "Yeah, she's crazy about him, too."

"Is that who she's on the phone with?"

"Probably," she said. "I'm sure you'll hate this, but we got her her own cell phone."

He groaned.

"And she's going for her driver's test next weekend."

"She is?" He'd always imagined he would be the one to teach her to drive.

"So she'll be asking for a car sometime soon."

He sat back in the chair. He was missing everything, and he'd already missed so much. *I shouldn't have taken this job.* He was sure that bastard Neil was teaching her. Add it to the list of reasons he hated the guy.

"I'll buy it. Let me take her car shopping."

"Sure. She'll love that." Melinda looked at him, crossing her arms over her chest. "You okay?"

"I just feel left out of their lives."

"I don't want you to feel left out, Richard. That's why I'm talking to you now."

"I know." He ran his hands through his hair. "I guess this isn't so easy for me." He gestured with his hand to indicate the space between the two of them.

Her expression softened. "Oh, hey," she said. "I'm sorry."

"Naw. Don't feel sorry for me."

"I didn't mean—"

The door to the garage opened and Neil walked in. "I'm home," he called down the narrow hallway. Melinda and Richard stood as he entered the family room. Nora sprang up too, but stayed by Richard's side.

If Neil was surprised to see Richard inside the house, he didn't show it. "Hey, how are you, Richard?" He gave him a firm handshake before kissing Melinda hello.

"Okay. How are you, Neil." Richard hadn't meant his voice to sound so flat.

"Very well, thanks. How's things up north?"

"It's colder up there, but otherwise, it's not bad at all," Richard said. "Keeping busy with work, you know."

"And he has a girlfriend," Melinda chimed in. Richard looked at her. She smirked.

"Great, Richard." Neil flipped through the mail on the kitchen island without looking up.

It was official, things had progressed to the Twilight Zone. "I'll go put the girls' suitcases into the car," he said. "You can send them out whenever they're ready."

Melinda frowned. "Okay."

Richard walked outside, set the bags on the ground, and lit a cigarette. He inhaled and blew smoke towards the darkening sky, trying to calm his frayed nerves, trying not to think about how good a whiskey would taste. He wondered what Natalie was doing right now. Closing his eyes, he pictured her fiery blue eyes, her smooth skin, her honey-blonde hair, wishing he could be with her this weekend instead of feeling bewildered by his ex's behavior.

The front door opened. Melinda walked outside with both girls, along with Nora on her leash.

"Sorry I took so long, Dad." Hannah reached up for a hug.

"It's okay, darlin'." He kissed the top of her head, looking at Melinda as the girls got into the car. He turned to pet Nora, rubbing her head. She poked her wet nose into his palm. He bent to kiss her head. "Goodbye, sweet girl."

"I'm sorry," Melinda said, gesturing towards the house as he straightened up. "I think we should try and be friends. For the kids' sake."

Friends. Was that even possible? He tried to come up with a response, but couldn't.

"I'll see you on Sunday, okay?" Melinda's voice was soft.

"You bet."

Her pale eyes shone. "Drive safe, now."

"You enjoy your weekend."

-10-

Sunday night brought another family dinner at her sister Christine's house. This time, Natalie said goodbye and bolted out the door, not giving anyone time to answer or hand her anything.

She got into her car and started the engine. The lights flickered and the car sputtered for a few seconds before coming to life.

"Don't you start on me," she said out loud to the little red Focus, easing her foot down on the gas pedal to encourage its compliance.

She pulled out of the parking spot and continued to the corner, turning right to head back towards the interstate. Halfway down the next block, the car shuddered and gave up. She had just enough momentum to pull off to the side of the road as everything shut off.

Shit.

She closed her eyes and pressed her head against the steering wheel. She sat in the silence, listening to the sound of her own breath and the occasional car driving past. *Maybe I'll just live here forever.* It seemed like a reasonable solution. The thought of having to ask her dad or either brother-in-law for help was too much. It would be like admitting she couldn't manage on her own. And the absolute last person she wanted to call was Ben.

She picked up her cell phone and flipped it open, scrolling through her contact list. She pushed a button, chewing on her bottom lip.

"Hey, Natalie." Richard sounded amused.

"I'm sorry to bother you."

"You're never a bother."

"I know you were away this weekend, but I was wondering, um... Are you back in town yet?"

"It's your lucky day. I'm about to walk in my front door."

"You are?"

"What's up?"

"My car broke down."

"Where are you?" She could hear him opening and closing the door of his truck and starting the engine.

She told him her approximate location. "It's a block or two down from the park where—"

"Sure, I know where it is. I take that road all the time. Sit tight. I'll see you in a few."

She thanked him and flipped her phone closed, relieved.

Within a few minutes, he had popped her hood, taken a look around with the aid of a giant flashlight, and diagnosed the problem. Her battery had died, he explained, due to a snapped alternator belt. He pulled it out and held it up to show her. The frayed ends were scratchy against her fingertips.

"The good news is, it's a pretty simple and cheap repair. I can do it myself, if you want."

"What's the bad news?" she asked, bracing herself.

He wiped his hands off on a rag. "Well, it's a little after nine on a Sunday night. Not too many places to go pick up an alternator belt."

"Right. Shit." She leaned against the side of her car.

"Tell you what." He stood in front of her. "I'll drive you home tonight. Then tomorrow, I'll pick

up the part, come pick you up, and bring you back to the car."

"You would do all that?"

"For you, baby girl? Anything."

She cringed at the nickname. "I have to work until three."

"Me too. I'll pick you up from there."

"Thank you." She gave him a crooked smile.

"Aw, shucks, ma'am, it's no problem at all," he drawled.

She laughed, locked her car, and got into the passenger seat of his truck.

"So how come you called me?" Richard maneuvered the truck onto the highway. Traffic was light, and he was comfortable accelerating a few miles per hour above the posted speed limit.

"Because I needed help?" Natalie answered, her voice thick with sarcasm.

"Right, but why me? Don't you have family right nearby, that I'm assuming you were spending time with before this happened?"

She groaned and looked out the window.

"Or were you doing your nightly patrol of the park, looking for kids stuck in trees?"

Natalie laughed.

"Don't get me wrong, I'm happy to provide the rescue. I'm just curious."

She hesitated before answering. "I left my sister's without saying goodbye. I didn't want another lecture about how I've ruined my life."

He glanced at her. "Ruined it by..."

"Leaving my marriage, of course." She rolled her eyes. "You can't just run away from a problem, Natalie. You have to try and work things out," she added in a put-on voice, imitating some unknown relative.

"I see," Richard said.

"I'm the youngest in my family," she continued. "They all see me as this sweet, innocent child who can do no wrong, but can't take care of myself. And I guess I've always gone along with it. Now they don't know what to think. I might as well have shaved my head and joined a motorcycle gang, or something."

"I'd tell you not to shave your head and join a motorcycle gang, but it sounds like you don't need anyone else telling you what to do."

The miles sped by as they talked. Richard parked in front of her house and walked her to the door. After she unlocked it, he took her free hand and turned her around so she was facing him. He was close enough to feel her breath on his face.

"I thought maybe you called me because you finally realized how much you like me."

She tilted her head to one side. "Oh, is that what you thought?" The dimple appeared next to her smile.

"Uh huh."

"Are you flirting with me?" Her eyes sparkled under the porch light.

He let go of her hand, taking a step backwards. "Oh, I'd never be brave enough to flirt with you, Miss Natalie."

She crossed her arms over her chest, leaning against the door frame. "So how come you agreed to help me?"

Richard blinked, caught off-guard by the question. "As if I could say no to you."

"Well, I'm very grateful. Thank you for being my knight in shining armor, once again."

"My pleasure, ma'am." He grinned. "I'll meet you outside school tomorrow, about three thirty?"

"I'll be there." He opened his arms for a hug, and she kissed his cheek. "You're the best."

"I'm glad someone thinks so."

Her phone rang at three thirty-five the next afternoon.

"Sorry I'm late," Richard said.

"I'll be right out." Natalie put her jacket on and grabbed her bag, locking her classroom door behind her. The sound of her footsteps reverberated through the empty hallway.

She passed Lauren's classroom on the way. Her friend looked up from her desk.

"Hey, I didn't know you were still here."

"Just heading out," Natalie replied.

"Hang on, I'll walk with you." She grabbed her things and turned off the light. They walked towards the door. Lauren eyed her. "You look nice."

"Thanks." She'd touched up her makeup after the kids were dismissed.

"Going somewhere?" Lauren raised an eyebrow.

"I'm not sure yet."

Lauren narrowed her eyes. "You're being mysterious."

They walked out the front door and around the corner towards the parking lot. Richard stood next to the open door of his truck.

He looked up and grinned when he saw the two women.

"Hi." Natalie returned his smile.

"Ready to go?"

"Oh my god." Lauren stopped, her eyes wide. She looked at Natalie. "Is this Rhett Butler?"

Natalie blushed as Richard looked at her, raising his eyebrows. "Rhett Butler?"

"I'm Lauren." She extended her hand.

"Richard," he said, shaking it. "Nice to meet you."

"Same here." Lauren turned to Natalie. "We'll talk later."

"Definitely."

Lauren glanced at Richard one more time, put her hand up to hide her face, and mouthed, "He's cute!"

Natalie gave her a playful glare. "Get out of here."

She got into the truck. Richard started the engine.

"Rhett Butler, huh?"

"You know, from *Gone With—*"

"I'm from Atlanta, Natalie," he interrupted with a laugh. "I know who Rhett Butler is. I just didn't know *I* was Rhett Butler. Wow."

"Shut up." She laughed, settling back into the seat.

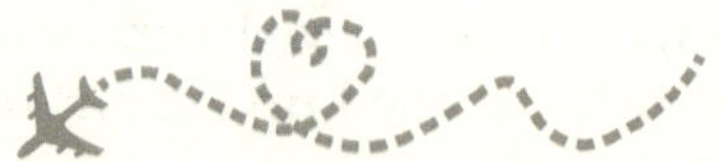

Natalie held the flashlight while Richard worked under the open hood of her car. The repair was a bit more complicated than he'd thought it would be, but after some effort, he got the belt into place. Natalie turned the key, clapping her hands when it started.

"Thank you so much." She got out of the car and gave him a hug. "What do I owe you for the part?"

He closed the hood, wiping his hands on a damp rag. "Not a thing. It was my pleasure, Miss Scarlett." He winked.

She rolled her eyes. "I'm going to kill Lauren."

He laughed. "I'm sorry."

"I was going to offer to buy you dinner, but now you're making fun of me."

"How about a cup of coffee?"

"Okay."

"Follow me." He got back into his truck and she followed behind in her car until he turned into the parking lot of a tiny café.

"I know you Philly people like your Wawa, but this place has the best coffee around," he told Natalie as they walked in the door.

"Hey, Richard," the girl behind the counter said with a smile.

Richard grinned. "How are you today, Gina?"

"Can't complain. Before you even ask, yes, we have the raspberry scones today."

"How many did you save for me?"

She eyed the cake display. "I've got four left."

"We'll take two. And one for the road."

"And a medium Americano? How about your friend?" She nodded in Natalie's direction.

"The same," Natalie said. "With lots of cream."

"I'll bring them to your table."

"Thank you, Gina."

"This place is cute." Natalie looked around as they sat down at one of the small tables. "And your little barista friend is cute, too," she said, hanging her jacket on the back of her chair.

"Is she? I hadn't noticed."

"Uh huh."

Gina brought the drinks and scones to the table, handing Richard the check. "Whenever you're ready. I threw in that last scone so it wouldn't be lonely."

"Thank you, darlin'," he said as she walked away.

Natalie snatched the check out of his hand. "My treat," she insisted.

Richard put his hands up in mock surrender.

"Try this." He pushed the small plate towards her.

She broke off a piece of raspberry scone and tasted it. "Oh my god. This is so good."

"The best." Richard took a bite of his.

She sipped her coffee. "How was Atlanta?"

"Weird."

"Oh yeah?"

"The good part is spending time with my daughters. But it's strange having to make small talk with the person who stomped on your heart."

"Yeah, that sounds awful."

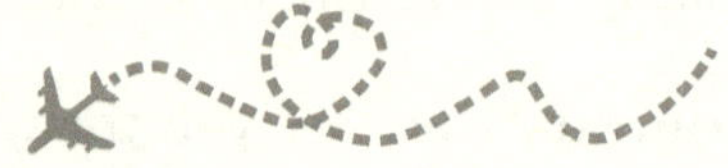

They lingered in the cafe until it was ready to close, talking and laughing.

"I guess we should have gone for dinner, after all," Richard said as they walked out the door.

"Next time." Natalie unlocked her car. "It's funny."

"What's that?"

"I like it better when you rescue me than when we actually go out. It's more fun."

"You're right."

"So I'll see you Saturday?"

"Unless you have another catastrophe before then."

She laughed. "You never know."

"Call me and let me know you got home safely."

"I will." She gave him a hug. "Thanks for fixing my car."

"Anytime. Shining Armor Auto Repair and Taxi Company, at your service."

-11-

By Saturday, Natalie was nervous about going out with Richard again. He'd called her every night since fixing her car. They talked for hours about nothing in particular. He told her stories and made her laugh. She found herself looking forward to his calls. She worried the next date would be as awful as the others had been, but more than that, she worried she was getting way too attached to him. What had started as a crush, a flirtation, was now turning into something more.

"I should cancel," she said to Lauren, over the phone.

"Tell him you're not feeling well."

"He won't believe that."

"Well, if you don't want to see him again, who cares what he believes?"

"Yeah, but he's been so nice to me, I don't want him to think I'm being mean."

Lauren groaned. "So say you forgot some other plans you already had."

"I guess that would work."

"Sounds to me like you *do* want to go out with him. You just think you *shouldn't* want to."

Natalie didn't answer.

"That's what I thought. Now go get ready."

"I like him, Lauren. I know I shouldn't, but..."

"Maybe it's not up to you." Lauren was a hardcore romantic. "Maybe it's meant to be."

Natalie hung up the phone, grateful for Lauren's friendship. All her other friends had taken Ben's side of things. Lauren was the only one she had left.

She dressed in jeans and sneakers, pulling her hair into a ponytail. She wasn't going to make any special effort this time. Tonight she was going to be herself.

Richard rang her doorbell at seven sharp. He was wearing jeans, too.

"I missed you." He held out his arms and she gave him a quick hug.

"It's only been a couple of days."

"Even so."

"So where are we going tonight?"

"You'll see." He opened the door of the pickup for her.

Richard drove in the direction of the suburb where he and Natalie's sister both resided. He turned off the highway, made a few quick turns, then pulled into a driveway in a small townhouse community. He turned off the engine.

"Where are we?"

"Welcome to my humble home."

"I don't know, Richard..." Her stomach tied itself in a knot.

"Come inside. I'm just going to cook you dinner. I promise I don't bite." He looked at her face, seeming to sense her apprehension was real. His expression turned serious. "Natalie, you can trust me."

She thought about the hospital, and how he'd taken her home afterwards and treated her with kindness. She trusted him, but what about herself? "Okay." She took a breath.

Natalie stepped out of the pickup and followed Richard to the front door. The entrance was on the ground floor, and they continued down a narrow

hallway, past a laundry room, and up a flight of steps into the main living space.

The house was cozy, but clean and tidy. It was obvious he didn't spend a whole lot of time at home. The front rooms were large and open, with no real separation between the living room, dining area, and kitchen. Richard walked into the kitchen to stir a big pot on the stove, turning the flame on underneath. The aroma of garlic, tomato and herbs filled the air.

"Smells good." She dropped her jacket and purse on a nearby chair.

"I hope you like pasta," he said. "I'm not a four-star chef, but I do make a mean plate of spaghetti and meatballs."

Natalie laughed. "I like spaghetti and meatballs." She looked around the living room. Above the fireplace were several framed photographs of two smiling, dark-haired girls. "Are these your daughters?"

"Yeah, that's Hannah, my oldest," he said, pointing. "She just turned seventeen. And my baby, Bella. She'll be thirteen next month."

"Pretty girls. And they're still in Atlanta?"

He nodded. "I see them every other weekend, and when I fly down for work. They have a room here for when they visit." He pointed down the long hallway leading towards the back of the house. "But so far they've only been here once."

"This isn't what I expected your place to be like," Natalie said.

"What did you expect?"

"A bachelor pad apartment with leather furniture and a great sound system?"

He shook his head, an amused smile on his lips. "That's not me."

She wandered around the room, noticing the comfortable-looking furniture, the big-screen TV, the shelf of CDs next to the stereo. On the opposite wall was a small bookcase.

She walked closer to view the titles. A handful of classics as well as a few current authors. "A Hemingway fan."

"My favorite."

"I didn't know you were a reader."

"Well, I wanted to pass the first grade, so I thought I'd learn how."

"Funny."

"I have more books in storage, back home. These are the ones I can't live without."

Richard walked over to the stereo and hit play on the CD deck. Elvis. Of course. Natalie smiled. He took her hand, put an arm around her waist, and danced her across the living room, singing along as she shook her head.

"So corny," she said, laughing.

"I've been called worse. Let me get the water boiling for the pasta. I'll be right back."

"I'll come with you." She followed him towards the kitchen, sitting on a stool at the center island, watching him as he filled a pot with water, added some salt, and set it on the stove to boil.

"That smells delicious," she said. He cut a small piece off a baguette, using it to scoop up some of the sauce. He blew on it before holding it towards her mouth. She took a bite. "Yum." She tasted olive oil, basil and oregano. "You said you weren't a four-star chef," she teased.

"I don't like to brag."

"I'd brag if I could cook anything that good."

Richard turned his attention back to the stove. Natalie got up from the counter and walked out

the double doors onto the deck, which overlooked a wooded area. There were a couple of chairs and a small table with an ashtray on it. She stood at the railing at the edge, looking out at the wooded area behind the row of houses.

Richard walked up behind her.

"It's nice out here," she said. "A lot quieter than my neighborhood."

"No backyard, but at least I have some outdoor space. The deck gets a good amount of morning sunlight. I want to plant some herbs out here, maybe even some tomatoes. I'm just waiting for it to get a bit warmer."

"I like it. The backyard is the only part of my old house that I miss."

He put his hands on her shoulders, but she stiffened and pulled away. She heard him light a cigarette, then exhale.

"Sorry. I'm..." She paused. "I'm not ready for this whole thing."

"Not ready for what? We're just having dinner."

"You know what I mean."

"Natalie." He took a step closer, reaching for her hand. He turned her to face him. "Look at me. I just want to get to know you. That's all this is. You're a fascinating woman." She rolled her eyes. "You *are*. And I want to spend one evening with you that doesn't involve head injuries, or broken down cars, or strange women hitting on me."

"Okay, first of all, I'm not all that interesting. And secondly, you, sir, are a world-class flatterer and incorrigible flirt."

He gave her a sheepish smile. "Guilty as charged."

"So do you expect me to believe you didn't bring me here hoping I'd sleep with you?"

"Ouch." Richard chuckled. "Okay, I won't deny it. The thought crossed my mind. How could it not? You're beautiful. You have a gorgeous body. And I might be a nice guy, but I am a man." His eyes traveled from her face down to her toes, and then back upwards.

Natalie blushed.

"But I'm much more interested in what's in here." He touched his index finger to her forehead. "And in here," he said, pointing to her heart.

Natalie's lips curled upwards against her will.

He took her hand. "I like you."

"You like everyone." She laughed, rolling her eyes.

He took a step closer to her. "But you're special."

"You barely know me."

"Don't I? I know you, Natalie," he said, his deep voice soft and gentle. "I know those blue eyes are like fire and ice, pushing me away and pulling me in all at once. I know the way your cheeks flush red when you're angry, or embarrassed. I know you're not afraid to call me out on my bullshit. I know you have secret wounds you try to hide behind snarky words and daggered looks. You're extraordinary. You just can't see it in yourself."

Natalie felt a sharp pinch in the center of her chest. She turned away, unable to keep his words from working their magic on her. And while her logical, reasonable side told her otherwise, something inside her wanted to believe he wasn't just trying to flatter her. She turned back, looking over her shoulder at him. He was still looking right at her.

The timer went off in the kitchen, and they both smiled as the apprehension between them dissolved.

"Shall we?" he asked, opening the door for her.

Dinner went well, or so Richard thought, despite his revelations on the deck. He hoped he hadn't scared Natalie off with all that he said, and he trembled inside with all the things he hadn't had the nerve to say. But she seemed more relaxed now, and she opened up to him a bit over their meal. He asked her easy questions about the trivia of her life, about her job, her family. He didn't care as much about the answers as he wanted to listen to her talk, to watch her expressions, to read her body language.

"I have two sisters," she said. "Christine is the oldest. She's the one who lives here. She has four kids and she's basically Supermom. She's head of the PTA, organizes all the school fundraisers and special events, and she has her kids in a million activities. They're always running from one thing to another. Lisa is a little more laid back. She lives close to me, in the city. She does freelance photography and she shoots weddings and portraits, too. She has two kids."

"So which sister are you more like?"

"I wanted to be just like them when I was younger, but it turns out I'm not really like either one of them." She twirled spaghetti onto her fork. "What about you? Brothers and sisters?"

"One sister. Rose." His throat got tight. He hadn't talked about Rosie in years.

"Older or younger?"

"A year older. She died when we were kids."

"Oh my god, I'm so sorry."

"Thanks."

She touched his forearm. "Is this for her?"

His rosebud tattoo. He'd gotten it while he was in the Army. He nodded. "We moved around a lot. She was my only friend most of the time."

"What happened?"

He hesitated. "You know, I don't want to tell my sad stories tonight."

"You're right. No sad stories."

He stood up and began clearing the dishes. She got up to help, but he waved her away. "I've got this," he said. "Relax."

"I don't mind helping."

Natalie cleared the table as Richard put away the leftovers and loaded the dishwasher. His heart pounded and he had to steady his hands so as not to drop the dishes as she handed them to him. He wasn't quite sure what to do next. He'd half-expected things to end in disaster before dinner was over, and hadn't planned anything for afterwards. Although he could think of a few things. *Stop it,* he told himself. *Keep your hands to yourself...at least for now.*

"Sometimes I go for a walk after dinner," he said a few minutes later, drying his hands on the dish towel.

"Are you telling me you think I need exercise?" She raised an eyebrow at him, and he laughed.

"Natalie, don't you know by now? I think every inch of you is gorgeous."

She grabbed her jacket and put it on. They walked downstairs and outside to the driveway. Natalie shivered.

"Are you cold? That jacket's not very warm. I can get you a sweatshirt or something."

"Thanks. Shit, that reminds me, I still have your sweatshirt at my place."

"Don't worry, I've got plenty." He walked inside and pulled an orange hooded sweatshirt from

a hook by the front door. He marveled that she was cold while he was sweating bullets just being close to her.

"Another University of Tennessee shirt?" She pulled it down over her head. Like his black sweatshirt, it hugged her curves in all the right places.

"Yep. I bleed orange," he said with a grin as they started down the front steps. Richard turned left and she followed, walking beside him at a leisurely pace.

"Did you go there, or are you just a fan?"

"Proud alum. And a die-hard fan. Especially football."

"I went to a tiny little Catholic college in Philly. No football team, I'm afraid."

"What?" He feigned shock, which made her laugh. "Imagine going to a college without a football team." He made a disapproving sound. "College football is a way of life where I'm from."

"I like hockey and baseball, though. And the Flyers wear orange."

"I guess I can deal with that." He winked, playing it cool, hoping she didn't see how nervous he was. They walked together in silence for a few minutes. At some point he reached down and took her hand. "Is this okay?"

"It's okay." After a few blocks, they arrived at the edge of the park. Natalie looked around. "This is where we met, isn't it?"

"It sure is."

"Does Logan's mom know how close you live to her house?" She flashed him a teasing smile.

"If she ever finds out, I'll know who to blame." He nudged her shoulder with his.

They stopped when they reached the tree where Logan had been stuck that first night, and sat down next to one another on the bench. He opened his mouth to say something, but found himself speechless for once.

Natalie put her free hand on top of the one holding hers. He hoped she didn't notice the clamminess as her fingers intertwined with his. His stomach rolled over, his heart beating faster.

"Listen. About what you said earlier," she began.

"Yeah?"

"You're sweet." He made a face. "No, seriously. And I'm flattered by what you said. I'm not used to a guy being so open about his feelings. It's kind of refreshing."

"I mean it, Natalie. You're an intriguing woman. I like being with you."

"I like being with you, too." She squeezed his fingers, then let go of his hand. "I like *you*. More than I should. But I want to be honest."

He waited for the sucker punch he was sure was coming.

"You shouldn't be wasting your time on me. I'm not worth it."

Her words made him ache. How could she think so little of herself? He touched the side of her face. "Natalie," he said. "Please. Don't say that about yourself."

"Listen. That night at the hospital, when you said you were divorced, I told you I was going through one, too. That's not exactly true. We're separated. I left him. It was only a few months ago." She paused. "But we haven't filed papers, or even talked about divorce. I honestly don't know what the future holds, for Ben and me. I'm supposed to be getting some space and figuring it out, but right now I'm kind of avoiding the whole thing."

"You're stuck in a holding pattern."

"I guess I am." Natalie looked away. "I just wanted to tell you the truth about where things stand with me."

"Thank you."

"I don't know if I can offer anything more than friendship right now."

A car drove past, its headlights illuminating the space between them. She turned her head in his direction.

Richard smoothed the hair from her forehead, gazing into her eyes. "I don't want to push you into anything, Natalie. It's like you said, I enjoy being with you. If friendship is all it can be, then that's okay."

"Everyone else in my life is mad at me. I could use a friend."

"Me, too," he admitted. "Being alone in a new city is tough."

"I can imagine." She turned to face him. "So, friends?" She put out her right hand.

"Friends." He shook her hand.

"I'm sorry I can't promise more."

"Don't be. I'm happy to have you for a friend." Her eyes misted over, and he panicked. "Hey now, I said I was happy."

"I know." She covered her eyes with her hands. "I'm sorry," she whispered, tears coming harder. "Shit."

Richard fumbled in his pockets for a tissue, but couldn't find one. He wiped her tears with the cuff of his sleeve, then wrapped his arms around her. Natalie buried her face into his shoulder. He smoothed her hair. "It's okay," he said. "You're okay."

"I'm so sorry, Richard." Her voice was muffled by his shirt. "That's embarrassing." She sat up and swiped at her nose. "I'm a fucking mess."

"No. No, I don't think so. I think you're someone who's had a lot of pain in her life. And I know what that's like." He paused. "If you ever want to talk about it, I promise to listen."

Her eyes softened. "Thank you." She rested her head on his shoulder. He would have given anything to kiss her, but he held back. He could be her friend. That would be enough. They sat together for a while, then began walking back towards Richard's house.

"Would you like me to take you home?" he asked as they approached his driveway.

"Trying to get rid of me?" she teased.

"Never."

"I guess I *should* go, but I wouldn't mind hanging out a little longer."

He unlocked the door and asked if she wanted coffee.

"Yes. With cream, no sugar."

"Comin' right up." He went into the kitchen to start the coffee maker. Natalie kicked off her shoes and sat on his couch, tucking her feet underneath her.

Richard fixed them each a cup and brought out some chocolate chip cookies. Natalie found an old black-and-white movie to watch on PBS. While they watched, she snuggled next to him on the couch, her head resting against his shoulder. He put his arm around her and stroked her hair as they watched, laughing at the same parts. At some point, he looked down and saw that Natalie was fast asleep.

-12-

atalie awakened to the sound of her cell phone ringing. She opened her eyes, looking around before realizing she was lying on the couch in Richard's living room. *Did I fall asleep here?*

She reached into the back pocket of her jeans and checked the display. It was Ben. Oh. *Shit.*

"Hello?"

"Good morning, beautiful, come down and answer your door."

Oh, no. No, no, no. "Um..."

"I brought coffee and bagels." He sounded so wide-awake and cheerful. *God, I hate morning people...wait...that's so not the thing to focus on. Think!*

Her stomach twisted in a knot. "I'm actually, uh, not at home."

"But your car's here."

Think faster. "I'm out to breakfast."

"With who? Lisa?"

"No..."

"Nat?" His voice rose. "Were you out all night?"

"Wow, okay. Yeah." She heard Richard's footsteps approaching and turned to look at him, a finger on her lips. He gave her a thumbs up and walked into the kitchen.

"The guy from the hospital again, right? You're sleeping with him now?"

"Ben..."

"When did this start happening? I think I have a right to know." His voice was like a little boy's.

She lowered her voice. "Nothing's happening, okay? I'm not sleeping with anybody."

"Then where are you?"

"Can we talk about this later?"

"You're with him right now?"

She pressed her thumb and forefinger to her temples. "I'll call you back." She flipped her phone shut. "Jesus." A wave of humiliation ripped through her. She hated how angry he'd sounded. *But maybe getting angry is the only way he'll realize he needs to move on.*

"Is the coast clear?" Richard asked from the kitchen.

She sighed. "Yeah."

He walked out carrying a cup of coffee and set it on the table in front of her. "Mornin'."

"Thanks." She reached for the coffee cup, taking a sip. He'd remembered, cream, no sugar. "What happened last night?"

"You were out cold." He sat next to her. "I tried to wake you."

"Sorry. I don't usually sleep that deeply, or for that long either." She noticed the clock on the wall read nine thirty. She'd slept more than ten hours. "How long have you been awake?"

"An hour or so." He was freshly shaved and showered.

"You should've woken me up." She tucked her legs underneath her before taking another sip of coffee. "I feel like I slept for a hundred years."

"Well, welcome back." He motioned to the phone. "Everything okay?"

"I don't know. It was Ben. He shows up at my place sometimes. He brought bagels." She rolled her eyes. "Sorry I fell asleep."

"It's okay."

"You must think I'm the most boring girl in the world."

"Nah. I was flattered."

"Shut up." She laughed.

"No, I'm serious. You felt comfortable enough to fall asleep—that means you trust me. And I'm glad." He looked pleased with himself. "Plus, you're adorable when you're sleeping."

"Wait. Where did you sleep?"

"Well, you fell asleep with your head on my shoulder, and I didn't want to disturb you."

"So you slept right here? Sitting up?"

"Pretty much."

"Pretty much? What else happened?" She feigned alarm.

He held up his hands, chuckling. "Nothing, I promise. After a few hours, I covered you over with a blanket and went to my own room. I'm a gentleman, remember?"

"A true gentleman would have taken me home," she chided. "Would it be terrible if I asked you to take me home now?"

"No, not terrible. We can go whenever you're ready."

"I'm sorry. I should go home, though."

"Why do you keep apologizing?"

"I don't want to be a bother."

"Maybe you haven't realized this by now," he said, one eyebrow raised, "but I want to be bothered by you."

She blushed. "I think I'm starting to realize."

"Good." He pulled her towards him, wrapping his arms around her. She relaxed into him. He kissed the top of her head.

She looked up at him. *I could get used to this.*

His eyes lingered on her mouth. She shifted and turned away.

"Let me make you breakfast before you go."

She thought for a minute. "Okay. But then I need to go home."

"Deal."

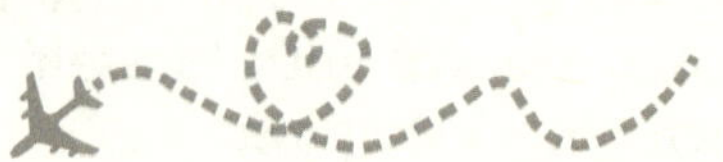

Richard drove Natalie home after breakfast. He followed her inside and up the steps.

"You don't have to come in. I mean, you can if you want to."

"I want to make sure you're okay."

Sushi greeted them at the door, meowing. Natalie bent to pet her head. "I know you're hungry."

Richard followed her into the kitchen, watching as she filled the cat's bowl.

"Can I get you a drink or something?" She opened the fridge and looked inside. "I have...well, I have milk and water. Or I can make coffee."

"I'm okay." He stood close behind her.

She closed the refrigerator door and turned to face him, seeming surprised to see him so close.

"Hi."

"Hey," she murmured. He wrapped his arms around her and she relaxed against him, resting her head on his chest. He kissed the top of her head, his lips lingering on her silky hair. She lifted her head as he bent towards her, his eyes on her mouth, but she pulled back. "I can't," she whispered.

He shifted his eyes away from her face. "Sorry," he said. "I know we agreed we're just friends, but I thought I'd take a chance."

She blushed. "It's pretty hard to say no."

"That's good to know, at least." He let go of her. "I guess I should head out."

"Unless you want to stay and help me do laundry."

"That doesn't sound too bad," he said. "But I have some work to catch up on. I'll leave you to your laundry."

"Thanks for dinner." She walked him to her front door. "And breakfast."

"When can I see you again?"

"Soon."

"Promise?"

"Promise." They shared a hug. "Call me tomorrow."

He called her a few hours later. "Is it tomorrow yet?" he asked.

She laughed. "You're a little early."

"Work is boring. I should have stayed to do laundry with you."

"It's tons of fun."

"So are these schedules I'm making."

"Sounds exciting." He could tell she was walking down the stairs by the change in her breath. "What should we talk about?"

"Ask me anything."

"Okay. Let me think." She paused. "If you could live anywhere in the world, where would it be?"

"That's a good one."

"You've traveled a lot."

"I've seen a lot of the insides of airports." He considered her question. "I've always thought someday I'd live on my boat, right off the Georgia coast."

"You have a boat?"

"I do. It's a good fishing boat. But I'd buy a bigger one. With a little cabin I can sleep in."

"Living right on the water?"

"Yeah. I could fish all day. Run around the beach with my dog."

"You have a dog?"

"Had a dog. The prettiest chocolate lab. Nora. She still lives with my kids. We got her when they were little. She was just a puppy."

It had been during one of his many attempts at sobriety. Before the divorce. Before AA. He and Hannah had driven out to a farm, and Hannah had picked Nora out of a litter of five, scooping her up. "This is the one, Daddy!" She'd been rewarded with a million puppy kisses on the face.

"Sounds like you miss her."

"I do. Now, are you one of those people who think a dog person and a cat person can't get along?"

"I like dogs," she answered. "I just prefer the quiet kind that don't jump on people, or bark at the mailman. Or need to be walked."

"I think the kind of dog you're talking about is called a cat."

Natalie giggled.

They stayed on the phone for over an hour.

"I guess I'd better get back to work," Richard said.

"If you insist."

"I'll talk to you soon."

She hung up, and dialed Lauren's number. "I'm in trouble," she said when Lauren answered.

"I'm so happy for you!" Lauren replied.

"I knew you would be."

-13-

On the second Sunday in May, Natalie awoke early after a long night of tossing and turning. She would have liked to cross this day off the calendar, but every year it showed up, reminding her of what she wasn't.

Her phone rang as she stood in her kitchen, making coffee.

It was Ben. "Hey, kid."

"Hey."

"How are you?"

"I'm okay."

"I wanted to..." He paused. "I mean, I know this day is hard for you. I wanted to let you know I'm thinking of you."

A twinge of warmth flickered in the center of her chest. He remembered. That was something. "Thank you."

"You never called me back after the last time we talked."

The early morning phone call replayed in her mind. "I'm sorry."

"I just want to know what's going on."

"You want me to call and tell you I met somebody?"

"No. But at least tell me the truth."

She swallowed hard. "It's like I told you before... He's a friend."

"Then why did you spend the night with him?"

"We were watching something and I fell asleep. That's all."

A long silence followed.

"Is that all? Or is it just what you're telling me?" He softened his voice. "Do you like him?"

She chewed her lower lip. "I don't know," she murmured. "Yes."

"What about me?" His voice quivered. "You know I love you, right?"

"I know." She hesitated for a moment. "I love you, too. I always will, Ben. But it's too hard. You could find someone else."

"I don't want someone else, Nat. I want you. I'm not giving up on us. No matter what happens. I know we can fix this if we try."

Natalie said a quick goodbye and hung up. That had always been his focus: fixing it. He was incapable of accepting things the way they were.

A few weeks after the last miscarriage, he came home from work, excited. "I was talking to one of the other guys at the office. Guess what? He and his wife adopted a little girl from Vietnam. He showed me pictures." He grinned. "She's two years old and so cute, with these chubby little cheeks and dimples."

Natalie managed a half-smile. She was back at work, making it through her days with a comfortable predictability, and had even stopped for groceries on her way home so she could cook dinner. She stood in the kitchen, waiting for the oven timer to beep while she cut up vegetables for a salad.

Ben continued. "He gave me the name of the agency they used and the social worker who helped them through the process. He said she's great and we should give her a call."

"Ben."

"Yeah."

"I'm not ready to talk about that yet. I'm not even ready to think about it. You said you would give me some time." She kept her tone gentle.

His face fell. "I'm sorry. You're right."

Later, in bed, he kissed her goodnight. When the kiss lingered, he reached for her, but she pulled away.

"I thought you were feeling better."

"I am. But I can't..." She rolled onto her side, away from him.

He snuggled close behind her, kissing her neck, his hands on her body. "I just want to make you feel good."

"No." She pushed his hands away. "I can't risk getting pregnant again."

He was quiet for a minute. "What if we used birth control?"

She sat up. "How can you even say that to me?"

He scoffed. "So what are you saying, we're never going to have sex again?"

She didn't answer.

"This is crazy." His voice sounded sad.

"I'm sorry."

"Natalie, I love you. I want to be with you."

"No. I'm not taking that chance." She stood and walked towards the door.

"What are you doing?"

"Leaving."

He jumped out of bed, standing between her and the doorway. "Natalie. I'm sorry. Please." He put his hands on her shoulders. "Don't go. Come back to bed."

She looked down at the floor. "I think I should be by myself for a while."

"No. Go back to bed. I'll...sleep on the couch or something."

A few days after that incident, the house phone rang as Natalie arrived home from work. She set

her keys down on the table and grabbed the receiver. "Hello?"

"Hi, is this Natalie?" a woman's voice asked.

"Yes?"

The woman introduced herself as April, the social worker from the adoption agency Ben had mentioned to her the other night. "I spoke to your husband yesterday, and I wanted to touch base with you and see if you had any questions for me."

Natalie's mouth went dry.

April continued, undeterred by Natalie's silence. "I told him we're having an open house next month for clients who are new to the process, to meet some of our families and get to know our agency and how the process works. It's December third, at six o'clock, at our offices. We'd love to have you and Ben attend."

"Oh, um, I'm not sure what our schedule looks like right now."

"That's okay, you can get back to us any time before the first to RSVP."

"Okay." The room was spinning.

"In the meantime, do you have any questions for me about our programs? Like I told your husband, we facilitate both domestic and international adoptions, with programs in six different countries." She rattled off some statistics as Natalie sank into a dining room chair, unable to pay attention to what this woman was saying in her annoyingly perky voice. Ben had called this woman without telling her about it. Gone behind her back. Her attention quickly shifted back to the phone call when she heard the woman mention her miscarriages.

"I'm sorry, what?" Natalie interrupted.

"I was just mentioning that so many of our families have had similar experiences as you and your husband, with infertility, multiple miscarriages.

It's nice to get to know one another, know you're not alone."

Alone. That was exactly what she was. She had trusted Ben, and he had called this woman, told her personal things, when she had told him over and over she wasn't ready.

She took a deep breath. "I'm so sorry, April, you know what, I'm just coming in the door from work and now's not a good time. I know my husband has your contact information, so we'll be in touch. Thank you." She slammed the phone down. The walls were closing in on her.

She hated this big, empty house. She hated the small bedroom they had painted buttery yellow and hung white eyelet curtains in when she'd gotten her first positive test, years ago. She hated her stupid, broken body. She hated her husband most of all. She grabbed her keys and walked out the door.

She started her car and stared straight ahead for several seconds before heading for the interstate. The anger felt like liquid fire, burning as it coursed through her body. She steered her car onto the highway. She couldn't remember ever being so mad. She drove north, away from the city, away from Ben, away from the house, away from the adoption agency, away from the doctors and their dire predictions. She would drive all the way to Canada if she had to. She cranked up the volume on the radio as loud as she could stand it.

When she had driven for almost an hour, her heart rate had returned to normal and she could breathe again. She pulled the car into the parking lot of a convenience store. She was calmer, but she couldn't drive forever. This was stupid. She needed a plan.

She went into the store and bought a Coke and a small bag of potato chips. She took them to the car and got back inside. The Coke tasted good. She

munched a chip and reached for her cell phone. She had missed four calls from Ben, two from her mother, and one from her sister Lisa. She flipped it closed, putting it down on the seat next to her. Almost immediately, it began to ring again.

"Hey, Lisa."

"Are you okay?" She sounded out of breath.

"I'm fine. Tell my asshole husband he can call off the search party."

"Look, I don't know what happened with Ben, but it doesn't matter right now. Nana's in the hospital. She had a stroke. It's pretty bad, Nat. You need to get here quickly."

Natalie's blood ran cold. "I'm on my way."

She drove as fast as she could, cursing herself for having gone so far. Not Nana. Please, God. Ben and Lisa met her an hour later at the entrance to the ER, but Nana was already gone.

"No." Natalie shook her head. Lisa gathered her into her arms.

"It was quick. She didn't suffer."

"I want to see her."

Lisa glanced at Ben. "I'll take her in," he said.

She walked beside Ben towards the room where Nana was, not looking at him, not talking. As they approached the entrance, her steps slowed, her feet seeming to not want to move forward. The various adult members of her family milled about, grief evident on their faces, greeting her with a wave or a brief hug. Her mother held her tight, unable to speak.

"I'm so sorry, Mom."

Ben pulled back the curtain, gently, so she could step into the cubicle where her Nana lay on a gurney, so still, silent machines still hooked up to her chest and arms.

Natalie put her hand on top of Nana's. It was still warm. "Nana," she whispered.

"I'm sorry, Natalie," Ben said.

She turned to look at him. "Were you here when it happened?"

"Yes," he replied. "Your mom called me. I was on my way home from work. We kept trying you. I didn't know where you were."

She turned back to Nana. "I should have been here." Her voice broke as tears spilled down her cheeks.

Ben put his hands on her shoulders.

She shrugged him away. "Don't touch me."

"What?" He reached for her again. "Natalie..."

"I said don't touch me!" She sobbed. "I should have been here, not you! I hate you for this!"

He looked at her, bewildered.

Her brother-in-law George stepped into the cubicle. He and Ben exchanged a glance.

"Hey guys. What's going on?" He turned to her, putting his hands on her upper arms. "Natalie? Are you okay?"

She collapsed against him. "I should have been here."

"Shh." George held her close. "I know, sweetheart. I know."

A nurse poked her head into the cubicle. "Everything okay?" she asked.

Natalie nodded, sniffling. "I'm sorry."

The nurse gave her a polite smile. "Grief is hard." She handed her a small box of tissues.

"Thank you," Natalie said, embarrassed. The nurse stepped back out of the room.

George looked at Ben. "What's going on?"

"I wish I knew," Ben answered.

She slept in the guest room that night. In the morning, she couldn't look at Ben. She sat at the

table, staring into her bowl of cereal. He kept trying to talk to her, acting as though everything was fine, but she couldn't bring herself to answer.

"Are you going to tell me why you're so mad?" he finally asked as he rinsed his coffee cup.

"Fuck you."

"Natalie." His voice had an edge of impatience. She knew if he didn't leave now, he'd be late for work. "Please talk to me."

She looked up from her cereal. "How could you do that?"

"What did I do?"

"What did you do? Your friend, the social worker, called me."

He sighed. "I was going to tell you."

"How could you go behind my back and tell her those things about me?"

"What things?"

"The miscarriages."

"Nat, she's an adoption worker. I'm sure she's had plenty of clients who have dealt with the same stuff." He glanced at the clock. "Look, I've got to go. Can we talk about it later? I was only trying to help. To move things along. I thought you'd be happy about this."

"I'm supposed to be happy you're on the phone with some other woman telling her your wife is defective?" Her eyes burned.

"God, Nat. I didn't think about it that way." He stood close to her. "We both want to be parents. Isn't that what this is all about? Having a child to love?"

"I asked you to give me some time."

"I know you did. I was trying to help you feel better."

After work that day she moved all of her clothes and personal items into the guest bedroom. Except for the funeral, she avoided him.

It was hard to think about, even now. Of course he hadn't meant to hurt her, but it had been impossible for her to let it go.

Richard waited as the phone rang at Melinda's house. Four rings, then five, and finally the answering machine picked up. "We can't get to the phone right now," Bella's voice chirped. "Leave a message!"

The machine beeped. Richard took a breath to speak, but then hung up instead. They might be out to breakfast, or engaged in some other happy family scene he didn't want to imagine. He frowned and walked into the kitchen to pour himself another cup of coffee.

The phone rang. "Daddy? Did you just call?"

"Hey, Bella. Yeah, that was me."

"We were all outside on the deck. Neil made breakfast."

Richard gripped the coffee mug. "That's cool. Hey, uh… Can I talk to Mom for a minute?"

"Okay." She put the phone down. "Mom!"

Melinda's rich voice came on the line. "Hello, Richard."

"Hi, Mel, how are you?"

"I'm well. How about you?"

"I'm okay."

Neither of them said anything for several seconds.

"We're in the middle of breakfast." Melinda sounded impatient. "Was there something you wanted?"

"I wanted to say happy Mothers' Day."

"Oh. Well, thank you."

"And, I thought about what you said. We should try to be friends."

Her voice got gentler. "Richard. Are you okay?"

He swallowed. "I'm okay."

"You're sure?"

"Absolutely."

Her voice fell to a near-whisper. "Why don't you go to a meeting today, okay? Are you going to your meetings? I mean, since you moved up there?"

"Of course." His face flushed. "I'm okay, Mel."

"Please? Promise me you'll go. Or at least call Mike and check in."

"Okay."

"Take care of yourself. I worry about you."

The words warmed his chest. "Thanks, Mel."

"I have to go now," she said. "Thanks for calling me. I... I miss you."

"I miss you, too."

"Bye."

He hung up the phone and looked at himself in the mirror. He hadn't wanted a drink before, but now...

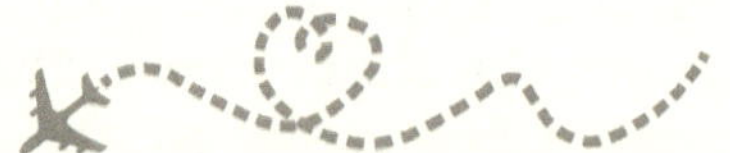

Natalie stood at the sink in her mother's kitchen, rinsing romaine leaves. She dried them with paper towels before ripping them into smaller pieces and dropping them into the big blue salad bowl on the counter.

Her sisters, Lisa and Christine, were on either side of the kitchen table, threading chicken and vegetables onto skewers for the grill. Christine was particular about hers, repeating the same pattern of

meat and vegetables over and over again with each skewer, while Lisa threaded hers with whatever she happened to pick up.

Growing up, her sisters had been the objects of her deepest admiration and envy. Both several years older, they'd always been closer to one another than to her. But they doted on her, making her feel special whenever they included her in what they were doing.

She had served as bridesmaid in each of their weddings while still a teenager herself, caught up in the romance, enraptured with the idea of love lasting forever. She was the godmother of Lisa's son, Connor, and Christine's daughter, Madeleine. She'd held them each as they were baptized and loved making an extra fuss over the two of them.

Christine was talking about her oldest son, Tyler, who was eleven and already had girls calling him.

Lisa laughed and shook her head. "Oh, stop. You had boys calling when you were that age, too. I remember."

"Things are so different now, though. They do stuff a lot earlier." She shuddered.

Lisa, whose children were a few years younger than Tyler, smirked. "You were only a few years older than that the first time you *did stuff*."

"Lisa!" Christine's eyes went wide.

"What?" Lisa shrugged. "Nat, how old were you the first time you kissed a boy?"

"Shhh!" Christine admonished as Natalie snickered. She glanced towards the living room, where her sisters' husbands were watching the Phillies game with her father. They hadn't heard.

"I don't know... Twelve or thirteen?" Natalie answered.

"See?" Lisa reached for a triangle-shaped piece of green bell pepper to thread onto one of the skewers.

"Fine, but still." Christine shook her head. "He's my baby."She walked to the sink and washed her hands, drying them on a dish towel.

Natalie looked out the window at the handsome boy with the sandy blond hair, kicking a soccer ball around with his cousin and his brother in the tiny backyard of her parents' home. Tyler was the oldest of the bunch, followed by nine-year-old Connor. Jack was Christine's next oldest at eight, then Madeleine, and Lisa's daughter, Callie. The girls were both six years old and upstairs playing princess with Natalie's mother.

"Don't let him hear you call him a baby."

"Oh, heaven forbid." Christine rolled her eyes. "Only baby I have left is this one." Her youngest, almost-three-year-old Owen, toddled into the kitchen.

"Can I have a tomayo?" he asked.

Christine cut a grape tomato in half and handed it to him, then patted him on the bottom. "Go play with Daddy."

"Wait." Natalie bent to scoop Owen into her arms. "I haven't had nearly enough Owen kisses today." He giggled, pursed his lips and gave her a juicy kiss, complete with tomato seeds. "Oh, thank you." She set him back down. She ran her fingers through his silky blond curls before he made his way out of the kitchen. Christine and Lisa fell silent for a minute, watching her.

"A woman in Kevin's department just adopted a little girl from China," Christine offered.

"*Christine!*" Lisa hissed.

"Well? I'm just saying."

Natalie forced a smile. "That's great for her." She sliced a cucumber into the salad bowl over top of the lettuce.

"It *is* something to think about," Lisa said after a minute.

"I hear you." She'd never told them about the call from the adoption worker. They'd have taken Ben's side, anyhow.

"Okay, sorry," Christine said. She took the platter of skewers outside to the grill.

Lisa turned to Natalie. "So what's going on with you?"

"Not much."

"Are you sure?"

Natalie felt her lips curve into a smile. "Actually, I met someone."

Lisa raised one eyebrow at her, grinning. "I know."

Natalie looked at her, baffled. "You do?"

"Ben said something to George."

"He did? What did he say?"

"I don't know, exactly. Just that you went out with someone."

Natalie scoffed. "Why was George talking to Ben?"

"They still hang out all the time."

"They do?"

"Well, yeah, Natalie, they're friends. They coach the soccer team? They have the Phillies season tickets together, remember?"

"Right." She guessed it would have been too much to expect George to take her side.

"Is this the guy who took you to the emergency room?"

"Oh my god! Is there anybody in this family who doesn't talk about me behind my back twenty-four seven?" She shook her head. "Who else knows?"

"Just me and George."

"For now."

Lisa nudged her with her elbow. "So what's he like?"

"What's who like?" Christine walked back into the kitchen, the now-empty platter in her hands. She went to the sink to wash it.

Natalie shot Lisa a look.

"Oh—uh, the new gym teacher at Nattie's school."

Christine grinned. "Oh? Is he young and handsome?"

Natalie laughed. *Nice save, Lisa.* The gym teacher at her school was a sixty year old woman who looked like she ate rusty nails for breakfast. She pinched Lisa's arm.

"Ow!" Lisa rubbed her arm, looking at Natalie as if to say their conversation wasn't finished.

Their mother walked into the kitchen along with the girls. "Announcing, their royal highnesses, Princess Maddie and Princess Callie!" She made a sound imitating a trumpet fanfare as the girls, overdone in their grandmother's makeup, jewelry, and high heels, twirled through the kitchen. Natalie and her sisters clapped in appreciation.

"Now, if you're princesses, you'll need tiaras." Natalie grabbed a roll of aluminum foil, shaping a piece into a tiara for each girl's head. They giggled and thanked her before prancing into the living room to show their daddies.

"Everything looks great, girls." Kathy smiled at her daughters. "Need me to do anything?"

"Relax, Mom, we've got it," Lisa assured her.

"How about some wine?" Kathy took the corkscrew out of a drawer.

"I'll take some." Natalie got four wine glasses from the cabinet while Kathy opened a bottle of Pinot Noir.

Christine poured, handing them each a glass. "To Mom," she said. "Happy Mother's Day."

"To my girls." They all clinked glasses and drank a sip. "You're such wonderful mothers." She looked at Natalie. "And you will be too, of course."

Natalie took a gulp of wine.

"Is Ben spending the day with his mother?"

Natalie coughed, and the wine burned her throat. "I don't know what he's doing today."

"Have you spoken to him recently?"

Natalie groaned. "He called me this morning."

"That's wonderful, honey," Kathy said. "Let him know we miss him."

She took a deep breath, her spine stiffening.

"He's a good man, Natalie. I know you two have had your differences, but you have to be willing to try and work on things before you throw your marriage away."

Natalie looked her mother in the eye. "Mom, every time I look at Ben I feel like I want to die. It doesn't make things easy."

"Whoever said marriage was easy?" Christine muttered.

Lisa shot her a look. "Don't you start."

"I just think she should give Ben another chance."

Of course she did. They all did. They adored him. She gulped another mouthful of wine.

"We can all say what we think she should do, but it's Natalie's life," Lisa said.

Natalie looked at her sister, surprised. Kathy and Christine drifted out of the kitchen and into the backyard without another word.

"Thanks, Lis."

"I'm tired of hearing about what they think you should do."

"It's all they talk about, isn't it?" Natalie realized.

"Pretty much." Lisa rolled her eyes. "I love Ben, you know that. But I love you more."

"Thanks, Lisa," Natalie said, touched by her sister's words.

Lisa gave her a playful smile. "Now, tell me more about this guy." They both laughed.

Natalie proceeded to tell her about Richard, but all she wanted to do was leave. To get away from her mom, her sisters... all of them. They thought they knew what was best for her, but they were wrong. They didn't know. She barely knew herself.

She only knew she was sick of being the good little sister. She wanted to be bad for a while. To do things she knew were wrong. Something completely out of character, just to see if it made her feel good. *I miss feeling good.*

She thought of Richard, of the way he looked at her, like he wanted to kiss her. She wondered how it would feel, how his lips would taste.

"You like him." Lisa grinned.

Natalie blushed.

-14-

"You said you like baseball, right?" Richard asked Natalie over the phone.

"Yes," she replied.

"Did you know the Phillies are playing the Braves this Friday night?"

"You want to go to the Phillies game?"

"Well, no," he said. "The game is in Atlanta. But you could come over and watch with me."

"Okay, that sounds like fun."

"Yeah?"

"Yeah. I'll bring cheesesteaks."

"Cheesesteaks?"

"You know what a cheesesteak is, right?"

"Meat and cheese on a bun?"

Natalie laughed. "Okay, first of all, it's a roll, not a bun."

"Sorry."

"I can't believe you've been in Philly almost four months and you haven't had a cheesesteak."

"I need someone to introduce me to the local culture."

"You do."

On Friday evening, she arrived at his house with two cheesesteaks and an order of fries. "This is iconic Philly food," she informed him as she pulled the foil-wrapped sandwiches from the paper bag.

"Like a Georgia peach," he suggested.

"Yes. Only better, because it's greasy and salty and smothered in melted cheese."

"I can't wait."

Richard took two plates out of the cabinet as Natalie cut the sandwiches into halves. They ate in the living room, seated on the couch in front of the TV.

Richard took his first bite of cheesesteak. The cheese stuck in his mustache, and Natalie giggled as she handed him a napkin. "What do you think?"

He finished chewing before he answered. "Delicious. I fear what it will do to my cholesterol level, but this is good."

"You're officially a Philadelphian now."

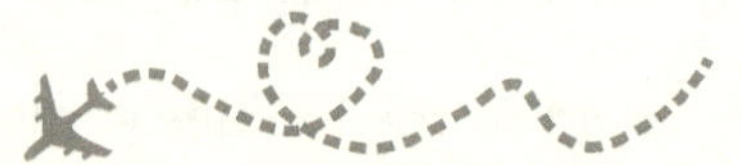

When the game was over, and the Phillies had won five to one, Natalie stood up with a yawn.

"I guess I should head home."

"Stay a little longer," he said, pulling her back down to the couch.

She laughed. "It's late. I'm already sleepy, and it's a long drive..."

"I'll make you a coffee," he offered. "Or you could stay."

"Stay?"

He shrugged. "Stay with me."

"Richard... I can't stay with you. Besides, we agreed, we're just friends."

"Just stay the night. You don't have to do anything you don't want to. I sleep better when you're here."

She recognized the feeling he described. She'd slept more soundly that night on his couch than she had in her own bed for...well, years. But she was certain he had more on his mind than sleep.

She sighed. His eyes pleaded with her to say yes.

"I should really go."

He made a face. "Okay," he conceded.

"Okay?"

"Yes. But only if you let me kiss you goodnight."

She opened her mouth to object, but couldn't find the words. *I should probably bolt right now,* she thought. And yet a part of her—a bigger part than she wanted to admit—wanted to stay. Wanted him to kiss her.

But it was so unromantic. Asking for a kiss, planning it ahead of time. Why not just wait for the right moment and go for it? She realized the moment had come and gone several times, but she'd always pulled away or said something snarky to deflect him.

What was the big deal about kissing, anyhow? It was fun when she was a teenager, but that was before she had done any of the things that kissing led to. It was just putting your lips against someone else's, and—

"One kiss," he said, interrupting her thoughts.

"Now?"

He nodded. When she didn't object, he moved closer to her on the couch.

"May I?"

"Okay," she whispered.

Richard's eyes focused on her mouth. He put his fingertips on either side of her face, closed his eyes and kissed her. The kiss was gentle at first, his lips grazing hers. She closed her eyes. One hand cupped the back of her head as the other slipped around her waist, pulling her closer. Their lips parted. His fingers slid into her hair.

Oh.

His mouth tasted smoky, but it wasn't unpleasant. As he traced her lower lip with the tip

of his tongue, her muscles relaxed, limbs softening into jelly. Richard's lips traveled down her neck, across her collarbone, planting soft, wet kisses on her skin. Her pulse sped up. He put his mouth on hers again, less gentle this time.

She grabbed a fistful of his shirt, leaning against the back of the couch, pulling him towards her. He slipped one hand inside her shirt as she wound her fingers into the hair at the back of his neck. She'd forgotten this feeling, this longing, this melting of lips and bodies into one another. She let herself sink into it, his hands on her body, heat rising within her.

He slid his hand up her inner thigh and reached for the button on her jeans.

"Wait." She grabbed his wrist, pushing him back. "We should stop."

Richard pulled away, sitting up straight. He put his head in his hands, taking a slow breath in. "Okay."

"I'm sorry." She waited for him to look at her.

His eyes were kind. "Don't be. We got a little carried away, that's all." He opened his arms. "Can we sit together for a few more minutes?"

She curled up next to him, resting her head on his shoulder.

"You're irresistible, you know," he murmured, his lips on her hair. "It's not fair."

She resisted the urge to deride the compliment with sarcasm. "Thank you."

"Can I ask you a question?"

She couldn't resist. "I think you just did."

He poked her in the ribs. "Silly girl."

"Okay, ask away."

"What is it you're so afraid of?"

She turned her head, staring at the ceiling. "It's complicated."

"Because of your ex."

She shifted her body away from his. "And...other stuff."

"Did he hit you?"

"Ben? No, no, never."

"But you're afraid of him."

"No. Richard. Stop. It's not like that at all. You don't know him. I'm not afraid of him. He's not the bad guy."

"You can tell me what happened. We're friends, remember?"

"Yes. Just friends. I remember. Do you?" She gave him a pointed look.

"Right." He looked wounded.

"I should go."

Richard didn't reply. She stood up.

"Natalie..."

She waited.

"Don't leave angry. Stay for a few more minutes. I'll be good. I promise." He opened his arms and she sat back down on the couch, his arm around her shoulder.

"Someday, maybe, I'll tell you."

He stroked the curve of her cheek. "You can trust me, you know."

"I do."

She rested her head on his shoulder. Her eyelids felt heavy. She began to drift off. She wasn't sure how much time had passed when she became aware of the sound of Richard's gentle snoring. She smiled to herself, snuggling into him.

He made a contented noise and buried his face into her hair. "Stay with me," he murmured.

And she did.

SUMMER 2005

-15-

atalie leaned against the doorway to Richard's bedroom, watching as he packed for a trip to Houston. His carry-on lay at the foot of the bed, next to a garment bag containing two suits. He stood in front of an open dresser drawer, counting pairs of socks.

"You can come into the room." He glanced at her. "I promise, I'll behave myself."

She giggled, taking a few steps past the threshold. "That's as far as I'll go."

Richard shook his head, chuckling. He'd been in Boston and Chicago earlier in the week, and had one night in Philly before he flew out again. After Houston, he would be in Atlanta for the weekend. Natalie hated to admit it to herself, but she missed him when he was away. She was glad they'd had dinner together tonight. She didn't want to go home.

"When will you be back?" she asked.

"Sunday night. I'll be here all next week."

"Good."

He turned to look at her. "You going to miss me?"

She gave him a shy smile.

He stood in front of her and put his hands on her shoulders, sighing. She rested her hands on his.

"Come with me," he said.

She laughed and shook her head. "I have work tomorrow."

He hung his head, pretending to pout. "Okay." He turned his attention back to packing.

She took a few more steps forward, standing next to him. "I will miss you, though." She nudged his shoulder with hers.

He nudged her back. "I'll miss you, too." He zipped the suitcase shut and sat on the edge of the bed. He reached for her hand and pulled her closer. "Stay tonight." He laced their fingers together and kissed the back of her hand.

"I can't." She bent forward and gave him a quick kiss on the mouth. "It's late. "

"All the more reason to stay." He grinned.

"You don't give up, do you?"

"Never," he said, pulling her back in for another kiss. "Coffee? Before you go?"

"Okay." She followed him into the kitchen.

They drank coffee and shared a slice of apple pie. As Natalie was leaving, Richard kissed her again. She let her lips part as the kiss became deeper, more intense, his hand sliding down to her backside. "I should go." It came out as a breathy whisper.

He leaned her against the doorframe, kissing her neck, his lips brushing her earlobe. Her muscles melted into a pile of mush. Her knees were weak. If she didn't stop herself now...

She pulled away. "What time is your flight on Sunday?"

"I'll try and be back by suppertime."

"I'll stop over Sunday night."

"Call me when you get home."

By the time the school year ended two weeks later, she was spending more time at Richard's house

than her own. She never planned it that way, of course. It just sort of happened. Aside from the time he spent traveling for work or to see his daughters, they were together more often than not.

When he was in town, they saw each other almost every day. They'd meet for dinner, usually at his place. She'd bring takeout, or he would cook. Sometimes they went for a walk after dinner. They'd have coffee and wind up talking for hours. And kissing.

It was easy being with him. He listened when she talked. Paid attention. Asked questions. He told stories about places he'd traveled to, people he'd met. He told her about his time in the Army, about his job, about the volunteer work he did as part of his recovery. He was kind, gentle, unassuming. He wasn't only interested in what she could do for him.

She knew, of course, that it was unwise to be this infatuated with someone she'd just met, especially given the fact that she and Ben were still married. Not to mention, Richard's job in Philadelphia was only temporary. But being with him put her at ease in a way she hadn't felt in a long time. For most of the past year she'd alternated between grief, anger, and numbness. When she was with Richard, she could tune out those feelings. With him, she felt almost alive again. Happy? Maybe even that.

She took him into town on the Fourth of July to see the fireworks and listen to Elton John perform on the Ben Franklin Parkway. They ate hot dogs and kettle corn, sitting on a blanket in the middle of the closed-off street, watching as the sky lit up.

The next night, Richard had to pack for yet another trip. This time it was Denver, then St. Louis. He would be gone for five days. Natalie sat on his bed, cross-legged, her bare feet tucked beneath her.

She pouted. "Don't go."

"Come with me."

"You're funny."

"I'm serious. You don't have work again until September. Come with me."

She made a face. "And do what? Sit in the hotel room while you're working?"

"There's a pool."

"No way," she said, laughing.

"One of these trips, I'll get you to come with me." He sounded sure of himself.

"Sure." She remained unconvinced.

"Where would you want to go?"

"I don't know."

"The beach?" he suggested.

Her lips curved into a smile. "Maybe. But not on a work trip."

"Okay, okay. Not on a work trip." He thought for a minute. "We could go to the Georgia coast. I could take you out on my boat."

"Keep talking." She stretched out on her right side, propping her head up with her arm.

"Palm trees. Fresh seafood. A moonlit walk on the fishing pier."

"That sounds pretty perfect."

"Next weekend."

"Really?"

"I'll make it happen."

"I'd have a hard time saying no to that."

"Then say yes." He zipped his suitcase closed and set it on the floor, lying down behind her on the bed. He swept the hair from her neck, pressing his lips against it. "Stay with me tonight."

"I can't," she whispered, but didn't pull away.

He rolled her onto her back and kissed her on the mouth. When she kissed him back, he pulled

closer. Their open lips moved against each other as his hands traveled along the curves of her body. He lifted her shirt, kissing the soft flesh of her belly and breasts before returning his mouth to hers. Her body ached for him.

"I want you so much." He slid his hand inside her pants.

Oh, God. She wanted him, too. Her breath came faster as he touched her, awakening things in her she'd tried to lay to rest.

"I know," she said. "I'm not ready..."

"You feel ready," he murmured.

She pushed his hand away. He groaned and rolled away from her.

She sat up. "I'm sorry, Richard." He kept his back to her. "I can't."

No response. She went into his bathroom, shutting the door behind her. When she came out, the room was empty, the bedspread smooth. She could hear Richard moving around in the kitchen.

She walked through the short hallway to the kitchen. He was wiping down the countertops. "I should probably go home."

He glanced at her. "Drive safe."

Ouch. "Okay...bye." She waited, but he didn't respond. She walked to her car alone, blinking back tears.

She met Lauren for dinner the next night, venting over Indian food and a bottle of wine. "I don't even know what happened. I shouldn't have let it get that far. I know I tend to blow things out of proportion, but I mean, we're not even...we're just friends."

Lauren smirked. "I don't think you can claim to be just friends anymore. I don't think you ever were."

"I guess we're dating, then."

"Nope. You two are in a relationship." She took a sip of wine.

"We are?"

Lauren raised an eyebrow at her. "You've been spending every waking minute with him for, what, over two months now? And you're still telling me it's just friendship, and you're *not* head over heels in love with the guy?"

"First of all, it hasn't been *every* minute."

"Oh, excuse me."

Natalie laughed, relaxing a little. "Second of all, regardless of how I feel about him, he's being a jerk."

"I didn't say he's not being a jerk. He is, or at least he was last night. But I think you're so afraid to let yourself be happy that you're looking for any excuse to push him away. And from what you've told me, he sounds like a pretty fantastic guy, Nat."

"He *is* fantastic." Natalie poked at a piece of chicken with her fork. "I know. I'm not afraid to be happy..." she trailed off. "I'm just a mess."

"I know. But you are."

"What?"

"Head. Over. Heels," she said, drawing it out.

"Shut up." Natalie laughed again.

After dinner, she returned to the quiet of her own apartment, thinking over what Lauren had said.

She'd been careless with Richard, letting him kiss her, hold her, touch her body when she couldn't follow through. Never thinking about how he felt. She shouldn't have let him get so attached to her.

She never should have let herself develop feelings for him. Solitude was what she'd chosen. *Better to be alone than continue to make another person miserable.* She'd hurt Ben. She didn't want to hurt Richard too.

She could have made herself say *no* when he asked her out the first time, or even the second time, but she hadn't wanted to. She hated that she was a sucker for his proficient flirting. But she enjoyed the attention. She enjoyed *him*. He made her feel like maybe she wasn't a worthless failure after all. And despite her intention to forever close off her heart to any kind of emotions, Lauren was right. She'd fallen for him.

She walked into her bedroom, kicked her shoes off, and lay down on the bed. Sushi hopped up onto the bed and curled up next to her, purring. "Poor thing," Natalie crooned, stroking the cat under her chin. "Sorry I've been ignoring you."

Natalie's eyes filled with tears. She tightened her hands into fists until her nails made deep imprints in the skin of her palms. *No crying. Dammit.*

In the living room, her cell phone rang.

Richard spent most of the day sitting in on meetings at Denver International, paying little attention to what was being said, too busy beating himself up.

He knew Natalie had been hurt. She didn't like to talk about it, but he knew. She'd drawn the line at friendship. And he had pushed and pushed, acting like a spoiled child, entitled to something he knew she wasn't ready to give. Alienating the one friend he'd managed to make in Philly.

A nice, smooth whiskey would taste good right about now. How many bars were right here in this airport? He could slip out of the office, have one drink, and come back relaxed and self-assured. Just one. Nobody would know, or even care. The thought was enough to make his mouth water.

Damn.

He excused himself from the meeting, stepping into an empty office down the hall. He opened his cell phone and scrolled through his contacts to find the number.

"Richard." The sound of Mike's deep, jovial voice helped alleviate the chaos in his brain.

"Hi, Mike."

"How are you?"

"Not so good, I guess." He told Mike about Natalie, how they'd met, how much he cared for her, the time they'd been spending together, and what had happened the night before. Mike listened to all he had to say. "I was sitting here and all I could think about was how I screwed up. I started making a plan to go get a drink. I haven't felt that way for a while."

"I'm glad you called me instead of getting that drink."

Richard exhaled. "Me too."

"Give yourself credit for that."

"I'm trying."

"You know what you need to do next."

"Apologize to her."

"Well, yeah, but also, you need to be honest with yourself. If friendship is all she's willing to offer, you have to accept it, or let her go. Otherwise, you're torturing yourself, which isn't going to help your recovery. What's the most important thing here?"

"Staying sober. Being able to see my kids."

"That's what it's all about."

"Thanks, Mike."

"Talk to her. Be honest. If you love her, you have to respect her. And you have to respect yourself. You know?"

"I hear you."

"Good. Okay. I love you, man."

"I love you, too."

He got back to his hotel after seven o'clock. It was two hours later in Philly. He debated with himself for a few minutes before dialing Natalie's number.

"I'm so sorry," he said as soon as she answered.

"So am I."

"You don't have anything to apologize for."

"I'm still sorry," she said.

"Can I come by your place Sunday night after I get in?"

She hesitated. "I don't know if we should."

"I'll keep my hands to myself, I promise."

Her soft laugh warmed his insides. "Okay."

<h1 style="text-align:center">-16-</h1>

atalie's doorbell rang Sunday night. She chewed her bottom lip as she walked downstairs. Richard stood outside her front door, a bouquet of pink roses in one hand and a bag of take-out Chinese food in the other. She opened the door to let him in.

He stepped inside, holding out the flowers. She took them from him and held them up to her face to breathe them in. "Thank you."

"I'm sorry," he said again.

"I'm sorry, too."

He followed her up the steps and into the kitchen. She filled a vase with water and arranged the flowers in it, setting it on the table, while he grabbed two plates from the cabinet.

"I'm trying hard to be a better person than I used to be. I let you down and tried to make you feel bad about it. I feel like an asshole." He took the food containers out of the bag.

She sat at the table, not answering.

"I get why you wouldn't want me. I'm old. I have a lot of baggage. You don't feel the same way about me as I do about you, I know that." He sat down across from her, offering her an egg roll.

She took it and set it on her plate. "You don't know how I feel."

"Okay, maybe not."

"I'm not mad at you, Richard."

He smirked. "You sure about that?"

"Yes, I'm sure. You can stop beating yourself up about it. I'm mostly mad at myself."

"What for?" He opened a container and spooned some shrimp and vegetables onto her plate, then his own.

"For letting things get as far as they did. That wasn't fair."

"Was it terrible?"

She shook her head, a faint smile on her lips. "No."

"It's me, right? I'm terrible."

"No. You're incredibly wonderful."

"Mind if I start printing that on my business cards?"

"You can, but it'll cost you." She took a bite of the egg roll.

"I can afford it," he teased. "So if I'm so wonderful—allegedly—why is it a bad thing to be with me?"

"I can't lie down on your bed and let you kiss me and not think you're going to want more. And I can't give you more. And I'm so busy feeling sorry for myself that I didn't consider your feelings at all." Her eyes burned. "I fucked up," she murmured. "I didn't mean to hurt you."

"Well, you didn't fuck up too badly. I'm still here."

"Don't worry, I'm capable of fucking up a lot worse." She speared a piece of broccoli with her fork and ate it, chewing slowly.

"Natalie." His eyes softened. "What happened to you, to make you think so badly of yourself?"

She shook her head.

"Don't shut me out." He gave her a crooked smile. "We're friends, remember?"

"It's not like you think, not at all. You think Ben was a terrible husband, or he didn't treat me right, but that's not true. You'll think I'm stupid and selfish for leaving. Everyone does. Including me." She looked up at him.

"Try me." He took a bite of his food, watching her face as he chewed.

"It's not easy to talk about." She took a breath. "There's something wrong with me," she began. "With my body. It doesn't work the way it's supposed to."

"You mean, you can't—"

"No, not that." She took a breath. "Okay, listen. We got married right after college. We bought a big house with four bedrooms and a swingset in the backyard. We always wanted lots of kids. It was all we talked about. But..." She trailed off.

"But it didn't happen that way."

"No." She looked away. "It took a long time to get pregnant, and once I did, I had a miscarriage."

"That's terrible. I'm so sorry."

"We went to see a fertility doctor, and we found out I had all these things wrong with my body. My hormones are messed up. I have little cysts on my ovaries, and scar tissue everywhere else. Nothing works the way it's supposed to.

"We tried medications, treatments, surgery. Our whole life revolved around getting pregnant. When conventional medicine didn't work, we tried acupuncture and herbs. Anything we heard about, we tried. And every once in a while, I would get a positive test. But I lost the baby, every time.

"People would say the most awful things. 'It wasn't meant to be'. 'Everything happens for a reason'. 'You're lucky not to have kids'." A tear rolled down her cheek, and she wiped it away,

sniffling. Richard passed her a napkin. "Sorry," she said, blowing her nose.

"It's okay."

Natalie lowered her voice. "The last one was in November. I lost a lot of blood, and I had to have emergency surgery. The doctor told us we should stop trying. It wrecked me. Ben started talking right away about adopting, or using a surrogate. He thought he could fix it somehow, but I..." She stopped herself, taking a sip of water. "I felt like a failure."

Richard nodded, his eyes sad.

"Nothing is wrong with Ben. Just me. He should be able to have kids. He's great with them. Instead he has five dead babies, and it was my body that killed them. And don't tell me they weren't babies yet. I'm a good Catholic girl. They were babies."

"Of course."

"Someone Ben works with adopted a baby, and gave him the contact information for the agency. I told him I wasn't ready, but he went ahead and called them anyway. When I found out, I got angry. I can see now I blew it out of proportion, but it was the last straw for me. I couldn't stand being in that big empty house anymore. My grandmother's neighbor told me she had this apartment for rent, and I took it. I moved out without even telling him. I know it was a terrible thing to do, but I couldn't stay." She paused, lowering her voice. "He shouldn't have to miss out on having children because of me. He's still young. He can find someone else." Her throat tightened. "Obviously I'm not meant to be a mother. But the problem is, I don't know what I'm supposed to do instead."

Richard was quiet for a few seconds. "I don't think it works like that. I think we make our

choices and we make the best of them. Sometimes things work out the way we want, sometimes not. But I don't believe in 'meant to be'."

"I don't know. I feel like I must have done something to deserve this."

"Sometimes bodies don't work the way they're supposed to. What happened wasn't your fault."

"I wish I could believe that."

He gave her a sympathetic look.

She hesitated, trying to think of a delicate way back to the real subject of this conversation. "I couldn't let him touch me after the last miscarriage. I can't risk it. I don't ever want to go through that again. I promised myself I wouldn't."

"I understand."

"I'm sorry," she said. "I wish it could be easier."

"It's okay," he replied.

She smiled, but frowned again. "So I don't know where that leaves us."

"I don't know, either. I don't know if we have to put a label on it. But I do know how I feel about you, Natalie. I like being with you, even when you're sullen or sad or angry at me. I like eating dinner with you, drinking coffee with you, walking in the park. Do I want more than that? Sure. But I'm not going to demand anything from you. You don't owe me anything. I want to be with you, however I can. Even if it never moves beyond what it is right now." He reached for her hand, and she gave it to him. "You own whatever's left of this old heart."

His hand was warm, gentle, his touch reminding her of the other night, before she'd pushed him away. Maybe punishing her body with a lifetime of celibacy was a little unrealistic. It felt good to be wanted.

"And this may be a bit awkward, and, I don't know if it changes anything, but in case you ever change your mind," he said, looking away, "it wouldn't be an issue with me. I've already had my children. Got snipped after Bella was born."

She felt her cheeks flush. "Oh."

He smiled, brushing a finger over her cheek. "But Natalie, please believe that I'm happy with what we have. Even when you lie on my bed with me and let me kiss you and then push me away. It's okay."

"It is?"

"Yes." He chuckled. "Do you believe me?"

"Yes."

"Then come here and give me a kiss, because I missed you all weekend. Especially those gorgeous lips of yours." He tugged gently on her hand.

She got up from her chair, slid into his lap and kissed him, wrapping her arms around him.

"You're really interfering with my plan of being miserable and lonely for the rest of my life," she said.

"Maybe we could be miserable and lonely together." He rubbed her back as she put her head on his shoulder. "You've had your heart broken, and it's okay to wallow in it for a while. But someday, believe it or not, it won't hurt as much, and life is waiting for you to live it."

She kissed him again. "Thanks for understanding."

"I'm crazy about you, you know," he said.

"I do know." She smiled. "I kind of have a thing for you, too."

"Can we still go to the beach next weekend? I promise to be a gentleman."

"I'd love to."

Richard piloted his boat along the narrow waterways, towards the ocean, until they were far enough from the shore that the beach was a thin line between the water and the sky. He dropped the anchor, securing them in place.

Small waves lapped at the bottom of the boat. Natalie took her book and stretched out in the sunshine as Richard cast his lines into the water.

"I could get used to this," she said.

"I'm just enjoying the view." He took his time looking her up and down while her face was buried in the book.

She wore a black bathing suit splashed with white flowers, dark green shorts, an unbuttoned white shirt over top and, well, damn. Just...damn. She looked sexy as hell. He wanted to kiss her, to touch her skin, but he held back. He understood, now, why she was afraid. He had promised himself he would wait for her to make the next move, if ever there would be one.

She seemed to be enjoying the trip so far. He'd arranged for them to fly first class, and booked an oceanfront suite at the nicest hotel on the beach. A separate bedroom, two baths, a full kitchen, and a private terrace with an ocean view. He knew Natalie wasn't materialistic, but every woman enjoyed being spoiled a little, at least in his experience. He wasn't above trying to impress her.

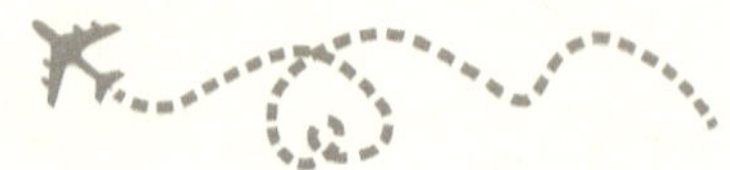

Last night he'd taken her for a late dinner at a local seafood restaurant and they'd gone for a stroll on the fishing pier. Back at the hotel, he gave her the bedroom and took the pull-out couch for himself, like the gentleman he'd somehow convinced her he was. If things went well, maybe he'd sleep next to her tonight. Even if it was only sleep. He wouldn't let himself hope for more.

He turned back toward the water as he felt a sharp tug on the line. He reeled it in, but the fish was too small. He threw it back and cast the line again.

This morning they'd packed some snacks in the cooler and gotten an early start to the marina. He was excited to show off his boat.

"*The Hannabelle*." She read the name painted on the side out loud, grinning.

"The one thing I got to keep in the divorce," he answered.

Natalie put her book aside after a few minutes. "Okay, it's official—reading on a boat makes me seasick," she announced.

"Grab a Coke from the cooler."

She climbed back towards the helm, found a can and popped the top, taking a sip. "That helps."

"Sorry," he said. "I should have warned you. That happens to Hannah, too. First time I took her fishing she heaved over the side of the boat."

"Thanks for that visual." Natalie made a face. She perched next to him and watched as he fished.

"They'll be flying up to Philly next weekend. Hannah and Bella. They're staying with me for two weeks."

"That sounds nice," she said.

"I should have told you sooner."

"It's okay."

"I'd love for you to meet them." He shifted his fishing rod to the opposite hand. He pulled a cigarette out of the pack in his shirt pocket and lit it, inhaling.

She made a face. "Isn't it a little soon for that?"

"I'm not going to introduce you as their wicked stepmother," he teased.

"Stop." She laughed.

"I think you'll like them. Hannah's smart and snarky, like you. Bella's the quiet one. We'll keep it casual. Come over and have pizza with us one night."

"I guess I can do that."

He smiled.

"So, what's their mom like?"

His stomach lurched. "Melinda?" He shrugged. "What do you want to know?"

"Everything. Come on. I told you my dirty laundry, but I don't know yours."

"Yeah, but my laundry's a hell of a lot dirtier than yours. Filthy. Disgusting, really."

A cloud passed across the sun, casting a shadow over the boat. Natalie turned her face towards the sky, shielding her eyes with her hand.

"Plus, I didn't ask you what your husband was like," he said, trying to lighten the mood.

"True." She pursed her lips. "So tell me how you met."

"At a party. Stole her away from the guy she was dating."

He remembered Melinda's platinum blond hair and the tight skirt she'd been wearing. She'd laughed at all his stupid jokes. Her eyes were gray, so pale they were almost white. The color of moonlight. He'd never seen eyes like those before. When she put a cigarette to her lips, he lit it for her, and she said something trite about how few real Southern

gentlemen there were in Atlanta. She was from some little town on the Gulf coast of Mississippi, and things were different in the big city.

After they'd both had a few too many drinks, he whispered in her ear, telling her how beautiful she was, how much he wanted her, that his apartment was just across the courtyard. They left the party, stumbling into his small bedroom and peeling each others' clothes off. He spared Natalie those details.

"And then what?"

"It's a long story, baby girl. And I'm the villain, not the hero."

"Did you love her?"

He looked away from her. "Sure. Very much."

"Do you still?" Her voice was timid.

He raised one eyebrow at her. "Do you still love Ben?"

"Okay. Fair enough."

"I wanted to make her happy, and sometimes I did, but I was wrestling with my own demons. Melinda deserved a lot better." He turned back to the water. He didn't want to tell her any more. He wanted to shield her from the truth about himself that would make her jump off the boat and swim back to the shore as fast as she could.

But she wanted to know him. Something about that made him hopeful.

"I was a shitty husband and father. I had a shitty childhood myself, but that's no excuse. I didn't have a perfect family growing up, like you did. Now, I don't mean your family doesn't have their flaws. But what you had is what every kid should have. Parents who love each other and put their kids first. I know they're not your favorite people right now, but you know deep down the reason they worry about you is that they care about you so much.

"I barely had a family. I never knew my father. My mother dragged me and my sister around, from one stepdad to another, and each one was a bigger asshole than the one before. I left home when I was fifteen. Joined the Army the day I turned eighteen. Worked my way through college and grad school. I was a hard worker. Self sufficient. But I didn't know what it was to be a man, let alone a husband and a father. I did some pretty terrible things, and I paid the price for what I did. I lost everything."

"Why did you leave home? When you were a kid, I mean."

"Oh, god." He groaned. "I'd rather talk about my ex-wife." He took a last drag on his cigarette and stubbed it out in the ashtray.

"My mother was...unstable," he said. "She couldn't support herself. My father left her at age twenty with two babies in diapers. All I know about him is his name, because I'm named for him. My sister Rosie was eleven months older than me. My mom resented us. Used us both as punching bags. It wasn't a great way to grow up." He cleared his throat. "The only good times were when we would stay with my grandmother. But that never lasted long.

"Rosie had a hard time of it, harder than I did, but she was always protective of me. If she saw my mother coming for me, she'd always step in." He lit another cigarette. "Anyway. She OD'd on her sixteenth birthday. I don't know if it was intentional or not."

"Oh my god. Richard. I'm so sorry."

"I left home the next day. Hitchhiked all the way from Tallahassee to Knoxville. My grandmother lived there. She was the only other family I had. I hadn't seen her in years. But when I got there, it turned out she was in a nursing home, so I couldn't stay with her. I got a job bussing tables and washing dishes at a restaurant, and the owner let me sleep in the stock room. I visited my grandma every chance I got. She died a couple years later. I didn't go to her funeral. I didn't want to see my mother. I haven't seen her in thirty years. I don't even know if she's still alive."

Natalie took a long sip of her soda. "I can't believe you sat and listened to me whine about my miscarriages when you had all that happen to you."

"Grief is grief. You can't compare your pain to someone else's. It all sucks."

"Still. I can't imagine how hard that was."

"Do you feel better, now that you know my dirty laundry?"

"Well. You still didn't tell me about your marriage."

"You're relentless." He shook his head. "Grab me a Coke out of the cooler? Please?"

She grabbed a can and popped it open for him. He reached for it, but she held it back. "Are you going to tell me?"

He laughed, turning away from her to check the lines.

"I don't know what there is to tell. We got married after she got pregnant with Hannah. A few years later we had Bella. I'm sure from the outside we looked like a happy family. We had a big, pretty house, and we spent weekends down here on our boat. But I worked long hours, and I traveled a lot. I'd go out after work with people from the office and we'd hit the bar for a few hours. I didn't even need anyone to go with me. There were always people around, and I was always the life of the party. I loved being that guy. I could be best friends with anyone as long as the drinks were flowing. If someone was holding drugs, even better. Especially coke."

"Cocaine?"

"Yeah. That became a regular habit, too. That's how I saw it. A habit, not a problem. I had this idea in my head that an addict was someone who couldn't hold their life together. But I worked hard, the bills were paid on time, the girls had everything they needed, so I thought I had it under control. But Melinda knew I didn't. She was the one who had to deal with it. She was the one who found me passed out in the bathroom, or the backyard. She would get on my case about it, and that made me want to be around her less. I know how awful it sounds, believe me."

Natalie frowned, and he continued, "I tried to quit a bunch of times. I could go for months without drinking or using. And things would be good for a while. But I always went back. I lied all the time about where I was and what I was doing. Sometimes I'd wake up someplace and not know where I was. The cops brought me home more than once.

"Eventually, Mel just kind of gave up on me. I didn't know, but she'd met someone at work. I came home one day and she had my bags packed. I tried begging, but her mind was made up. She said she was in love with somebody else." He sighed.

"I was pissed. I left without anything. Went to a bar and got drunk, of course. Went home with a woman I just met. She kicked me out the next night. I found my way back to the bar on foot. Got wasted, again. Spent the night in my car, in the parking lot, and it was the worst night of my whole life. I knew I was sick. I had lost everything that mattered. I didn't know if I'd see my kids again.

"A cop woke me up at five in the morning, tapping on the window. I was scared. But he was nice. Gave me information about a local AA meeting. Before, I'd always thought I was strong enough to get sober on my own. Turns out there's no shame in asking for help.

"I bought some clean clothes, checked into a hotel, took a hot shower, and went to my first meeting. I met my sponsor that night. Mike." He sat next to her and pulled a photo out of his wallet of himself and a man with dark brown skin and warm, crinkled eyes, about a foot taller than Richard. The two men had their arms around each other, huge smiles on their faces.

"I always say he saved my life, but the truth is, he helped me save my own life." He looked at the photo. "Mike would say, it wasn't him, or me, it was the Lord. I'm more of a skeptic, but whatever it was, I'm grateful. He and his wife are like family to me now.

"I've been sober ever since. It will be three years this summer. But it was hard, in the beginning. I knew I didn't want to lose my kids, so I went back to Mel and I had to apologize. That was the hardest part. Going to her and saying, I know I fucked up. I've been a selfish asshole, and I'm sorry, and I don't expect you to believe me, but I'm going to show you that I can do better.

"She got married again two years ago. Neil is a decent guy. A little younger than her. He's an administrator at the hospital where she works. Smart guy. Quiet. He's good to my kids. If he wasn't the bastard who took my wife away from me, I might actually like him." He smirked.

"You didn't try to get her back?"

He shook his head. "'Grant me the serenity to accept the things I cannot change'. She's happy with

him, and she deserves that after all those years of misery with me. I'm okay with it." He wished that were true. Maybe someday it would be.

Natalie looked out at the water, not saying anything.

"See what I mean? Now you don't even like me."

She shook her head. "I still like you."

"Even though I'm a liar and an alcoholic?"

"You're not like that anymore."

"Well. I try not to be, anyhow." He stood. "I don't like to dwell on the past. What's done is done, I can't change it. I can only make the decision to forgive myself for my mistakes and be better than I was before."

"I wish I knew how to do that." Her voice sounded sad. "I think that's what makes marriage so hard. You're promising a lifetime to someone when you don't even know what tomorrow is going to be like."

"There are some good marriages, though."

"Yeah, I guess. My sisters both seem to have them."

"What about your parents?"

"They do everything together, but I've never seen them be, I don't know, affectionate."

"Affection is important," he said.

"It is."

He took her hand and pulled her up so she stood in front of him. "Especially kissing." He leaned in to kiss her.

"Agreed." She kissed him back.

"I like this bathing suit, did I tell you that?" He traced the straps with his fingertips. He eased her shirt off one shoulder, brushing his lips against her collarbone. Her breath caught.

He held her for a few seconds and then turned back towards the water. He wouldn't push her,

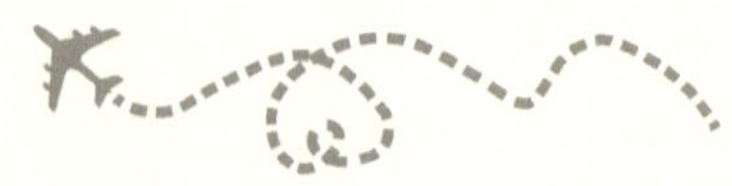

tempting as it was. Picking his fishing rod back up, he baited the hook, waiting for her to make the next move.

She stood close to him. "Show me how to fish."

He laughed. "You'll have to get your hands dirty."

"I'll live."

He showed her the basic setup: the hook, the line, the lure, and the bait. "Now, you cast the line into the water. Hold your hand on the rod like this," he said, placing her fingers above and below the reel and wrapping his hand over hers. He wrapped his other hand around her waist. "Now you open up this part with your other hand, pull back a little, and then let it fly." He watched as the line hit the water, not taking his hand off hers.

"And now we wait?"

"And now we wait."

She turned her face in his direction. "Am I doing it right?"

"Yes." He eased his hand off hers and took a step back. "Mm-hmm. You look good, holding my rod."

She giggled. "Wait, I feel something."

He stood close behind her and put his hands over hers. "That's just the current. When you've got something, it'll feel like it's going to jump out of your hand." He took his hands off but kept his body pressed against hers, and she leaned into him. He tried to breathe normally.

"How about now?"

"Just relax. You have to give it some time." He put his hands on her hips.

"This is nice." She nestled the back of her head into his chest. "It's peaceful out here."

"Mm-hmm." He inhaled the scent of her hair, stroking her upper arm.

The line jumped. "Now!" they both said at the same time.

Richard helped her reel in a decent-sized red drum. "Not bad for your first catch."

She grinned, but frowned as he pulled the fish from the hook. "Do we have to kill it?"

"We can't eat it if it's still alive, darlin'."

She looked sad.

"You can close your eyes while I put it into the cooler," he offered.

They stayed on the boat for a few more hours, catching a few more fish, but releasing them. The fish she'd caught would be more than enough for them for dinner tonight, and he was looking forward to cooking it. Back at the marina, he cleaned the fish while Natalie browsed in the shop.

At the hotel, Richard washed up and changed clothes. It felt good to be in the cool air conditioning after hours in the sun.

"I'm going to stretch out for a few minutes while you change," Natalie said, yawning.

When he came back to her room, she was sound asleep.

-18-

Natalie woke up hours later. Something smelled delicious. She walked out of her room and into the kitchen. Richard had cooked the fish and he served it with salad and a loaf of crusty bread.

"Did you go to the grocery store?" she asked as they sat at the table.

"I tried to wake you up and tell you, but you were out cold."

Natalie took a bite of the fish. "This is amazing." It was well-seasoned, meaty but tender.

"Well, you're the big strong fisherwoman who caught dinner, I'm just the chef."

"We're a good team." She took a sip of water and then yawned. "Sorry I slept so long. I guess we missed the beach."

"Nah. We have about an hour of daylight left. Besides, night swimming in the ocean can be fun."

"In the dark? Sounds spooky." She shuddered.

"You've never been swimming in the ocean at night?"

"No."

"You'll love it. I'll keep you safe. I promise."

It was a few minutes after sunset when they got to the beach. A few people strolled along the water's edge. They set their towels on the sand and watched as the moon rose over the ocean.

"That's beautiful." Natalie said, watching the light reflect off the water.

"A dip?" Richard took off his t-shirt.

His shoulders and arms were more well-defined than she'd expected. Soft-looking dark hair covered his chest and abdomen, thicker just above the waistband of his swim trunks. She resisted the urge to reach out and touch it, to see if it was as soft as it appeared. He saw her looking and she felt her cheeks redden.

They walked to the water. It swirled around their ankles, washing over their feet.

"The ocean never gets this warm at the Jersey shore."

"Southern hospitality." He ventured ahead of her, jumping through the breakers and plunging his whole body into the water. "Come on out," he called to her. When she caught up to him, he swam further away, splashing in her direction. "Can't catch me."

She laughed, swimming towards him. They played and splashed each other as the sky grew dark. Natalie floated on her back, letting the waves rock her body, watching the stars as they peeked through the darkness.

"You were right. This is kind of amazing."

Richard didn't answer.

She turned and looked around. "Richard?" Her heart pounded.

He grabbed her from behind. "Boo." His lips brushed her ear. She yelped and pushed him away.

"I don't like you anymore." She turned to glare at him, pouting.

"Yes you do." He scooped her into his arms, holding her close. "Give me those pouty lips."

"No way." She put her palms against his chest with a laugh and held her face away from his.

The next wave pushed her out of his arms, and she swam away. "You'll never catch me," she teased.

He caught up with her much faster than she had with him. Damn those muscled arms. He wrapped them around her, pulling her close. She pressed her lips to his. He tasted salty.

This kiss was different than their other kisses had been. She didn't hold back. Her fingers curled into the wet hair at the back of his neck.

She hadn't stopped thinking about their conversation in her kitchen. Knowing it couldn't end the way she feared, she allowed herself to enjoy the way he made her body feel. Gentle waves rocked them back and forth, but they held on to one another, the rhythm of the tide pushing them together. The impulse to pull away had dissolved beneath the waves.

Richard put his hands under her bottom and lifted her to him. "Is this okay?"

"Yes." She wrapped her legs around his waist, enjoying the weightlessness of her body in the water. He pulled her closer so she could feel him pressed against her. She let out a soft moan.

"Let's go back to the room," she said.

"You're sure you want to?"

"I'm sure."

They emerged from the water. The sky was dark, the beach deserted. Richard picked up a towel and wrapped it around Natalie's shoulders, kissing her again.

They walked off the beach towards the hotel, hand in hand, Richard trying hard not to break into a sprint.

"I'm going to take a quick shower and rinse off the salt water," she said once they were back in their suite.

His heart sank. "Okay. Me too, I guess."

"Hey." She gave him his favorite half-smile. "Meet you on the terrace when I'm done?" She pulled him in for another kiss.

"I'll see you in a few minutes."

Richard rushed through his shower and threw on a clean t-shirt and jeans. He flipped the TV on, hoping to catch the next day's weather forecast. As the talking heads droned about sports and local news, his thoughts returned to those moments in the water when Natalie let her guard down and allowed herself to be with him, without stiffening or pulling away. Although she had relegated their relationship to only friendship, it had evolved into something quite different, and not only in his mind. It was obvious something had shifted for her, too.

After listening to her story about struggling to have a child, his heart broke for her. He understood the pain of failure, and almost wished she'd stayed and fought, persevering through the obstacles until she reached her goal. He realized, however, if she hadn't walked away from her husband, he wouldn't have had the incredible luck of meeting her. The thought of Ben made him uneasy, but he shoved it aside.

The weather forecast began, a welcome distraction from the contents of his mind. Sunny tomorrow, high of eighty five. Perfect. They'd play on the beach some more, and he'd take her out for dinner again before they had to fly home Sunday morning.

He turned the TV off, stepped out onto the terrace and lit a cigarette. Leaning against the

railing, he looked in the direction of the water. Moonlight sparkled on its surface. Warm breezes drifted through the night air, causing the branches of the nearby palms to sway. He could hear the waves crash against the shoreline in the distance.

He took a drag of his cigarette, trying to be patient as he waited for Natalie. He knew better than to have any expectations, but he couldn't help hoping.

Natalie stepped out of the shower and grabbed a towel. She looked at herself in the mirror, trying hard not to cringe at the reflection. Ample tummy and dimpled thighs, soft and jiggly, streaked with faded stretch marks. Would Richard still think she was beautiful if he saw her naked? Was he going to see her naked? *Yes.*

She wrapped her hair in one towel and dried her body with another, pushing away any misgivings as she opened the bathroom door. The air conditioning in the bedroom chilled her bare skin. She ran a comb through her damp hair and applied deodorant. Unzipping her suitcase, she located the pale blue nightgown with spaghetti straps she'd purchased for the trip.

Underwear, or no? *No.* She slipped the nightgown over her head. The fabric was thin and clung to her body, leaving little to the imagination. She turned to look at herself from every angle. Not too terrible. She took a deep breath and opened the door.

"Damn," Richard said under his breath as she stepped onto the terrace.

She blushed.

He ground out his cigarette. "You look good." He eyed her from head to toe as she approached. "You smell good, too."

She nestled herself into his arms, looking out at the water along with him. "So do you."

Richard smoothed the damp hair off the back of her neck, inhaling as his lips brushed against her skin. She arched her back, reaching for his face. He lowered his lips to hers. She turned her body to face him, pulling him closer. Their kisses were hungry, demanding. He slid his hand to her waist, resting it on her hip.

"You're not wearing anything under this," he said.

"Nope."

He made a deep, growling sound before kissing her again, turning her knees to jelly. She put her hand in his, taking a step backwards, in the direction of her room. He followed, keeping his eyes locked on hers.

They stood beside the bed, the room illuminated only by the faint moonlight streaming through the screen door. Natalie took Richard's face in her hands, kissing him again.

"Are you sure about this?" he asked her again as their lips met.

"I'm sure." Her body ached for him.

He slid his hands up the backs of her thighs, under the hemline of her nightgown, pulling her closer. "Can I take this off?"

She nodded. Richard pulled the nightgown up and over her head. She crossed her arms over her belly.

"Stop." He eased her arms away and took a step backward. "Let me see you."

She relaxed her arms, allowing him to look at her. She watched as his eyes traveled down her

body, all the way to her toes, then back up to her face, her cheeks flushing. She felt awkward and beautiful all at once.

"You're exquisite."

He stepped closer, putting his mouth back on hers. She lifted his shirt over his head. Her fingers traveled down his bare chest to his waist, unbuttoning his jeans, sliding them off.

Somehow they made their way onto the bed. She'd already turned the sheets down in anticipation. He pressed against her in the darkness, sliding one hand between her thighs, touching her as he had that night on his bed. She didn't push him away.

"Does that feel good?"

"Mmm-hmm," she managed, her body responding to every touch.

Salt air blew through the screen door, across her face, lifting wisps of hair off her forehead. His lips traveled over every inch of her skin. She closed her eyes, toes curling against the thin cotton of the sheet.

Richard moved back, reaching for his jeans. He pulled a condom from the pocket. Natalie froze.

He glanced at her face. "You look nervous."

She motioned towards the hand holding the condom. "You said you had a vasectomy."

"I did. But, um. I haven't exactly been an angel. I want to keep you safe."

"Oh," she said, not wanting to think about what he meant by that.

"Is that okay?"

She nodded.

"Are you sure? I can stop if you're not."

"I guess I am a little nervous." She took a deep breath and blew it out, slowly. "I've only ever been with one person."

Richard shifted his body, lying down next to her, turning her to face him. "We don't have to do anything you don't want to." He tucked a lock of hair behind her ear.

She smiled. "Now you look nervous."

He laughed. "I guess I am."

She pulled his face to hers, kissing him again. His lips moved down to her neck. The hollow of her throat. Down her torso, to the back of her thigh, just above the knee. He brushed the tip of his tongue against her skin. She whimpered, her anxiety melting away. She moved one hand down the center of his body. He groaned as she touched him.

"I want you so much," she whispered. She rolled onto her back, pulling him on top of her. She heard the rip of the condom packet. He lowered his body to meet hers, moving slowly at first, paying close attention to what elicited a response from her.

She closed her eyes, feeling the touch of his lips, his hands. Waves of heat rippled out from the center of her body. Her breath came faster, in time with the motion of Richard's body against hers. She put her hands on his thighs, pulling him closer as every muscle in her body tightened, then released.

"Natalie," Richard murmured, his lips against her neck.

He gave her a tender kiss, trying to catch his breath as he turned onto his side. They lay together, their heads on one pillow, inches apart. He stroked her hair. She put her hand on his, threading their fingers together.

"Are you okay?" he asked.

She smiled and nodded. "Better than okay."

"You're incredible," he said, his voice soft.

"You're pretty incredible, too."

-19-

Natalie sat up in bed as morning sunlight began to fill the room, trying to reconcile the conflict churning within her. Her heart fluttered happily within her chest. Meanwhile, a lead weight had settled in the pit of her stomach.

Richard slept next to her, prone, his head turned away from her, the sheet pulled just below his waist. She watched the rise and fall of his back as he breathed.

I did this. I can't go back now. It was exhilarating. And disconcerting.

She kissed his cheek and slipped out of bed, leaving him asleep as she pulled on some clothes and went for a walk on the beach.

The sunlight reflected off the water, stinging her eyes. Her sunglasses only helped a little. She stood at the ocean's edge, sandals in her left hand, a folded towel under her arm. A salty breeze drifted across her face. She waded in the surf, letting the water pool around her ankles and then retreat. Her thoughts ebbed and flowed in rhythm with the ocean as she processed the events of the night before.

Richard was good in bed. Different, but good. Patient. Attentive. She'd been nervous, uneasy, not knowing what to expect. But he'd paid attention to what she liked, making sure she was satisfied.

Her thoughts drifted to Ben. Their first night together had been the first time for both of them.

It was clumsy but tender, neither of them really sure what to do beyond the basic mechanics, but they laughed their way through it, figuring it out as time went on. They'd gotten pretty damn good at it.

But that was before sex became a science experiment, and her body the laboratory. Prescribed by the doctor at certain times, prohibited at others, eventually an unbearable chore. She pushed Ben from her mind.

It was obvious Richard was much more experienced, but that was both reassuring and unsettling. She wondered how many women he had slept with. She wasn't sure she wanted to know.

It was hard to reconcile the man she knew with the one he'd described to her yesterday. The Richard she knew was kind, considerate, hardworking. He was the type of man who would sit with a stranger in the hospital in the middle of the night and see them safely home. She couldn't imagine him as an addict, a liar. She was glad she hadn't known him like that, but she had to admire how hard he had worked to put his life back together when it seemed like no hope was left. Maybe, someday, she would be able to do the same.

The beach was mostly deserted, except for the occasional jogger or dog walker. Natalie spread out her towel and sat a few feet from the water's edge, burying her toes in the sand. She stretched backward, resting the weight of her torso on her elbows as she tilted her face toward the sun.

She wasn't sure how long she sat, looking out at the water, the sun warming her skin. Sensing Richard's presence, she turned and saw him walking towards her. He extinguished his cigarette and sat down beside her.

"I woke up and you were gone."

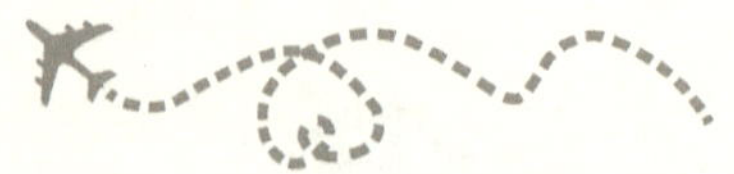

"Sorry. I didn't want to wake you."

"Everything okay?"

She leaned her head on his shoulder. "Better than okay. I don't ever want to go home. Let's stay here."

"Deal." He kissed the top of her head.

She started to speak, then hesitated. "I... Um..."

"You're not ready for this whole thing?"

"Funny." She nudged his arm with hers. "I was going to say I had a good time last night."

"Me too." He leaned in to kiss her.

"We should do it again sometime."

"And we will." He made a growling sound as he kissed her neck. She giggled. He lay back on the towel, pulling her on top of him.

"Richard!" She laughed, pulling away.

"I hope you know how much you mean to me," he said, his voice deep and serious. "You make me so happy, baby girl." He wrapped his arms around her.

She was glad he couldn't see the tears that sprang into her eyes. She squeezed them shut, willing the tears away as she held him close.

"Me too," she whispered.

-20-

ichard was waiting at the gate when the girls landed. They smiled when they saw him, and he stood with his arms open as they rushed towards him. Hannah hugged him first.

"Hi, Dad," she said as he put his arms around her.

"Hey, Princess. Look at you." He took a step back. "Every time I see you, you're more grown up."

She smiled.

"And my baby." He turned his attention to Bella. He barely had to bend to hug her. She stiffened in his arms and pulled back a little, scrunching up her nose at his kiss. "What?" He pretended to take offense.

"You hug too hard."

"I'm sorry, ma'am, I didn't realize how fragile you were," he drawled.

Bella giggled.

"Let's go get your bags."

He hoisted their suitcases into the back of the pickup and drove towards his house, the three of them crammed together in the front seat.

"So what are we doing this week?" Bella flipped the stations on the radio.

"What would you like to do?

"I want to meet your girlfriend," Hannah replied.

"My girlfriend?"

"I heard you talking to Mom about her, remember?" Bella chimed in.

"So you two have discussed this."

"Dad," Hannah said. "Don't be embarrassed. It's good you have a girlfriend."

"Yeah, Daddy. We're worried about you being here all alone."

It was sweet of them to worry. He guessed he had given them ample reason. But Natalie was hesitant about meeting the girls. She didn't want to intrude on their time. Then again, he couldn't imagine going two weeks without seeing her.

"Maybe we can invite her over for dinner one night."

"Tonight," Bella said.

He laughed. "Okay, okay."

Once they arrived at his house, and the girls were busy unpacking their suitcases in their room, he called Natalie.

"The honor of your presence is requested by their royal highnesses Hannah and Isabella."

"How can I refuse an invitation like that?" She laughed. "I'll be right over."

The girls loved Natalie right away, and it seemed the feeling was mutual. Over the next two weeks, every plan they made, every place they went, the first thing they asked was "Can Natalie come too?" She accompanied them to the Liberty Bell and Independence Hall. They explored the Art Museum. They wandered through the shops of South Street and visited the Magic Gardens.

Natalie was a breath of fresh air into his relationship with his kids. He got to see a side of them he hadn't seen since they were little. They were relaxed, happy.

They took a day trip to the Jersey shore and walked the boardwalk. Hannah and Bella rode the roller coasters. When they pulled into his driveway at almost one in the morning, the girls were asleep in the back.

"Stay tonight." Richard took her hand in his and kissed it.

"I can't." She glanced at the girls.

"They're already asleep. Don't worry about it." He put his hand on her knee. "Just stay."

"I don't want them to see me in the morning and think I'm some kind of—"

"Human being?" He slid his hand up her leg.

She put her hand on his.

"Stay. Please." He kissed her.

"Just do it," Hannah said from the backseat, her voice sleepy.

Natalie's cheeks flushed as she burst into laughter.

"My lawyer," Richard said, sounding amused.

"Your kids are great."

"They are," he agreed. "You're so good with them. They love you." He smiled at her. "I can't blame them. You're easy to love."

"Flirting again, huh?" she teased.

"Never," he said with a grin.

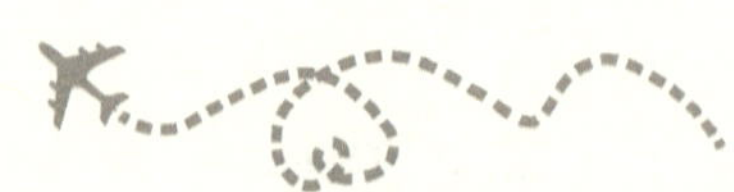

FALL 2005

-21-

Richard was glued to the Weather Channel at the end of August as Hurricane Katrina dominated the news. He watched each day as the storm grew larger and conditions on the Gulf coast intensified.

"Mel's family lives there," he said.

"It always looks worse on TV," Natalie tried to reassure him.

"Usually I'd be inclined to agree with you, baby girl. But look at the size of that thing." Natalie watched the image of the swirling cloud mass replaying again and again on the screen. Richard was pacified once he heard Mel's parents had traveled to Atlanta ahead of the storm and would remain there until the danger had passed.

The hurricane interfered with their plans to spend the last weekend of August on the boat, as Richard was swamped at work with helping to deal with one crisis after another.

"I'll make it up to you," he promised.

Up until that point, their summer had been perfect. Natalie spent all her nights at Richard's place when he was in town, and they spent a few more weekends on the boat. She even joined him on a few work trips, relaxing by the pool while he was at meetings, spending evenings walking around cities she'd never visited before. They were sealed inside a perfect bubble of happiness and romance and sex it seemed nothing could damage.

"It's okay," she said. One little disappointment couldn't take away from her overall contentment. She was finally feeling like herself again, thanks to Richard, and although she didn't know how long it would last, she was grateful to be feeling anything other than the shame and disappointment that had plagued her for so long.

On Labor Day weekend, her sister Christine had a party to celebrate their mother's birthday. Natalie spent the night before at Richard's.

"Do you want me to go with you?" he asked.

"No, I like having you all to myself." She kissed him.

"Come on, I want to meet these people. I showed you mine," he teased.

She hesitated. "Probably not a good idea. My family is still unhappy about my separation. If I bring you along, it might send my mother over the edge."

"Give me a chance. I'm good with people. Even moms."

"Okay, but I'm warning you—they're going to hate it. They'll be nice to you, but later, I'll get all kinds of shit."

"They have to get used to the idea that you have someone new in your life at some point."

Natalie wasn't so sure. She and Richard had been together for a couple of months now, but it was only temporary. By the end of the year he would be gone. She hated to think about him leaving, what life would be like afterwards. Instead, she focused on living in the moment, happy with what they had.

When they arrived at Christine's house the next day, her husband Kevin answered the door. Natalie introduced Richard and the two men shook hands.

"Good to meet you." Kevin looked at Natalie. "Does your sister know you were bringing your...friend?"

She laughed and shook her head no.

"Good luck, man," Kevin said to Richard, laughing. They followed him through the house, towards the sliding doors that led to the backyard. "Richard, can I get you a beer?"

"I'm okay, thanks." Richard winked at Natalie.

Kevin slid the door open and stepped onto the deck. Natalie peered out, hesitant.

All the kids were in the pool, along with George, Lisa's husband, who was jumping up and down to make waves. The kids shrieked and begged for more. Her sisters and parents sat on the far side of the deck, drinking beers, eating snacks and talking, as the Phillies game played on the radio.

"Might as well get this over with." Natalie took a deep breath and stepped through the doorway.

The entire yard fell silent when they saw Natalie and Richard. Lisa leaned in to say something to Christine, who stared at them, mouth open. The only sound was the crack of the bat over the radio. The broadcaster announced a home run as the crowd cheered.

George turned to see what the sudden quiet was all about. He saw Natalie, grinned, and hopped over the side of the pool to greet her.

"Hey, there's my gorgeous sister-in-law!" He ran over to wrap his arms around her.

"George!" she protested, laughing as her clothes soaked through with pool water.

"Sorry, I can't help myself around you," he flirted, planting a juicy kiss on her cheek. George was the only member of the family that hadn't made Natalie feel bad for leaving Ben. On the contrary, he joked, now that she was single, Lisa had competition. He held his hand out to Richard. "Hi, I'm George."

"Richard." He shook George's hand.

"Don't mind George, he ate a few too many paint chips as a child." Lisa handed Natalie a towel. "I'm Lisa. It's great to finally meet you, Richard." She shook his hand as George rejoined the kids, who were eyeing Richard with suspicion. Natalie knew it would be a hard sell.

She walked towards the side of the pool. "Hi, guys."

"Hi, Aunt Nat," a few of them answered.

"Can you guys say hi to my friend, Richard?"

Richard gave a friendly wave. The older boys managed polite hellos, but Maddie crossed her arms over her chest, pouted her lips and turned away.

"Maddie." Natalie frowned. She knew how much her niece adored her Uncle Ben. All the kids did.

"It's okay." Richard patted her shoulder.

"Oh no, a sea monster!" George made a growling noise and the kids all began shrieking and laughing again.

Natalie and Richard approached the table. Her parents stood to greet them. "Mom, Dad, Christine. This is my friend, Richard. These are my parents, Bob and Kathy, and my sister, Christine."

"Good to meet you, Richard." Christine gave him a wide smile. "I wish Natalie had told me you were coming." She shot Natalie a look.

"She's full of surprises." Richard shook each of their hands, calling her father "sir." He wished her mother a happy birthday, and she smiled and thanked him. "It's good to meet you all."

"We're happy to have you." Lisa opened the cooler to grab herself another beer. "Can I get you something to drink?"

"Oh, that's okay, I'll help myself. Are the Phillies winning?" He took a can of Coke from the cooler and popped the top, handed it to Natalie, and grabbed another for himself.

"One-nothing. Bottom of the third," Natalie's father answered.

"Pull up some chairs, guys," Lisa said.

Before dinner, Richard watched as Natalie helped her sisters get the kids out of the pool and dried off. She cuddled Owen in an oversized beach towel, tickled his feet and blew raspberries on his cheeks. She sat with Maddie for a while and talked to her, giving her a big hug. Watching her with the children sent a tender throbbing to the center of his chest.

He looked away. Natalie's mother stood alone by the other side of the pool. He strolled towards her. "Sure is a beautiful day."

She took a sip of wine. It wasn't her first glass, and Richard could tell she was feeling pretty good. "Would you like a glass of wine, Richard?"

"No, thank you, ma'am."

"You don't drink at all?"

"Not for three years, now, no. One day at a time."

"Oh." She straightened up a bit, understanding. "Congratulations. Three years. That's an accomplishment."

"Thank you."

She lowered her voice. "You seem like a good man, Richard."

"Thank you, ma'am." He knew where this conversation was headed.

"I have to assume you're aware my daughter is a married woman."

"Separated, yes. I'm aware."

Kathy looked in Natalie's direction and pressed her lips together in a self-satisfied half-smile. "So I'm sure you realize we all have concerns about this relationship." She gave him a pointed look. It was obvious where Natalie got her fiery eyes.

If he hadn't expected it, he might have been wounded by her words. But he'd been preparing for this moment. "Oh, I know, I know." He chuckled. "I don't blame you one bit."

"No hard feelings, then."

"Naw. She's your daughter, you only want what's best for her. I've got two daughters of my own. I understand."

"Oh? How old are your daughters?"

"Seventeen and thirteen. Love 'em to death, but teenage girls are a handful. I guess you should know."

"Only too well."

"It's tough being a parent. You know what I mean. Anytime I see one of them about to make a mistake, I want to say, no, wait! Don't do it that way!" He held up his hands, palms out, to illustrate. "But sometimes I gotta let them do what they're gonna do. And sometimes, I think they learn a lot more from their own mistakes than they ever could have learned if I'd told them what to do. Sometimes, what I think is a mistake might even end up being the right thing for them."

She nodded, but her eyes were focused on her daughter.

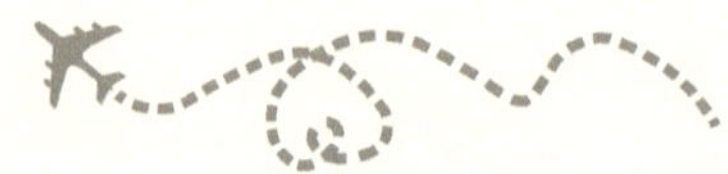

Richard was a perfect Southern gentleman throughout dinner, helping Kevin at the grill and praising Christine's cooking. After dinner, he helped serve the birthday cake. When Natalie's father went out front for a cigarette after the meal, Richard joined him.

As soon as he stepped outside, Natalie was cornered by her sisters in the kitchen.

"I can't believe you didn't tell me you were bringing your boyfriend!" Christine elbowed her in the arm.

"It was a last minute decision. Plus I thought you'd say no if I asked."

"I wouldn't have said no."

Natalie and Lisa looked at one another, laughing in disbelief.

"Yes, you would have," Lisa said. "Well, I like him. He seems nice, he's funny, and he's clearly crazy about you, Nat."

"I didn't say I don't like him. It was just a surprise," Christine said. "How old is he, anyway?"

"He's forty-six."

"Gosh, Nat."

Their mother walked into the kitchen and they all fell silent. Natalie held her breath and waited for the lecture.

"Don't let me interrupt," Kathy responded to the silence.

"It's okay, Mom," Christine said.

"Richard's a very nice man, Natalie. I'm glad I had the chance to meet him."

Natalie blinked, certain she had heard wrong. "Um..."

"He obviously cares for you quite a bit."

"Well, yeah."

Christine and Lisa stared at their mother in amazement.

As Richard and Natalie's father re-entered the kitchen, she smiled and shook her head. "How did you do that?" she whispered in his ear.

"What did I do?"

"My mom just told me she was glad to meet you."

"Told ya." He grinned.

-22-

A few nights later, Richard and Natalie parked out front of her apartment after an early dinner and got out of the truck. Richard unlocked her door and handed back her keys.

"Hey." A voice came from behind them. "Natalie."

Richard glanced at Natalie, who froze. "Ben," she whispered before turning around.

Richard turned too, his heart in his throat.

Ben stood at the edge of the porch. He was a good-looking guy. Tall, a little over six feet, with brown hair that fell across his forehead and scruffy facial hair somewhere beyond five o'clock shadow, but not quite a beard. He leaned against the railing, glanced at Richard, sized him up, and looked back at Natalie.

"I heard you brought him to meet the whole family." He indicated Richard with a flick of his chin.

Natalie took a step in his direction, positioning herself between the two men. "Who told you that?"

Ben shrugged, crossing his arms over his chest. "Doesn't really matter, does it?"

"It does to me," she said. Ben didn't respond. "Okay, I guess you're not going to tell me." She turned to look at Richard. "Richard, this is Ben. Ben, Richard."

Richard held out his hand. "Good to meet you."

Ben looked at his hand and smirked. "Sure," he replied, shaking it. "So you two are finally past that whole 'just friends' thing, huh?"

Natalie turned to Richard. "How about if you wait inside while I talk to him for a minute?"

"I don't think so."

"It's okay. I'll come in, too," Ben said.

"What?" Natalie asked.

"Sure. We can all hang out for a while. I'd like to get to know the guy who's fucking my wife."

"Hey, whoa." Richard held up his hands and took a step towards Ben. "Take it easy."

"Don't you fucking tell me to take it easy." Ben looked Richard in the eye for the first time. His hands clenched into fists. "She signed this lease for six months. Did you know that? It was up in June. We would be back together now if it wasn't for you."

"Ben." Natalie took a step toward him and put her hand on his chest. Her voice was calm. "Look at me. Please. You need to go."

"No, I want to stay and talk about this." His eyes locked with Richard's. "I think you should hear what I have to say."

"I think you should listen to Natalie." Richard maintained his composure.

"Oh, is that what you think?" Ben took a step towards Richard, who stood still, unflinching.

"That's right." He would knock this kid out if he had to. He prayed it wouldn't come to that.

"Hey." Natalie raised her voice. "Stop it. Both of you. Can we please try to remember we're all grown-ups here, for a minute?"

She took a breath and looked at Ben. "Let's go for a walk. Just you and me." She turned back to Richard. "You can wait for me inside or you can go."

He stared at her, surprised. *She's choosing him over me?* His stomach ached.

"I'll wait for you." He would give her three minutes with this asshole and then he would come and find her.

She handed him her keys and walked past Ben down the steps.

Ben threw a smirk at Richard and followed Natalie. The two of them walked down the street talking, although Richard couldn't hear what they said. He watched until they rounded the corner, noticing how similar their mannerisms were, the way they fell into step with one another. The ache in his stomach grew. He turned away, opening the door.

"What the fuck, Ben?" Natalie said once they were far enough away. "You're stalking me now?"

"I stopped by to see you. I didn't know he would be here."

"Please." She shot him a look.

"I figured since everyone else got to meet him, I should have a chance, too."

"Are you serious?"

"Yeah."

"Do you know how fucked up that sounds?"

"I'm part of this family too, Natalie."

"It's my family."

"But they're my nieces and nephews, too."

They turned a corner. Natalie led him on a zigzagging path along the side streets, past narrow row houses with flower pots on their front sidewalks, past a cluster of teenagers smoking on a street corner. Away from where she thought Richard might look for them, if he decided to follow.

They turned onto a wide avenue, cars whizzing by. She stopped in front of a bakery. Although it had closed hours ago, the sweet smell of cakes and pastries hung in the air. She turned to face Ben,

who leaned against the brick wall, hands in his pockets.

"What did you think would happen back there?"

"I don't know."

"Did you think if you showed up like that I would realize what a terrible mistake I made by leaving you? Or were you planning a duel to the death on my front porch?"

He kicked the ground with the toe of his sneaker. "I didn't think. I just..." His eyes shone.

"Ben." She crossed her arms over her chest. "If you want to talk, call me, okay? We can talk. But this is bullshit. You can't show up at my house and start acting like a dick." She softened her tone. "Did you think about how it would make me feel?"

He scoffed. "You think you're the only one who has feelings."

"You never say how you feel, Ben, except for 'I love you'. You're always pretending everything is okay. Like I'm on some extended vacation or something."

He stepped forward, taking her hands in his. His wedding ring was still on his finger. "I just want you back, Nat. I'll do anything. I want everything back the way it was before."

"I can't."

"Why?"

"I'm with Richard now."

He let go of her hands. "So we're over? That's it?"

Was that it? She looked into his eyes, seeing the past thirteen years of her life looking back at her. Every decision she had made centered around him, around having a family together, and where had it gotten her? Heartbroken, bleeding on the bathroom floor. She didn't want to hurt Ben, but more than anything, she didn't want to hurt anymore.

"I don't want to live without you, Nat."

"Try."

The pain in his eyes sliced her through the heart.

He turned, walking back towards her house. She followed, staying a few paces behind. When he reached the silver Jeep Liberty parked a few doors down from her house, he paused, glancing behind him to see if she was there.

"Is this your new car?"

He nodded.

"It's nice."

"Thanks."

She took a step towards him. "Ben..."

"Don't." He put his hand up. "Please."

"I'm sorry."

He sniffled. "You take care of yourself, Natalie."

"You, too." She watched as he drove away.

She sat down on her front step, still seeing the hurt in Ben's eyes. She wiped her eyes with the heel of her hand, sniffling.

Her gaze drifted across the street, to her Nana's house. Her refuge. After Nana's funeral, Natalie had begun going there every day after work instead of going home. Wishing she could connect with Nana somehow. She always felt better after talking things over with her grandmother.

One night not long after the funeral, she stood in the bedroom with a roll of painter's tape in one hand and a black Sharpie marker in the other. The brass-framed bed was still perfectly made, as if Nana would be sleeping in it again tonight. The drawers and closets had been emptied, clothes given to charity, jewelry divided among her female descendants. It seemed heartless. She'd only been in the ground for two weeks.

Natalie sat down on the bed and ran her fingers over the silky bedspread, tracing the seams. The room still smelled of Nana's perfume, as if she were right behind Natalie, talking to her as she penciled in her eyebrows at the little antique vanity table, a cigarette dangling from her lips. How many hours had Natalie spent in this room with Nana, playing dress-up, trying on her makeup?

"The baby will come in its own time," Nana had assured her, at some point during their struggles. "Be patient. It will happen when you least expect it." Unlike all the other well-meant things people had said to her, Nana's words comforted her. No advice, no platitudes. Only compassion. But now Nana was gone, and there would never be a baby. The life she thought she would have was gone, buried in the ground like Nana's body. And Natalie was as empty as this house would soon be.

She'd been instructed to tag any items she wanted for herself. Both of her sisters, her aunt, and her mother had claimed what they wanted. Natalie was welcome to whatever was left. The rest would be picked up and donated.

The furniture in the living room and dining room was marked with color-coded Post-its, indicating which family members wanted which items, but this bedroom was still mostly unclaimed. Maybe they could keep the room as it was, a memorial to Nana, and visit her here, instead of a stone marker in the cemetery. Instead of emptying the house and letting a stranger buy it. Nana had lived most of her eighty-five years here, fifty with Pop and then fifteen without him. Now it would belong to someone else.

"I wish I could keep it," she said out loud. She could live here by herself, like Nana had done since Pop died. If only they would let her.

She began tearing off strips of blue tape, writing her initials on them. NMK. She stuck one on the vanity table. NMK. The dresser. NMK. The desk. NMK,

NMK, NMK. Both nightstands, the TV, the lamps, the brass bed.

Where will we put it all? She could hear Ben's voice inside her head.

No. It's not for us, it's for me. It's for my place. Her own voice. Her heart pounded. The hairs on her arms stood up. My own place. The thought was exciting and terrifying all at once.

She walked into the second bedroom, which Nana had used as a sitting room. She tagged the small couch, the end tables, the bookshelf.

What else?

She went downstairs to the kitchen. Dishes, glasses, flatware, pots and pans. The coffee maker, the toaster. A spatula, a wooden spoon, a ladle. She was giddy with adrenaline. What would her mother say? Nobody else wanted this stuff, anyhow.

Her cell phone buzzed in her pocket, interrupting her tagging frenzy. She flipped it open. "Hello?"

"Hey, where are you?" Ben. She glanced at the clock on the wall. Almost six.

"Nana's."

"You coming home soon? Want to grab something for dinner on your way? Or I can meet you someplace."

How long would he pretend everything was fine between them? "You go ahead and get yourself something."

"Are you sure?"

"Yes."

"You okay?"

She didn't answer. She couldn't. Was she okay? How could he even ask? A few weeks ago she'd been okay. Better than okay. Happier than she'd ever been. She was pregnant, Nana was alive, no doctor had told her to give up trying, no adoption worker had called her on the phone.

She was not okay.

"How about if I meet you there? It must be hard being there by yourself. I can help you with stuff."

"No," she said. "I'll be home later." She flipped her phone closed.

All the energy that had coursed through her body a few minutes earlier was suddenly gone. She was tired. Deflated. Defeated.

What the hell am I doing? *She looked at all the items she had blue-tagged. NMK. She would have to start pulling them off.*

She walked into the living room and sat down on the couch. What a crazy, stupid idea that had been. As if she was going to go home, pack her things, and move out. She'd never done anything so bold.

Nana had been bold. She dyed her hair red and smoked Marlboro cigarettes. She worked as a public school teacher until she was sixty-five and then continued on as a volunteer until she died. She said fuck *all the time and was never afraid to tell anyone exactly what she thought.*

Then again, she went to Mass every Sunday, baked cookies for her great-grandkids, and put doilies on top of her furniture. She played Bingo with the other ladies at church. And she'd stayed married to her husband for almost fifty years. Who knew what she would have said to Natalie now, trying to figure out her life?

Her stomach growled. I'll go home, *she decided.* I'll go home, eat dinner, and get some sleep. I'll come back tomorrow and take off all these stupid tags.

She grabbed her coat and purse, making sure to turn off all the lights before opening the front door. She turned the key in the lock and stood on the porch, her heart heavy in her chest. It was quiet and cold outside. Snow fell from the sky, dusting the pavement. She took a deep breath of the frosty air.

"You're one of Kathy's girls, right?" The voice came from across the narrow street. Natalie looked over and saw her grandmother's neighbor, standing on her porch, smoking.

"Yes." She crossed the street. "I'm Natalie. You're Jean?"

"That's right." Jean stubbed out her cigarette in an ashtray. She walked down the three steps from her porch and shook Natalie's hand. "I'm so sorry about your grandmom, hon. She was a good friend. I miss her."

"Thank you. She talked about you a lot."

"Did she? That's sweet. I try to look out for some of the older ones on the block who are alone. Never thought of Evelyn as old, though. I was so surprised to hear she had passed."

"It was a shock."

"How are you? You doing okay?"

She shook her head as tears filled her eyes. "I'm a mess."

"Oh, shit, I'm sorry, honey. I didn't mean to make you cry." Jean gave her a hug, sniffling. Her arms were strong and warm.

"It's okay," Natalie said. "I carry tissues all the time now." She pulled a small package out of her coat pocket. She handed one to Jean, who dabbed at her own eyes.

"I'd invite you in for a cup of coffee but I'm waiting to show the upstairs apartment. The guy better get here soon. I'm freezing."

"You have an apartment for rent?" A strange flutter began in her chest, like the feeling of waking up on Christmas morning.

"You interested? Want to take a look?"

"Yeah. I do."

"Come on, I'll show it to you." She looked at her watch. "This guy is twenty minutes late. If he shows up, he can wait for me." She grinned.

She followed Jean through the front door and down a narrow hallway. "This is me." She indicated a door on the right side of the hall. On the left side were two more doors. She unlocked one of them and pointed towards the other. "Laundry's in the basement. And some storage space if you need it."

Jean opened the door and began walking up the stairs. "The front porch would be yours. I don't use it. The yard out back is mine." Natalie followed her.

Jean told her the rent, when it was due, what day was trash day.

The apartment was small, but cozy. One bedroom, a living room, an eat-in kitchen, and a bath. There would be enough room for all the furniture she'd tagged at Nana's. She just had to figure out a way to get everything across the street.

"Water and heat are included, electric is separate," Jean continued.

Natalie looked around the kitchen, peeking inside the cabinets.

"I like the space."

"It's good for one, but I don't know if it's big enough for two." Jean pointed towards Natalie's ring finger.

Natalie looked down at her hand. "It would just be for me," she said softly, putting her hand in her coat pocket. The reality of what she was doing finally occurred to her. Her eyes filled again.

"Hey, it's okay." Jean put her hands up. "These things happen."

"I've been thinking about it, I haven't made any plans or anything..."

"Does he know?"

"Nobody knows."

"I see."

Natalie took a deep breath. "I'm sorry. I guess I wasted your time." She swallowed hard, looking

around the room again. For some reason, it already felt like home.

"If you want the place, hon, it's yours. I'd rather have you than a stranger." Jean patted her shoulder. "Come on downstairs and have a cup of coffee. I'm a pretty good listener, if you want to talk about it."

Natalie followed her down the stairs and into her cozy living room. An hour later, she had signed a six-month lease.

"You can move in whenever you're ready." Jean handed her the keys.

"Thanks." Natalie tried to stay calm as her heart threatened to beat out of her chest.

"My son will be here this weekend if you need help moving stuff."

"Oh," she said. "I need to move a few things from across the street."

"No problem, hon. I'll have him bring one of his friends."

Natalie smiled. "Thanks."

Jean gave her a hug. "I know it's hard. Been through it myself. Twice. I'm here anytime you need to talk."

She left feeling better than she had in months. She had her own place. She could start her life over.

But her problems hadn't magically gone away the day she moved her things into Jean's. Her family was confused and worried. Ben was hurt and angry. Instead of feeling closer to Nana, she'd never felt so alone.

By the time Natalie came back, Richard had imagined about a thousand scenarios in which Ben had hurt her in some way. He recalled the first time

he'd seen Melinda and Neil together, how it felt like someone was tearing his heart into pieces. If he hadn't been so desperate to see his daughters, he'd have loved to kick the guy's ass. Just once.

She hadn't hesitated about taking him to her sister's because of what her family would think. It had been because she didn't want Ben to find out.

He stood by the window until he saw them walking back. They stopped in front of his car, but their voices were too soft for him to hear what they were saying. He watched Ben get into his car and drive away before he went back into the living room.

It took longer than he expected for her to come upstairs. She opened the door and stepped inside. Her eyes were puffy, her nose and cheeks a blotchy pink.

"Are you okay? I was worried."

"I'm fine."

"Are you sure?"

She walked into the kitchen. "I need water. You want some?"

"Okay." He followed her. "I think I get it now."

She glanced at him as she filled the glasses with water from the fridge. "What?"

"Why you didn't want me to go. I didn't realize."

"Yeah, well." She handed him a glass, not meeting his eyes.

"And I thought your mom was intense," he said, an attempt at levity.

"You could have been a little nicer."

"I was trying to be nice. He practically lunged at me."

"Well, it didn't help that you couldn't listen to me and let me talk to him for a minute."

Her tone surprised him. "Natalie, I wasn't about to leave you alone with him."

"Why not?" She looked him in the eye.

"I, um—he was—" he stammered, realizing he had no good reason. "I guess I was worried he would hurt you."

"I told you before, he's not like that." She took a sip of water. "You don't know him. He doesn't always think before he does stuff. He needed to walk it off. He was upset –"

"Upset I met your family." His stomach churned.

"He's close with my family. He and my brother-in-law George are, like, best friends. The kids adore him. My family is...well, we're all tangled up in each other's lives. I don't know." She paused. "Ben's a good guy. He's a big kid, he doesn't always think things through, but he's sweet and considerate. He would never hurt me. He's just really sad. And it's my fault." Her eyes misted over.

Richard set his water glass down on the table. "Oh."

"What?"

The realization hit him like a punch in the gut. She was still in love with her husband, whether she was aware of it or not.

"I'm sorry. I guess I was wrong about him."

"I knew taking you over there would stir up drama. I should have said no."

"I pushed you into it," he admitted.

"I have work tomorrow, I should probably—"

"Yeah. Me too." He picked up his keys. "I'm sorry."

"I'll call you tomorrow, okay?"

"Okay." He hesitated, not wanting to leave with the tension between them unresolved.

"What?" It was clear she was irritated with him.

"I guess I misunderstood."

"It's okay." She walked him to the front door and he gave her a quick kiss goodbye.

"I'll talk to you tomorrow."

He wanted to say more, but he turned and walked towards his truck, feeling like an idiot. She'd told him from the beginning that she wasn't sure if things were over with Ben, but he'd seen it as a challenge he was sure to win.

After this evening, he wasn't sure at all.

-23-

The first two weeks of school were as chaotic and exhausting as usual. By the time Natalie got home in the afternoons, she was ready to drop. It wasn't a bad thing that Richard's travel schedule had picked up, giving her the ability to go to bed early. But she missed him.

They finally got together for dinner on a Saturday night in late September, at a restaurant near his house.

"How are the girls?"

"Good," he replied. "Hannah's in her senior year. She wants to apply to all the Ivy League schools. Pre-med."

"She's a smart girl. I'm sure she'll get in."

"The tuition's a little steep," he said.

"If she goes to Penn, she can live here with you."

"If I'm still here."

"Right." His job here was still temporary. At first, that had seemed like a positive thing, but now... "How about Bella?"

"She's okay. I think middle school is tough no matter how smart and pretty you are." He avoided her eyes.

"Richard. Is everything okay?"

"Yes."

"Are you sure?"

He took a sip of water. "I'm sure."

"I don't think so." She put her fork down. "You're mad at me."

"It's this thing with Ben and your family."

"Oh."

"I don't have a family, like you do. I know that's not an excuse," he began. "It's hard for me to understand the dynamics of it."

"Well. They all need to learn to mind their business and back off. I'm sorry it got weird."

"If it's going to be this hard for you—"

"I've been thinking about it a lot and you were right," she interrupted. "They all need to get used to the idea that I have someone new in my life. I'm not just going to do what they think is best."

"Okay." He looked relieved.

"Why, what were you going to say?"

"I guess I was going to try and give you an easy out."

A lump formed in her throat. "You were going to break up with me?"

"I don't want this relationship to cause you so much stress."

"This relationship," she said, pointing to him and then at herself, "is the only thing keeping me sane."

"Really?"

"Yes."

He exhaled. "Okay. Good."

"I'm crazy about you." Her lips curved upwards, dimple showing.

"You are?"

"Um, yeah." Her tone was teasing, sarcastic.

"I missed you," he said. "Let's go somewhere next weekend."

"Fishing?"

"Perfect." He grinned.

-24-

onnor's soccer game was scheduled to begin at ten. Natalie arrived at the playground a few minutes early, hoping to find Lisa before it started. She grabbed her lawn chair out of the trunk of her car and walked towards the field.

The morning air was chilly, even for mid-October. She shivered inside her sweatshirt, wishing she had thought to bring a blanket. Lisa spotted her, waving from about twenty feet away, where she stood with Callie. Natalie raised her hand in response. As she approached, she saw Ben standing close by, talking with some of the kids. He wore shorts and a red team sweatshirt, his hair falling into his eyes as he spun a soccer ball between his hands.

Should she keep walking towards Lisa and pretend she didn't see him, or should she stop and say hello? She wasn't sure. His head turned, as if pulled by gravity in her direction. He grinned and set the ball down on the ground.

"Hey, I didn't know you were coming today." He stepped forward to give her a hug. God, he always smelled so good.

"I heard my godchild was the starting goalie."

"*Our* godchild." He grinned.

"Our godchild. Of course." An image flashed through her mind from Connor's christening day. The memory flooded her senses: holding Connor's warm little body in her arms with Ben at her side, chubby pink baby cheeks nestled against a sea of white, the smell of incense and oil, the trickling sound as the priest poured water over his head.

"You coming out for pizza after the game?" The referee blew the whistle. The game was ready to start.

"Oh. Um, maybe?"

"My treat. I insist." He jogged away from her, stopping to scoop up the ball on his way to the field. Natalie watched him go. *I miss him,* she thought, surprising herself.

Connor waved to her. "Hey, Aunt Nat!"

"Hey, bud! Good luck!"

"Hi," Lisa said from right beside her, startling her.

"Oh, hi."

"The assistant coach is cute, huh?"

"Sure. Not as cute as the head coach, though." She nodded in George's direction. She turned back to look at Ben. "I haven't seen him for a while."

Lisa looked at her, then at Ben. "He looks good."

"Yeah," she replied, not taking her eyes off him.

"Where's Richard this weekend?"

"In Atlanta, visiting his kids," she said. "So who else is here?" They began walking.

"Just me and Callie. And Mom."

Natalie stopped. "Oh, shit, you didn't tell me Mom was coming."

Lisa laughed.

"Did she see me talking to Ben? Of course she saw me talking to Ben."

"Why do you think I came over to grab you?"

Natalie groaned and looked in the direction of where she'd seen Lisa standing earlier. Her mother was beaming at her. "This should be fun."

Connor's team won five to two, and the kids and their families went out for pizza after the game.

The pizzeria was crowded, joyful and chaotic, with what seemed like hundreds of kids in dirt-stained soccer shorts running around, high-fiving one another and cheering. Ben sat with Natalie and her family, but was frequently distracted by the kids on the team. It was obvious they all adored him.

Her mother made sure to get in a few comments to Ben about how wonderful it was to see him, how much they missed him, how he should keep in touch. Natalie stayed silent, chewing her pizza and pretending not to notice. Lisa stepped in and changed the subject a couple of times, and Natalie was grateful.

After they finished eating, Ben asked her to step outside for a minute.

"Your mom gives you a pretty hard time, doesn't she?"

"Yeah, well. What else is new."

He looked at her face, crossing his arms over his chest. "How have you been?"

"I'm okay. September is always exhausting, you know, but I'm settling in."

"That's good.You look good."

"Thanks. You do too."

"Look, I know we didn't exactly leave things on good terms the last time I saw you. And before you say anything, I know that was my fault. I'm sorry."

"Apology accepted."

"I miss you, kid."

"Me too." She smiled. "I'm glad I got to see you today."

"Do you think maybe we could be friends? Like we were before?"

"We can try."

"Where's Mister Wonderful this weekend?"

She made a face.

"Sorry."

"He's in Georgia, with his kids."

"He goes back down there a lot?"

"A couple of times a month."

"So then what are you doing tonight? Want to grab dinner?"

She chewed on her bottom lip for a minute, thinking it over. She wanted to, but would it cause them both more heartache?

George poked his head out the door and looked at Natalie, then at Ben. "Hey, guys, sorry to interrupt," he said. "Liam's mom wants to talk to you." He looked in Ben's direction. "When you get a minute."

"Okay, I'll be right in."

"Take your time." George winked at Natalie, letting the door shut.

Ben turned to go inside. "You hanging out for a while, or..."

"I think I'm gonna take off."

The door opened again. A bunch of the kids were leaving. "Bye, Coach Ben!"

Ben handed out high fives as they passed him by. "Good game, guys. See you Tuesday." He turned back towards Natalie. "So, dinner later?"

Why did she have butterflies in her stomach? "Sure."

"Great." He gave her a quick hug. "I'll call you."

She followed him inside so she could say goodbye to her family. Ben walked to the other side of the pizzeria and found the woman she presumed was Liam's mom. She was pretty, with long, dark hair and a huge smile that showed off her perfect, white teeth. Natalie's stomach twisted as the woman smiled at Ben, touching his left arm. He wasn't wearing his wedding ring any more.

Her mother caught her watching Ben. "How long do you think you can push him away until he finally gives up and moves on?"

"Mom. That's what I want him to do."

"You don't sound so sure."

Ben picked her up and took her to their favorite sushi restaurant. She'd agonized over what to wear, trying to look nice without looking like she was trying. Which was stupid. She didn't need to impress Ben. This wasn't a date.

"Pizza and sushi in one day. I'm a lucky girl," Natalie joked.

They drank hot sake and ordered their favorites on a big platter to share. It was easy enough to slip back into the friendship that had always been the foundation of their relationship.

Natalie had to know the answer to something that had been bothering her for weeks. "Can I ask you something?"

"Sure."

"Was it George who told you I took Richard to Christine's house that day?"

"Why, are you going to kick his ass?" he teased.

"I just want to know."

"It wasn't George. Although I did grill him pretty hard about it once I knew."

"So who was it?"

"It's bugging you, isn't it?" He smirked. "Okay, you tell me something first."

"Go ahead."

Ben thought for a moment. "What is it about him? He's so much older."

"He's a grown-up."

He winced. "Wow. That was mean."

"Sorry."

"I get that he's got more money than I do, but..."

"You know I don't care about money."

"You don't seem to mind it, either."

"So now you're not answering my question, and you're insulting me."

He put down his chopsticks. "Shit." He sat back in his chair, breathing out. "Sorry. It was Connor."

"Connor?" She raised her eyebrow at him.

"At soccer tryouts. I asked about you, and he mentioned it. He wasn't trying to rat you out or anything."

"Oh. I guess I can't be too mad, then."

"I saw you two getting out of his truck, smiling and laughing. We used to be like that, Nattie."

"A long time ago, maybe."

He frowned. "So now do I get an answer to my question?" He picked up his chopsticks and popped a piece of spicy tuna roll into his mouth.

"I don't know, Ben."

"Why him, and not me?"

"How am I supposed to answer that?"

"Be honest. Come on, we're friends, right?"

"I wasn't out looking for someone else. He helped me out when I was hurt, and, I don't know, we sort of clicked. He makes me happy. We have fun together. It's easy being with him."

"And it's not easy being with me."

"He doesn't see me as a problem to be fixed."

He dropped his chopsticks onto his plate and put his head in his hands. "You think that's how I see you."

"Do you remember what happened?"

"I think I remember it differently than you do."

"You called that woman without telling me," she said.

"And you left without telling me. You didn't even give me a chance."

"I tried to talk to you. You wouldn't listen to me. I told you I needed time. But you were already onto the next thing."

He looked at her. "That's how I am. You know that."

"I needed you to be different."

"It's hard for me, Nat."

She narrowed her eyes. "Well. God forbid you should have to go through anything hard, Ben. All those injections and doctor's appointments were a fucking walk in the park for me."

He didn't answer.

"I'm gonna go. I'll call a cab. Thanks for dinner." She stood, grabbed her purse and turned to leave.

"Nat, wait." He got up from his seat. Natalie stopped, but didn't turn back toward him. "Please wait for me outside. I'll take you home."

She waited outside the restaurant, taking deep gulps of the crisp fall air, swiping at the tears that burned her eyeballs. Ben came up beside her. "You have to stop running away because things get uncomfortable."

She didn't answer. They walked to his car and got in. Ben turned the engine on, but left the car in park.

"Nattie." He pinched the bridge of his nose. "Nine years, we've been married. Next weekend is our anniversary. Remember?"

She stared straight ahead. "Of course I remember."

"Is this guy really worth throwing away our marriage for?"

"Our marriage was over before I met him."

Ben recoiled. "How can you say that?"

"Because it was, Ben. It's never going to be what we wanted. I'll keep letting you down."

"Only if you give up on us, Nat."

"Please take me home."

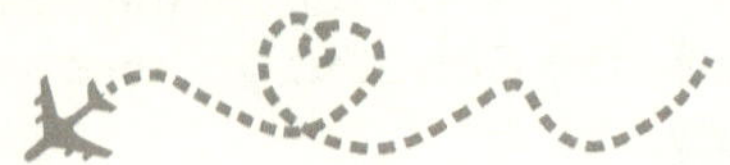

As they pulled up in front of her house, Ben was the one to break the silence. "I guess this was a mistake."

"I don't think we're ready to be friends," Natalie answered, trying not to cry.

"I'm sorry."

"Me too." She put her hand on top of his. *Fight for me, Ben.* The thought came out of nowhere, surprising her.

Ben pulled his hand away without looking at her. "Bye, Natalie."

She stared at him, her heart aching. "Bye." She got out of the car and watched as he drove away.

The truth was, she knew she had handled things badly. She hadn't told him she was leaving. She had Jean's son and his friend carry over the furniture from Nana's, paying them in pizza and beer. She packed up her clothes and a few other belongings, putting them in her car one day before Ben got home from work. The next day, she left for work and didn't come back. She came home to this little apartment instead.

He called her at about ten, in a panic. "Where are you? Will you be home soon?"

"I'm not coming home."

"You're not coming home? Where the hell are you?"

She tried to keep her voice steady. "I got my own place."

"What?"

The regret was instant. She closed her eyes and stiffened her spine. "I got my own apartment. I signed a lease. I'm not coming back."

She hung up the phone. He tried calling her back, but she turned the phone off. It was selfish. Cruel. She knew. She hated herself for it. But she couldn't live in that house anymore, and if she'd told him before she left, he would have found a way to get her to stay.

For the next few weeks, he begged her to come home. "I can't afford the mortgage on the house alone, Nat, you know that."

"So sell it."

"But this is our home."

"Not anymore."

She left him with all the responsibility of selling the house, of moving their stuff out. They'd signed the papers in March, a few weeks before she and Richard had met. A couple with two young children and one more on the way had bought the house.

"Do you feel better now?" he asked her once the papers were signed.

"No." She watched the new owners of their house smile and hug each other. It hadn't helped, selling the house. Instead, it was one more nail in the coffin of her dreams.

She unlocked her door and trudged up the stairs to her apartment. This had to get easier at some point, didn't it?

Richard flipped open his phone with one hand as he pulled his suitcase behind him with the other. He pushed the button to dial Natalie's number.

"I'm on the ground in Philly," he said when she answered.

"You caught an early flight?"

"Couldn't stay away. How was your weekend?"

Natalie groaned. "Awful."

"What happened?"

She paused. "Just...family bullshit."

"Well, it's not even five o'clock yet. Want to hang out for a while? We can grab some food."

"Sounds perfect."

"Where can I meet you?"

"I'll come to your place."

"I'll see you in a little bit."

Natalie showed up at his house an hour later. Richard grinned as he met her at the door, wrapping his arms around her. She dropped her bag on the floor.

"Do you want some dinner? I got Pad Thai and curry chicken..."

"I'm not hungry." She kissed him hard, pulling him closer.

"Okay, maybe later." He led her to the bedroom.

Natalie sat at the kitchen counter in pajamas, eating reheated Pad Thai while Richard poured them each a glass of water.

"That was a nice welcome home."

Natalie blushed. "Thanks."

He sat next to her and kissed the top of her head. "Thank *you*." He picked up a fork and ate a bite of Pad Thai. "So Hannah is taking pre-calculus this year."

"Oh, no. Does she hate it?"

"She's doing fine with it. I'm lost." He laughed. "She's showing me these problems, and, well, I took calculus in college, but I think I completely blocked it out because none of it looked like anything I remember..." He looked at Natalie, picking scallions out of her food with a faraway look in her eyes. "Hey, you." He waved a hand in front of her eyes.

"I'm sorry."

"Where'd you go?"

"Nowhere. I was listening. Pre-calc."

"Right."

"Sorry." She frowned, setting her fork down. "I saw Ben. I wasn't going to tell you. My nephew, Connor, was the starting goalie in his soccer game yesterday. Ben helps coach the team."

Ben. That was why she was all out of sorts. "What happened?"

"Do you think you can ever be friends with an ex?"

"Not really. Hurts too much." He tried again. "What happened?"

"My mom was there, and it got weird. She kept saying stuff."

"To you or to Ben?"

"Both."

"Oh, man. She doesn't quit."

"It's not just her. It's all of them." She chewed on her bottom lip. "I, um..." She looked at him, then averted her eyes.

"What happened?" he asked a third time, his stomach in knots.

"He asked me to have dinner. He said he wanted to try and be friends."

She'd gone out on a date with him. *Damn.* He kept his expression neutral. "And it didn't go well."

"It started off okay, but once we got to talking, it was the same as always. He wants me back, he doesn't understand why I'm with you."

"Sounds like the guy is still pretty hurt."

"Yeah." She glanced at him. "Are you mad?"

"That you went out with him?" He shrugged. "You're a grown-up, Natalie, you can have dinner with whoever you want."

"Are you sure?"

"Did something happen that you think I'd be mad about?"

"What? No," she said, looking surprised.

"Just checking."

She put her head down. "I want to move to Canada." Her voice was muffled. "No, that's too close. Maybe Australia."

"How about Atlanta?"

She looked up, surprised. "Atlanta?"

"It's nice there," he said. "Doesn't get too cold. People are friendly. Great food. Low cost of living."

"I thought you were starting to like Philly. You said Hannah was thinking about Penn."

"I like the people here. One in particular." He winked. "But it's hard being so far away from my kids. I'll be glad to move back."

She swallowed. "When?"

"Probably after the holidays." *Maybe you'll come with me.* He thought it, but was afraid to say the words out loud.

"I don't like to think about you leaving." Her voice was soft.

"Hey." He leaned forward to kiss her lips. "It's not for another couple of months. Forget about it. I don't know why I even brought it up. Did I tell you how thick Hannah's pre-calculus book is?" He held up his hand, his thumb and forefinger about

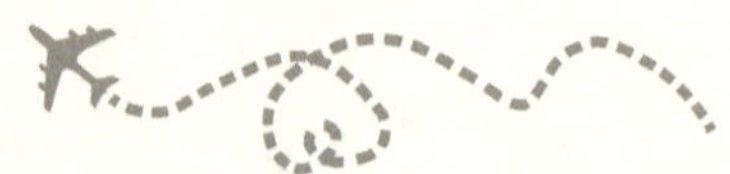

four inches apart. "I don't know how she carries that thing around. You teachers are mean."

"Second time this weekend I got called mean," she said. "I promise, my third graders' books are not that big. Although they're pretty big."

He cupped her chin in his hand and kissed her. "I'm sorry you had a rough weekend. Next weekend will be better."

"I'm holding you to that."

-25-

Natalie walked into the tiny tea shop near Lisa's house on a November afternoon. Her sister had called a few days ago and asked her to meet Friday after work.

"What's the occasion?" Natalie had asked.

"Just to hang out and talk," Lisa said. "I never see you anymore now that you have a boyfriend," she teased.

"Ha, ha."

Lisa was waiting for her at a wooden table near the front window. Natalie walked up to the counter and ordered a chai latte, then sat down across from her sister.

"Hey," Lisa said. "How was work?"

"Boring. How are George and the kids?"

"They ran away to join the circus. It was only a matter of time." She was trying hard to be her usual jovial self, but something was off. She fidgeted with her cup, avoiding Natalie's eyes.

"What's going on?"

"Am I that easy to read?"

"I've only known you for thirty-one years. Seriously, Lis. Tell me what's wrong."

"I guess there's only one way to tell you." Lisa took a deep breath. "I'm so sorry, Natalie. I'm pregnant." She breathed out slowly. "I'm planning on telling Mom and Dad and everyone at Thanksgiving dinner, but I didn't want you to find out that way."

A knife twisted in the center of Natalie's chest. "Wow." She tried to sound happy. "Well, congratulations." She forced a smile.

Lisa's eyes filled with concern.

"It's not like it's the first time, Lisa. I'll be okay."

"Yes, but it is the first time since… You know. Since what the doctor said, and your separation, and Nana dying. The last thing I want is to cause you any pain." She began to cry. "Goddamn hormones. I'm sorry."

She handed Lisa a napkin.

"Thank you." Lisa dabbed at her eyes.

Natalie willed her voice not to crack. "Are you happy?"

Lisa let go of a breath it seemed she'd been holding since Natalie had walked in the door. "I am. We weren't planning on any more. But, yeah. I'm happy."

"Then I'm happy for you."

"Really?"

"Yes. You and George are great parents. You deserve it."

"I'm so sorry, Nattie."

"Don't be. I'll have another niece or nephew, right? So, it's all good."

Lisa blew her nose. "I would have one for you, you know."

"Let's get through this one, okay?"

"I'm serious, though."

"Thank you." Natalie took a swallow of her tea.

"Are you sure you're okay? God, I was so worried about telling you. And George! The first thing he said when I told him was 'Oh no, what about Natalie?'"

She set her cup down, trying to hold on to her composure. "How far along?"

"Ten weeks. I'm due June eleventh. I wanted to tell everyone on Thanksgiving, because by then I'll be in my—"

"Second trimester." They finished the sentence in unison.

Natalie blinked and looked away.

"Right," Lisa said.

The second trimester had always been the promised land for Natalie and Ben. A fairytale place where the risk of miscarriage plummeted. She never made it that far. Twelve weeks was the closest they got. The last one. The one where they said to stop trying. Next week, it would be a year since that day.

Natalie shook off the sorrow threatening to consume her. "Are you feeling okay?"

"Tired, mostly. A lot of morning sickness, but I feel okay the rest of the day. More like I felt with Callie than with Connor, so maybe this is another girl."

Natalie smiled, a genuine one this time. "We need more girls in the family."

Lisa grinned. "Yes. We do."

She waited until after they said goodbye to fall apart. She pulled her car onto the highway, heading towards Richard's house, wiping at her eyes and sniffling. It was unfair, and it wasn't Lisa's fault, but it hurt. Like someone had kicked her in the ribs. Repeatedly. With steel-toed combat boots.

The drizzle that had fallen from the sky all day turned into a steady rain, hammering the roof of her car. She'd tried hard to stay numb while she was with Lisa. She couldn't give her a reason to feel worse than she already did.

She pulled into the driveway behind Richard's truck, taking a quick look at herself in the rear view mirror. She looked hideous, eyes swollen, nose

bright red. She couldn't go inside like this. A fresh wave of tears overtook her, and she buried her face in her hands.

Richard tapped on the window of the little red Focus. Natalie turned her head. He opened the passenger side door and got in.

"What happened?"

Her lips began to quiver. He held out his arms, and she collapsed into them, sobbing. His jacket was wet from the rain, but she didn't seem to mind. He listened as her breathing got deeper and more normal.

"I'm sorry," she said.

"For what?"

"For not coming in right away."

"It's okay. You want to come in now?" he murmured.

She nodded.

He guided her inside, took her jacket and keys from her, and led her to the kitchen. "Want some coffee?"

"Okay."

He put a pot on to brew. Once it finished, he poured two cups. He added cream to Natalie's cup and set it in front of her. She wrapped her hands around the mug and blew across the top before taking a sip.

Richard sat next to her. Even with puffy eyes and a red nose, she was beautiful enough to make his heart flip over in his chest. He would slay dragons for her if necessary. He would welcome the challenge.

"Lisa is pregnant," she said, her tone flat.

There it was. They must have tried to break the news to her gently, and in so doing made it impossible for her to have an honest reaction, for fear of hurting their feelings.

"I'd say I'm sorry, but that sounds so empty."

"You don't have to say anything. Knowing you understand helps."

"I do. You don't have to be strong in front of me."

"Want to know the worst part of having people feel sorry for you? You always wind up being the one to try and make them feel better, instead of the other way around."

"That does sound pretty terrible."

She rubbed her temples. "She's making the big announcement at Thanksgiving, so she wanted to give me a heads up." She made a face. "That should be a fun day."

He had an idea. "What if we went someplace else that day?"

She brightened a bit. "A holiday without my family? My mom will probably flip, but..."

"The past few years, I've had Thanksgiving dinner with my sponsor, Mike, and his family. His wife is the best cook in Georgia. I'm serious. How do you feel about going to Atlanta for the holiday?"

"I'd like that. Would we get to see the girls?"

"Sure. We'll stay the weekend. We can go Christmas shopping."

She gave him a grateful smile. "Thanks for coming to my rescue for the millionth time."

"I'm only repaying you for rescuing me, baby girl."

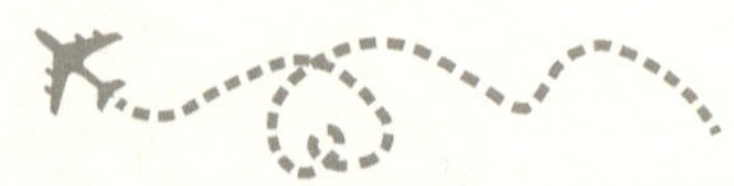

-26-

They flew into Atlanta on Thanksgiving morning.

He rang the doorbell at Mike and Ruth's house.

"You look nervous." He squeezed Natalie's hand. "Don't be. You're about to meet the two best people on the planet. Trust me."

Mike opened the door. Natalie recognized his face from the photo Richard had shown her. He had warm, crinkled eyes and graying hair. He towered over them both.

He grinned, wrapping Richard in a bear hug. "Richard, I'm so glad you're here. Happy Thanksgiving."

"Happy Thanksgiving. This is Natalie."

Mike took Natalie's hands in his. "The famous Natalie. Welcome. It's so good to finally meet you. Can I give you a hug?"

"Sure." She smiled as he wrapped his arms around her. "Thank you so much for having me."

"It's our pleasure. Ruth is in the kitchen. Follow me." They walked down a wide hallway, past a formal living room. She could smell the turkey roasting in the oven.

"There's our long lost boy," Ruth said as they entered the kitchen. The long center counter was laden with pans, bowls, and casserole dishes. Richard handed her the flowers he'd brought. "For me? You shouldn't have."

"Shouldn't have gotten you such a small arrangement, I know. Next time I'll try and do better, Miss Ruthie." He grinned and hugged her, both of them laughing.

"You're too much. Introduce me to your beautiful young lady." She turned towards Natalie. Ruth had warm eyes and a kind smile, like her husband.

"Ruth, this is Natalie. Natalie, this woman loves me for reasons I don't quite understand."

"You're pretty lovable," Natalie said. "Ruth, it's so nice to meet you. Your home is beautiful. Thank you for having me."

Ruth hugged her. "We're happy to have you. Welcome to the family."

"Can I help with anything?" Richard asked.

"You can get this man out of my kitchen so he stops picking at the food." Ruth looked at her husband, who had peeled back the foil on a casserole dish and popped a piece of cornbread dressing in his mouth. "That's not even cooked yet." She swatted him away from the counter. "Go watch football."

"I'm happy to help," Natalie said as the men exited the kitchen.

"Thank you." Ruth put an apron over her dress and handed one to Natalie.

"I'm not much of a cook," she warned Ruth as she tied the apron over her clothes.

"That's okay, sugar. You keep me company, and I'll show you what to do."

By the time dinner was ready, the house was full of guests and Natalie and Ruth had become friends. They laid out the dishes buffet-style on the long kitchen counter, and each guest fixed their own plate.

There were three other men and two women from their AA meeting, along with Mike and Ruth's adult children and their families. They had four

grandchildren, including one sweet little girl who was just learning to walk. Natalie offered to hold her so her mother could help her other children fill their plates. Her chubby, dimpled hands wrapped around Natalie's fingers as she pulled her down the long hallway, giggling with pride at each step she took.

When they turned at the end of the hall to walk back towards the kitchen, Natalie saw Richard, watching her. She grinned, scooped the baby into her arms and nuzzled her dark hair. "I'm in love."

"So am I," he said.

Dinner was delicious. As Richard had said, Ruth was an excellent cook. The food was divine. The biscuits were light as air. The candied yams were spicy-sweet and melted in her mouth. Natalie tried foods she hadn't had before, like collard greens and sweet potato pie. She went back for seconds, despite being full.

They stayed until late in the evening. She and Richard helped Ruth clean up, and they were the last ones to leave.

"I had a wonderful time." Natalie hugged Ruth goodbye. "Everything was delicious. Thank you, again."

"Anytime, sugar."

Richard threw his arms around Ruth and kissed her on the cheek.

"You behave yourself, now," she teased. "Your girlfriend's watching."

Natalie laughed.

"Bring her back to see us again."

"I will."

Mike walked them to the car.

"I'm so glad I got to meet you. Richard talks about you all the time."

"He's a good guy," Mike replied. He gave Natalie a hug. "You make him very happy."

She blushed. "Thank you."

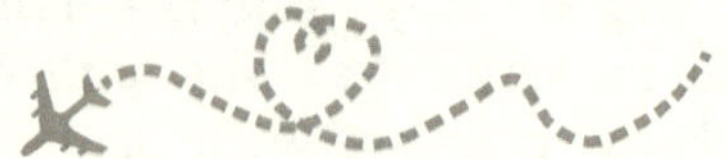

On Friday morning, they picked the girls up from Melinda's.

"Wow," Natalie said, staring at the house. It was massive and beautiful, with tall white columns on the front porch, and white-shuttered windows as large as doors. Four huge, glossy-leaved magnolia trees full of creamy white blossoms stood towering above the lawn.

"We planted those the year we moved in," he said, pointing to the trees. "And that balcony, off the second floor? I built that myself." His face had a wistful look as he showed it to her.

"You miss it," she said.

The front door opened and the girls came out, pulling suitcases behind them. Richard got out of the car to hug them. They piled into the backseat, happy to see Natalie.

They spent the rest of the weekend with Hannah and Bella, Christmas shopping and looking at lights displays. The girls showed her all their favorite places in the city. Richard loved being with all three of them, together. Like a family.

Before they flew home on Sunday afternoon, Richard dropped the girls off at the front door of the house. Melinda asked him to wait for a minute after the girls went inside.

"I need to talk to you." She stepped outside and closed the door behind her.

"Sure." He expected she wanted to talk about the girls' holiday break, which she'd agreed to let them spend in Philadelphia.

"I need a favor. Please hear me out before you say no."

"Uh oh."

"You know my parents have been staying here since Katrina," she began. "They flew home to meet with the insurance adjuster and the house is a total loss."

"I'm so sorry, Mel." That was the house where she'd grown up. He knew she was upset.

"Thank you."

"Are they going to live here permanently, then?"

"No." Melinda gave a sarcastic laugh. "God, no."

Richard chuckled.

"They're moving back and getting a condo, close to the beach. Anyhow, we were going to fly down the weekend after next and help them go through the house and see what can be saved, if anything. Furniture, clothes, pictures, you know. I figured it was your weekend with the girls. But then Neil—" she stopped and rolled her eyes "—went and dislocated his shoulder on Friday night."

"How did he do that?"

"Fell off a ladder hanging Christmas lights."

"Jesus."

"Yeah. He's waiting to see if he's going to need surgery. We meet with the orthopedist on Tuesday."

"Yikes," Richard said. "So what's the favor?"

"Would you be willing to come with me and help them pack up their things? My brother and Nikki will be there, too, and my nephews."

"Oh, God, Mel." He hesitated, running his hand through his hair.

"I know it's a lot to ask."

"I'm not their favorite person."

"Y'all have had your differences over the years."

"Mel... I'm sure they hate me. Shit, if I were them, *I'd* hate me."

"Richard, please don't make this about you." *Ouch.* "They don't hate you. You're their grandchildren's father. They need help. I'll be perfectly honest with you." She lowered her voice. "I'm a little tired of having them stay here with us. So are the girls. Try to see it as something you're doing for your daughters. For me." Her eyes pleaded with him to say yes.

"Okay. I'll go."

"I really appreciate it, Richard."

"No problem."

She looked at the car. "Where's Natalie?"

He blinked. "Natalie?"

"What? Isn't she here with you? I was hoping to get a chance to meet her."

"You wanted to warn her about me, huh?"

"The girls showed me pictures of her from the summer. My god, Richard. She's a kid."

"She's thirty-one."

"She doesn't look it. And thirty-one is closer to Hannah's age than yours."

He sighed. "And?"

"I guess it's none of my business."

"That's right. You have a good night, Melinda."

"Hey. I'm sorry. You'll still come next weekend?"

"I'll be there."

He got into the car. Melinda waved as he backed out of the driveway.

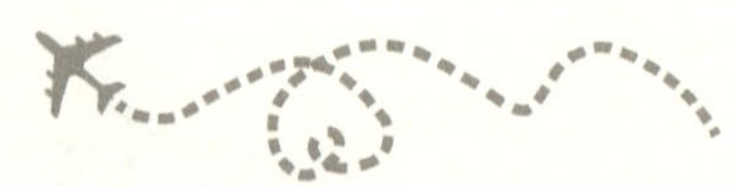

-27-

Melinda's parents moved around their house like grief-stricken zombies. On the lower floor, it was easy to see the marks on the walls from the flood water, the beginnings of mold at the edges of the carpet. Every room seemed to contain some irreplaceable item destroyed by the storm. Her mother's eyes filled with tears.

"Why don't you take Mom back to the hotel?" Melinda asked her father. "We can handle this."

Richard and Melinda worked together in her parents' bedroom on the second floor, where almost everything was salvageable. They spent their time gathering and organizing clothing, linens, and personal items, sorting them into bins and boxes for the movers to retrieve. Richard manned the dresser drawers while Melinda pulled things from the closet.

"Hey, how come I'm the person who gets to deal with your mother's underwear?" He grabbed a handful of bras from a drawer and shoved them into a bin, his head turned to the side, trying not to look.

"Richard." Melinda turned around, holding up a white photo album. "Look what I found."

"Oh no." He laughed.

She brought it over for him to see. Melinda stood on the beach in a white sundress, flowers in her hair, baby belly just beginning to show. Richard was at her side, dressed in white trousers and an untucked dress shirt. Both of them were barefoot. Suntanned. Smiling.

"Feels like a hundred years ago," she said.

"And five minutes ago."

"Time is weird like that, isn't it?" They continued to thumb through the album, laughing at the fashion choices, getting quiet when they saw the photo of their first married kiss.

"We should get back to work." Melinda's voice was thick.

They worked until late Friday evening and most of the next day. On Saturday night, her parents took the whole group for dinner to a little bar and grill across the street from the motel. The servers brought the food family style, in big bowls, and they stuffed themselves full of shrimp, crawfish, and oysters. The seafood was so fresh, it tasted like it had just been pulled out of the water. Melinda's family ordered pitchers of beer and shots of whiskey, but she didn't join in. Richard nodded his appreciation, and she winked at him.

As the evening wore on, the beer and whiskey kept flowing, and Richard could sense it would be a long night. He excused himself, thanking his hosts and apologizing, claiming he was tired.

"Thank you so much for your help, Richard," Melinda's mother said, getting up to give him a hug. "It made a big difference."

"We appreciate you." Her father shook Richard's hand.

"Glad I could help," he said, embarrassed.

"I'll walk you back to the motel." Melinda got up to follow him. "Think I'll turn in, too." She hugged her parents.

Richard stopped outside the door and lit a cigarette, Melinda following behind him.

"Can I get one of those?"

He raised an eyebrow at her. "I thought you quit years ago." He handed her one and then lit it for her.

She took a drag, inhaled, and blew out the smoke. "Every once in a while I get a craving."

They began walking together, their pace unhurried.

"Thanks for coming down this weekend. It means a lot."

"You're welcome," he said. "How's Neil?"

"Better. He doesn't need surgery, just some rest and PT."

"That's good."

"Yes."

"You could have stayed with your family," he said. "I don't need a babysitter."

"I'm not babysitting you. I wanted to get out of there before they all get drunk and start telling stories. Alcohol's not as glamorous to me as it once was."

They crossed the narrow highway and strolled towards the side of the motel where both their rooms were. A chorus of frogs sang out as the crickets chirped. The warm breeze blew Melinda's hair back from her face. She took one last drag on the cigarette, dropped it on the ground and crushed it with her sandal.

Richard looked at her, letting his eyes drift from her face down to her body, clad in a tiny black tank top and tight blue jeans. "Did you look this good when I was drinking?"

She laughed and elbowed him. "I wish I had known kicking you out of the house was the answer. Would have kicked you out a lot sooner."

"Ouch." He rubbed the spot on his arm where her elbow had hit.

"I'm sorry... I didn't mean that the way it sounded."

He stopped walking, moving closer to her. "What did you mean?"

She tilted her head to one side as she studied his face. "I guess...sometimes I wish it had turned out differently."

Her eyes were fixed on his mouth, her lips parted. Richard's heart pounded. He knew that look. He shifted his eyes away from her face. "Yeah, well. Seems like things turned out pretty well for you, anyhow."

"I don't know. I guess everything's been crazy, having my parents staying with us. It's been hard."

"On you and Neil."

"Yeah." She looked down, frowning.

"Well, I may not be his biggest fan. But this guy took on raising two teenage stepdaughters, plus taking in your parents for almost four months. He should probably be nominated for sainthood."

Melinda chuckled.

"You'll work it out."

She took his hand. "Thanks." Her voice was almost a whisper. She stroked the side of his hand with her thumb. He watched, hypnotized by the movement of her skin against his.

"Sometimes I think—"

"Mel." He pulled his hand away. "Don't do this."

"Do what?"

"Get caught up in nostalgia and say something you can't take back."

"I guess we should call it a night."

He walked her to her room. She gave him a hug and kissed his cheek.

"Do you want to come in for a little bit?" she whispered in his ear. She stepped back and took his hand again, watching his face.

It would be easy enough. Nobody would know. How long had he wished for this moment? How many times had he longed to see her looking at him the way she was right now? God, he wanted to. The feel of her hand in his was driving him crazy. He pictured their bodies tangled together in her bed, sheets and pillows in disarray.

Wait.

He forced himself to think about the lies he would have to tell. Natalie. Neil. Even Mike, who he'd sworn he would never lie to. He pictured his daughters' faces. This had the potential to tear their world apart. Again. They didn't deserve this. He couldn't do it.

Richard pulled back, clearing his throat. "I think we should say goodnight."

Her smile faltered. "You sure you don't want to?"

He hesitated. Maybe for a few minutes. He would leave before anything— *No.* He wasn't that strong.

"I didn't say I don't want to. I'm just saying goodnight. I'll see you in the morning." He kissed her on the forehead.

"Shit." She looked away. Her cheeks flushed. "Forgive me?"

"Nothing to forgive, darlin'."

"You must really love her."

He swallowed. "Yeah. I do."

"She's a lucky girl." She squeezed his hand. "Goodnight, Richard."

<h1 style="text-align:center">-28-</h1>

Natalie parked her car about a mile from the mall entrance, wondering for the millionth time why she had agreed to meet her sisters here. She hated shopping, especially at this time of year. Too many people, too hot inside the stores, too much fake cheerfulness. Still, it was a rare chance to spend time with just her sisters. Maybe it would be a good day.

She met Christine in the mall, and gave her a hug. "Lisa running late?"

"Of course." Christine rolled her eyes. "We missed you at Thanksgiving."

"I'm sorry." The guilt was instant.

Christine shook her head. "Oh, no, I didn't mean—" She put a hand up as if to stop herself. "I sound like Mom, don't I?"

"Little bit."

"Sorry. What I meant to say was, how was Atlanta?"

Natalie laughed. "It was nice. The food was amazing. The city is beautiful."

"What about Richard's family? What are they like?"

"They're great. I love his daughters."

"How old are they?"

"Seventeen and thirteen."

"Oh, seventeen," Christine said, a wistful look on her face. "Don't you wish sometimes you could go back in time?"

Natalie laughed, surprised. Perfect, hyper-organized, supermom Christine never dreamed of being a teenager again, did she?

Lisa showed up a few minutes later, looking flustered. "Sorry, guys." She gave them each a quick hug. "I'm exhausted. Callie was whiny about Daddy taking her to dance class, George is mad I'm going out, it was a whole thing." She looked at Natalie. "We missed you at Thanksgiving."

"Stop." Christine put her hand up again. "No channeling Mom today."

They all laughed.

They shopped for a few hours and then went to a restaurant outside the mall for lunch. Christine and Natalie each ordered a glass of wine.

"No fair," Lisa pouted. "Okay, I'm going to order two desserts and not even give you guys a bite."

"You do what you need to do." Natalie laughed and clinked her glass against Christine's.

"This is great, I'm almost done shopping." Christine double-checked her list after they ordered their food. "Just a couple more things for Maddie and something for Kevin, and I'm done."

"Show-off," Lisa said. "I still have to figure out what to get George."

"Why are men the hardest to buy for? I have no idea what to get for Richard," Natalie chimed in.

Christine and Lisa exchanged a quick look. "Well, what is he into?" Christine asked.

"Guy stuff. Fishing. Watching football. He travels a lot for work."

Lisa used her straw to stir sugar into her iced tea. "What do you think he's getting you?"

"No idea," Natalie answered. "He's good at picking out gifts, though."

Christine and Lisa looked at one another again.

"Hey, you know what would be great? If you guys didn't make those faces at each other every time I mention my boyfriend."

"Sorry, Nat," Lisa said. She looked at Christine.

Christine glared at Lisa. "Sorry."

"Thanks."

Christine took a sip of her wine. "How serious are you and Richard?"

Lisa looked at Christine. "I thought we decided not to talk about this."

"Wait," Natalie said. "You guys discussed whether to talk to me about Richard."

"I'm curious. I thought we both were," Christine said.

Lisa shrugged. "We want to know what's going on in your life."

"You do know what's going on. I'm separated from Ben. I met someone. We're dating. End of story."

Christine raised an eyebrow. "You're doing more than dating."

"And we're both adults." Natalie sat back and crossed her arms over her chest. "I thought you guys agreed not to channel Mom today."

"We're not, we just..." Christine paused. "Does everything I say come off judgy?"

"Yes," Natalie and Lisa said at once.

"I like Richard. We both do. You're spending holidays with him, introducing each other to your families, I think it's getting pretty serious," Christine continued. "I mean, where is this headed? Are you two in love? Do you see a future with him?"

Natalie squirmed. She asked herself these questions on the regular, but never brought them up to Richard. Back in spring, he had said he'd be in Philadelphia until the end of the year. Now, it was

only a few weeks until then. He hadn't mentioned moving back to Atlanta since that weekend in October, and Natalie didn't want to bring it up.

Her sisters both looked at her, waiting for an answer. They had her cornered.

She lied. "I'm not worried about where it's headed. I like him. We have a good time together. All I did when I was with Ben was think about the future, and I was miserable. Right now I'd rather live in the moment."

"What about Ben?" Lisa's voice was soft.

Natalie leaned forward, put her elbow on the table, and rested her forehead on her fingertips. She closed her eyes. "What about him?"

"Well...you two are still married."

"Yes. I know."

"I know you and Richard are happy and everything is wonderful, but you have to come back to the real world sometime."

"You both think I should just go back to Ben," she said, her voice flat. "Back to crying myself to sleep every night."

Lisa didn't answer.

Christine chimed in. "Nat, all we're saying is that you can't keep living in this fantasy world. There's other people involved here. Not just Ben, but Richard's letting his kids get attached to you now. Their feelings matter, too."

"I never said they didn't."

"What are you going to do?" Lisa asked.

"Are you asking because you want to know, or because Ben wants to know?"

Lisa looked away.

"If Ben has a question, he can call me." She stood, picking up her purse. "I'm going to the ladies' room."

"Nice job," she heard Lisa say to Christine as she walked away.

"You're the one who mentioned Ben!"

Natalie moved faster, resisting the urge to put her hands over her ears as her sisters continued to argue. She went into the bathroom and stood in front of the sinks, taking a slow breath in, then exhaling. *Don't cry.*

She opened her eyes. The bathroom was next to the exit. She could walk right out the front door of the restaurant without her sisters seeing.

She walked to the parking lot, got into her car, and drove away. She didn't care that she'd already ordered food and her sisters would get stuck with the bill. It served them right. Who did they think they were?

At the first red light, she fished her phone out of her purse.

"Hey, Natalie, what's up?" Ben sounded cheerful. She hadn't spoken to him since the night they'd gone for sushi, two months ago.

"If you want to talk to me, you call me. Okay? Don't send my sisters as your messengers." She flipped the phone closed and tossed it onto the passenger seat.

The phone began to buzz almost immediately. She flipped it open. "What?"

"What?" Ben was laughing.

"What do you mean, what? Are you serious?"

"What the hell happened? All I told Lisa was to tell you I said hi."

"That's it?"

"Yep. She asked if there was anything else, and I said no."

"Are you sure?"

"Nat... Yes. Gosh."

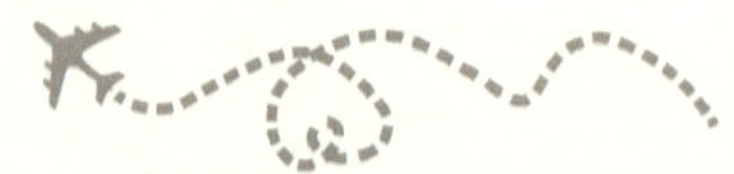

"She was asking me all these questions." Natalie paused. "I guess maybe I overreacted."

"You? Never."

"Shut up." She laughed, her body relaxing.

"Cheer up, kid. It's almost Christmas. Peace and good will and all that."

"Sorry I accused you."

"I'll forgive you this time."

"Thanks."

"It's good to hear your voice, anyhow."

"It's good to hear yours, too." A moment of silence passed between them. "Well, have a merry Christmas, if I don't talk to you again before then."

"You too, kid."

It was the most civil conversation they'd had in months.

About an hour after she got home, her doorbell rang. She went downstairs and opened the door. Lisa stood on the other side, holding Natalie's coat and a takeout container.

"Hey." Natalie held the door open so her sister could step inside.

"You left these."

"Thanks."

"It's okay," Lisa said. "I got a call from Ben. I'm sorry."

Natalie made a face. "Come on upstairs."

"We didn't realize you had left until he called." Lisa watched from the kitchen doorway as Natalie put the container into the fridge. "I thought you just went to cool down for a few minutes."

"I had to get out of there."

"I don't get it."

Natalie leaned against the kitchen counter. "Honestly, Lisa? I expect that kind of thing from Mom and Christine but for some reason I always thought you were on my side."

"I am on your side."

"Are you? Who was it that told Ben I brought Richard to Mom's birthday?"

"Connor mentioned it to him."

"And then he asked you and George for details."

Lisa rolled her eyes. "Okay."

"Did you know he showed up a few nights later and ambushed us?"

"I know. I told him it was a stupid idea."

"You knew he was going to show up here? Did you think to warn me?"

Lisa leaned against the doorway. "I'm sorry, Nat. I see it differently than you do. It's complicated, I guess."

"Enlighten me." Natalie crossed her arms over her chest.

"Can we sit? I'm so tired."

"Of course. I'm so sorry." Natalie narrowed her eyes, her voice full of derision.

Lisa pressed her lips together and looked away. "I guess I deserve that."

Natalie sighed.

"You're right. Okay? I'm sorry." Tears formed in Lisa's eyes.

"Shit." Natalie shook her head, defeated. "I'm sorry, too."

They went into the living room and sat on the couch.

Lisa took off her jacket and looked around the room. "Your place looks, um..."

"Yeah, I know. It's not much to look at."

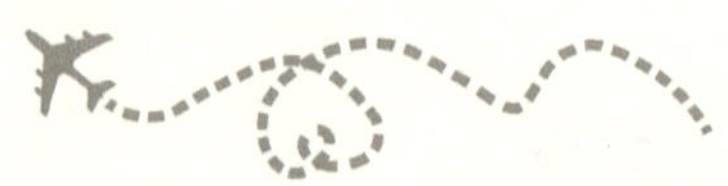

"It's nice to see some of Nana's things, anyhow." She ran her hand over the crocheted blanket on the back of the couch. "I'm sorry, Natalie. We're all worried about you and instead of being supportive, we act like assholes. Today was my turn, I guess. And I thought I could get away with blaming Ben, but you were one step ahead of me. It wasn't him, it was me."

"And Christine."

"Well, yeah, to some degree. But I keep putting myself in the middle and I'm not helping anyone. Ben is my friend, but you're my sister. So, on behalf of Christine and myself, we are sorry. And I am sorry."

"Okay."

"We would like to invite you *and* Richard to Christmas Eve dinner, at Christine's house."

"Are you serious?"

"Yes."

"Wow."

"We did miss seeing you at Thanksgiving. It wasn't the same. I understand why you didn't want to be there. I know this is hard for you." She pointed to her abdomen.

"Thank you."

"I hope you guys will come."

"I'll talk to Richard about it."

"Good."

"So how is Ben?"

Lisa laughed. "Are you kidding me? You can't have it both ways."

"Come on. You're *my* sister. I should get information, too."

"Well, he's doing better than I would be in his position. He was so sad, pathetic really, after he found out you took Richard to meet the family. He was over at our house all the time. I thought we were going to have to start claiming him as a dependent. But the past few weeks, it seems like he's doing a little better."

"Good," Natalie said, although she was suspicious of the way Lisa said he was doing better. As if she wanted to convey a specific reason he was doing better, but she didn't want to say what it was.

"Look, I know I said I wouldn't tell you what to do. It's none of my business. I just want to say one thing. Okay, two things."

"Okay. What?"

"You can't run away anytime things get difficult, Nattie."

"I haven't heard that before." She rolled her eyes.

"I'd rather you tell me to fuck off than disappear in the middle of an argument."

"I don't like to argue."

"Then say that. Be honest. Running away doesn't solve anything."

"What's the other thing?"

Lisa gave her a pointed look. "About Ben."

"What about him?"

"He's never going to be the one to bring this up. But if it's over between you two, you should end it. Make it official. Get a divorce. Let him off the hook."

Natalie didn't answer. Lisa was right, of course. But the thought of it gave her stabbing pains in her chest. Selling the house had been hard enough. Signing papers to officially end their marriage would be impossible.

"Okay, I'd better get home before George sends out a search party." Lisa stood and put her jacket back on. Her belly still looked flat, but Natalie noticed the gentle way she smoothed her jacket above her lower abdomen, like she was tucking a blanket around the baby.

"Is everything good? With the baby?"

Lisa nodded. "He's kicking now. Too early to feel it on the outside yet, but it's like little butterflies in my stomach."

Natalie smiled. "He? You seemed pretty sure it was a girl."

"I go back and forth. We'll know for sure in January."

"I'm still hoping for a girl."

"Me too."

There were tears in her eyes after Lisa left. Were they about the baby, or about Ben? She couldn't tell. It was all the same, anyhow.

Christine called a few hours later and apologized.

"Will you and Richard come to dinner on Christmas Eve?"

"I think so."

"It was nice spending the day together."

"It was. I'm sorry I took off."

"It's okay."

She stared at the phone after hanging up, wondering if her relationship with her family would ever go back to normal.

WINTER 2005-06

-29-

"Good morning," Richard said. "Merry Christmas."

Natalie stretched and opened her eyes, watching as he set a full mug of coffee on the nightstand next to her. She sat up as he kissed her lips.

"Merry Christmas." She reached for the coffee and took a sip.

"Santa Claus was here." His eyes twinkled.

"Ha, ha."

"Come on." He took her hand.

She sniffed the air. "What did you make?"

"Cinnamon rolls."

"You're the best boyfriend ever." She set down her mug and stood up. "I'll be right there." She kissed him again before making her way to the bathroom.

Christmas Eve dinner had gone better than she'd expected. Everyone was genuinely friendly to Richard, not just cordial. Even her dad, who was in a rare good mood. George dressed as Santa, as he always did, to the delight of the children. They were all smart enough to know who was under the fake white beard, yet innocent enough to enjoy the magic anyhow. Dinner included ham, pineapple stuffing, mashed potatoes, green beans, plenty of wine, a salad nobody touched, and enough pies to feed a small army.

After the gifts were opened and the mess cleaned up, Natalie and Richard made an early exit. Richard apologized, saying he'd been under the weather and needed some sleep. Her sisters must have threatened their mother to keep her thoughts to herself, because for once, she said nothing critical to Natalie, just hugged her and wished her a merry Christmas.

Natalie walked into the living room, coffee mug in hand, just as Richard put a plate of hot, gooey cinnamon rolls on the table. A warm fire glowed in the fireplace. Next to it, an assortment of wrapped gifts sat piled beneath the tiny tabletop tree. Most of them were for Hannah and Bella, but Natalie had placed a few gifts for Richard under the tree last night. She picked one of them up and handed it to him.

"Open," Natalie insisted.

"Okay." He took the present from her. It was a flat package, wrapped in candy-striped paper with a huge green bow.

She took another sip of her coffee and watched as he unwrapped her gift.

Inside was a picture frame that held a photo she'd asked someone to snap at the marina on their first fishing trip. The two of them stood in front of Richard's boat, Natalie holding up the fish she'd caught, his arm around her, both of them sun-kissed and smiling.

He grinned. "I love this. Thank you. Now you have to open one." He handed her a package. "Wait." He handed her a napkin. "Wipe your fingers first."

"Yes, sir." She licked icing from her thumb before taking the napkin from his hand.

Natalie ripped off the paper and opened the box. Inside was a blue crocheted scarf. "It's the color of your eyes," Richard explained. "I saw that at a craft market in Atlanta and I had to get it for you."

"It's so soft," Natalie said, touching the buttery yarn. "Thank you."

"Try it on. No, wait. Let me put it on you."

She laughed. "Sure."

Richard draped the scarf around her neck so a bit of the length hung down over each shoulder. "Beautiful."

They each opened more gifts, watching and enjoying the other's reactions.

"Okay, this is the best one." Natalie handed him a small box and clapped her hands.

"Saved the best for last, huh?" He untied the ribbon. "Tickets to Radio City Music Hall?"

"I'm taking you and the girls to New York. We'll go see the Christmas show, go ice skating, drink hot chocolate."

"Sounds perfect."

"I made a hotel reservation so we can stay overnight in the city."

"The girls are going to go nuts."

Natalie grinned. "Good. I can't wait to take them."

"You're incredible."

"I try."

"It means a lot that you want to make my kids happy."

"They deserve it. They're great kids."

"I have one more thing for you. Well, actually two, but you can only open one of them." He handed her a small square box.

Her eyes widened as her heart started to pound inside her chest. "What is this?"

"Open it."

She tore off the wrapping, taking the lid off the box. Inside was a circle-shaped gemstone pendant suspended on a white gold chain. "Richard..."

"Let me put it on you." His voice was much more serious than when he'd said the same about the scarf.

She touched the pendant with her fingertip. It sparkled in the firelight. "Are those diamonds?"

"Yes."

"It's too much." She looked at him. "Richard. It's beautiful, but you shouldn't have—"

"You're worth it," he interrupted.

Her heart flipped over.

Richard took the box from her hand and pulled the scarf from her neck. He fastened the necklace, his lips brushing her skin above the clasp.

She touched the pendant again. "I don't know what to say. Thank you."

"There's more."

She waited.

"I want you to move to Atlanta with me."

"You do?"

He looked down, fidgeting with the jewel box. "I've been wanting to talk to you about this for a while now. My time in Philly is done. I'll be based in Atlanta after New Year's." His eyes met hers. "I was hoping you'd come with me."

Natalie didn't say anything.

"My lease on this place is up at the end of January. You can come with me then, or wait until the end of the school year, if you want to finish with your class. I know some people who can help you find a teaching job. I think you'll like living there." His eyes sparkled. "And I want to buy a house. I mean, we'll pick it out together, of course. It'll be your house, too. But a house that's ours, with a front porch, and a garden. A bedroom for each of the girls, so they can spend whole weeks with us, not just weekends." He paused to take a breath. "What do you think?"

"Wow," she whispered.

It was overwhelming. This was her chance to leave the past behind her and make a fresh start.

To create a life for herself away from everyone else's expectations.

"Talk to me." He sounded nervous.

"I didn't realize you were even thinking about this."

"Of course I am. I want us to have a future together." He kissed her. "I'm in love with you, Natalie."

He'd never said that to her before, not outright. She threw her arms around him and kissed him.

"I would love to."

"You would?"

"Yes." She pulled back to look at him. She reached for the necklace, running her fingertip over the diamonds. Tears sprang to her eyes, surprising her. She blinked.

"You're crying." He tipped her chin up with his finger.

She smiled, sniffling. "I'm happy."

"I'm happy, too," he said. "I'm the happiest man in the world." He kissed her on the lips, soft, lingering. "I love you." He pulled her closer.

"I love you, too."

You're worth it.

Richard's words echoed in Natalie's mind. He'd told her he loved her, and that was significant, but after years of feeling worthless, those other three words meant everything. He didn't just mean she was worth the expensive necklace—he meant she was worth building a future with.

She undressed in front of the bathroom mirror, waiting to take the necklace off until last, tracing the circle with her fingertip.

As she showered, she thought of another small, square box she'd been given, this one on a warm summer evening more than eleven years ago. On one knee, Ben held it out to her, visibly nervous although they had picked out the ring together a few days before. She said yes with happy tears in her eyes, and he slipped it onto her finger. She was only twenty years old and about to begin her junior year of college, but certain they would live happily ever after.

Natalie looked at her left hand, touching the spot Ben's ring used to occupy. Her skin was still indented at the base of her finger. The ghost of the ring. An eternal reminder. It was tucked in a box, along with the plain gold band that accompanied it, inside a dresser drawer in her apartment. She'd taken them off the day she moved out. One more dream that hadn't come true.

She closed her eyes as the water rinsed the conditioner from her hair. When she'd envisioned happily ever after, it never included so much heartbreak and pain. It had never included her own body rejecting the one thing she wanted most.

The one thing I wanted most.

She opened her eyes. Was that still true?

She shut off the water and stepped out of the shower. As she wrapped a towel around herself, she looked at her reflection in the mirror. *It can't happen,* she reminded herself. *It doesn't matter how much I want it.* She had her nieces and nephews, her students, and now Hannah and Bella. That would have to be enough.

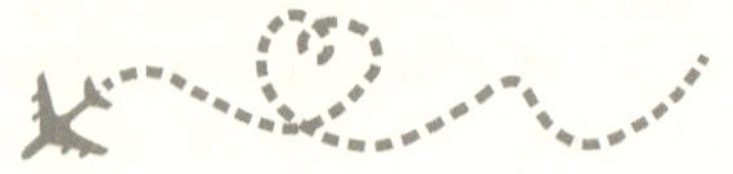

Richard walked back to the kitchen, rinsed out Natalie's coffee mug, and covered the cinnamon rolls with a piece of tinfoil before pouring himself another cup of coffee. He wiped down the already clean countertops. A nagging ache in his back had been troubling him all morning, but he wasn't going to let it bother him.

She had said yes. *Yes.* She wanted to move to Atlanta with him. His heart swelled thinking about it. And yet... Had he imagined the flash of hesitation he'd seen in her eyes right before she'd said yes? Or was it just that he'd been so nervous about asking her?

The ache in his back tightened. He stretched and tried taking a deep breath, but it started him coughing again. He was so sick of this goddamned chest cold. He'd brought it back from Mississippi and hadn't been able to shake it since. That, or the uneasiness still plaguing him over the moment he and Melinda shared. He gripped the edge of the counter as the coughs shook his body.

When he began to catch his breath, he poured himself a glass of water. Coughing left him worn out. He walked to the couch and sat down, propping his feet on the coffee table. He would sit for a few minutes and then start preparing for the rest of the day. He was excited to have the girls here for Christmas dinner. He planned on making roast beef, with red potatoes, glazed baby carrots, and a green salad. Chocolate cake for dessert.

He didn't realize he had dozed off until he felt Natalie's warm hand against his cheek. "Hey, sleepyhead."

"Hey." His voice was raspy. He looked up at her. She was still wearing the necklace. It sparkled against her skin, above a pretty red sweater cut low enough to make her look irresistible. He tried to clear his throat, but another coughing fit began. *Damn.* He hated when it happened in front of her. Her eyes grew large.

"You should go to the doctor about that cough," she said as the coughing eased.

He made a face. "They're closed today."

"Tomorrow," she said. "Okay?"

"I'll think about it."

She crossed her arms over her chest.

"I'll go, I'll go, you can stop with the fire eyes."

"If we're going to live together, you'll have to deal with me nagging you," she teased.

"Yes, dear," he said, feigning annoyance.

"What time do you need to put the roast in?"

"Is it that late?" He glanced at the clock. It was past noon. "Shit."

"You were out for a while."

"I'm sorry." He stood and walked towards the kitchen.

"I know you're not feeling well. Tell me what to do, I'll get it ready."

"No way."

"Well, let me help, at least."

"You can cut the potatoes."

"That's it?" She pretended to pout. "That's how little faith you have in my culinary skills?"

He grinned and patted her bottom. "You have other skills, darlin'."

After the roast was in the oven, the potatoes washed and cut, the carrots prepped and the salad made, Richard showered, dressed, and took some cough medicine. They drove to the airport and made their way to the gate to welcome the girls. They were both excited to see Natalie, and they were thrilled when she told them about the trip to

New York. They talked about it during the short drive home and all through dinner.

When dinner was over, they gathered in front of the fireplace so the girls could open their Christmas gifts. Natalie curled up next to Richard on the couch. It wasn't the family she'd always longed for, but maybe she could be happy with the family they had. He knew he was.

He kissed Natalie on the cheek and put his arm around her, wishing he could freeze this moment, seal it away somewhere, keep it forever.

-30-

On the day they were supposed to go to New York, Richard woke up with a fever.

"One hundred and two," Natalie read from the thermometer. "Looks like you're going to the doctor instead of New York."

"I'll be fine," he croaked. He shivered and pulled the blankets up to his chin. "Just let me get warmed up."

She shook her head. "You're not fine. Why are you being so stubborn? Find out what's wrong, get some meds."

"It's a cold. I'll take some Tylenol," he said. "I don't want the girls to miss New York."

She crossed her arms over her chest and raised her eyebrow at him. "This isn't just a cold. Look at you, you can't even get out of bed."

He closed his eyes. "Will you take the girls?"

"What? Without you?"

"Yes. If I go to the doctor, will you please take the girls to New York?"

"Please, Natalie?" She turned and saw Bella standing in the doorway of Richard's bedroom. "We'll be good, I promise."

Hannah appeared behind her sister.

"You, too?" Natalie asked.

Hannah gave her a half-smile. "I want to go to New York."

Natalie looked at Richard. "I can't leave you like this."

"I'm a big boy," he said. "I can take care of myself. I promise."

"What about Melinda?"

"I'll call her," Bella said. "She won't mind." Richard looked skeptical as she took Hannah's phone and dialed her mother's number.

Melinda was less than thrilled. Natalie could tell by the way the girls spoke to her, in hushed tones, glancing up at her every so often.

"She wants to talk to you, Dad." Hannah handed the phone to Richard.

"Hey, Mel. No, I know. I'm sick. Caught a cold after I got back from your parents' place." Natalie turned away, uneasy, as she always was when Richard talked to Melinda. The woman had his heart for almost twenty years. She'd lived with him, given birth to his children. Plus she was beautiful and had a perfect body. Natalie had seen photos. Living in Atlanta would mean interacting with her on a regular basis.

"Yes. Look, she's a teacher. She's great with kids. She has a horde of nieces and nephews. Of course I trust her." Richard looked at Natalie, shaking his head. "Do you want to talk to her?"

Natalie's eyes widened and she shook her head as Richard handed her the phone. "Please," he whispered.

Perfect. "Hi, Melinda." She used her teacher voice.

"Natalie." Melinda's voice was syrupy sweet. "I'm so glad to have a chance to talk with you. My daughters think the world of you."

"I feel the same way about them."

"I'm a little nervous about sending them off to a strange place to stay overnight with someone I don't know. I'm sure you can understand."

"Absolutely." She glanced at the girls. "Listen, I bought the tickets for them as a Christmas gift, and we don't have to stay in the city overnight. I'll take them to the show and then bring them right back here. If it's okay with you, of course."

Hannah's face fell. "No, wait, we want to stay. We've never been to New York."

"Please, Natalie?" Bella chimed in.

"Tell Bella I can see her puppy dog eyes through the phone."

Natalie laughed and motioned for them to hush.

"Natalie, listen. I know I don't know you very well, but I need you to be honest with me," Melinda said. "Answer yes or no, please."

"Yes."

"I'm sure Richard has told you he's a recovering addict and alcoholic."

"Yes."

"Is he drinking or using at all, that you know of?"

Natalie glanced at Richard. "No."

"I want to trust you, because I know my girls love you, but please understand. If he's not sober, it's crucial that I know. Their safety is number one."

"Yes, ma'am. I agree."

"Okay, good," she said. "You're sure?"

"Yes."

"Have fun in New York," Melinda said. "Pass me back to Hannah, please."

Natalie handed the phone to Hannah.

"Sorry," Richard said.

"Get better quick, because I'm going to kick your ass."

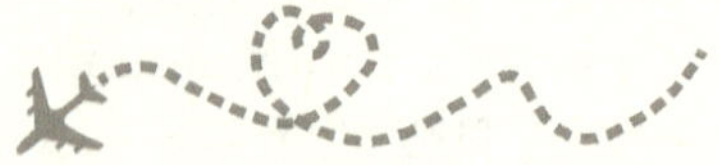

They made it to Radio City Music Hall in just enough time to be seated for the show. Their seats were in

the middle of a row, and they had to squeeze past a frazzled couple with three small children. The two little girls wore matching dresses, with red bows in their hair and black patent leather shoes. The boy, just old enough to walk, wore a red argyle sweater vest and bow tie. They giggled as they climbed over and under the seats, despite their parents' admonishments. Natalie's throat tightened as she watched them.

At intermission, Hannah and Bella got up to use the restroom. Natalie took a moment to look at the sleeping toddler, curled up in his mother's arms.

"He wore himself out." She gazed down at his sweet face, wishing she could run her fingers through his silken hair.

The mom rolled her eyes and smiled. "Tell me it gets easier when they can go to the bathroom by themselves."

"To be honest, I don't really know. They're my stepkids," she said, trying out the word for the first time.

"Oh, that makes sense. I thought you looked too young to have teenagers."

"I'll take that as a compliment."

The girls came back with a box of popcorn and a Coke. Bella glanced across Natalie at the little boy curled up in his mother's lap.

"He's so cute." She looked at Natalie. "I always wanted a little brother."

"Bella!" Hannah nudged her. "Sorry," she said to Natalie.

Natalie gripped the armrests of her chair. It was an innocent enough remark. The girls didn't know anything about her history. "It's okay."

"He is cute, though," Hannah agreed.

Natalie forced a smile. She was grateful when the lights went down and the music began.

After dinner they checked into the hotel, got into their pajamas, and snuggled in bed with the TV on, tuned to a sappy Christmas movie Bella insisted on watching. After her sister was asleep, Hannah tiptoed over to Natalie's bed.

"Can I ask you something?" She kept her voice quiet.

Natalie sat up straight and glanced over at Bella to make sure she was asleep. "Sure." She patted the bed next to her, and Hannah sat, tucking her legs underneath her. "What's up?"

"Is everything okay with my dad?"

"He's just feeling sick," Natalie said. "It's a cold, a bad one. He's had it since he came back from helping your grandparents."

"You're sure? He's not drinking again?"

"No, Hannah. I'm sure."

"I mean, this is how it used to be." Her voice cracked, her dark eyes shimmering. "We would have something special planned, and then he would be sick—" she used her fingers to make air quotes around the word "—and my mom would have to take us by herself. But he wasn't sick, he was drunk. Or hung over. Or detoxing."

"No, I promise, he's actually sick."

"Is he going to his meetings?"

"Yes." The response was automatic. She wanted to reassure Hannah, although if she was honest with herself, she couldn't remember the last time Richard had mentioned going to a meeting.

"I'm sorry." Hannah sniffled. "I don't mean to sound ungrateful that you brought us. I worry about him."

"No, it's okay." Natalie handed her a box of tissues from the nightstand. "I can't imagine how hard that must have been on you. And Bella."

"It's better now. I miss him, though."

"I know you do." She wondered if Richard had told them yet that he was moving back to Atlanta. She didn't want to spoil the surprise if he hadn't. "I know he misses you, too, and he wanted to come with us."

"Thanks, Natalie."

Hannah gave her a hug and got back into her own bed, leaving Natalie to wrestle with her thoughts. If she was honest with herself, she didn't know if she'd be able to recognize the signs if Richard did start using again. He seemed to be serious about his recovery, but what if he slipped? She'd never considered it before.

She glanced over at the other bed, her heart heavy for the little girls who'd grown up watching their father struggle with addiction. They knew the signs. Hannah even knew enough to ask. It was strange that someone half her age could have so much more wisdom.

Natalie watched the girls sleeping in the glow of the TV screen. *Stepkids.* The word had come easily enough. It would be nice to live close by and see them as often as they liked. A house where they could come and stay. They could be a family.

But her thoughts drifted to the children seated next to them at the show. The sweet blond-haired baby boy snuggled on his mother's lap, so like the baby she and Ben had dreamed of. The baby she would never have.

She closed her eyes, pushing it from her mind.

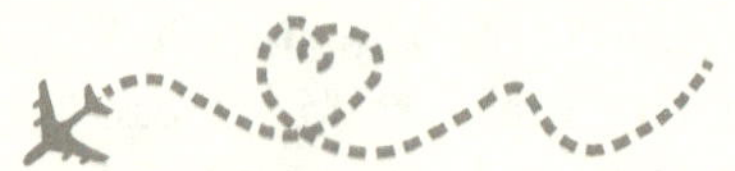

"Bronchitis," Richard told her on the phone, early the next morning. She was sitting in a diner with the girls, finishing breakfast. "They gave me an antibiotic and a decongestant and I slept for twelve hours. I feel better already," he insisted.

"I'm glad you went," Natalie said.

"Me, too. I'm sorry I missed New York."

"So are we."

"Let me talk to the girls." She passed the phone to Bella.

"Hi, Daddy." Bella began chattering about everything they had done and seen in New York.

Hannah looked at Natalie. "You look relieved."

"Yes," she admitted. "It's bronchitis."

"I'm glad. I mean, not that he has bronchitis, but..."

"I know."

"Now if we can get him to stop smoking." Hannah grinned as Bella handed her the phone.

-31-

By the time Richard sent the girls home to Atlanta, early in the morning of New Year's Eve, he was himself again. The cough lingered, but was more of a nuisance than anything else.

He and Natalie ordered dinner in. They toasted with sparkling cider at midnight, curled up in front of the fireplace.

"Happy New Year." He clinked his glass against hers.

"Happy New Year."

"Almost as good as the real stuff." He looked into his glass.

"Hey, can I ask you something?"

"Sure."

"Are you going to your AA meetings?"

Richard straightened up, setting his glass on the table in front of him. "Yes. Mostly when I'm in Atlanta. I may have missed one or two with the holidays and the kids being here. But I'm still sober."

"Okay."

"What made you ask?"

She shrugged.

"Did Melinda say something?"

"I'm not supposed to tell you she asked."

"She's a good mom. She has every right to be worried about her kids."

"Are you mad?"

"No." He kissed her forehead and stood up. "Thanks for being concerned about me."

"Hey, I like you a little bit." She followed him into the kitchen.

"You do?" He cleared the counter and rinsed out their glasses.

"Mmm. Nope. I'm madly in love with you."

"So come to Atlanta with me." He trailed his hand along the length of her arm, lacing his fingers with hers.

"I said yes."

"Say it again." He wrapped his arms around her.

"Yes."

"No, the other thing."

"I love you."

"I love you. So much."

Something darkened her face, causing her mouth to turn down.

"What's on your mind?"

She got quiet for a minute, shifting her gaze away from his face. "When we were at the show, there was this couple next to us with these three little kids. They were so cute. Two girls and a little boy. Bella said she always wished she had a baby brother."

She glanced at him. He kept silent.

She spoke in a low voice, the words rushed. "Have you ever thought about having another one? Another baby, I mean?" When he didn't respond, she continued. "I know you had the vasectomy, but I've read they can be reversed."

"Oh. Wow." The question caught him off guard. He tried taking a deep breath, but it made him cough.

"Are you okay?" Her face was concerned.

"A little surprised, I guess." He cleared his throat. "I don't know why. I should have seen that coming."

Natalie shrugged and looked away. "I was just sort of wondering."

Sure. Just wondering. *Before I rearrange my whole life for you, could you give me everything I've ever wanted?*

"Natalie." He put his hands on either side of her face. "I'm sorry."

She gave him a sad smile. "It's no big deal."

But it was. It was everything to her. He could see it. This was where the hesitation was coming from. She wasn't ready to give up her dream. And why should she? For him?

He was an idiot.

"I know how much you love being a dad, so I thought maybe," she said. "It probably wouldn't work, anyhow, with everything that's wrong with my stupid body."

He could hear it in her voice. He'd failed her.

He pulled her into his arms. "I love you so much, Natalie."

"I love you, too."

He sighed. *I wish it was enough.*

"Let's go to bed," she said after a minute, pulling away.

"I'll meet you there, okay?" He pulled a cigarette from his pack.

She raised one eyebrow at him.

"What?"

"Don't you think you'd get rid of your cough a lot sooner if you stopped that?" She pointed to the cigarette.

Richard looked down at the cigarette, then back at her. His heart sank. He could do this one thing for her. He tucked it back into the pack. "Okay." He had stopped drinking. This would be a breeze compared to that. Maybe, just maybe, he still had a chance with her.

"Really?"

"You're right. I should cut this shit out." He crumpled the pack in his hand. "Consider it done. It'll be my New Year's resolution."

She shook her head as he tossed the pack into the trash can. "I'm impressed."

He took her hand. "Let's go to bed."

-32-

Richard was in Atlanta at the beginning of the week, and then he had meetings in Boston and Raleigh. Natalie said she was grateful for the solitude. The first week after winter break was always exhausting, anyhow.

They had worked out a plan: he would move back to Atlanta at the end of January. Natalie would stay at her job until the school year ended in June. In the meantime, they would see one another on alternating weekends, some in Philly, some in Atlanta. This would give them time to find a house and Natalie time to pack and look for a job.

Richard wasn't looking forward to their separation, but he assured himself it would only be a short time until they were together. He'd even started looking at engagement rings, although he knew it was much too soon to ask. Maybe next Christmas.

When he arrived back in Philadelphia the second weekend of January, he was drained. The cough was still lingering, despite finishing the antibiotics. He hadn't smoked in two weeks. His meetings had been more stressful than he expected. And now he had the chore of packing up his things and moving out of the townhouse. Thankfully, it was only clothes, books, and linens. The furnishings would stay with the rental.

Natalie met him at his place on Friday after work. She'd picked up dinner. After kissing him hello, she told him to sit while she put the food on their plates.

"You don't look so good." Natalie put his plate in front of him.

"It's been a long week, baby girl. Dealing with a lot of miserable people." He closed his eyes and pinched the bridge of his nose. "Doesn't help that I can't smoke anymore." He tried to make it sound like a joke, but he saw the hurt on her face.

"I'm sorry."

He forced a laugh. "Naw, it's okay. I couldn't if I wanted to, with this damn cough."

"Maybe you should go back to the doctor."

"I think I just need some sleep."

"I'll go home after dinner. You can catch up on rest."

"Natalie."

"It's okay. I'll come back another night this week. If you want."

"You're hurt. I was trying to make a joke. It came out wrong."

She looked skeptical.

He put his hand on hers. "I want you here. Stay with me."

"I didn't make you stop smoking. I only suggested it."

"I know." He squeezed her hand. "Forgive me. Please. Look." He got up and grabbed a stack of papers from his briefcase.

"What's this?" she asked as he handed them to her.

"Real estate listings." He grinned. "Let's pick out our dream house."

Natalie gave him a cautious smile and took the papers, looking over the first one.

"I really like this one," he said. "It has a front porch swing—see?" He pointed to the photo. "Four bedrooms, so we'd have space for guests."

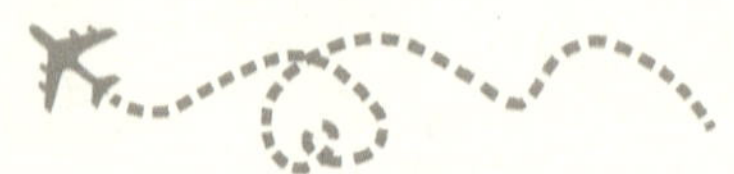

"It's pretty." She turned to the second listing.

"This one is nice, a big backyard, but the house itself is a little bit smaller. And the driveway is kind of small for both of our cars plus Hannah's."

Natalie made a face. "Right. My car."

"What's wrong with your car?"

"Nothing." She flipped to the third page. "My car is registered in Ben's name. I'll have to get it transferred over, I guess."

"Oh," he said. "Well, we can get you a new one if you want."

"Everything's in his name. Car insurance, health insurance. Cell phone plan. Everything except my apartment." She paused. "I'm going to have to talk to him."

He blinked. "You weren't going to tell him you were moving?" His stomach began to hurt.

"I know I have to, I just don't want to." She avoided his eyes. "But technically we're still married."

"Just on paper."

"Right, I know. But still."

"Well. You should talk to him."

"I guess so."

"Natalie." She looked at him. He raised his eyebrows at her.

"I don't want to hurt him." Her voice was soft.

"You already hurt him, darlin'. Let the poor guy have some closure instead of hanging on to false hope." He hesitated. "Unless it's not false hope."

"I'll call him next week."

Neither of them ate much. After cleaning up from dinner, they went to bed early. Richard was too tired for anything but sleep.

Natalie looked anxious. "You're mad at me."

"I'm not mad." He held her close as she drifted off.

The truth was, he was nervous. Lately, any form of exertion made him cough, and he didn't want it to happen in bed with her. The coughing spells sometimes brought up a few flecks of blood. He'd read an article that said some people who'd been in areas damaged by the hurricane had developed respiratory problems because of exposure to mold. He knew he needed to see a doctor. He didn't want to go to the doctor here in Philadelphia, yet again, complaining of a cough. Besides, he had too much to do. He would wait until he was back in Atlanta. Maybe by then, it would clear up on its own anyhow.

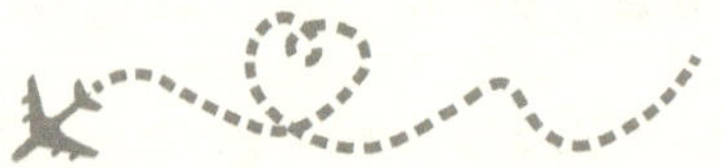

Natalie dialed Ben's number, hoping he wouldn't pick up.

"Hey, Nat." He answered after the fourth ring, sounding cheerful.

"Hey, how are you?"

"Not bad. What's going on?"

"I was wondering, um..." She paused for a moment. "Can we get together and talk? Maybe grab some coffee?"

"Sure. How about Saturday?"

She glanced at her calendar. Richard would be in Atlanta. "That will work."

"The Flyers are playing that night. Want to meet up at Quinn's for wings and beer? It is almost Valentine's day, you know," he said, his tone playful.

She laughed. "Oh, yeah," she said, though Valentine's Day was almost two weeks away. Quinn's was a bar not far from his brother's house. She and Ben shared a dislike of the forced sentimentality

of Valentine's Day. It had always been one of their traditions to go out to the most unromantic place they could think of. A hockey game, a Chinese buffet, a sports bar. Once, they had taken their nieces and nephews to Chuck E. Cheese's. That, they decided, had been taking things too far.

"I'll meet you there? Around seven?"

"I'll see you then."

Her heart sank as they hung up the phone.

"I talked to Ben," Natalie said. They stood in the kitchen of the townhouse, giving it a quick once-over before Richard took the keys back to the rental office. He would spend tonight at her place and drive to Atlanta tomorrow.

"What did he say?" He watched her face as he wiped down the countertop one more time.

"I asked him to get together and talk." She avoided his eyes. "I didn't want to tell him over the phone."

He rinsed the sponge with warm water, squeezed it out, and put it next to the sink. "He's going to try and get you to stay." He dried his hands on a paper towel.

"I know." She looked at him. "It'll be okay."

"Are you sure?"

"Don't you trust me?"

He balled up the paper towel, putting it into the garbage can under the sink. "I trust you. It's him I don't trust."

"You don't know him."

"I know he's a hotheaded kid who doesn't think before he reacts."

"That was one time—"

"And what if it wasn't?"

"He would never hurt me. I've known him my whole life."

"What if he tries to talk you out of it?"

"You have to trust me. I trusted you to go spend that weekend with Melinda in December."

He sighed, thinking about the moment outside Melinda's room. "Are you ready to go?"

"I guess so."

"Okay." He glanced around the room before turning off the light and walking downstairs. Natalie followed a few steps behind him. "I'll drop the keys and we can go get some dinner," he said as they reached the door.

She didn't say anything.

"Hey." He reached for her. "I'm sorry. I know it's hard."

"I wish we could skip this part. I'm ready for it to be June. I hate winter." Her eyes filled. "I don't want to be away from you."

"June will be here before you know it. I promise."

-33-

"Pneumonia," the doctor said. She'd heard his list of symptoms and listened to his chest. "You'll need an x-ray to confirm, but I'm certain of it." She was beautiful, tall, with thick black hair, pale skin, and a hint of an accent he couldn't quite place. Italian? Greek? She wore a wedding band, so it seemed likely Thompson wasn't the surname she was born with. Portuguese? "Mr. Rung?"

"I'm sorry." He shook his head. "What were you saying?"

"Given your low oxygen level, I'd like to admit you to the hospital this afternoon."

He balked. "The hospital? I'm not that sick, am I?" It was a cough. Hospitals were for old people. For people so sick they couldn't get out of bed. For dying people.

"Yes. This is serious. I want you to have some more tests, to figure out what's going on and to rule out any other problems. You told me you've had this cough since you came back from an area damaged by Hurricane Katrina."

"Yes."

"You may have been exposed to mold. Some people in that area have been diagnosed with fungal infections."

"But why does that mean I have to go into the hospital? Can't you write me a prescription?"

"It means we have to find out exactly what's causing the pneumonia before we can treat it effectively. We have to work a little harder to figure out what drugs to use."

"And I have to go to the hospital for that?"

She gave him the kind of smile he had seen Melinda give the girls when they were trying her patience. "We need to run some tests. It will be quicker to have them done in the hospital than outpatient, and we want to get you on the correct course of treatment as quickly as possible. Okay?"

"Okay."

"I'm going to make a few calls and arrange for a bed for you, and I'll be right back." She walked out of the exam room, closing the door behind her. He could hear her footsteps echoing down the hall.

He reached for his phone, but hesitated. He didn't want Natalie to worry about him. He'd be fine. It was only some tests to figure out what kind of germs were making him sick, like the doctor had said.

He needed to let Melinda know he wouldn't be able to take the girls this weekend. She would be angry. The girls would be disappointed, too. Maybe he could stay one night and be out on Saturday.

Dr. Thompson reappeared, knocking at the door before she opened it. She went over the details with him as he tried to pay attention to what she was saying.

"I'll check in this evening to make sure everything is okay, and then I'll come see you tomorrow."

"How long will I be in the hospital?"

"I can't make any promises, Richard," she said. "I'll try to have you home in a couple of days. Okay?" She handed him some papers. "You'll go down to the ground floor here and have a chest x-ray first, to confirm the pneumonia. Then I want you to go home, pack a bag, and head to the hospital."

After the x-ray, Richard drove back to his hotel in a daze. He wanted answers, but this was overwhelming. He packed his personal things and checked out. In the truck, he flipped his phone open.

"Hi, Richard."

"Hey, Mel. I know it's last minute—"

She cut him off. "You're not taking the girls this weekend."

"I haven't been feeling well, and—"

"Sick again, huh?"

He let out a heavy sigh.

"Tell me the truth, Richard. Are you drinking?"

"No."

"Using?"

"Mel. No."

"You were too sick to take them to New York. Now you can't take them this weekend. I've been through this before, Richard. I'm not stupid."

He squeezed his eyes shut, swallowing the shame threatening to derail the conversation.

"I want you to take a drug test. I'm not letting you see them again until you do."

"Jesus. Mel. I'm not using. I swear. Look. I told you. I'm back in Atlanta permanently now, okay? I'll take them the next two weekends. I'll take them for a whole week. You and Neil can go take a trip. Give me this weekend. Please."

"I still want you to take a test. And then you'd better be willing to follow through on all these big promises."

"Will you listen to me for a goddamn minute?"

She didn't say anything.

"I have pneumonia. The doctor wants me to have some tests done because I might have been exposed to mold while we were in Mississippi. I'm going to get them done this weekend so I can get on the right course of treatment."

"Oh my god," she said.

"Yeah."

"Shit. I'm sorry. I had no idea."

"Well, now you know."

"Is there anything I can do?"

"I don't want the girls to worry about me."

"I'll do my best."

"Thanks. I owe you."

"Just get better."

-34-

atalie stood outside Quinn's, watching other customers come and go, fighting the urge to pace the floor or tap her foot. Ben was ten minutes late. That wasn't like him. She tried calling, but his phone went straight to voicemail.

At what point do I give up? She wondered if he'd sensed what she wanted to talk about and changed his mind about showing up. She wondered if she'd have the guts to go through with it.

She frowned and opened her phone again. As she began to dial, Ben finally appeared.

He grinned when he saw her, and she couldn't prevent her own face breaking into a smile in response. He looked good. Freshly shaved, hair trimmed and slicked back from his face, wearing a wool jacket and scarf she'd never seen.

"Hey, beautiful." He put his arms around her and spun her around. He smelled so good she was a little dazed by it.

She closed her eyes and relaxed into his embrace. *This is probably the last time he'll ever hug me.* "You look great."

"Thanks." He laughed. He seemed happy, almost joyful. "So do you, but you always do." He pulled back and looked at her without letting go. "Sorry I'm late."

"It's okay."

"Let's go inside."

The bar was noisy, but not crowded. They found a small table near the back and ordered two beers, a plate of hot wings and some fries. They chatted about their families and work, catching up like old friends. Natalie was surprised to find herself laughing and enjoying his company for a change. She dreaded the part where she would have to steer the conversation towards more serious issues.

As if he could sense her apprehension, Ben looked her in the eye. "Tell me what's on your mind, kid."

Kid. Why did the men in her life insist on giving her these diminutive nicknames? He'd always called her that, from the time they first met, even though she was only a few months younger. Ben had been a grade ahead of her in high school, and he envisioned himself much older and wiser. They'd known each other for so long, neither had a clear recollection of the day they met. They seemed to have always been in each other's lives.

They were close friends for years, and then it evolved into something more. It took her by surprise the first time he kissed her, while playing video games together one night in his parents' basement. Natalie had turned towards him, expecting their customary high-five, but instead he took the controller from her hand and planted one on her lips.

Before that moment, she'd never thought of him as anything more than a friend. Her best friend, Ben. But his lips were soft, his hands gentle. She remembered feeling stunned, but at the same time, as if it was what they were supposed to be doing all along. When their lips parted, she'd looked into his eyes, overwhelmed with the realization that he was the person she was meant to be with. It hadn't taken long before they became a couple. She'd never had another boyfriend as devoted and sweet. He adored her, and the feeling was mutual.

She chewed her bottom lip and looked down at her plate, dissecting a French fry with her fingers. The waitress came by and put another two bottles of beer in front of them. Natalie took a long swallow of hers.

"Come on. You said you wanted to talk."

She took a deep breath. "I want to talk about moving forward with a divorce."

She hated the word as it left her lips. She hated the feel of it in her mouth, the sound of it in her ears. She hated the way Ben's face fell when the word reached his. A wave of nausea washed over her. *Too late to take it back.*

Ben sat back in his chair, took a deep breath and blew it out. "Is that what you really want?" He looked her in the eye.

No. Her eyes burned, surprising her with sudden tears. Ben kept his gaze locked on her.

She blinked. "Yes." Her voice was tight.

He pressed his lips together. "Okay."

"Okay?" She swiped at her eyes with a napkin. She'd prepared herself for a fight, an impassioned plea, a discussion at the very least. She never thought he would just agree to a divorce.

"Yes. Okay." He shrugged. "I figured this was why you wanted to talk."

"I'm moving to Atlanta," she said. "In June."

"So you want this taken care of quickly."

"Yeah."

"We'll get started on it this week. I'll call a lawyer on Monday."

"Thanks." Her heart was heavy in her chest. "I'm sorry."

"Me too." He took a sip of his beer.

She blinked and looked away. This was even harder than she'd imagined.

"It's okay. I'll live. It's not like it's completely out of the blue, right? Let's not talk about it anymore tonight, though. Every time we talk it gets so heavy," he said, drawing out the last two words. "We can sort out the details later. Let's just hang out for a while."

"Oh, okay, I guess. I had a whole speech prepared."

"I wouldn't expect anything less," he teased, grinning.

She laughed, the tension easing.

"I don't want to fight with you anymore, Natalie. Your mind is made up. I can't change it."

"I don't want to fight with you, either."

"Well then, I wish you the best." He held his beer bottle up, smiling. She held hers up and clinked it against his.

"Thank you," she said, her voice soft.

He gave her a sad smile. "This is what I miss the most." He took a sip of beer. "Just hanging out with you. We used to have so much fun. I feel like I lost my best friend. How long have we known each other? Fifteen years? Twenty?"

"Something like that. Still friends?"

"Still friends." He held up his bottle again. "To Valentine's Day. I think this one might be the least romantic of them all." He furrowed his brow as he drained the last of the beer from the bottle.

"I think you're right."

He ordered them another round.

"So tell me something, Benjamin. Why are you being cool about this divorce thing?" she asked after the waitress walked away. As soon as the words exited her mouth, she recoiled in fear of the answer. "Oh, god. Never mind, I'm not sure I want to know."

Ben smirked, raising his eyebrows.

She squeezed her eyes shut. "So you're seeing somebody?"

The waitress put two new bottles onto the table. Natalie lifted the bottle to her lips and took a long sip.

He shrugged, tilting his head to the side. "Yeah. I am."

"How long?"

"Couple of months."

She examined his face. "You're serious about her."

"I don't know. Maybe. We're taking things slow, but so far, so good."

"Who is she?"

"She's nice. She's sweet. I like her. A lot." He smiled. "She's not you. But life goes on, right?"

He wouldn't give her any more details. A fierce wave of jealousy coursed through her. For all her talk about wanting Ben to move on, she realized she'd never thought he would actually do it.

"I need another beer," she said, emptying her bottle.

"We just got these."

"But look!" She turned the bottle upside down. A single drop splashed out onto the table.

Ben laughed. "That's a problem." He signaled the waitress. "Two more," he said. He took a long gulp to catch up.

A few of the patrons cheered. Natalie and Ben both glanced at the nearest TV screen to see the Flyers had scored.

"Do you remember that one game we went to in ninety-three?" he asked. "There was a blizzard, and they shut the game down? We had to walk home from the subway station. All the buses had stopped running."

"Oh my god. I remember. That must be a five mile hike. How did we make it home without freezing to death?"

"That old guy picked us up."

"Right. His truck reeked of cigar smoke." She made a face.

"But he got us home."

"To your house, anyway."

"You were stranded at my house for three days."

"Your mom was *not* happy."

"Yeah, well." He took a sip of beer. "You were supposed to be sleeping in my brother's old room, and yet somehow every morning she found you in mine." He gave her a wicked grin.

"Funny how that happened."

"She thought you were corrupting me."

Natalie giggled. "Your mom is the only person who ever thought I was a bad influence." Her eyes widened. "Let's do a shot."

"You'd better slow down."

"Come on, we're having fun, right?"

He looked at her, one eyebrow raised. "Okay. What are we shooting?"

"Jameson," they said in unison, and laughed. The first time either of them had tried alcohol had been a bottle of Jameson they'd snuck from Ben's father's liquor cabinet when they were still in high school. They'd each taken three shots and Natalie had promptly gotten sick, which had been hilarious to both of them at the time.

Maybe they should have stayed best friends. Maybe becoming a couple was where things had gone wrong.

The waitress brought them the shots and two more beers. They clinked glasses and gulped down their shots. The whiskey burned her throat. She coughed and took a sip of her beer.

"One more?"

He shook his head. "Talk about a bad influence. Maybe my mom was right."

Ben was different from the way he'd been the last few times she'd seen him. More relaxed, more at ease than he'd been in a long time. Less sad. No longer consumed by a constant need to bounce from one thing to the next. When she spoke, he listened, instead of talking over her.

Maybe the girl he was dating was having an effect on him. She looked at him, imagining his hand in someone else's hand. His lips kissing some other woman's lips. It made her queasy.

He waved his hand in front of her eyes. "You're staring at me."

She pointed her beer bottle at him. "You're different."

"Good different, or…"

"I don't know. Good, I guess. But you're different."

"And you're drunk."

"Maybe a little." She held up her thumb and index finger, about an inch apart.

"Water for this one," he told the waitress.

It was almost midnight when he called a cab to take them home.

"I don't want to leave my car here," she slurred.

He looked at her and crossed his arms over his chest. "No way, kid. I'm not driving, and you're definitely not driving."

She pouted her lips.

Ben took her by the hand as she stood. "You can come back and get your car in the morning. If you can get out of bed."

She wobbled on her feet. Ben steered her towards the door, his hand on her back. The bar was crowded now. Too many people milling around.

Someone stepped into Natalie's path. She stumbled backwards against Ben.

"Whoa," Ben said as she lost her footing. He held onto her shoulders for a minute.

Natalie turned her face towards his. "Thanks," she murmured, her lips so close to his they almost touched. For a few seconds, neither of them was able to move.

"Let's get out of here." He took her hand and walked in front of her, leading the way.

The entrance to the bar was surrounded by a thick cloud of cigarette smoke. Ben led her away from the crowd, towards the curb. The night air was bitter cold against her face. Sobering. She shivered and pulled her scarf up to cover her mouth and nose.

"You feeling okay?" He pulled a knit hat over his ears.

She nodded, although she felt strange, disconnected from her body. It wasn't just the alcohol, either. She kept her eyes on Ben as he watched for the cab, studying his face, his jawline, his mouth. She'd never kiss that mouth again.

Again, she thought of him kissing another woman. She had to be younger than Natalie. Prettier. Definitely thinner. She imagined this person, pressed close against Ben, her hands on his body. *Oh, God...I'm going to be sick.*

"Nat?" He reached towards her face, pulling the scarf down from her mouth. His fingertip brushed against her lips, lingering for a second. Was it accidental, or had he meant to— "Natalie?"

She blinked, watching his face.

"Are you crying?" He wiped a tear off her cheek with his fingertip.

"What? No." She hadn't realized her eyes were wet. "It's freezing out here." She searched her coat pocket for a tissue and dabbed at her eyes.

"Natalie," Ben said, softly, eyes fixed on her, full of concern.

"Stop," she said. She turned towards the street. "I'm fine. I just feel a little, um…"

"What?" His voice was soft.

She shook her head. "Nothing. Just cold."

"Here." He put his arm around her shoulders. "I'll keep you warm." She looked up into his eyes, her lower lip trembling. He gave her a lopsided smile. "It's gonna be okay, kid."

"Ben," she whispered.

His lips parted to speak, but then the cab pulled up to the curb. He raised his hand to signal the driver, reached for the door and opened it for her.

Natalie got into the cab. Ben followed, pulling the door shut behind them. He started to give the driver her address. "Wait." She put her hand on his arm.

He turned toward her and started to say, "What?" but her mouth was already on his. She put her hands on either side of his face. His lips parted, melting against her own.

"What are you doing?"

"I don't know." She kissed him again. He put his arms around her, pulling her closer. His hand slid down to her thigh. "Come home with me," she said.

Ben pulled back, staring into her eyes.

The cab driver cleared his throat. "Where to?"

"Sorry," Ben said to the driver, straightening up. To Natalie, he whispered, "Are you sure you want to do this?"

"Yes." She started to give the driver her address.

"No, wait," Ben interrupted. "My place is closer." He gave his own address, a few blocks away. "Pull up out back," he said when they got to the end of his block. He handed him a twenty and thanked him.

Ben took Natalie's hand and helped her out of the cab. "Shh." He put a finger to his lips as he led her towards the house.

He unlocked the back door, turning the light on so they could see their way towards the front of the basement. He led her by the hand to where his makeshift bedroom was, behind a tall partition made of a plywood panel. He turned on a small lamp by the side of his bed, pulling her towards him, putting his lips on hers. His fingers fumbled with the buttons on her coat, and she helped him, giggling.

"Kissing in the basement," she said. "Like when we were kids."

"You're noisy," he whispered.

"Shh. I'm sorry." She bit her lower lip and hooked her fingers into the belt loops of his jeans, pulling his body to hers. He put his hands on her shoulders, gazing down at her. He hesitated.

"Nat... You've had a lot to drink. So have I. Maybe we should talk first."

She put her hands on either side of his face and kissed him again. "I don't want to talk."

"Promise me you won't regret this in the morning." He kissed her neck below her ear.

"I promise."

Their lips met again as he lowered her onto the bed, peeling her clothes away from her skin. She pulled his shirt over his head and unbuttoned his jeans, not paying attention to anything but the way his body felt against her own.

His hands roamed her body, seeking out the places that longed for his touch. They joined together, finding a familiar rhythm. Any hesitation she might have felt was eclipsed by the soft wetness of Ben's lips, the warmth of his skin, the touch of

his hands that knew her body so well, the weight of him on top of her.

She crushed her mouth against Ben's. Her hands gripped his hips, her breath quickening with his touch. He leaned in closer, pressing his cheek against hers, his breath warm on her neck, matching the pace of hers, moving faster, until they were both sweaty and satisfied, gasping for air, clinging tight to one another.

Ben pressed his lips against hers. He kept his eyes locked on hers as he reached for the sheet, pulling it over them. Natalie rested her head on his chest. He held her close, trailing his fingertips along her upper arm.

"You okay?" he asked, his voice soft, a million other questions remaining unasked.

"Yes." She looked up at him, her hair falling in her face. "Are you?"

He smoothed her hair back with his hand and kissed her forehead. "Yes." Her eyelids were heavy. She snuggled in close to Ben, inhaling his scent, listening to the sound of his breath. As she slipped into sleep, she heard him whisper, "I love you."

"I love you, too," she whispered back.

-35-

The nurse entered Richard's room just after seven. She checked his IV and listened to his chest, then told him he was going for another test and they'd hold his breakfast until afterwards. Yesterday he'd had three other tests, the rest of the day spent in bed hooked up to this damned oxygen, watching mindless, crappy TV. But at least they'd fed him.

"How about just coffee?"

"Nothing by mouth, sorry. They have to sedate you for the test."

"Any chance of getting out of here today?"

"We'll see what the tests show. Your oxygen level has been pretty good. But it's up to the docs."

It was going to be a long day. As she left the room, he thought about calling Natalie. It was too early, though, on a Sunday morning. She'd still be in bed. Melinda? No, she'd be in bed, too, or else getting ready for church. It was hell being stuck in the hospital on the weekend, with nobody even aware of where you really were. He drummed his fingers on the bedside table. *Mike.* He picked up the phone.

Natalie awoke with Ben's lips on the spot where her neck and shoulder met.

"Morning," he murmured, pulling her close.

She opened her eyes as her mind flashed through the events of the night before. It seemed like a dream. The bar, the cab, being here with Ben. Now it was daylight, and she could hear the sounds of his nephews running around upstairs. She wasn't dreaming.

Oh. Shit.

She turned her head. A jolt of pain drove itself between her eye sockets. She closed her eyes. "What time is it?"

"Almost nine," he answered, his lips still on her skin. He made a trail of soft kisses along her shoulder, towards her neck. His hand cupped her breast. It felt good. *Too good.* She waited for a wave of guilt to wash over her, but it remained absent.

"Wait." She eased herself away from him. "I have to pee." Her head throbbed. She squeezed her eyes shut. "I need coffee," she said. "Oh, God, and ibuprofen."

"Okay. But first..." He took her face between his hands and kissed her lips.

"Hey, Ben, are you awake?" The door at the top of the basement steps opened, followed by quick footsteps on the wooden stairs. Their heads both turned towards the noise.

"Shit," he whispered. "Michelle." His sister-in-law.

Ben put a finger to his lips. He yanked on his discarded jeans as he answered in a loud voice. "Be right there." He dashed to the edge of the partition and peeked his head out. "Hey." He kept his tone casual. Natalie pulled the blanket over her head.

"Hey," Michelle said. "The kids asked for pancakes, so I thought I'd see if you wanted to join us."

"Oh, thanks. I'm gonna pass, though. I'm still pretty beat."

"Are you sure?" She sounded skeptical.

Ben gave a short laugh. "Yeah."

"Okay. What time did you get in last night?"

He exhaled. "I don't even know. Late."

"I didn't see your car this morning."

"I took a cab home."

"Ouch." She laughed. "That kind of night."

Natalie listened from the bed, praying Michelle would go back upstairs. The need to use the bathroom was becoming urgent, but it was at the other end of the basement, by the back door. She pulled the blanket away from her face and slid her body toward the edge of the bed, causing the springs to creak.

"Wait, do you—" Michelle hesitated for a few seconds. "Do you have somebody in there with you?" She sounded amused.

Ben made a sound somewhere between a sigh and a laugh. "Um, yeah. Sorry."

"Oh no, it's okay. I don't care if you bring someone home." She lowered her voice. "Who is it?"

He hesitated, turning to glance at Natalie, who was pulling on her underwear. She froze, her eyes wide.

"Is it—" Michelle began.

"Natalie," he interjected, his voice loud enough to drown out whatever name Michelle had been about to say. "It's Natalie."

"Wait, what?" Michelle was surprised. Ben turned to look at her again, mouthing *sorry.* "Natalie?" she called out.

"Hey, Michelle," she replied, trying to keep her voice casual, as if this happened every day. The words *walk of shame* went through her mind as she yanked Ben's Flyers jersey over her head.

"Aunt Nat's here?" Ben's nephew, Charlie, called from the stairs as he ran down. Ben caught him at the edge of the doorway.

"Whoa. Hang on, bud." He turned to look at Natalie, his face apologetic.

Natalie looked around for her jeans, finding them on the floor next to Ben's side of the bed. She grabbed them and pulled them on.

"It's okay," Natalie said. "Hey, Charlie." She waved him into the room. He ran in to hug her. "Look at you, you're getting so big!"

"I lost another tooth." He opened his mouth to show her. Both of his top teeth were missing. She crouched down to take a closer look. He was six now, and in first grade. She'd missed a whole year of his life.

"Aunt Nat!" Charlie's older brother, Ryan, came down the stairs next. Would they still call her *Aunt Nat* after she and Ben were divorced? *I'll probably never see them again.* Her chest ached.

Natalie gave Ryan a hug and kissed the top of his head. "You guys are having pancakes for breakfast, huh?"

"And bacon!" Ryan said.

"That sounds pretty good."

"You better get back upstairs before your dad eats them all," Ben said.

The boys scrambled back up the steps.

"Morning, Natalie," Ben's brother, Jason called down from the top of the stairs in a teasing tone.

"Morning, Jason." She waved at Michelle as she made her way past.

She shut the bathroom door. *Relief.* She exhaled. She could hear Michelle and Ben talking in hushed tones. She heard phrases like "thought she had a boyfriend" and "getting back together" from Michelle.

Natalie cringed. Like her sister Lisa, Michelle loved gossip and drama. She couldn't make out Ben's responses.

She wondered what name Michelle had been about to say when Ben interrupted her. It was clear the relationship was serious enough for Michelle to know who he was dating, and to expect *she* would be here, in Ben's bed.

She glanced at herself in the mirror as she washed her hands. Her hair was a mess. Dark, smudgy mascara circles ringed her eyes. She wiped as much off as she could with her fingers, rubbed some toothpaste across her teeth, and rinsed her mouth, waiting to exit the bathroom until she heard Michelle start back up the stairs.

"If you change your mind about pancakes, you're welcome to them," Michelle said. "You too, Natalie."

Ben sat on the edge of the bed, still wearing only his jeans. He looked up. "Hey." He reached for her.

She sat next to him. "Sorry."

"For what? Stealing my jersey?" he asked, tugging on the sleeve.

She pointed up. "Your family? Michelle?"

"Oh, don't worry about it. The kids were happy to see you. Michelle will get over herself in a day or two."

"Yeah, but she likes to talk. She's going to tell your mom. Oh God, and your mom will call my mom." She put her head in her hands.

"I'll talk to her." He put his hand on her thigh. "Are you okay?"

She looked up. "I think so. My head hurts and my mouth is dry."

"Mine too." He turned towards her. "Let's go get coffee."

"I should go home."

"Or you could stay here." He kissed her behind the earlobe, moving down to her neck, then her collarbone.

"Ben."

"Mmm-hmm."

"Your family is right upstairs. And your room doesn't even have a door."

"We'll be really quiet." He pulled her face to his.

"Ben..." She meant it as a protest, but it came out too softly.

He took that as an invitation to continue. He eased her down onto the bed. Her lips parted beneath the warmth of his kisses. Ben unbuttoned her jeans, planting kisses on her belly as he eased them down.

"Wait." She nudged him away. "I should go. I have to pick up my car..."

"Not yet," he said. "Stay a little longer."

"Ben. I'm serious."

"So am I. Last night was...incredible."

"It was." Her insides grew warm, her cheeks flushing. She couldn't remember the last time it had been like that between the two of them.

"But..." He waited.

"But, we were both pretty wasted," she reminded him, sliding out from underneath him. "I didn't exactly..." she trailed off, pulling her jeans back up.

"What?"

"I didn't plan that."

"I know." He turned her to face him, kissing her again. "But I'm not sorry it happened."

"Me neither." She turned her head, laying her cheek on his bare chest for a minute. "You're going to make me feel bad now, aren't you?"

"Feel bad? No, I want to make you feel good." He slid his hand up her thigh.

"I don't think we should."

"Is this because of Michelle? I'll go up there right now and tell her not to—"

"It's more than that, Ben."

He let go of her. "Right." He backed away from her, watching from the edge of the bed as she stood and began gathering her clothes. "Are you going to tell your boyfriend you cheated on him with your husband?" The teasing words failed to disguise the edge in his voice.

She turned her back to him, pulled off his jersey, and put on her bra and top. "Very funny." She gave him a playful nudge on the upper arm as she sat to put on her shoes. The weird thing was, it hadn't felt like cheating at all. It had felt like falling into place. Like coming home.

She forced herself to stand back up. She needed to go back to her own place. Take a bath. Clear her head.

She looked around the makeshift room, half-filled with storage bins and cardboard boxes. The only furniture was the bed, a nightstand, and a tall, skinny chest of drawers with a TV on top, surrounded by various video game controllers. His work clothes hung from a water pipe just below the ceiling.

She made a face. "You could afford your own place, Ben."

"It's not as bad as it looks," Ben said. "I'd rather be here than be alone."

He watched her as she put on her coat and wrapped her scarf around her neck. His eyes held all the questions she knew he was too afraid to ask.

"Don't go."

She sat next to him. "Last night was great, Ben. But the longer I stay, the harder this is going to be."

He put his head on her shoulder. She kissed the top of it and stood to leave.

"Wait." He got up, pulling on his own clothes. "Mind if I walk with you? I have to get my car, too." He slid his feet into his sneakers.

"I guess that wouldn't be so bad."

Ben put on his coat and hat. They stepped outside into the crisp February morning. "Oh, it's too bright." Natalie squeezed her eyes shut.

"Wait, I think I have a pair of sunglasses in my pocket." He handed her a pair of silver-rimmed aviators.

"Don't you want to wear them?"

"I have another pair," he said, holding both hands above his eyes. She giggled.

They walked at a brisk pace, not talking much. Across the street from the bar was a donut shop.

"Coffee?" Ben asked.

"God, yes," she answered. They walked inside.

Ben ordered coffee for each of them. He turned to her. "Cream-filled donut? Icing and sprinkles? Pretty good hangover cure." He said the last part in a teasing voice, grinning at her.

"Twist my arm." They walked across the street to the parking lot of the bar, to-go cups in hand. Natalie's car sat a few spaces away from Ben's Jeep.

"So what time does his flight get in?" Ben asked. It occurred to her she'd never heard him say Richard's name.

"He won't be back until next weekend." Why was she telling him that?

She blew air into the small opening of the coffee cup and took a tiny sip. It was too hot.

"Then why the hurry to get home?"

"I'm tired. I need a shower. I..."

"What?"

She swallowed. "I have to go." She pushed the button to unlock the doors and set her coffee in one of the cup holders. Ben handed her the bag with her donut inside. "Thanks."

"You're welcome." He took the lid off his coffee cup and blew across the top before taking a small sip.

She took off his sunglasses and handed them to him, squinting as she looked up at his face. "Here," she said. "I think I'm okay."

Ben set his coffee on the roof of her car. He wrapped his arms around her. She buried her face in his chest, clinging to him. "I had a good time," he said, smoothing her hair.

"Me too."

He gave her a tender kiss on the lips. She didn't pull away.

"Can I just ask one thing?"

"Okay," she said, still wrapped in his arms.

"Was this your way of saying goodbye? Or does this mean maybe I still have a chance?"

She closed her eyes. "Ben," she whispered. The question made her heart ache.

She looked up at his face. Her husband's face. His soft lips. His warm, brown eyes. The dark hair that fell across his forehead, the hint of stubble that seemed to be there no matter how closely he shaved. The rush of love she felt for him surprised her.

He'd always had a chance.

"Can I call you later?" he asked, not waiting for a response to the previous question.

She put her hand on his cheek. "Call me tonight."

"I will." He picked up his coffee cup.

"I love you," she said.

"I know." He smiled. "I love you, too." He kissed her once more before she got into her car and drove away.

-36-

*R*ichard closed his eyes and covered them with his hand as they wheeled him back to the room. The anesthesia had nauseated him, and he was still groggy.

"Here we are," the nurse announced as he was pushed into the room. "And you have a visitor."

Richard opened his eyes. Mike. "Hi," he croaked.

"Hey." Mike stepped forward. "You look terrible."

"Thanks," Richard said.

The nurse helped him back into the bed. "Let me know if you need anything," she said once he was settled.

Mike shook his head. "How long you been in here?"

"Since Friday."

"Friday!"

"I know. I should have called you."

"Mister tough guy." Mike chuckled. "Now, I forget, does going through hard times by yourself make you less likely to start drinking again, or not?"

"At least I called you."

Mike leaned in to hug him. "It's a good thing you did."

Natalie woke up from her nap, hair still damp from the shower she'd taken when she got home from Ben's. Her head still ached. *I'm never drinking again.*

She glanced at the clock on her nightstand. It was almost three o'clock in the afternoon. She groaned, sitting up. The cat jumped onto her bed, demanding to be petted. Natalie stroked her head, trying not to get sucked down into the churning whirlpool inside her brain, threatening to drown her.

She got out of bed and used the bathroom. In the kitchen, she put a pot of coffee on to brew and a slice of bread in the toaster. She grabbed a bottle of water from the fridge and took a sip.

Ben wanted her to tell him last night meant something. Richard, if he found out, would be angry and hurt and say *I told you so*. If he even continued to speak to her.

She barely understood what had happened, except she'd been jealous and afraid of losing Ben. Which didn't make any sense. She'd already left him, told him it was over. She had someone else. And now, so did he. She couldn't lose something that was no longer hers.

She thought about the way Ben's face had looked under the streetlight. That split second in the cab when she had the irresistible urge to kiss him. Heat surged through her body as her mind replayed the memory of being in his bed, the way his skin felt against hers, the way everything seemed right when they were together.

But their marriage was over. Wasn't it? They'd been separated for over a year. She was in love with Richard. She wanted to move to Atlanta and start a new life with him. She'd said yes to him. They'd made plans. It was too late to try and go backwards.

And yet, the second she said the word *divorce* to Ben, the whole thing had felt wrong to her.

He was dating someone else. That felt wrong, too.

She was losing it.

She flipped open her cell phone and pushed the button to dial Richard's number. She would tell him everything. *He's going to hate me.* She hoped he could forgive her.

His phone went straight to voicemail. She thought about leaving a message, but hung up before the tone sounded.

She drained the last of the water from her bottle and put her head down against the cool wooden surface of her kitchen table. The toaster dinged. She took the toast out, buttered it, and took a bite while she poured coffee into her mug. In the cabinet, she found a bottle of ibuprofen. She shook two into her hand and swallowed them down with coffee.

Her phone began to buzz. Her heart skipped a beat. *Richard.* She grabbed it, looking at the display. It was Ben.

"Hey," she answered. She took another sip of coffee.

"Are you at home?"

"Yeah. I just woke up."

"Listen, I know you said to call you tonight, but I'm around the corner and I was wondering if I could stop by. I just want to talk."

Of course he wanted to talk. She knew she shouldn't say yes, but she owed it to him to explain what had happened. Problem was, she didn't know how.

"I don't know if I'm ready to talk."

"You don't have to. But I have a couple of things I want to say."

"Ben..."

"Please?"

She sighed. "Sure. I'm just having some coffee."

"Okay, great. Pour me a cup. I'll be there in a minute."

Natalie took another bite of toast and poured a cup for Ben, preparing it the way he liked it, with cream and extra sugar. She'd always teased him that it tasted more like a coffee milkshake that way.

She stopped in the bathroom to check her reflection in the mirror. Not too bad, but her hair was a mess and her eyes were a little puffy from sleep. She ran her fingers through her hair and splashed some cool water on her face before walking down the stairs.

She would tell him she was sorry, it was all her fault, and they should go ahead and move forward with the divorce like they'd planned. That was the smart thing to do.

Ben stepped onto the porch as she opened the door. Last night flashed through her brain, speeding up her pulse, flooding her body with heat. *Oh.*

"Hi." He stepped inside.

"Hi." She shut the door behind them and turned to face him. Her hands reached for his face and pulled it down, crushing her lips against his. He put his hands on her waist, pulling her body against him. They made their way towards the stairs and up to her apartment.

"Wait, I don't think we should do this," he murmured, making no move to stop what they were doing.

"No, we definitely shouldn't." She kept kissing him, unzipping his jacket, pulling him towards the bedroom.

"This isn't why I came over," Ben said into her ear, kissing her neck.

The two of them lay curled together in her bed, the quilt pulled over them, as their heart rates returned to normal. The cat lay at the foot of the bed, purring at Ben's feet.

"It isn't?" Natalie teased.

"Well. Maybe a little." He kissed the back of her neck. She turned her head, putting her hand on his cheek. Their lips met. Natalie turned her body towards his. "Wait." He pulled back.

"I know." She groaned. "We need to talk," she said, imitating his voice.

"I don't know. I kind of like not talking." He pressed his lips to hers.

"Mmm. Me too. Kissing is better than talking."

"Agreed." He kissed her again.

"You're pretty good at it."

He kissed her again, pushing her lips open with his. She put her hands on him, pulling him closer as she turned onto her back.

He laughed. "You have to give me a few minutes."

"Just kiss me."

Someone came into the room to drop off a dinner tray. Richard looked at it and made a face. "I don't know what that is, but I don't think it's food."

Mike laughed. "Now, you know my wife wouldn't let me come to see you empty-handed." He picked up a grocery bag Richard hadn't noticed before. "Beef stew and homemade biscuits." She'd sent paper plates, napkins, even a jar of sweet tea.

"I love that woman," Richard croaked.

"You're telling me. Let me go ask the nurse where I can warm this up. I'll be right back." He ambled out of the room, carrying the casserole dish.

He was grateful Mike had been waiting for him after the procedure. He'd told him on the phone that he sensed things were more serious than what the doctors and nurses were telling him. They'd stopped giving him much information. It was the weekend, and he knew they didn't have as many people on hand – years of being married to a nurse had taught him how hospitals worked. Still, it was frustrating. And to be honest, he was scared.

He shifted in the bed. His back ached. The oxygen made his face itch. He hoped he'd be able to get out tomorrow.

He picked his phone up off the tray table where he'd put it after he'd shut it off. He pressed the power button. A voicemail notification popped up.

Bella. "Hey Daddy, hope you're having a good weekend. Call me back. I love you!"

He hated being nearby and not being able to see the girls. But he couldn't let them worry. At least not until he knew if there was anything to worry about.

His finger hovered over the button to call Natalie's number. It was getting late in the day; usually he called her by now on a Sunday after dropping the girls off at home. Was she worried about him? He needed to hear her voice. To tell what was going on. Like Mike had said, going through difficult things alone wasn't good for him or his sobriety.

He pushed the button. The phone rang a few times, then went to voicemail. "Hey, Natalie." He cleared his throat. "Just checking in. I'll call you tomorrow. I love you." He flipped the phone closed.

Natalie's stomach growled. Ben laughed. "You hungry?"
"I'm fine."

He groaned and pulled away. "Come on, let's get dressed and go get some dinner. I bet you haven't eaten since that donut." He stood, pulled on his underwear and headed for the bathroom.

"I had a piece of toast right before you got here. Well, a bite of toast."

He laughed and shut the bathroom door. "That's what I thought," he called from behind the door.

Natalie took a breath in, sat up, and ran her hands through her hair. She listened to the sound of Ben washing his hands, trying to push down the uneasiness she felt. This didn't mean anything. She was just having a very strange reaction to the fact of getting divorced. They would have dinner, talk, part ways, Richard would call, and everything would be fine.

Ben opened the bathroom door. "So he keeps a toothbrush here."

"Ben..."

"Shaving cream, razor..."

"He doesn't have his own place in Philly anymore."

Ben sat on the edge of the bed. "He's living here?"

"No," she said. She pulled the sheet around herself. "He had to move back to Atlanta. For work. He's going to stay here when he comes up."

"He moved back?"

"Yeah."

"Oh." He stared straight ahead.

She moved closer to him, kissing the side of his face, hoping to distract him. Talking to him about Richard felt strange.

"But you're not moving until June, right? That's what you said."

"Well, yeah. I want to finish the year with my class."

"So how's that going to work?"

"We'll see each other when we can. It's only a couple of months."

"And then what?"

She raised one eyebrow. "You really want to hear about this?"

He shrugged.

"And then he wants me to move down there. He wants to buy a house, so his kids can stay with us half the time."

"And what do you want?"

She hesitated. "What do you mean?"

"*He* wants to buy a house. *He* wants his kids to come and stay. I don't hear you in there at all."

"Stop," she said. "Don't do that."

"It's your life, too."

"You don't have to worry about me. I'm fine."

He looked at her, putting his hand on the side of her face. His eyes were so sad. She put her hand on top of his. They looked at each other for what felt like several minutes.

"I'm thinking a cheeseburger sounds really good right now," Ben said, breaking the silence.

Natalie giggled. "That does sound good."

"With onion rings."

"Or maybe cheese fries. And pie."

"And coffee."

"Or a chocolate milkshake."

"We'll have to get dressed, though."

"Or we could order in and stay in bed," she offered.

"I'd be stupid to say no to that."

"Very stupid." She lay back, pulling him down with her. Her stomach growled again.

He shook his head, laughing. "I think you need to eat."

"I'll call and order some food. Be right back." She kissed his lips and stood up, pulling on her underpants and a t-shirt.

"Hurry back," he said, lying back against the pillow.

Natalie walked into the kitchen and picked up her cell phone from the counter where she'd left it. She opened her junk drawer, fishing for a takeout menu. As she flipped open her phone, she noticed the voicemail icon. She pushed the button.

She closed her eyes, listening to Richard's voice. *Oh, fuck. What am I doing?*

"Hey." Ben was behind her. "I thought maybe you got lost." He put his hands on her hips.

She didn't turn around.

"Nat? What happened?"

"Nothing."

"Did you call and order?"

"Not yet." She held up the phone. "Sorry. I had a voicemail on my phone."

"Oh." He wrapped his arms around her waist and rested his chin on her shoulder. She could feel his breath on her neck. "Do you need to call him back?"

"No." She turned to face him.

"Are you okay?"

She buried her face in his chest. Her eyes burned.

He didn't say anything as he took the phone out of her hand.

"Ben. Wait. What are you doing?"

He picked up the menu she'd put on the kitchen counter. "You need to eat." He flipped her phone open and dialed. "Delivery," he said into the phone, and gave her address. He gave them the order, said thank you, and flipped the phone closed.

"Thank you."

He wrapped his arms around her. "No problem, kid."

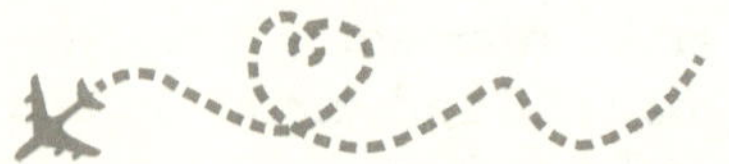

Mike took Richard for a walk down the hall and back. It felt good to get up and move. When they got back, Mike tidied up the room and packed up Ruth's dishes.

"You going to be okay?"

"I hope so," Richard said. "The doctor's supposed to come in tomorrow morning and give me a clue about what's going on."

"Want me to come back?"

"No, that's okay, I know you have work."

"I'll go in late. You're more important."

His eyes burned. "Thanks, man. That means a lot."

"I'll be here first thing in the morning. Let me pray with you before I go."

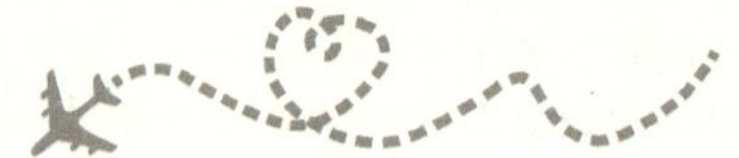

Natalie took a bite of her cheeseburger. "Oh my god, this tastes so good."

They sat together at her kitchen table, both fully clothed. It seemed smarter than eating in bed. Less messy, too.

Ben looked at her. "Feel better?"

She nodded. "Thank you."

He passed her the fries. She took a handful.

The voicemail from Richard kept replaying in her mind. How was she supposed to survive until June? Maybe she should quit her job and head down there now. Tonight. *This is fucked up.*

"You want to talk about it?" Ben was staring at her. She couldn't imagine what her face must look like.

"No."

"Soon?"

"Not tonight."

After dinner, Ben cleaned up the trash and did the dishes while Natalie dried them and put them away. "Some of these dishes have been here for a few days." He gave her a look.

"I never was a great housekeeper."

"I guess I should go home." He rinsed the dishrag, wrung it out, and hung it over the faucet. He took the towel from her and dried his hands on it.

"You don't have to," Natalie said.

"You're insatiable, woman." He pulled her towards him, kissing her.

She laughed, blushing. "I didn't mean it like that. Just... you could stay. If you want to."

Ben turned her so her back was against the kitchen counter, putting his hands on either side of her. "What's going on, Nat?"

Natalie looked away, blinking. "Nothing. You can go."

He looked at her face like he was trying to solve a puzzle. Finally, he gave up and kissed her. "Come on, kid. We'll watch some TV."

They curled up together under a blanket on the couch and watched sitcoms. Ben's phone buzzed in his pocket, but he made no move to answer it.

"Do you need to get that?" She tried to keep the question casual.

"No." He kissed her forehead. The buzzing stopped.

Natalie slid out from his arms and turned to look at him. "Ben..."

"Don't worry about it."

Natalie's stomach did a flip. "Do you want to call her back?"

He shook his head, smiling. "No."

"Why not?"

"Why do you not want me to go home?"

Her heart pounded. "I just want to be with you right now," she said, her voice timid.

He lowered his lips to hers.

-37-

The nurse came in to wake Richard early. "Good morning, Mister Rung. I'm Abby." She wrote her name on the whiteboard on the wall opposite his bed. She was young and pretty, with short brown hair and freckled cheeks.

"Nice to meet you, Abby," he said. "Am I allowed to get up and go to the bathroom?"

"Of course."

"Without this?" he asked, pulling the oxygen from his face.

"You should be okay without it for a few minutes. I'll stay here and wait."

He got up, used the bathroom and washed his hands. He looked at his face in the mirror, running his hands over his stubble. What he really needed was a shower and a shave.

"The doc's supposed to come in and see me this morning, right?" he said as he came back into the room.

"That's right."

He sat back down in the bed and Abby helped him put the oxygen back in place. "What time do they come in?"

"It could be anytime. You're in with pulmonology, right? They're usually early."

"What's early?"

"Before eight."

"I'm holding you to that."

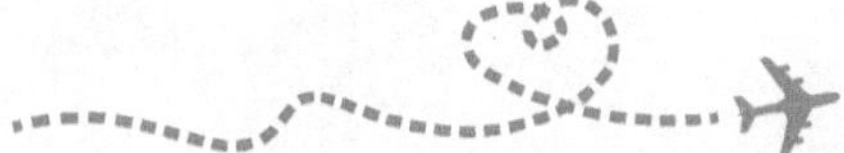

She laughed as she turned to leave. "Oops! Excuse me," she said to someone as she exited the room.

"That's okay," said a voice he'd know anywhere. She appeared in the doorway, arms crossed over her chest.

"Mel."

"Nice outfit." She nodded towards his hospital gown. "I can't believe you thought you were going to get away with not telling me about this." Her words were harsh, but her tone was gentle.

"Who told you? Mike?"

She shook her head. "I've got ears and eyes everywhere, darlin'."

"This is a violation of my privacy rights." He'd intentionally chosen a doctor who wasn't affiliated with the hospital she and Neil worked at, but he guessed someone had seen his name and called her.

"What's going on, Richard?"

"I told you. Pneumonia."

"You didn't say you were in the hospital."

"The doctor thought it would be easier to do the tests inpatient. Turns out it was your run of the mill regular pneumonia, anyhow. They put me on some fancy antibiotics. I feel a lot better. Just waiting on the rest of the test results and then they should spring me."

She walked towards the bed. "What kind of tests?"

"All of them. I think I've had every test there is."

"Be specific."

"I don't know. Chest X-ray. CT scan. Bronchoscopy. PET scan."

"PET scan?" She looked alarmed.

"Is that bad?"

"Depends on what they're looking for." She put her nurse face back on.

"The doctor should be in soon."

"Will you let me know what they say?"

"Look, Mel, I didn't want to worry you. Or anyone. I'm fine. I just couldn't get over this damn cough."

"Maybe this will finally get you to stop smoking," she said.

"Maybe I already did."

"Maybe I know you too well to believe that."

Mike knocked on the door. "Am I interrupting?"

Melinda turned towards him. "Hey, Mike."

"Melinda." He wrapped her in a hug. "Haven't seen you for a long time."

"Not since this one skipped town. Now he doesn't even call to let me know he's in the hospital. No manners anymore."

"He's becoming a northerner," Mike teased.

"You guys are hilarious," Richard said.

"You guys!" Melinda laughed. "Listen to him!"

A woman came in carrying his breakfast tray. "Mister Rung?" He nodded and she set it down in front of him.

"Thank you." He took the lid off the coffee cup. He looked at Mike and Melinda, who were still laughing. "*Y'all* can get out of my room, now."

"I'm leaving, anyhow," Melinda said. "I have to get to work. Will you call me and let me know what the doctor says, please?"

"Yes, ma'am."

She bent to kiss his cheek. "Take care, Mike. Good to see you." She hugged him again.

"Oh, sure, you get two hugs and all I get is a peck on the cheek," Richard said as soon as she was gone.

"What can I say? I'm adorable."

He poured cream into his coffee as Mike sat down in the chair next to him. "Thanks for coming."

"How are you feeling this morning?"

"Nervous. I'm wishing I had a cigarette and a shot of whiskey right about now."

"How about a homemade blueberry muffin?" He handed Richard a paper bag. "Sent with love."

"I won't say no to that." He pulled the muffin out and took a bite. "Thanks."

"We're gonna give it to the Lord, okay?" Mike said a short prayer, then they recited the Serenity Prayer together. "Whatever it is, I've got you. We're going to get through it together. Okay?"

"Thank you, Mike." He sipped his coffee.

A knock on the door turned both their heads. "Good morning, Richard." Dr. Thompson stepped into the room along with his nurse, Abby, and two more doctors. Abby gave him a sympathetic smile and patted his leg.

"Hey doc." Richard set his coffee down. "How soon can I get out of here?"

"Let's talk about that," she said. She turned to Mike and extended her hand. "Anita Thompson."

Mike shook her hand. "Michael Foster."

"My best friend," Richard said.

"Very nice to meet you." She introduced Dr. Patrick, from pulmonology, who'd admitted Richard, and Dr. Reed, from oncology. "We're here to talk to you about your test results, okay?"

Richard's mouth went dry. "Oncology?"

Dr. Thompson nodded. "I'm afraid it's not good news, Richard."

Natalie's phone rang as she parked her car at the school. *Richard.* She fished it out of her bag and

flipped it open without checking the caller ID. "Hello?"

"Good morning," Ben said. He sounded cheerful. She'd sent him off last night with a kiss and a promise that they would talk today.

"Hey. I just got to work."

"Can I take you out for dinner tonight?"

"I guess that would be okay." Her voice was flat.

"Cheer up, kid."

"Can't. It's Monday."

He laughed. "I'll pick you up at six?"

"See you then." She flipped the phone closed and took a long sip of coffee from her cup. He would want answers, and she didn't know them. Nothing made sense anymore. She got out of the car.

"Hey," Lauren called from behind her.

She turned. "Hey." They walked together towards the building.

"How was your weekend?"

Natalie didn't answer.

"What's wrong?"

Natalie shook her head. "Nothing." She blinked back tears and gave a nervous laugh.

Lauren gave her a look. "That bad?"

"I don't even know." She sniffled, looking away.

"Nat? Oh my god, what happened?"

Natalie stopped and turned to face her friend. "I slept with Ben."

Lauren's mouth fell open. "Shut up."

Natalie didn't respond.

"Seriously?"

"Yes."

"Holy shit," Lauren said, drawing out all three syllables.

"I know." They started walking again, up the steps, past the office.

"We'll talk at lunch," Lauren said, looking at her watch. "Okay?"

Natalie nodded, looking down.

"It's gonna be okay," Lauren called back towards her as she hurried down the hall, giving her a thumbs-up.

Richard couldn't make sense of the words they were saying to him. Biopsy. Tumor. Malignancy. Metastasis. Lymph nodes. He knew what the words meant. They'd had meaning to him when he'd heard them with regard to someone else. But hearing them about himself, the words suddenly seemed foreign.

"Palliative care? What does that even mean?" Richard asked.

"It means we work to ease your symptoms as much as possible. Pain management, oxygen, respiratory support," Dr. Reed, the oncologist, said.

"I don't understand," he said. "What's the treatment? Chemo, radiation, surgery?"

"We're not recommending treatment," she said. She was about his age, with cropped chestnut hair and wire-rimmed glasses. Her face had a worn, tired look, like she had given patients this news far too many times.

"You're not recommending treatment?"

"With this type of cancer, especially at this advanced stage, treatment is rarely effective," Dr. Patrick said. The pulmonologist was a guy about his age, stout and balding.

"Rarely. That means it does work some of the time."

Dr. Reed answered. "Any type of treatment at this stage is going to make you sicker, cause you more pain, diminish your quality of life."

"As opposed to the cancer, which will have exactly the same effect?"

"Our recommendation is that you try and make the most of the time you have left," she said.

The time I have left.

"How much time?" he asked.

"We need to do some more tests," Dr. Patrick said.

"I don't want any more tests. Give me your best guess."

"We can do the tests outpatient," he offered, glancing at Dr. Thompson.

"A number."

Dr. Reed stepped in. "Three to six months. But with supportive care, it could be longer."

Three to six months. He could be dead before summer. Before Natalie finished the school year. Before Hannah's graduation.

"I want a second opinion."

"Richard," Dr. Thompson said. "We know how difficult this is to hear."

"You don't know shit." His voice was thick. "You don't know me. I have two kids. I have a girlfriend. I have a job I love. I'm not going to roll over and let this thing take me out."

"Easy," Mike said. "Slow down. Take a breath."

"Take a breath," he muttered. "Into my shitty, diseased, cancer-ridden lungs." He slammed his fist on the bedside table.

Abby turned away, facing the window, holding her hand up to her face. Dr. Thompson discreetly handed her a tissue. Richard looked away. He hadn't meant to upset her.

Mike stood and took Richard's hand into both of his. "I've got you, okay? Look at me. Richard. I've got you."

Richard looked up into Mike's warm brown eyes. The same eyes he'd looked into after the worst night of his life. The eyes that had helped restore him to sanity.

"Doctors," Mike said, turning to address them. "How soon can Richard go home?"

"Today," Dr. Thompson said. "We need to get some paperwork together, and set up some appointments, but there's no reason you can't be out of here this morning."

"That's good." Mike looked at Richard. "Richard? That's good. Right?"

Richard nodded. His mouth was dry and his throat ached.

He tried to pay attention as the doctors described the next steps, but in his mind he had left the room, left the hospital, left Atlanta. He was driving south on the highway at a hundred miles per hour, a fifth of whiskey stashed under the seat in a plain brown paper bag.

He closed his eyes, imagining the smell of the salt air as he pulled the truck up to the marina. It would be empty except for a few local fishermen, who'd nod hello and leave him alone as he climbed onto his boat and steered it towards the open sea. He imagined opening the bottle, emptying the whiskey in a few quick gulps. It would burn his throat at first, but the warmth would course through him, washing away the pain, the fear. Walking towards the stern, one foot in front of the other, the waves crashing into him as he hurled his body into the icy surf...

"Richard?" One of the doctors stood in front of him, her hand extended. The tired-faced one.

He couldn't remember her name. It didn't matter. None of it mattered, did it? Three years of sobriety, rebuilding his life, finding love again, and for what? He was going to die.

But not without a fight.

As soon as the lunch bell rang, Lauren appeared in Natalie's doorway. "Hey."

"Hey," she answered.

Lauren sat across from her and pulled a container out of her lunch bag. "You must be flipping out."

"Trying not to, but, yeah."

"Tell me everything." She took a bite of her sandwich.

Natalie told her about the bar, about Ben agreeing to get divorced, about the cab ride home and spending the past two nights with him. Lauren listened, not saying anything.

"This is bad," Natalie said. "Right?"

Lauren raised her eyebrows. "Yes, you have two men desperately in love with you. It's terrible. Every woman's nightmare."

"Not helping," Natalie said, laughing. She was grateful for Lauren's ability to listen to her without judging. She was judging herself enough.

"So Richard is still in Atlanta?"

"Yeah. We're playing phone tag."

"Or are you avoiding each other's calls?"

"Maybe a little of both."

"Wow. I didn't see this coming."

"I know. Me neither."

"So was it, like, a goodbye fuck that lasted all weekend, or is it more than that?"

"I don't know." Natalie shook her head. "I really fucked up."

"It's an understandable lapse in judgment. You've loved the guy for more than a decade. It's got to be hard to say goodbye. Don't beat yourself up about it."

"Should I tell Richard?"

Lauren laughed. "I'd say that's a hell no."

"You're right. Thanks for listening."

"Anytime."

-38-

"I put fresh sheets on the bed," Ruth said, as Richard set his bags down in Mike's spare bedroom. "And there's a towel and wash rag here on the dresser."

"Thank you, ma'am," Richard said. "I told Mike I could go to the hotel."

"Don't be ridiculous. And don't you dare call me ma'am. We're family."

"I appreciate it."

"My husband's been doing this a long time. He brings around some interesting characters. You know, you've met some of them." She raised her eyebrows, and Richard attempted a smile. "Don't tell anyone, but you're my favorite." She winked.

"Thank you."

She looked him over. "You need anything, let me know."

He nodded, afraid his voice would crack if he said anything else.

"You okay, Richard?"

Richard shook his head. *No.*

She sat on the bed and patted the spot next to her. "Come here." She opened her arms. He hesitated. "Come here, sugar." He let her hold him as sobs shook his body. She cradled him like a child. "It's okay. Let it go."

"I'm sorry."

"Don't you apologize," she said. "There's no shame in crying. Not in this house."

"I just got my life back. And now it's over."

"You're still breathing. You still have people who love you."

"It's not fair."

"You're right about that." She kissed his head. "Michael and I are here for you. However we can support you, we will."

"I appreciate it."

"This is what family does."

Ben took her to a diner near her apartment. As they finished eating, he asked, "Are you ready to talk yet?"

"Here?" She looked around the diner.

He shrugged. "Sure."

"Maybe we should go back to my place."

"I think we both know what will happen if we go back to your place."

"Right." Her cheeks flushed.

"Are you blushing?" he teased.

"Shut up." She laughed.

Ben took a deep breath. "I didn't call the lawyer today."

"Right. God. I forgot about the lawyer."

"I wanted to check and make sure you still wanted me to."

Natalie stared down into her coffee cup.

"Nattie. Listen. I'm trying not to be an asshole here. Because the past few days were kind of incredible, and I'm actually feeling pretty happy right now. But that scares me. Because I don't know if I should feel happy. This whole thing is starting to fuck with my head."

"I didn't mean to fuck with your head."

He continued, speaking quickly, "I mean, you started out the other night telling me you want to move forward with a divorce, and then later, we ended up in bed together. And I wasn't the one who made the first move." He raised one eyebrow at her. "Maybe we drank too much on Saturday, but you weren't drunk yesterday afternoon. Or last night. And anyway, I know you, kid. Natalie doesn't do anything she doesn't want to do."

Ben was right, of course. She fidgeted in her seat. She didn't know why the urge to be with him had taken her over, why she hadn't been able to stop herself from acting on it. She'd always shut it down before. His question from the other morning echoed in her mind. Had it been her way of saying goodbye? Or was it that she didn't want to?

"So you tell me."

She blinked. "What?"

"If you still want me to call the lawyer." He looked her in the eye. "Or if maybe something changed."

She didn't answer.

"I can't read your mind, Nat. I need you to tell me what's going on inside your head. I know I was a dick that day when I came by and he was there, and I'm sorry. But other than that I've been pretty patient. I think I deserve to know what you're thinking."

"I'm not sure I can say anything to make you feel better right now."

"So then don't try to make me feel better. Be honest with me." He paused, waiting for her answer. When she didn't respond, he continued. "You always say I don't tell you how I feel. Well, I feel like what happened the other night maybe means there's a chance for us to work things out. I'm not crazy, right? You feel it, too." He reached for her hand.

"I..." She pulled her hand back. She knew what he wanted her to say, but her thoughts turned to Richard, the plans they had made, the future she was looking forward to. "I told him I would go. I made a commitment to him."

"You made a commitment to me first."

"God, Ben... I know that."

"Sorry." He paused, thinking. "How about this? Why did you kiss me in the cab? Why did you want me to stay last night?"

"I don't know." She put her face in her hands.

"I think you do. But maybe you can't admit it."

She looked at him. His gaze was intense. The truth of his words resonated deep within her. He was right, she wasn't ready to admit it, not even to herself.

"I get the feeling your mind isn't as made up as you pretend it is."

Her stomach twisted. "I'm just worried about moving."

"Is that all?"

"No," she admitted. "I don't know."

"Listen." He reached for her hand again, and she let him have it. "I'm not going to beg you. I'm just going to be honest. I'm not perfect, Natalie, but I'm willing to try. I still love you and you still love me. That's got to be worth something." He leaned forward. "I don't want to get a divorce. I know I said okay, and I'll do it if it's what you really want, but I don't want to. I want to be married to you, Natalie. That's never changed."

"What about your girlfriend?" she asked, her voice thick with sarcasm.

"She's not you." He took her other hand. "It's that simple."

Her heart flipped over in her chest. She looked at his face. His eyes shone.

"I love you, Ben. It probably sounds stupid now, after everything, but I do."

"I know you do," he said. "You know what I want, you know what he wants. I think you need to figure out what you want. What you really want."

Natalie chewed her bottom lip. "Okay. Can we go?"

"Yeah, sure."

The drive home took less than three minutes.

"Do you want to come in?"

He pulled her close. "Of course I do. But you need some time to think."

They shared a brief kiss, and she got out of the car. She turned when she reached her front door, giving him a quick wave before he pulled away.

"So we have the consult on Thursday morning." Mike took a bite of his eggs. "And then we'll meet with Melinda and the girls on Friday after school."

"You don't have to do all of this with me."

They sat together at Mike's kitchen table, early Tuesday morning.

"I want to. I told you I'd be there for you. Don't be a tough guy."

"Well, I appreciate it."

"Now, what about Natalie?"

Richard took a long sip of coffee. "I can't talk to her about this yet. Not until after I start treatment."

"Richard." Mike's face was stern. "You have to tell her the truth."

"She's been through so much pain and loss. How can I add to that?"

"Pain is a part of life, man. You can't have love without loss. It's a part of the package."

Richard shook his head.

"So the real question is, do you still want to go through with having her move down here? Buying a house together? Knowing what the doctors said?" Mike took a sip of his coffee.

"I don't care what the doctors said. I'm doing treatment. If this doctor on Friday says no, we'll go to another one. I'll go to as many as I need to."

Mike looked at him, sadness in his eyes, but he pressed on. "But what about Natalie? She's making arrangements, packing her things, thinking she's moving down here in a few months to live happily ever after with you."

Richard's stomach churned. It would be selfish, he knew, to have her move here. Maybe the best thing would be to let her go. Make a clean break. But he wasn't ready. "I'll talk to her after the consult."

Mike didn't press him any further. "You sure you're okay to go to work today?"

"Work is the only thing I think I can handle today."

"You need me, call me, okay?"

Richard nodded.

"I'm serious."

"I appreciate it."

"I love you, man. I'm here for you."

"Thanks. I love you, too."

-39-

Natalie couldn't sleep. It was Wednesday night. Two days since she'd seen Ben. Three days without talking to Richard. He'd left her a voicemail this afternoon, calling when he knew she'd be in class, saying he was swamped at work and he'd be in on Sunday. It made sense that he wanted to stay through the weekend so he could spend time with the girls, but why had he called when he knew she couldn't answer? Why wasn't he answering her calls? Did he suspect something had happened between her and Ben?

Ben. She smiled at the thought of him, then frowned.

She turned from her belly to her back, staring at the shadows cast on the ceiling by the streetlights. The lights from a passing car changed the pattern for a few seconds. She wished the car was Ben's. She reached for her phone, but hesitated. Ben wanted her to make a decision, and she wasn't even close. And Richard... If she talked to him now, she'd probably start crying.

She rolled to the side, trying to slow her breathing. Sushi jumped onto the bed and curled up at her feet, purring. Natalie closed her eyes.

She had just begun to drift when her phone rang. *Ben.* Her heart leapt.

"Hey," she said, her voice sleepy.

"Hey, beautiful. Are you home?"

"Yes."

"Are you alone?"

"Yes."

"Come downstairs," he said.

"I'll be right there." She got out of bed, checked herself in the mirror, and went down to open the door.

Ben pulled her towards him and kissed her.

"Hey," he said. He ran his hand down her back to her waist, pulling her closer. She smelled beer on his breath. "Let's go upstairs."

"Wait, are you sure?"

"Shh. Don't talk."

They lay together in her bed, quiet, her head on his chest. Ben ran his fingers along her spine as she listened to the sound of his breath. He kissed the top of her head.

"I missed you yesterday," she said.

"Me too. I know I said I would give you some time, but I really wanted to see you tonight." He rolled onto his side, propping his head up on one arm to look at her.

She laughed. "What?"

He shook his head. "Nothing. I'm just looking."

"Stop." She gave him a playful nudge and turned away.

"No fair." He kissed the back of her neck.

"I'm glad you're here." She snuggled close to him.

"Thanks for letting me in."

"Can you stay the night?"

"If you want me to." He curled up next to her, wrapping his free arm around her.

"I want you to."

"You do?"

"Yes." She turned her head and kissed him.

"I love you, kid."

"I love you, too."

She listened as his breathing grew slower and more shallow. When she was sure he was asleep, she slid out from under his arm, sat up, turning to look at him in the faint light streaming through the window, watching him as he slept.

It was so easy when she looked at him. She loved him. His words from Monday night echoed in her mind. *"It's that simple."* And it was.

"Hey. Natalie." Ben's lips grazed her forehead.

She opened her eyes. It was still dark. Ben was fully dressed, standing next to the bed. "What time is it?"

"A little after five. I've got to go, I have an early meeting. I'll let myself out. You go back to sleep."

"No, wait," she said. "Give me a minute." She pulled on the pajamas she'd left on the floor last night and used the bathroom. "Can you stay for coffee?"

"Not today. But I'll call you later."

"Okay." She walked with him down the stairs, to the front door.

He gave her a hug. "Go get some more sleep, kid."

She reached up for a kiss. As their lips parted, she saw a long, dark hair caught in the fibers of his wool jacket. She pulled it off, looked at it, and held it up. Her heart skidded to a halt. "This isn't mine."

He took it from her and put his hand in his pocket. "Sorry."

"Were you with her last night? Before you came here?"

"That could have been there for a while."

"Sure," she said. "So that's a yes?"

Ben rested his hands on her shoulders. "Natalie."

She looked away.

"Yes. I had dinner with her. After work." He touched her cheek, turning her face back to his. "But then I went home. Alone. I couldn't stop thinking about you. I wanted to be with you."

"Does she know?"

"What?"

Natalie shrugged.

"Did I tell her about this weekend, is that what you want to know? No. I didn't want to hurt her."

She winced.

"Nat, please."

"I can't," she whispered, pulling away from him.

"Can't what?"

"I can't think about you with someone else." She crossed her arms over her chest.

Ben rested his forehead against the door frame. "I have to look at your boyfriend's toothbrush when I pee, and you're upset about one brown hair."

"Do you love her?" Her voice was tight and squeaky.

He was quiet for a minute, peeling a piece of flaked paint from the wood. "I love *you*."

That wasn't an answer.

"Come here." He pulled her into his arms. "I'll call you after work, okay?"

He kissed her forehead and left.

She stopped for coffee on her way to work, picking up a muffin, too, even though she felt like she might throw up at any second. Last night she had been so sure, but this morning had left her rattled.

She pulled into her parking space with a few minutes to spare. Richard would be up, on his way to work if he wasn't already there. She grabbed her phone and pushed the button to call him.

It went to voicemail after two rings. What did that mean? She closed the phone, not leaving a message. Had he rejected her call? Was he avoiding her on purpose? They had never gone this long without talking, not since they'd been together.

She was being paranoid. Or was she?

She dialed Lisa's number.

"Natalie? Are you okay?" She sounded out of breath. Natalie could hear the kids in the background.

"I'm fine," she said. "Do you have a minute?"

"I'm trying to get the kids out the door."

"Oh, right. Sorry."

"What's up?"

"How much do you know about Ben's girlfriend?"

"Oh, shit. This is going to take more than a minute." Lisa sounded amused.

"You're right. It was stupid of me. Please don't tell him I said anything. I'll talk to you later."

"Nat, wait." Natalie heard her ask George to put Callie's shoes on. "Honestly, I don't know much. He told George he was dating somebody, and that's all I know. George hasn't met her, or anything." She paused. "Wait. How do you know he has a girlfriend?"

"He told me."

"I didn't know you two were talking."

Natalie was tempted to tell Lisa what had happened between her and Ben, to ask her for some guidance in sorting it out, but she held back. "You know what? Don't worry about it. I'm sorry I called so early."

"Natalie. Come on. You called me. Tell me what's going on."

"Go take the kids to school. I'll talk to you later."

"I'm calling you back tonight, okay?"

"Okay."

Taking a deep breath, she gathered her things and got out of the car. *That was a mistake.* She didn't need to talk about it. What she needed was to get out of her head, get to work, feel normal for a little while.

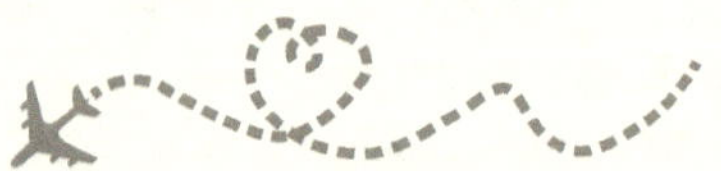

Richard sat holding the phone for several minutes after Natalie's call. *I should have just let it go,* he thought, knowing she would realize he'd pushed the button to reject her call. He couldn't put off talking to her forever, but he wasn't ready. Not yet.

Maybe she'll get angry enough to break up with me. Finally her fiery temper could come in handy. But she wouldn't, not as long as he was her escape from the things she didn't want to feel.

Work was good. It was dull and predictable and kept him busy. It didn't take his mind off anything, not for a second. But at least it made sense.

He would wait until after the consult, after he knew what his next steps would be. He couldn't go back to her without hope.

-40-

As Natalie walked in her front door, the scene from the morning repeated itself in her mind. So stupid, getting worked up over a fucking brown hair. What right did she have, after everything she had put Ben through?

Her phone rang. "Hello?"

"Hey," Lisa said. "Are you home?"

"Yes."

"Good. I'm coming over, and I'm taking you out for dinner."

"You don't have to do that. I'm fine."

"Well, I need some time with my sister. Okay?"

She showed up an hour later and drove to a tiny Polish restaurant a few blocks away.

"This is going to make me cry," Natalie said as they walked in the door. It smelled like their Nana's kitchen: sausage, onion, cabbage.

"I figured you could use a little comfort food." Lisa took off her jacket before sitting at the table. Her belly was just beginning to protrude. "Just don't tell George. He's not letting me eat anything salty because of my stupid blood pressure."

"Deal." Natalie examined the menu.

"So tell me what's going on," Lisa said after they had placed their order.

"It's nothing."

"You don't call me before eight over nothing. I thought someone died."

"Sorry I scared you."

Lisa gave her a stern look, crossing her arms over her chest. "Talk."

Natalie hesitated.

"When did Ben tell you he's dating someone?"

"Saturday."

"How did it happen?"

That night already seemed so long ago. "We went out for a beer. I told him Richard asked me to move in with him, and I said I wanted a divorce." She left out the part about moving to Atlanta. She hadn't told anyone but Lauren yet.

Lisa set her fork down. "You did?"

"Yes."

"What did he say?"

"He said okay."

"He did not."

Natalie gave a short laugh. "I was as surprised as you are."

"Wow." Lisa shook her head. "So that's when he told you?"

"He didn't tell me. I figured it out. He just confirmed it."

"Oh," Lisa said, understanding. "He must really like this girl."

"Evidently," Natalie said, her voice flat.

"Are you jealous?"

"Crazy jealous," Natalie admitted.

Lisa smirked.

"What do you know about her?"

"Nothing. I don't know much about her at all."

"If you did, would you tell me?"

"Nat... yes. I'm on your side, here, believe it or not."

"Do you know how they met?"

Lisa made a face. "Well..."

"Oh, God, is it that one soccer mom? With the big teeth?"

"No," she said, laughing. "It's someone who works in his building. But, yeah, I remembered one more thing about her. She has kids."

Natalie's stomach rolled. She put down her fork.

"I can't believe you're getting a divorce," Lisa continued. "It makes sense, but I always thought you guys would find a way back to each other. Wishful thinking I guess."

She kept talking while Natalie pictured Ben with the dark-haired woman and her children. She wondered if he was already involved with them. Taking them to the playground, helping them with their homework. They could have another child, or two. Ben could be a father.

"Hey. Natalie."

Natalie blinked. "What?"

"You were on another planet."

"I'm sorry." She chewed her bottom lip for a minute. "Do you think he's in love with her?"

"Oh, wow, Natalie. What's going on?" She sounded concerned.

Natalie hesitated.

"You're having second thoughts about divorcing him."

"Yes," she admitted.

"Did you tell him how you feel?"

"Well, in a way." She looked away, trying not to smile.

"Oh, shit." Lisa laughed. "You fucked him."

"Shh," she said.

"Who's gonna hear?" She took a bite of pierogi. "Well, no wonder."

"No wonder what?"

"No wonder you're all screwed up."

"Hey, thanks."

"You know what I mean. Does Richard know?"

Natalie shook her head.

"What are you going to do?"

"I don't know. Last night I felt like I wanted to get back together with him, and then this morning I found his girlfriend's hair on his jacket and it nearly killed me. Like, before that she was an idea, but suddenly she became an actual person. With long, dark hair. And kids."

"Wait. This morning?" Lisa looked at her, eyebrow raised.

Whoops. "Yeah." She buried her face in her hands.

"So he's been coming over every night?"

"Not every night."

"Natalie. Jesus."

She looked up.

"Honestly, is there a chance of you guys getting back together, or are you just jealous of this girl?"

Her throat felt tight. "I don't know."

Lisa gave her an impatient look.

"I still love him, I always have. But he never understood what I was going through. He never even tried. Everything was so damn hard. I need to know it wouldn't be like that again."

"But it will be like that, Nat. Marriage is hard. That's how it is. Some days are good, some are really good, but a lot of the time you can't stand each other and you don't even know why."

"You and George aren't like that."

"Trust me, we are. And eventually, you and Richard will be, too."

Natalie frowned. "It's different with him."

"Sure. It's all fun and romance in the beginning. I remember. But sharing a life is hard, and there's

no way around it. You start fighting about whether the peanut butter goes in the fridge or the pantry, and the next thing you know, you're wondering what the hell you ever saw in this person. I love George, but he drives me crazy. I'm sure he feels the same way about me. Sometimes you have to remind yourself your life is better with them than without them."

Natalie chewed her bottom lip.

Lisa looked uneasy. "Look, I know I said before that I wouldn't get in the middle of this. I'm not going to tell Ben anything you told me, but I want to say one thing."

"Okay."

"You've been saying you wanted him to move on, and now he has. He has someone who he likes. Don't ruin that for him. Don't fuck with his head. Don't string him along because you're jealous, or because you feel bad about asking for a divorce."

Natalie felt like her chair had been pulled out from under her. She'd expected Lisa to be happy. Wasn't this what all of them had wanted, from the moment she'd left Ben? For her to give him another chance? She'd never thought Lisa would tell her to back off. She set her fork down and looked away.

"I'm sorry, Natalie."

"No, you're right. It's not fair." Tears filled her eyes, but she blinked them away.

"Oh, God. Hey. I didn't mean to sound harsh."

"I don't know what to do."

"Look, Nat, this is real life, not a romance novel. There's no hero or villain. No magical neon sign is going to fall out of the sky with an arrow pointing to Ben or to Richard. You have to make a choice, and then make the best of it. And whatever it is, I'll support you."

After Lisa dropped her off at home, she checked her phone. Two missed calls from Ben. Nothing from Richard. She stood on her porch for a minute, drumming her fingertips on the wrought iron railing, letting the cold numb her body and her mind.

She grabbed her keys and got into her car. She didn't know if he'd be home, she didn't know if he'd be alone, but she knew she had to see him, even if she didn't have anything figured out.

His car was in the driveway. She knocked at the back door of his brother's house, praying he'd be the one to answer. After a minute of waiting, she knocked again.

She had pulled her phone out of her pocket and was about to call when the door opened.

"Natalie." He was barefoot, wearing a t-shirt and sweatpants. "What are you doing here?"

"Were you asleep?" It was only eight-thirty.

"No." He yawned. "Maybe." He grinned. He opened his arms to hug her, and she stepped into them.

"Can we talk?"

"Sure."

She followed him to the bedroom. He switched on a lamp, turned off the TV, and sat down on the bed, patting the spot next to him.

"I'm sorry about this morning," she said.

"It's okay."

"No, it's not. I don't have any right to be upset that you went out with your girlfriend, Ben. And..." she faltered, her voice beginning to shake. "We shouldn't be doing this. We should have stopped after that first night."

"You want to stop." His voice was soft. Calm.

"Yes."

"Why?"

"It's not fair. To you. To anyone."

"Natalie." He groaned, putting his head in his hands.

"You're with someone else. You deserve...a chance...to be happy..." She tried to keep the tears at bay, but couldn't. "Do you think you could be happy with her?"

"Why are you asking me that?"

"She can give you what I can't."

Ben flopped backwards onto the bed and sighed, closing his eyes. "What do you mean?"

"She has kids."

He pinched the bridge of his nose. "One kid. And how do you know that?"

"Lisa told me."

"Lisa needs to learn to mind her own business."

"You should stay with her," Natalie said. "You deserve to have a family, Ben."

He sat up. "No offense, Nat, but you're full of shit."

She sniffled. "What?"

"You don't get to decide that for me. Did you ever consider that I wouldn't want to have a family if it wasn't with you?" His breathing quickened, his eyes shining. He blinked his eyes and sniffled. "The babies we lost... they were *our* babies. Having a family was *our* dream. And now you're talking about stepping aside so I can have a family with someone else. As if I could ever be that selfish...as if that was something I would ever want. All I want is *you*. Kids, no kids, it doesn't matter. *You're* my family."

His words only made her cry harder. It was everything she'd needed to hear since the last miscarriage, but it was so much more complicated now.

"Things got hard and you took off. I wish you would have stayed and tried to work on it with me, but we're here now. We can work on it, if you want to, but you have to stop running."

"I'm scared," she whispered.

"Natalie. Please. Look at me."

She looked into his eyes.

"I'm sorry about the hair, okay?"

She gave a sad laugh. "I'm sorry I got jealous."

"*You're* jealous?" He was amused.

"You're finally moving on with your life, you don't need me wrecking it."

"Nat. You're not wrecking it. Come here." He opened his arms, and she went into them. "I love you." He kissed her forehead.

She swiped at her nose. "What about your girlfriend?"

"Let me worry about her."

"You said you don't want to hurt her."

"She knows I'm still married. Nobody's going to get blindsided. Okay?"

Except Richard. She straightened up. "I don't know what to do."

"Me neither."

"We had a couple of fun nights together, but I don't know if that's enough."

"Enough for what?"

"Enough to jump back in and pretend everything is okay."

"I'm not asking you to do that."

"You're not?"

He shook his head. "Obviously there are a few things we both need to take care of if we're going to think about getting back together."

"Right."

"Let's give it some time. We can work on it together and see what happens." He smiled. "I love you, kid."

"I love you, too."

-41-

The doctor took a long look at all the scans and test results laid out on the desk in front of her, folding her hands.

"I understand what you're asking, Richard," she said. "I know this is a tough prognosis, especially for someone so young. Of course you want to fight. I'm going to be honest, though. Chemotherapy is very hard on the body. It destroys your immune system. It compromises your vital organs. You're talking about a slim chance it will be helpful, while dealing with a one hundred percent chance it will make you weak, and sick, and unable to fight off infections. I see you've already been treated for bronchitis and pneumonia recently."

"But if the chemotherapy can shrink the tumors, won't my lungs improve?"

"There's no guarantee it will shrink them. More likely, it won't."

"I have to take that chance."

She looked at him, tilting her head to the side.

"I have kids," he said. "Two beautiful girls." He pulled their photo out of his wallet. "Hannah and Isabella."

She glanced at the photo. "I understand. I have children, too."

"So imagine you were told you're going to die and leave your children behind. Wouldn't you fight for the chance, even a tiny one, to not have that happen?"

The doctor gave him a sad smile.

"Please," he said. "I'm in love. Her name is Natalie. She's incredible. Smart, funny, beautiful. I don't know what she sees in me, but she loves me, too. She just agreed to move in with me. We're buying a house together. We have plans for the future." His voice threatened to crack. "I don't care what the odds are. I'm determined to beat this thing."

"The cancer is going to take your life, Richard. You might be able to slow it down temporarily—"

"You really think so?"

"I like you, Richard. You don't give up."

"Never," he agreed.

"This is against my better judgment, you understand. I'll give you three treatments, and then we'll re-evaluate. If there's any improvement, we can continue treatments, but if things are the same, or worse, please reconsider palliative care."

"Of course," he said. "Thank you. I appreciate you taking a chance on me."

He listened as the doctor explained how the chemotherapy would work, and made sure he understood he would have to take steps to decrease the chances he'd be exposed to any kind of infection. "No airline travel for a while, I'm afraid."

His heart sank. No airline travel would make his job challenging. But it also meant he couldn't go back to Philly again once he'd started treatment.

When he got back to Mike's, he took out his phone. Natalie answered in a cheery enough mood.

"Hey. I thought you forgot about me."

"Never," he said. "I'm sorry I haven't called."

"What's going on?"

"Look," he began. "I have to tell you something."

"Okay." She waited.

"You know I was sick when I came down here. Well, it turns out I was really sick. I was admitted to the hospital last weekend."

"The hospital?" She sounded alarmed.

"I had pneumonia."

"You were in the hospital? And you didn't tell me?"

"I tried to call on Sunday. I left you a message."

"You didn't say you were in the hospital."

"I didn't want to tell you in a voicemail. And I didn't want you to worry. I knew you had other stuff going on."

"I can't believe you didn't tell me."

"I'm sorry. I'm okay now." *Liar.* He couldn't tell her over the phone. He changed the subject. "How did it go with Ben on Saturday?"

She hesitated. "It went okay."

"Did you talk to him about everything?"

"I did."

"Was he upset?"

"He was okay, but..." She paused. "It turned out to be a little more complicated than I thought it would be."

Something was different. He could hear it in her voice. He closed his eyes, remembering the way she looked at Ben when he'd confronted them outside her house. "Did something happen?"

She was silent.

"Natalie?"

"When are you coming home?"

He winced at the word *home*. "I'm going to spend the weekend with the girls, and then I'll try and be in Philly for a couple of days, early next week."

"We'll talk when you get here."

"Yeah. I'll give you a call when my flight gets in, okay?"

"Sunday night?"

"That's the plan," he said. "I'll talk to you then."

"Okay."

"Bye." He flipped his phone shut and closed his eyes.

Something had happened between her and Ben. And why shouldn't it have? They were still in love with each other, even if they were too stupid to see it.

For the first time, he allowed reality to sink in. Could he let her move here, divorce Ben, uproot her entire life, when the prognosis was so grim? She was better off without him.

And she loved Ben. The man had been patient long enough.

He got up and went downstairs. Mike was sitting at the kitchen table, working. He looked up. "Hey, I'm glad to see you. I was just about to take a coffee break." He started to stand up.

"Coffee sounds good. Don't get up, I'll make it." He measured out the water and coffee. Once it was ready, he poured them each a cup and sat down at the table.

Mike cleared his papers away. "What's on your mind, Richard?"

"I spoke to Natalie." He sipped his coffee.

"Did you tell her?"

"I want to tell her in person." His throat tightened. "And then I've got to let her go."

"Are you sure that's what you want to do?"

"It's not what I want to do. It's what's right. She deserves to have a life, not to come all the way here to play nursemaid to a cancer patient."

"It's not an easy decision. I know you love her."

"I'm crazy about her. But honestly, I'm pretty sure she loves somebody else."

"The ex-husband."

"Yeah."

"Is he a good guy?"

"He is. And he loves her."

Mike gave him a sympathetic smile. "Tell her the truth, Richard. She's stronger than you think."

"I know she is." He closed his eyes and put his head in his hands. "What I am to her, is what drinking and using was to me."

"What do you mean?"

"I'm an escape. I'm a distraction from her real life. She's hiding from stuff she doesn't want to face, by being with me." He shook his head. "I've known it for a long time. But I was so happy to be with her that I didn't care."

"Being honest with yourself is never easy, my friend."

"You don't know how badly I want a drink right now," he said, his voice breaking.

Mike stood, patting Richard on the shoulder. "Come on. It's still early. Let's go to the meeting over at the Methodist church."

"Thank you."

-42-

Richard rang the doorbell of the house that had once been his, sweating bullets.

"Relax, man," Mike said.

"Can't do it." He shifted his weight from one foot to the other.

"Breathe."

He'd packed his things that morning, thanking Mike and Ruth for their hospitality. This weekend he would have the girls, at the hotel by the airport where he usually stayed. He guessed at some point he would have to find a permanent address nearby.

Melinda opened the door. "Richard? It's only one. The girls won't even be home for—" She caught sight of Mike, who had stood off to the side. "Mike." Her eyebrows went up.

"Hi, Melinda."

"Come on in." She held the door open. "Can I get you some coffee? Sweet tea?"

"A glass of tea sounds good," Mike said. "Richard?"

"Sure."

Melinda walked into the kitchen. The two men followed her. "Have a seat." She motioned towards the table. She took three glasses out of a cabinet, filling the first one with ice from the dispenser in the refrigerator door, but her hands were shaking. The ice spilled onto the floor.

She set the glass down. "I'm sorry."

Mike stood and put his hands on her shoulders. "Come and sit down, Mel." His voice was gentle.

She sat at the table. Mike began to pick up the ice that had spilled.

Melinda looked at Richard, her eyes already damp. "Just tell me."

"It's lung cancer."

"Shit." She looked down at the surface of the table. "What stage? Is it treatable?"

Richard glanced at Mike, who was setting glasses of sweet tea in front of them. "The doctor's going to do three rounds of chemo and then redo some of the scans."

"Okay. Are you going to have the treatments here in Atlanta, or..."

"Here," he said. "I told you before. I'm back permanently."

"The girls told me you and Natalie were making plans to buy a house."

The mention of her name sent a stabbing pain through his gut. "Well. Those plans have changed."

Melinda's eyes reflected his pain. "I'm so sorry." She put her hand on top of his.

He lifted the glass of tea to his lips and took a long swallow, avoiding her eyes.

"Richard, you wanted to ask Melinda for some flexibility with your custody arrangement," Mike reminded him.

"Of course," Melinda said. "Whatever you need, Richard. I can go to appointments with you if you want."

"That's okay." He held his hand up. "I don't need you to take care of me."

She folded her arms over her chest. "Still as goddamn stubborn as ever."

Anger rose in his throat. "Look. I don't want your pity and I don't need anyone coddling me. I can take care of myself."

"Oh, no doubt about that," Melinda replied, her voice dripping sarcasm.

"I think we're getting off track here," Mike interjected. They both looked away.

"I'm sorry," Melinda said.

"Why don't we start over?" Mike suggested.

Richard cleared his throat, but remained silent.

"Richard?"

"I'm sorry," Richard managed.

"You wanted to ask Melinda something," Mike said.

"I'd like to ask you for some flexibility with our custody arrangement," he said, keeping his voice flat. "After next week, I'll be here in town. I won't be traveling for the foreseeable future."

"What are you asking for?"

"I'd like to be able to see the girls as often as possible. A few days a week. Maybe more."

"That's fine with me."

"But I know the treatment will make me feel tired and sick, so sometimes I may have to change plans at the last minute."

"That's okay, too."

He hadn't expected her to agree so easily. "Thank you."

"You're welcome."

"I'd like to speak to them when they get home from school today. Together. If you don't mind."

"Okay."

"Thank you."

"I wasn't offering help because I pity you, Richard. I'm offering because I care about you."

He looked at her face. It was a fine line between care and pity, he knew. Still, some of the love they had shared was still there.

"I'm sorry." He sighed, running his hand through his hair. "I don't like asking for help."

"No shit."

"Okay," Mike said. "So we're all on the same page, then?"

"Yes," they said in unison.

"Good," he said, his voice cheerful. "We're gonna give it to the Lord, okay?" He took one hand from each of them in his, closing his eyes, and began to pray out loud.

Richard looked at Melinda, who reached for his hand. He gave it to her. Hers was warm and soft. Mike's prayer continued in the background as he and Melinda locked eyes. He wished for the millionth time that he'd been a better husband. A better father. As if she could read his thoughts, she gave his hand a gentle squeeze.

-43-

Natalie opened the door. Richard smiled at her. Her heart sank. *Oh, God.* This was going to be harder than she'd thought. They stared at each other for a moment, not saying anything.

"Are you coming in?"

He glanced over her shoulder towards the hall. "Come on out here for a minute."

"Okay," she said, surprised. She stepped outside, pulling her cardigan around herself. He turned to face her, reaching for her hand. He looked sad, like he already knew what she was going to say.

Natalie shivered. "It's cold out here."

"I'm sorry."

She had to say it. Quickly, like ripping off a Band-Aid. He would be hurt, but she had to believe he would be okay.

"I need to tell you something."

He didn't answer right away. She pulled her hand away from his. The distance between them was growing. He remained silent, his eyes unable to meet hers. The wind blew cold against their faces.

"I have something I need to tell you, too," he said, his voice thick.

She stared at him. "Richard. What's wrong?"

"I got some test results back from the doctor and, well, I've had to change some plans. I have to go back home to Atlanta tomorrow. And I won't be able to come back." His voice was even. Flat.

Test results? She felt a lump of ice form in the pit of her stomach. The cold radiated out slowly to every part of her body. She shivered again. "What do you mean?"

He looked at her, swallowed, and finally spoke. "I have cancer."

"What?"

"I have lung cancer," he said. "They thought it was just pneumonia, but it's lung cancer."

"Oh my god." She pulled the sweater tighter around her body. "What did they say? What are they going to do? Is it—" Richard put his hand up, and she stopped short.

"Listen." He looked away. "I don't want you to worry. I have every intention of beating this thing. It's a disease, it can be treated and put into remission. I've already set up my first chemo appointment in two weeks." He paused. "But I need to be back in Atlanta right away, and I won't be able to travel for a while. I'm going back tomorrow morning."

She realized he was trying not to cry. Her heart ached. She squeezed her eyes shut.

I made the wrong choice, she thought. *I can't break up with him now. He needs me.*

Ben could stay with his girlfriend. They could have a child. They could have a good life. *Oh, God, that hurts too much to think about...*

She opened her eyes, exhaling. "Okay. I'll go with you. Just let me pack a few things. I'll come back for everything else later. Jean will understand. I can—"

He cut her off. "Natalie. No."

"All I have to do is throw some clothes into a suitcase. I'll let the school know Monday there was an emergency."

He shook his head. "No."

Oh. He didn't want her to go. Her eyes misted over. "You're breaking up with me."

"Natalie, please try to understand," he pleaded.

"I do understand." She gave a sad little laugh. "But it hurts."

"I know." His gaze locked with hers, his eyes wet, his voice rough. "I'm so sorry."

"I don't know what to say." Her voice broke.

"Don't say anything. It is what it is."

He took her apartment keys out of his pocket and handed them to her. He held out a shopping bag he'd brought with him. "Here, these things are yours."

Natalie took the bag from him, opening it. Inside was an assortment of her things he must have packed up with his own when he left the townhouse: pajamas, shampoo, toothbrush, books, CDs. At the very bottom was the framed photo of the two of them from their first fishing trip, the one she'd given him for Christmas.

"You don't want to keep this?" She held it up.

"You hang onto it."

She put it back into the bag and set it down. "Are you staying here tonight?"

Richard watched Natalie as she waited for his reply, chewing her bottom lip, her face full of anxiety. It made his stomach hurt.

I shouldn't have told her, he thought for the millionth time since the words had exited his mouth. He had wanted to tell her the truth, he had wanted to set her free, but now everything was harder. She wanted him to stay tonight, but only because she felt sorry for him.

He steeled his heart. "I don't know if that's such a good idea."

The pain in her eyes sliced him in two.

"Well, do you want to?"

He sighed, hearing the hitch in her voice. He was a weak man. A selfish man. He had accepted these things about himself. He could pretend she wanted him as much as he wanted her, that it wasn't pity and guilt driving her desire to spend the night with him. He could keep her away from the life she deserved, away from the husband who still adored her, by feeding into her indecisiveness and fear. But he didn't want her to feel sorry for him. He loved her, oh, God, how he loved her, but he loved her enough to push her away.

"No," he said.

Her face crumpled. "Why are you doing this?"

He feigned ignorance. "What?"

Tears spilled down her face. "Putting up this wall. Talk to me. Please. You're so far away already, and you haven't even left yet."

"I don't know what to—" The words caught in his throat. He squeezed his eyes shut, cleared his throat, and tried again. "I don't know what to say." He looked at her and took her hand. "I don't know how to say goodbye."

"Then don't." She took his other hand, stepping towards him. "Stay with me."

"I can't do that, Natalie."

"Then let me go with you."

"No," he said again.

"Why not?"

Because she didn't deserve to uproot her life to watch him get sicker. Because she had a good man who loved her, who had been patient long enough. Because deep down she knew she wanted to stay. One more push.

"I don't want you to."

Oh, God, the look on her face. She pulled her hands away and crossed her arms over her chest, looking down at her feet.

"I slept with Ben," she said.

She wanted to hurt him back. "It's okay."

"Stop! It's not okay!"

"It is. I'm not upset."

"How can you not be upset?"

His resolve began to crumble. "You know as well as I do that you belong with him. Not with me." He opened his arms. "Come here." She stepped into his embrace. "I want you to go back to your husband."

She pressed her face into his chest. "That's not up to you."

"Look at me. What were you going to tell me tonight, before I told you I was sick?"

"It doesn't matter now."

"Yes it does." He pulled a tissue from his pocket and handed it to her. "You said you had something to tell me."

She wiped her eyes and nose, sniffling.

He put his hand on the side of her face until she turned her eyes back towards his. "You want to stay here. You want to be with him. It's okay, I already knew. I knew it when I asked you to move to Atlanta with me. If I'm being honest, I knew before that."

She drew back from him. "I'm sorry," she whispered.

"Don't be. I've always known you still love him."

"I love you, too." Her eyes filled again. "I don't want you to go."

"I have to go. I have to get better," he said, his voice almost a whisper. "We'll see each other

again someday." He pulled her close and kissed her forehead.

"Here." Her hands reached up to unfasten her necklace.

"No." He put his hand on top of hers. "It's yours. You keep it."

"I can't, Richard. I know it was expensive."

"No. I won't take it back."

"You get to give me back the photo but I can't give you this?"

"Please." His voice cracked. He blinked back tears. "Keep it. Put it away somewhere. And maybe, once in a while, take it out and think of me."

He took her in his arms and kissed her one more time, letting go before he knew it would be impossible. She stood on her porch as he walked down the steps and got into the car, watching him go. He started the engine, trying to look away, trying to fight the urge to go back to her and take her upstairs, to lie down in her bed with her, to stay with her, to let whatever would happen, happen. He squeezed his eyes shut. He had to go.

He took one last glance before pulling away from the curb. Natalie watched him go, her arms crossed tight against her chest, her cheeks glistening with tears as the car rolled down the street. Richard let his own tears flow now that she couldn't see him. The doctors were wrong. It wasn't the cancer that was going to kill him, it was this.

<h1 style="text-align:center">-44-</h1>

On Tuesday night, the doorbell rang. For half a second, her heart leapt, thinking it was Richard. It had all been a mistake. He wasn't sick after all. He'd decided to stay.

She pulled herself back to reality. He'd been gone for two days. He hadn't called. He wasn't coming back.

She had replayed the conversation on the porch a million times in her mind, trying to make sense of it. Richard should have known better than anyone that she didn't need someone else deciding what was best for her. He hadn't even given her a choice.

Why had she let herself get so distracted by her jealousy over Ben that she hadn't answered when he called to tell her he was sick? And how could she face Ben now, knowing she would have tossed him aside so easily if Richard had wanted her to come along?

She opened the front door. Ben smiled. He looked so happy to see her. It made her heart hurt.

"You didn't answer your phone. I was starting to get worried."

"Sorry," she said.

He leaned in to kiss her hello. "Can I come up?" he asked, motioning towards the stairs.

"Sure."

He followed her upstairs. She moved her blankets from the couch to make room for him. He looked

around at the pile of blankets, the half-empty teacup, the discarded tissues on the coffee table. He grabbed her small trash can and began cleaning up the mess.

"Are you feeling okay?"

She sat down. "Just tired."

"I was thinking we could go get some dinner. Or maybe order in?"

"I'm not hungry."

"Maybe later?"

"Maybe."

"I tried calling a couple of times."

"I know. I'm sorry I didn't call you back. Things didn't go exactly the way I expected." Her eyes burned. She shut them, putting her thumb and forefinger over her eyelids.

"Wait, what happened? The last time we talked was Sunday morning. You said you were going to tell him you decided to stay."

She opened her eyes.

"Natalie." He took her hand. "Are you okay?"

"No, I'm not okay."

"Hey, what's wrong? Talk to me, kiddo."

"I can't," she whispered. "I don't want to talk to you about it, Ben. It's not fair."

He smoothed her hair back from her face. "I guess I can understand that."

"Why don't you go home and call me tomorrow?"

"Tell me what happened. Did he get angry, or—"

"Please, Ben."

"Natalie," he said, his voice anxious. "I just want to make sure. Did you break up with him, or not?"

"He broke up with me."

"Oh." He gave her a puzzled look."Same difference, right?"

"No." She shook her head. "Turns out he's sick. Like, really sick. He was in the hospital for

pneumonia and he had all these tests done while he was away and didn't even fucking tell me what was going on. He found out he has cancer. He came here to tell me he was going back to Atlanta and that he didn't want me to come with him and that I should get back together with you." Her throat began to tighten, and she stopped to take a breath.

"Wait...cancer?"

"Lung cancer. He's going for chemo. He says he's going to beat it, but I hear the word cancer, and..." She shivered.

"Right." He swallowed. "Jeez."

"Anyhow, he's gone. He left yesterday and he's not coming back." She put her head in her hands. "And I can't stop crying." A fresh batch of tears welled up.

"Hey. Come here." He wrapped his arms around her. She rested her head on his chest. "It's okay, kid. Let me be here for you." He rubbed her back and she tried to calm her breathing. "I missed you," he said, his voice low as he leaned in to kiss her.

She pulled back. "Sorry. I'm a mess."

They sat in silence for a few minutes.

"You can talk to me," he offered.

She gave a sad laugh. "Not about this."

"Try me."

"I'm worried about him. I mean, it's cancer."

"It's a terrible disease."

"I know." Ben's father had died of cancer when they were still in high school. She didn't remember what kind. One day he had seemed perfectly fine, and then he'd gotten sick. He'd died less than a year after his diagnosis.

"What can I do to help take your mind off it?"

"Nothing. That's the thing, I can't stop thinking about it. When he told me, I felt like..." she hesitated. Admitting it would change everything.

"Like what?"

She shook her head. "Never mind."

"Are you sad because he's sick, or because you still have feelings for him?"

"What?" She sniffled.

"Be honest with me."

"We just broke up. I'm sure you still have feelings for your girlfriend."

"No."

"What?"

"It was nothing compared to what I feel for you."

"I'm sorry I'm not as perfect as you," she muttered, crossing her arms over her chest.

"I didn't say I was perfect."

"You didn't have to."

"Jesus, Natalie."

"Look, I don't want to argue. Maybe you should go."

"Maybe I should." He was pissed. She didn't blame him. This fight didn't even make sense.

"Give me some time, okay?"

"How long?" He stood, putting his jacket back on. "How long am I going to have to wait for you? I thought we decided to get back together."

She sniffled and wiped her eyes. "I think we said we were going to give it some time. That we both still have some things we need to take care of first."

"I thought we were taking care of them!" He scoffed. "I was. I told my brother I was moving out, I broke up with Sarah—" A look of panic crossed his face as he realized he'd said his girlfriend's name out loud.

"Sarah." She narrowed her eyes. "That security guard from your building?" Of course. She sat at a desk in the lobby of Ben's office building and greeted him every morning. Long dark curls, pretty brown eyes. Natalie hadn't met her more than a handful of times, but when she had, she'd noticed the way Sarah looked at Ben, the way she laughed at his jokes. It made sense that he liked her.

"You remember her?"

"I could tell she liked you." She squeezed her eyes shut and shuddered, picturing the two of them together.

"Oh, does it bother you to think about it?" he asked. "Because it's a little hard to have sympathy after what you've put me through for the past year."

"Shut up."

"Give me a break, Natalie."

She didn't respond.

"Did you sleep with him?"

Her jaw dropped. "Oh my god. You're such a jerk."

"I'm a jerk? Seriously?" He gave a humorless laugh. "He breaks up with you, he lies to you, but he gets your tears, and I'm a jerk."

"Stop," she said.

"You know what, Natalie? Maybe I'm tired of being treated like a doormat."

"What?"

"I'm tired of begging you to take me back. I deserve better than this." He zipped his jacket and put his scarf around his neck. "You were the one who walked out on our marriage. You jumped into bed with someone else. You... You think you're the only one who's broken. You broke *me*, Natalie."

His words stabbed her in the chest.

"I knew this whole thing was too good to be true. I knew he would find a way to one-up me, and he did."

"Right. He got cancer on purpose to fuck with you, Ben."

He walked towards the door, then stopped and turned. "You're always going to have one foot out the door with me, aren't you?"

"What?"

"You're going to leave. That's what you do. Things get hard and you take off. Why don't you go ahead and go? Go to Atlanta. I can't do this anymore."

He opened the door and walked down the stairs. As he left, she called after him, "Now who's running away?"

She sat back down on the couch, pulled the blanket over herself, and sobbed.

-45-

Richard sat in an ugly beige recliner in the infusion suite. He had a bag the girls had packed for him with snacks, a blanket, and a book, but he'd brought his work laptop with the intention of keeping himself productive. This would be no big deal. Just some poison being pumped into his body while he was otherwise occupied.

He'd had blood drawn, had his vitals checked, been seen by the oncologist, and filled out about ten million forms. He'd looked out the window while the nurse accessed the port they'd installed under the skin near his collarbone. He'd received the pre-infusion medications to help prevent an allergic reaction.

The waiting had seemed interminable, but now that the nurses were standing in front of him, double-checking the actual chemotherapy medication, he was scared. For the first time, he wished he'd followed their recommendation and brought someone to sit with him.

"We're going to start the infusion now, Richard. I'll stay with you for the first few minutes so we can see how your body responds, and then you can work or watch TV or whatever you'd like to do." His nurse was a guy named Bobby, with scruffy brown hair and tattoos on his arms, wearing navy blue scrubs. He was about Natalie's age, or a little younger. His face reminded Richard of Ben.

Taking a breath, he relived the torment of letting Natalie go as the chemicals began to drip into his bloodstream. It was the right choice, the only choice, and yet he couldn't stop thinking about her blue eyes, her voice, the way her hair smelled after a shower.

"How do you feel?" Bobby asked, jolting him back into the present.

"I'm okay."

"Any itching? Shortness of breath?"

"No."

"Good. Tell me about your family."

"I have two daughters."

"Are you married?"

"Divorced."

"Who lives with you?"

"I'm on my own." He frowned, thinking of Natalie. He'd called her a few days after he got settled in Atlanta, but she hadn't talked very much. *I'm okay,* she'd said, her voice flat. She was hurt, that was obvious, and he hated that he'd had to hurt her. He hoped someday she could forgive him. He hoped she and Ben were doing well. Okay, so maybe that wasn't quite true. But he wanted her to be happy.

"Do you have someone you can call to check in on you?"

"My ex-wife and my friend Mike. Those are my people." Bobby wrote down their names and phone numbers.

His heart began to pound, and he felt a sudden chill. He shivered and reached for the bag with his things inside it.

"Here, let me get that for you." Bobby spread the blanket over him. The warmth made him sleepy. His head swam. "Relax. I know this is nerve-wracking."

"Thank you."

"Let me know if you need anything at all."

"How about a bottle of whiskey?"

Bobby smiled. "I wish."

"Hey," Natalie called from the doorway of Lauren's classroom. It was a Friday afternoon, and the kids had been dismissed. Richard had been gone for two weeks, and she hadn't spoken to Ben since the night they'd argued.

"Hey," her friend said, tilting her head. "How are you?"

She had spent the past two weeks walking around in a fog, going through the motions at work, much the same as she had done a year ago. Trying to stay numb. It was better than feeling. Always had been. But it was harder this time.

"I'm tired of sitting at home feeling sorry for myself. Can we go out tonight?"

Lauren feigned shock and delight. "You don't know how long I've prayed for this day to come."

"Very funny."

Lauren grinned. "Sure. Let's go out. Wear something cute. You're a single girl now."

"Times two," Natalie added. "Who gets dumped by two different guys in the same weekend?" She pointed both thumbs at herself.

"Forget about those two losers. We'll drink margaritas and flirt with cute boys."

"Perfect."

That night, she wore her least frumpy pair of jeans with a black cardigan over a low cut blue camisole. She put on some makeup and did her hair. *Not too bad*, she thought, looking at herself in the mirror.

She took a cab into town and met Lauren at a bar. They sat on stools at a high table near the bar, and Lauren ordered them both margaritas on the rocks.

"To being single." Lauren lifted her glass.

"Ha." Natalie clinked her glass against Lauren's.

"It's not so bad, trust me."

"We'll see." She took a sip of her margarita. "Damn. This is good."

"See? Single life agrees with you."

Natalie laughed.

"This guy keeps looking at you."

"Oh, God," Natalie said. "Which one?"

Lauren glanced over. "At the bar. Third from the left. Dark hair, stubble."

"Is he cute?"

"I'll tell you when to look. Wait." She watched him carefully. "Okay, now."

Natalie turned her head and looked out of the corner of her eye. The guy was looking right at her. He smiled.

"I'm gonna kick your ass."

"Sorry. He's cute though, isn't he?"

He was adorable. A little on the younger side. "He's okay."

"Okay? I mean, maybe he's not Rhett Butler, but..."

"Hi," came a voice from behind them. Natalie glared at Lauren. They turned to look. "I'm Dave." The guy extended his hand. Natalie looked at it, then back at her friend.

"Lauren." She shook Dave's hand. "And this is Natalie."

"Hi, Natalie."

She shook his hand. "Hi."

"This is Tom," he said, indicating the man to his left. Natalie hadn't noticed him until then. Tom was a bit shorter than Dave, skinny and shaggy-haired, with horn rimmed glasses and a kind smile.

A flurry of small talk ensued. Both men were funny and easygoing. Lauren laughed easily at their jokes. Natalie sipped her drink and tried to keep up.

Dave set his beer down on the table next to Natalie's drink. "We were thinking about ordering some food."

Lauren looked at Natalie, who nodded. "Sure, have a seat."

They guys sat at the table and ordered food and another round of drinks for the four of them. Natalie sipped her margarita and picked at the nachos. Fun nights out with friends, cute guys buying her drinks... Maybe single life wouldn't be too bad. She'd never really been single, she realized. Maybe she'd play the field for a while. Sleep with random guys and never call them again.

It seemed odd to her now that she'd only seen a choice between two men. She had never considered the third option of not choosing either one.

A live band started playing at ten, and the music was pretty good, although the volume made conversation a bit more difficult. Tom and Lauren leaned in so they could hear one another.

Dave slid his chair closer to Natalie's and took a sip of his beer. "You have really beautiful eyes, Natalie."

"Thank you."

"I noticed them from over at the bar. But you look sad."

She gave him a weak smile. "It's been a rough couple of weeks."

"I'm sorry to hear it." He glanced at Tom and Lauren. "Want to dance? Take your mind off it?" A handful of other people had made their way to the area in front of where the band played and were moving to the music.

"Sure." She stood up too fast. It made her dizzy. Her stomach turned over. She gripped the chair next to her.

Lauren laughed. "Careful. Those margaritas will sneak up on you."

Dave held out his hand, and Natalie took it.

"Thanks. I haven't been out drinking in a while," she said as they stepped onto the dance floor. A lie, of course, the last time having been a few weeks ago with Ben. Her body flushed with unwelcome warmth at the memory. Ben's lips, his hands, his skin pressed against hers.

She didn't want to think about that night, not now. Dave was a good dancer. He was smart and funny. She could let herself enjoy the attention. Let whatever happened, happen.

The music slowed. Dave put his hands on her hips. He pulled her closer. He was cute. He smelled good. She was enjoying herself...wasn't she?

No. Her stomach lurched. She took a step backwards.

"Hey, are you okay?" Dave asked, stepping back to look at her face. "You don't look so good."

"I'm sorry." She put her hand over her face. "Oh, God." She ran towards the ladies' room and made it in the door just in time to heave into the trash can.

Two women standing by the sink made sounds of concern. "Are you okay?" One of them brought her a handful of paper towels.

"Thank you." She wiped her mouth as another wave of nausea hit, then vomited again. She slumped to the floor and covered her face.

"Here." The other woman held a damp, cool paper towel to Natalie's forehead.

She started to cry.

"Shh, it's okay." The woman patted her shoulder.

"Natalie?" She heard Lauren's voice, then saw her shoes as she approached. "Oh my god."

"She should go home," the first woman said to Lauren. "Probably the flu, poor thing."

"Or one too many drinks," the second one said.

"Thanks for helping her." Lauren knelt down next to Natalie. "What happened?"

"I don't know, I just felt sick all of a sudden." Natalie looked at her. Another wave of tears began. "I don't want to be single."

"I know." Lauren squeezed her hand. "Do you want me to call Ben?"

She shook her head. "I want to go home."

But home was cold, and lonely. She shivered in her bed all night, tossing and turning, unable to sleep more than an hour at a time. In the early morning, she tried to call Ben, but he didn't answer. She hung up before the voicemail tone.

A few hours later, she woke to the sound of her phone ringing.

"Mom?"

"You don't sound too good," Kathy said.

"I'm sick."

"What's wrong?"

"A stomach bug, I guess."

Her mother was silent for a moment. "Do you want me to come over?"

Natalie's eyes filled with tears. "Yes."

Her mom showed up less than an hour later with ginger ale, crackers, and Lipton noodle soup. She put her hand to Natalie's forehead. "No fever," she said. "That's good." She looked at her daughter. "Smells more like a hangover than a stomach bug."

"I guess so."

Kathy chuckled, surprising her. "It's okay. These things happen." She put the soup on the stove to heat.

"This always helped when you were little." She ladled the soup into a mug as Natalie sat on the couch, wrapped in a blanket. Her mother brought her a tray and sat beside her.

"Thank you," Natalie said, taking a sip of ginger ale.

"Better?"

Natalie nodded and tried a small spoonful of soup. The warm, salty comfort helped settle her rolling stomach. "This is good, Mom."

"I was calling earlier to invite you and Richard for dinner next Sunday. For your birthday."

"Or maybe just me."

Kathy gave an exasperated sigh. "Honey, Richard is more than welcome. I know we haven't seen eye to eye about your relationship, but I have accepted it."

"We broke up," Natalie said. "He moved back to Atlanta."

"I had no idea."

"Yeah, well. I'm sure you're happy about that."

"I'm never happy to see you upset, Natalie."

Natalie waited for Kathy to launch into a lecture, but she held back. Instead, she stood. "Why don't I put some fresh sheets on your bed? You can finish your soup and then get washed up."

Her mother changed the sheets and cleaned up the kitchen as Natalie ate a few more spoonfuls of soup and drank the rest of her ginger ale. She took a quick shower and put on clean pajamas. That was enough to exhaust her.

Her mother had made the bed and turned down the covers, and Natalie slid between the cool, clean sheets. Her mother tucked her in and smoothed the hair back from her forehead before sitting next to her on the bed.

Natalie turned to look at her, expectant. Here came the lecture.

Instead, her mother surprised her. "Did I ever tell you I had two miscarriages? In between Lisa and you."

"Mom." Natalie sat up. "No, you never told me."

"Lie down," Kathy said, tucking her back in. "It wasn't something you talked about back then, you know. It just happened. Your father and I were upset, of course, but it was never expected that we would do anything other than accept it and move on." She looked at her daughter. "And of course, we did, and you surprised us a few years later. But..." She paused, her eyes damp. "I should have told you this years ago. It's hard for me to talk about it."

Natalie's heart ached.

"Anyhow, I guess the reason I'm telling you now is because I want you to know that grief, well, it doesn't end, but it changes. It softens, somehow, and even though you don't think you'll be strong enough, you move forward. I lost my babies. I lost my father, and then my mother." Her voice shook on the last word. Natalie's own eyes prickled with tears. "But life is still good. Full of unexpected joys. You're proof of that, Natalie Marie."

"Mom," Natalie whispered. A tear rolled down her cheek.

"Well." Her mother looked at her, a sad smile on her face. "You get some sleep. I hope you know how much I love you."

"I love you too, Mom."

Kathy leaned over and kissed Natalie's forehead.

Richard's phone made an angry buzzing sound. Although he'd set the ringer to silent, the vibration was loud enough to wake him. *Shouldn't be sleeping in the middle of the afternoon, anyhow,* he reminded himself. More than two weeks past his first chemo treatment, he hadn't been able to shake the fatigue that had settled into his bones.

The call went to voicemail before he could reach the phone. Damn. Everything went too fast, or he moved too slow. Maybe both. He stood up, stretched, and walked to the fridge for a Coke. A coffee would do him better, but lately it hadn't been sitting right. Not much had.

He took small, slow sips of the Coke. Anything that went down too fast had a habit of coming right back up. As he put the bottle back into the fridge, the phone buzzed again. He looked at it. *Natalie.*

"Hey, baby girl," he said, warmth spreading through his tired body.

"How are you?" She sounded like she was walking.

He'd spoken to her for a few minutes the day after his first treatment, keeping the call brief. He'd been almost too sick to move. The fatigue and joint pain were overwhelming. The nausea had come later, not as bad as he expected, but it had lingered. "I'll be honest, I've been better."

"Me too."

"It's good to hear your voice. I miss you."

"I miss you, too."

"How's the weather up there?"

"Is this what we're reduced to? Talking about the weather?"

He chuckled.

"Hang on for a sec." She must have covered the phone. He could hear her talking, muffled, and someone else's voice in response. "Okay, sorry about that."

"That's okay. Where are you?" The land line began to ring. "Damn," he said. "Now I need you to hang on."

She laughed. "Okay."

He picked up the phone. It was the hotel's front desk, telling him he had a package in the lobby. "I'm on a call. Can you hold it down there for me? I'll come down later."

"I'm sorry, Mr. Rung, you have to sign for it in person," the woman on the other end said.

"I'll be right down." Turning back to his cell, he told Natalie, "I guess you get to go for a walk with me. Evidently, I have a package in the lobby." He sat on the edge of the bed and put his shoes on.

"Oh yeah? What is it?"

"No idea. I didn't order anything." He grabbed his room key. Out of habit, he looked for his cigarettes before remembering. *Right.*

"Maybe it's flowers from your secret admirer."

"I've got so many of those." He pushed the down button for the elevator. "If I lose you, I'll call you right back."

"You'd better."

He stepped on the elevator and sure enough, his phone dropped the call. He flipped the phone closed, putting it into his pocket. He wondered what she

was doing. God, he missed her. Her curves, her soft skin, her lips, her scent. Her eyes.

The elevator doors opened, and there she was, pulling a suitcase behind her with a smaller bag over her shoulder. Her face lit up.

"Surprise."

He wrapped his arms around her and breathed her in. It was better than he'd remembered. Damn, just...damn.

"You're skinny," she said, her eyes full of concern.

"You're gorgeous," he replied, taking the suitcase from her.

She blushed and stepped onto the elevator. "Which floor?"

"Six."

She pushed the button. The doors shut. Richard stared at her, unsure if she was really there or if he was having a dream. She put her arms around him and kissed him. It felt real enough. Too real. He pulled his face back.

"Wait."

"What?" She gave him a smile, but her lip trembled. He had to be cautious. He'd already hurt her enough.

"Did you run away from home?"

She laughed. "I guess so."

He glanced at the tag on her suitcase, making a face when he saw she'd flown with a rival airline.

"I knew you wouldn't be happy about that."

"I'm offended."

"I was in a hurry."

The doors opened. He used his plastic key card to open the door to his suite. "Probably paid three times as much for your ticket, though."

"I got some money for my birthday to buy myself whatever I wanted. And all I wanted was to see you."

Well... damn. A dopey grin broke out across his face.

"Okay. Next question."

"Oh boy," she said, taking off her jacket and setting it down on a nearby chair. Richard stayed by the door, watching her. She crossed her arms over her chest and raised her eyebrow at him, an amused look on her face.

"Does Ben know where you are?"

She rolled her eyes at the mention of his name. "Nobody knows I'm here. Except you." She put her arms around his neck, kissing him again. *Damn.* He knew he should stop her, but he was weak. He couldn't resist. He put his hands on her hips, pulling her closer.

He turned, pressing her body against the door. His hand slid into her shirt, fingertips drinking in the warm softness of her skin. He moved his lips in slow motion over her neck, listening to the sound of her breath, savoring the taste of her.

When she reached for his belt buckle, he grabbed her hand, forcing himself to take a step back.

"Natalie."

She looked at him, her eyes full of so much anguish he had to look away. "Shit," she whispered.

"Come here." He drew her against him.

"I'm sorry."

"No. Don't be." He led her to the couch. "Here. Let's sit." He handed her a tissue, sitting next to her but leaving some space between them.

"Thank you." She wiped her nose, her voice quivering.

"Talk to me. What's going on with you?"

"I don't know."

"Why are you here?"

"What, I can't just drop in?" Her snarkiness was still intact.

"You can always drop in. But I know something's on your mind."

She paused, taking a breath. "I want to stay. I want to be with you. I bought a one way ticket. I brought everything I need and I'm going to have Jean ship the rest. I'll call Monday and quit my job. And we can get a house, like we talked about. Or not. I don't care. But I want us to be together." She put her hand on his. "This is where I want to be."

He forced a smile. "I wish that were true."

"It *is* true," she insisted.

He looked at her for a long time, not saying anything. He pictured it, the two of them in their own house, laughing as they cooked dinner together. Sitting on the deck with Hannah and Bella. Snuggling in front of the fireplace.

But it wouldn't be like that, not at all. He forced himself to see the reality of what it would be like. Natalie sorting his cancer meds, taking him to his chemo treatments, cleaning up his puke. Watching him die. *No.*

"What about Ben?" he asked, pushing her out of the fantasy.

She pulled her hand back. "We're not together."

"Natalie. Did you give him a chance?"

She rolled her eyes. "He left me."

"Tell me what happened."

"I don't want to talk about it."

He laughed, but his expression turned serious. "Natalie." He cupped her chin. "Try to listen to me. Just because two people care deeply for each other, it doesn't mean they belong together. Not even Rhett Butler and Scarlett O'Hara ended up together, remember? I'm not your happily ever after, sweetheart. Much as I would like to be."

She pouted. "Then what are you?"

He was her whiskey, her cocaine. He was her hiding place from the things she couldn't face. Didn't she see that?

He thought for a minute.

"When you're stuck in a holding pattern, circling for a long time, sometimes you need a safe place to land for a little while. You refuel, you get out and stretch your legs, but then you have to get back up into the air so you can get to your destination. You know?"

She pressed her lips together, nodding. "I'm sorry."

"It's okay," he said.

Her face fell. "Oh, God, it's not okay, is it? I don't know what I was thinking. It's so cold and so lonely at home. Nothing has been right since you left. I wanted to see you. I thought you would be... I mean, I didn't think..." She paused, taking a breath. "I'm so stupid. I didn't think about whether you wanted to see *me*. I forgot. You broke up with *me*." She paused, her voice softening. "Ben's right. I only ever think about myself."

"Of course I wanted to see you. Don't ever think otherwise." He closed his eyes for a few seconds, rubbing them with his thumb and forefinger. "I'm worried about you, baby girl. You get a little self-destructive when you're upset." He pulled her closer, kissing her lips again, less passionate this time. "But I'm happy you're here. No more questions. For now at least."

She snuggled against him. "Thank you."

"Feel better?"

"Yes. How about you?"

"Best I've felt in weeks." He kissed her forehead. "I'm sorry if I gave you the impression I wanted to do anything other than be right here with you."

She groaned. "Why do you have to be so wonderful all the time?"

"I'm not. But I'm glad I have you fooled."

"I miss this."

"Me too." If he sat this close to her for one more minute, it would break him. He stood. "Do you want something to eat? I've been existing on chicken soup and peanut butter and jelly sandwiches, but I can order something..."

"That actually sounds perfect."

Richard walked towards the kitchenette.

"Let me help," she said, following him.

He warmed the soup on the tiny stove while she spread slices of bread with peanut butter and strawberry jam.

"How have you been feeling?"

"A little better each day, but I'm tired all the time. I hate that."

"When's the next treatment?"

"Wednesday. So just when I start feeling better, I get to feel like shit all over again." He smirked. "Can't say I'm looking forward to it, but I've got to try and get rid of this thing, right?"

"Well, you look a little better."

He grinned. "You're a liar. But I don't care."

She poured some Coke over ice for each of them and ladled the hot soup into bowls. They sat at the table.

"This soup is good," she said.

"It's from Miss Ruthie."

"I should have known."

"She's been taking good care of me."

"That's good." Natalie's eyes filled, and she set her spoon down on the table. "But *I* should be the one taking care of you."

"Don't do that," he said. "I'm in good hands. I've got a good team of doctors and nurses taking care of me and I've got Mike and Ruth and I've got my girls, and even Melinda and Neil. And believe it or not, I'm pretty good at taking care of myself."

"I know," she murmured. "But I wish—"

"I know," he said, his voice soft. "Sometimes I wish it, too."

"You look tired."

"Yeah, I think you're right. Let me go close my eyes for a couple minutes."

"Of course," she said. "We can talk later. Go get some rest. I'll clean up."

He kissed the top of her head and went into the bedroom, closing the door behind him.

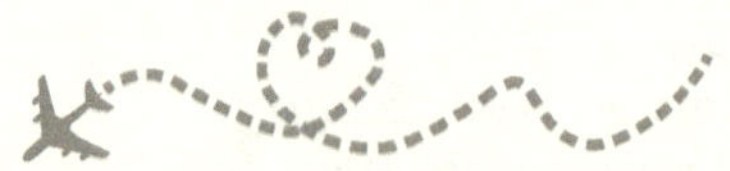

Natalie sat at the table, stirring the soup with her spoon. Richard seemed smaller to her. Not just thinner, but less substantial, as if a strong wind might carry him away. Watching him move around the hotel suite, she'd noticed how the fatigue hung on him like a heavy weight. Even kissing her had seemed to require extra effort on his part. Her heart hurt for him. He was convinced he'd be able to beat the cancer, but what if...

The icy feeling in her belly reappeared, sending shivers throughout her body. She blinked back the tears threatening at the corners of her eyes. Neither of them had eaten more than a few bites. The stomach bug she'd had last week had left her without an appetite, and Richard was probably still queasy from the chemo. What a pair.

She stood, clearing the dishes from the table. In the kitchen, she allowed the tears to fall as she poured the soup back into its container, wrapped

the sandwiches and stuck them in the fridge. After washing the dishes, she sat on the couch, flipping through the channels on the TV. She looked at the clock and wondered how long she should let Richard sleep. *As long as he needs to.*

She yawned. Between working through the sickness last week and traveling today, she was exhausted. Richard had the right idea, lying down for a nap. She opened the bedroom door and tiptoed to the side of the bed. She stared at him for a minute, watching him sleep, wishing their story could have a different ending, knowing it was impossible. She hesitated for a moment, then curled up beside him in the big bed. He smiled in his sleep.

-47-

Richard opened his eyes and looked at the clock next to the bed. He turned his head, content to see Natalie curled up next to him. He snuck out of bed and shut the bathroom door behind him. Mornings always began with a coughing spell. He turned the shower on to muffle the sound, holding a washcloth to his mouth.

He started a pot of coffee in the kitchen, and got back into the bed. Pulling back the sheet, he drank her in with his eyes, pausing to savor every curve of her body. God, she was beautiful, even with her hair in disarray and a little drool on her chin. How he wished he could be a selfish asshole and keep her with him until...well.

He took a breath. He had to send her home to her husband. Ben was a good guy, the poor bastard, and he would give her a good life, if they could both get over themselves and forgive each other.

He stroked her cheek, kissing the top of her head. "Wake up, darlin'."

She glanced at the window. "Oh my god. Is it morning?"

"Looks like it."

"Wow." She sat up and made a face.

"Feeling okay?"

"Yeah, I just feel a little dizzy." She shook her head. "Probably hungry. My stomach's been a mess lately."

"Mine too." A question flickered at the edge of his mind, but he swatted it away. "I made coffee. Do you want some?"

"Yes, please." He left the bedroom and brought two cups back with him.

Natalie took a sip. "Thanks," she said, setting the cup down on the nightstand.

He sat down next to her on the bed.

She glanced at the clock. "Did we really just sleep for like...fourteen hours?"

"Well, I did. Someone cleaned up and did the dishes."

"You know me. I'm a party animal."

He laughed. "I reserved a seat for you on the two o'clock flight."

"Okay," she said, her voice soft.

"I'd love for you to stay, you know that, Natalie."

"No, I get it." She hugged her knees to her chest.

He tucked a lock of her hair behind her ear, his hand lingering on the side of her face. She put her hand on his, giving him a sad smile.

"Tell me what happened with Ben."

She made a face. "I don't want to—"

"Please."

She chewed her bottom lip. "You may not realize this, but you kind of left me in a tailspin."

"I'm so sorry. I never wanted to hurt you."

"Why did you?"

"Now, wait a second," he said, chuckling. "You were going to break up with me. Remember?"

"But I didn't know you were sick. That changed everything."

"It shouldn't have."

"I would have gone with you." Her eyes filled.

"I know."

"And it wouldn't have been the right thing. Okay. I know that, but—"

"What happened with Ben?" he asked, again.

"I fucked everything up. My head was spinning for two days. I couldn't even make sense of it. And then he showed up and we started arguing. It was my fault. It was so stupid, and I couldn't stop myself. He got mad and he left."

Richard shook his head. "My little spitfire."

"It was bad. We both said some terrible things."

"I'm sure none of it was unforgivable."

"I don't know about that." She rolled her eyes. "I think it might be broken beyond repair."

His heart twisted in knots.

"Last weekend I went out with Lauren. It was supposed to be fun. We were going to drink margaritas and hit on cute guys."

"And what happened?"

"I drank margaritas. I met a cute guy. I danced with him. And then I got sick and puked my guts up."

Richard laughed. "Lucky guy."

"Yeah." She gave him a crooked smile. "I wasn't going to tell you about that."

He pressed on. "What was the fight about? With Ben?"

She looked away.

"You fought about me."

"It wasn't just that."

"But that was part of it."

"Yeah." She glanced sideways at him. "I got all mixed up. I thought I made the wrong choice, that I was supposed to go with you. I felt so bad."

"That you didn't go with me?"

"That I wanted to."

"And he's worried you'll leave him again."

"I guess."

"I can understand why he was upset."

"Well, I can, too."

"What else happened?"

"He was dating someone," she said. "It's someone I've met before, and I can't stop seeing them together in my head. He broke up with her, but she works in his building, so I know he still sees her every damn day. It makes me sick to my stomach. I want to stab her. Both of them. And don't tell me it means I'm a total hypocrite, because I already know that."

"Don't shoot me for saying this, but maybe now you can understand how he feels."

"I know," she whispered. "He made sure to throw that in my face. It feels horrible."

He raised his eyebrows. "I remember."

"Right."

"I think you have to let him off the hook for that one."

"Do I?"

"Yes. Nobody's perfect, Natalie."

"You are."

"Not at all." He shook his head. "Far from it. I had a moment," he confessed. "Back in December, when I was in Mississippi. It was late one night, at the motel, Mel and I were walking back from dinner. She and Neil were going through a rough patch. We got to talking, and there were all these feelings, and, I don't know—"

"Did you sleep with her?"

"Natalie." He didn't answer. It would be better to let her believe it had happened.

"Richard?"

"No. But I wanted to," he admitted. "My point is, this is one of those things humans do. We hurt and we seek comfort from the nearest warm body." He put his hand on her knee. "Or we jump on a plane and go find the warm body we want comfort from."

She laughed, then frowned. "I guess you're right."

"It's okay to want to escape for a little while. To numb the pain. But you can't live your whole life that way."

She looked away.

"Have you talked to Ben since the fight?"

"No." She twisted the edge of the blanket in her hand. "I can't talk to him like I can talk to you. It's not the same."

"Maybe you should try," he said. "And maybe you guys should talk to someone."

"You mean, like, therapy?" She wrinkled her nose.

"Might be worth it."

"Maybe."

"You gotta let that shit go, baby girl. Forgive him. He's a good guy, he's loved you since you were just kids, and he's only human. And so are you." He kissed her forehead.

"What about us?"

Oh, God, those eyes. "You and I will always be friends. You can't get rid of me. But I think it should be a while before we see each other again. Let Ben have you back."

"If he still wants me."

"He does." Richard chuckled. "How could anyone not want you?"

"Stop," she said, smiling.

"You two will go the distance. I promise. And you won't even think about me anymore."

"Except, once a year you and I will take a secret fishing trip to the Georgia coast," she said with a wicked grin.

"Are you flirting with me?"

Her eyes twinkled. "I'd never be brave enough to flirt with you."

Richard laughed.

"I guess I should go."

"Breakfast first. Then I'll drive you back to the airport."

"Thank you." She kissed his cheek.

"Have I ever told you you're a fascinating woman?"

"Repeatedly."

"I'm a lucky man, Miss Natalie, to have had you in my life."

"No, I'm the lucky one."

After breakfast, he drove her to the terminal, flashing his ID badge at the security guard to buy them a few extra minutes. He held her close, stroking her hair, kissing the top of her head, willing the tears to remain unshed.

"I want nothing but happiness for you, Natalie. Tell Ben how you feel. Get it all out into the open. Scream if you have to. Go to therapy if you have to. And give him space to get his feelings out. He's been through hell, too."

"Okay."

"Promise?"

"I promise."

"No more running away. It's time to stay and fight for what you want."

"I'll try."

"You're stronger than you think. Whatever comes next, you can handle it."

She nodded.

"And... I know it's not my place, but don't give up on your dream of having a family. Being a parent is the best thing that ever happened to me, and I took it for granted for way too long. Keep trying. You're meant to be a mother."

"You don't believe in meant to be."

"What the hell do I know?" He sighed. "Life is short, baby girl. It goes by so fast and then you realize what…" His voice crumbled. He paused, clearing his throat. "What really matters." Natalie looked up at him, her eyes shining, and he knew she understood.

She sniffled, her lower lip trembling. "This feels like goodbye."

"No. It's not goodbye. But it's time for us both to move on."

"Take care of yourself, okay?"

"I'll do my best."

"I'll see you later." She kissed him, her lips lingering for a few seconds, and then she was gone.

Ben was an idiot. He would let the guy have one more chance, and if Natalie showed up again…

No. He couldn't let himself think about her that way. He pulled away from the curb, swiping at his eyes with the cuff of his sleeve.

The airport was crowded and the lines were long. Natalie finally made her way through security and stopped at a food stand to buy a Coke before settling in a chair near her departure gate. She took a long sip of the soda and grabbed her phone out of her jacket pocket. She stared at it for a long time before flipping it open to make the call.

"Natalie," Ben's voice said at the other end.

"Hi," she said.

"Are you okay?"

"Yeah. How about you?"

"Hanging in there."

"Listen. I'm so sorry, Ben."

"I'm sorry, too."

She chewed on the end of the plastic straw. "I didn't mean to hurt you, but I know I did." She took a breath. "Can you forgive me for making you leave?"

"Can you forgive me for being an asshole?"

"You're not so bad."

"Tell that to my wife," he joked.

"Very funny." The way he said the word *wife* touched her heart. She would fight for him. "Can we get together? Sometime this week?"

"Sure."

"Dinner tomorrow night?"

"I'll bring a pizza."

"No, let's go out somewhere." She knew what would happen if he came to her place, and it would be better if they actually talked this time around. With clothes on.

"Let me know a time and place and I'll meet you there."

"I love you, Ben."

"I love you, too."

She flipped her phone closed and prepared for the journey home.

-48-

The next day, she met Ben for dinner at an Italian restaurant near his house. She spotted Ben sitting on a bench outside. Her face broke into a grin when he turned to look at her. He stood as she approached, smiling but reserved. Hesitant.

"Hey," he said.

"Hi," she replied, opening her arms to hug him. "I missed you."

He pulled her close for a moment, then let go. "You hungry?"

"Starving." She followed him inside. The restaurant was mostly empty, and they ordered right away.

"I'm so sorry, Ben," Natalie finally said after the waitress brought them each a glass of wine. "For everything."

He took a long sip of wine. "Listen. I talked to a lawyer."

Her jaw dropped. "You did?"

He looked down, fidgeting with his fork and spoon. "Yeah. He said our case is pretty straightforward, since we don't have any shared assets anymore, or custody issues. Your car is in my name, but I can sign it over. So as long as we're both in agreement about it, it's just a matter of signing the papers and then waiting for it to be finalized."

Natalie stared at him. She couldn't tell if he was testing her, or if he was serious. "Is that what you

really want?" she asked, her throat so tight she had to work to get the words out.

"I think it's probably for the best. I think we're better off as friends."

She took a deep, steadying breath before opening her mouth to speak. "No."

"No, you don't want to be friends?"

She shook her head. "No. I want to be your wife."

Ben sighed. "Natalie—"

"I want to work on our marriage," she said, interrupting. "Together. If you still want me."

She locked eyes with him. He was doing his best to appear calm, but his eyes were troubled.

"It's too hard. I can't trust you."

That was fair. She took a sip from her wine glass. The waitress brought their plates, but neither of them touched their food.

"Listen. I know I fucked up. I'm sorry. Let me show you that I can do better." She paused. "You're the only one I want. Okay? I don't want to sign any papers. I'm not going anywhere. I'm going to fight for us. Whatever it takes, however long it takes."

Ben's lips curved upwards for a second, but he reset them into a hard line.

"I love you," she said. "Please don't give up on me yet."

"What do you want me to say?"

"Say we still have a chance to work this out."

He shook his head. "I don't know, Natalie. I need some time."

SPRING 2006

-49-

Natalie sank down onto her couch, exhausted. She put her feet up and closed her eyes. Sushi settled down in her lap, purring as Natalie scratched her soft head. Her students had been particularly trying today. She couldn't blame them. The weather was warm, and they would rather be outside playing than stuck in a classroom. After years of teaching, she should have been better prepared. But lately she'd been tired. Defeated. Worn out.

Ben had asked her to give him time, and she had. Almost two months. They spoke often, and sometimes they would grab a bite together, or he would stop by for a beer or a cup of coffee. But they had settled back into the same awkward friendship they'd had a year ago. Only this time, it was Ben who needed time and space to figure things out.

Sometimes it seemed as though they were making progress, but then Ben would pull away and not call her for days. She wasn't sure where she stood with him. The anxiety was eating away at her. She was sick to her stomach all the time. Her sleep was troubled by bad dreams. She wondered if she had done so much damage that things couldn't be fixed. Maybe they should go ahead and get divorced.

At least the cat was content. Sushi had never been much of a lap cat before, but for the past few weeks, anytime Natalie sat down in the apartment, she was right there to snuggle into her lap. Maybe she sensed Natalie's sadness. Natalie was grateful for the comfort.

Reaching for the remote, she turned the TV on for something to take her mind off Ben, and gave the cat a gentle nudge off her lap before she walked into the kitchen. Sushi gave her an annoyed meow, but followed her. As she filled a glass of water, she realized she'd forgotten to pick up something for dinner on her way home, again. She wondered if she had anything edible in her cabinets.

As she stood in her kitchen trying to decide between ramen and cereal—neither of which was appealing—her cell phone rang. Maybe it was Ben and they could meet for dinner.

She walked back into the living room and looked at the display. An Atlanta area code, but she didn't recognize the number. She debated answering. Was it Richard? She hadn't talked to him in a couple of weeks. What if he was calling to tell her things were better? That he'd changed his mind? Or, someone else, calling to tell her he'd taken a turn for the worse?

The call ended before she had a chance to answer. *Shit.* She waited for the voicemail icon to pop up.

"Hi Natalie, it's Hannah. Richard's daughter?" She took a brief pause. "I need to talk to you. Can you call me back?" She left a number.

Natalie's chest filled with ice. If Hannah was calling, it couldn't be good news. Her finger hovered over the button. She took a deep breath and waited for Hannah to answer.

"Natalie?"

"Hannah? What's wrong?"

"My dad is in the hospital," she said, her voice shaking.

"Oh, no."

"He's not doing too well," she continued, crying. Natalie's own eyes began to burn. "He has a fever. He didn't want us to call you, but my mom said you would want to know."

"Is your mom there with you?"

"Yes," Hannah said.

"Let me speak to her." She knew she was the last person in the world Melinda wanted to talk to, but she needed the facts, and she didn't want Hannah to have to be the one to give them to her.

"Hello?"

"Hi, Melinda."

"Hi, Natalie." It was quiet for a moment, and then Melinda gave a short, nervous laugh. "I thought you'd prefer to speak to Hannah. I know this is awkward."

Natalie exhaled. "Yes," she admitted. "She said Richard is in the hospital?"

"He didn't want me to call you," she said. "I know you two aren't together anymore, but I know you still care for one another. We thought you should know what's going on."

Natalie braced herself. "Okay."

"He hasn't been honest with you about how sick he is. He wasn't honest with anyone, but now he's at the point where he can't pretend any longer. He thinks he's doing it out of love, protecting you from being hurt, but I think he just doesn't want to have to be the one to tell you."

Natalie squeezed her eyes shut. "How bad is it?"

"It's bad. Right now, he has an infection, probably just a virus, but between his lungs being compromised and the chemo, he doesn't have the immune system to fight it off. We don't know what's going to happen. But even if he recovers from this, honestly, Natalie, he's at the point now where they can't do anything more for him."

The floor was dropping out from underneath her. She needed to lie down, but she couldn't move. "Um…" She started to speak, but her throat tensed. She swallowed. "He's dying."

"Yes," Melinda said, her voice tender, motherly.

"Where is he now?"

Melinda told her the name of the hospital and the room he was in.

She scribbled it down. "I'll be there as soon as I can."

"Good," Melinda said. "Now, I know it might feel strange, but I don't want you to feel like there's anything between you and me. You're more than welcome here. My daughters adore you. Mike and Ruth do, too. We're all in this together, okay? You're part of the family. Truly."

"Thank you." Natalie tried to breathe. "I'm so sorry, Melinda."

"Me, too." Melinda gave Natalie her number and told her to call back when she knew her travel plans. "And for what it's worth, I don't think you should come alone," she said before they hung up.

Natalie flipped her phone closed and stared at it. Her hands tightened into fists. Her legs shook, her whole body tensed. She wanted to run. To scream.

Richard was dying, and he hadn't told her. He was dying, and he'd pushed her away, pretending he wanted her to be with Ben. *That motherfucker. I hate him,* she thought.

Oh God, but I love him.

She had to go. She would need to book a flight. She hoped she had enough room on her credit card for a last-minute fare. She didn't want to go alone,

but she had to. Nobody would agree to go with her. She got up to find her purse.

Was it fate or coincidence that the phone began to ring again?

"Ben?" she squeaked.

"Hey...what's wrong?"

She couldn't answer. Her body shook with sobs.

"Are you at home?"

"Mm-hmm," she managed.

"I'll be right there."

-50-

They drove through the night. Well, Ben did. Natalie dozed in the passenger seat for most of the trip. At first, she tried to stay awake, playing DJ and helping navigate. But somewhere around the Maryland-Virginia border, she gave up and allowed her exhaustion to take over. Every so often she opened her eyes and caught sight of Ben, his steady hands guiding them on their journey, his faithful heart taking on a task she was certain he never dreamed he'd have to endure.

"Why are you here with me?" she asked him, somewhere around sunrise.

"I thought you were asleep." He glanced in her direction.

She yawned, adjusting her seat to an upright position. "I was."

"Do you want to stop for coffee? I could use a break."

"Coffee sounds good. Food sounds even better."

"Waffle House?" he asked, spotting a billboard.

"Perfect." She yawned. "Where are we?"

"South Carolina."

Natalie looked out the window. "You didn't answer the question."

He laughed. "I said, South Carolina."

"No, the other question."

"What?"

"Why are you here?"

He shrugged, keeping his eyes on the road. "I've been wanting to take the new car on a long road trip."

"Very funny."

"It's true."

"Okay, but seriously. Ben."

"Because you asked me."

"Did I?" She couldn't remember saying the words.

"I think so," he said.

"You could have said no." She put her hand on his knee. "You could have told me to go alone, or take one of my sisters."

He shook his head and put his hand on hers. "I want to be with you."

"For this?"

"For whatever you need. You're still my best friend."

"Thank you." Her heart swelled.

But last night, he had been the one to say he'd go. She knew she hadn't asked him. He'd listened as she relayed what Melinda had told her and said, "I'll go with you." At first she protested, knowing how he felt about Richard, but he insisted. He said they could take his car, waiting while she threw some clothes into a suitcase. They made a brief stop at his house so he could do the same.

Ben pulled the Jeep off the highway at the next exit. They ate waffles and drank coffee at a sticky booth, surrounded by truckers and other road-weary travelers, probably on their way to Disney World, or Miami, or some other fun destination. Not on their way to say goodbye to someone who was dying.

Natalie drove the next shift, letting Ben doze in the passenger seat as she continued south along interstate eighty-five. She fiddled with Ben's car radio and tried not to think too much about what lay ahead.

Ben snored as she drove. She glanced at him, her heart swelling. For all she had put him through, he had every right to leave her on her own—to never speak to her again—yet here he was, by her side. That had to mean something. Didn't it? Then again, his delivering her to Richard's bedside could be the final blow that would destroy whatever was left of their relationship.

They arrived in Atlanta in the early afternoon and checked into a hotel just south of the city, a few miles from the hospital where Richard was. Natalie took a quick shower and changed her clothes while Ben dozed in front of the TV. She told him he didn't have to come to the hospital with her, that he should stay and get some rest, but he insisted he wanted to go.

She got a knot in her stomach as they got into the elevator that would take them to the intensive care floor.

"Oh, God," she muttered.

"What?"

"I don't know. It's too much." She choked back tears, fighting the urge to run back to the parking garage.

"Breathe, Nat. You'll be fine." He squeezed her hand. "Don't be scared."

The elevator door opened. Hannah was waiting for them and gave Natalie a warm hug.

"I'm so glad you're here," she said without letting go.

"Thank you," Natalie's eyes filled. She squeezed them shut, not wanting to cry in front of Hannah. She introduced Ben, who shook Hannah's hand.

"It's good to meet you, Ben." She looked back at Natalie. "You look nervous."

"A little."

Ben laughed. "A lot."

"Don't be, it's fine. My mom is anxious to meet you. I promise, she's nice."

"How's your dad?"

Hannah's face was sad. "It's still not looking good, but he's hanging on. The pain medication makes him pretty sleepy, so he's out of it a lot of the time. But talk to him. He'll be glad to hear your voice."

She led them down the hall and into a large waiting area. Bella was curled up on a wide chair with a video game device in her hands. The man and woman next to her stood as Hannah approached. Bella leapt up to give Natalie a hug.

"Natalie, Ben," Hannah said, "this is my mom, Melinda, my stepdad, Neil, and you know Bella." They shook hands all around. "And Mike will be here later, right, Mom?"

"Yes. It's so nice to finally meet you, Natalie. You too, Ben." She took Natalie's hand. "Let's you and me go talk for a minute, before you go in to see Richard." Her eyes were kind, her honeyed voice enveloping Natalie in comfortable warmth.

Natalie glanced at Ben. "I'll be okay," he said. He sat down next to Bella. "Is that the PSP? What are you playing?" Bella showed him the screen.

"I'll go sit with Dad until you're ready to come in," Hannah said to Natalie.

"She's barely left his side," Melinda said as she watched Hannah walk away. "I had to beg her to go home last night and get some rest, bless her heart."

Melinda led Natalie to a far corner of the room. "Have a seat."

Natalie obeyed. Melinda settled in the chair next to hers.

"How was your drive?"

"Long," Natalie said.

"I bet." She smiled. "You look nervous. I know it must feel strange, being here with me. I'm sorry about that. It's strange for me, too, I'll be honest. But I'm glad you came. It will be good for Richard to see you."

"Thank you."

"How are you doing?" Her concern seemed genuine.

"Honestly, I don't know. Exhausted. My head is spinning."

Melinda gave her a sympathetic nod.

"I saw him in March, and he was okay. Sick, obviously, but not like this." She took a breath and continued. "I talked to him after he had the second chemo. He called me and said he might have to take leave from work and he wasn't sure where he'd be staying. He was making these terrible jokes about being homeless." She shook her head. "But he seemed okay. I can't believe things went downhill so fast... I can't believe he didn't tell me."

"It's okay to be mad. He was dishonest with you."

"I'm mad at myself, too. I feel so stupid. I feel like I should have realized."

"I know. Me, too. I mean, I'm a nurse. I should have seen it." She gave a short, humorless laugh. "But he's known from the beginning this was terminal. He kept it from everyone. They gave him six months. He insisted on trying chemo, even though they told him he would be doing more harm than good. He was sure he was going to beat the odds."

"That sounds like him."

"He went for tests to see how well he was responding to the treatment, but the scans clearly showed the chemo wasn't working," Melinda said, looking toward the window. "He met with the oncologist, and she showed him the tumors hadn't budged. This kind of cancer is aggressive, and it's sneaky. By the time someone is diagnosed, it's almost always too late to treat." She looked sad. "Anyway. He started feeling sick while he was at the appointment, and they admitted him. The hospital called me after he lost consciousness. He had listed me as next of kin. Natalie, I had no idea how sick he was until I got here and I saw him."

Natalie could see the tears in the corners of Melinda's pale eyes. She wrapped her arms across her chest and shivered. "How is he now?"

"He's stable, but the fever won't quit. He's on antibiotics and some pretty strong pain meds. He's been in and out for the past few days. He gets confused about where he is and when it is. He tries to refuse the pain meds because he's in recovery. He's so goddamn stubborn. I'm sure you know." She glanced at Natalie, who rolled her eyes in agreement. "I'm so sorry, Natalie."

"I'm sorry, too."

"Mike and I have been alternating spending nights here with him. We didn't want him to be alone, you know, in case."

"Right."

"I was mad he left you and didn't tell you how sick he was, but he told me you and your husband are trying to work on things." She nodded in Ben's direction. "He didn't want to get in the way."

"Still. I wish he would have told me."

"Can I give you a hug?" Melinda asked, getting out of her chair.

Natalie stood and allowed herself to be embraced by the tiny woman. The strength of her hug was surprising. Natalie melted into it, allowing herself to be comforted.

"Okay, darlin', I know you didn't drive all this way to sit here and talk to me," Melinda said, pulling back from their embrace. "But I want you to be prepared for when you go in to see him. Cancer isn't pretty. Richard doesn't look like himself. He's thin and frail. He sleeps most of the time. He's on an oxygen mask. I didn't tell him you were coming. He didn't want me to call you, but I have a feeling that's because he wanted you to remember him the way he was, not like this." She paused. "My guess is he'll be happy to see you. He's still crazy about you, you know that."

Natalie smiled. "I know."

"Are you ready?"

"Yes. Not really, but…"

"Follow me." They walked back through the waiting area. Ben sat next to Bella, their heads huddled together over the tiny video game screen. He was playing the game as she kept watch, offering instructions. Neil sat across from them, reading the newspaper.

Natalie put her hand on Ben's shoulder. "You've got a friend for life now, Bella," Natalie joked. Bella grinned, but neither of them looked up.

"You going in now?" Ben asked.

"Yes."

"Hang on, Bella." He paused the game and looked up at her. "Do you want me to go in with you?"

"No."

"You okay?"

She shook her head.

He gave her hand a gentle squeeze. "I'll be right here."

Melinda led her through the swinging doors and down a short hallway, pointing out the ladies' room on the way. Near the nurses' station was a small room with the curtain drawn across, Richard's name written in dry erase marker on a small whiteboard at the entrance. Melinda stepped into the room and motioned for Natalie to follow. Hannah stood up from the chair when she saw them, letting go of her father's hand.

"I'll be back, Daddy." She bent to kiss his forehead.

The late afternoon sunshine streamed in through the window, casting diagonal beams of light across the narrow hospital bed. It seemed impossible that on this perfect, summer-like day, Richard could be dying.

Melinda was right. Richard didn't look at all like himself. What had happened to that dark, handsome man she'd met in the park? The man she'd played in the ocean with, the man who'd taught her to fish, the man she'd made love with? He was shrunken, faded, curled on his side with a pillow behind his back, looking like an old man and a little boy all at once. His hair, what was left of it, was shorter, thinner, and mostly gray. An oxygen mask covered his mouth and nose. His breathing was ragged. IV tubing and wires connected him to machines beside his bed. It hurt to look at him.

Melinda looked him over and then looked at Natalie. She put a hand on her shoulder.

"We'll leave you two alone," she said. "If you need anything at all, call my cell. I'll send Hannah back in to check on you in a little while."

"Okay." She held back her tears. "And thank you."

The tears began to flow as they left the room.

-51-

" Hey, sleepyhead."

Richard felt a warm hand on his forearm. The effort involved in opening his eyes was almost unbearable, but it would be worth it to see the face that belonged to that hand, that voice. He could make out her silhouette, perched on the bed alongside him. The afternoon sunlight illuminated her golden hair.

Her blue eyes came into focus. They were shiny, pink where they should have been white.

"Hi." She smiled as she saw his eyes open.

He smiled back at her. He reached for the oxygen mask and pulled it below his mouth. "I told them not to call you."

"I know."

He took both her hands in his. "I'm glad they did."

"Me, too." She bent to kiss his lips. "I missed you." Her eyes spilled over with tears.

He took her into his arms, shifting his body to make room for hers in the narrow bed. The effort was excruciating. She curled up alongside him, burying her head in his shoulder. He smoothed her hair back from her face and kissed her forehead.

"I know, baby girl."

"I'm so sorry," she sobbed.

"It's okay. Shh."

She tried breathing normally. It took some effort. Once she had it under control, she sat up, looking at his face. "I love you, Richard."

"I love you, too. So much."

"Why didn't you tell me?"

"I told you before, I don't know how to say goodbye." He put the oxygen back over his face for a moment, taking a breath.

Her eyes filled up again as she watched. "I hate that we can't be together."

"That was never in the cards for us anyhow, baby girl. You belong to someone else. You always have. I was too stubborn to see it. So were you. But I'm glad I had a chance to love you for a little while."

She looked away for a second. "Ben's here with me," she said. "He's playing video games with Bella in the waiting room."

"Good. I'm glad you're not alone."

She wiped her eyes.

"Things are okay with you two?"

"I don't know."

"But you're trying?"

"We're still stuck in a holding pattern."

"He came with you. That's something. Unless he wants to finally have a chance to punch me in the face."

She laughed.

"It's good to see you smile," he said. "He'll come around."

"We'll see."

He put his hand on her belly. "Does he know about this?"

She stared at him in disbelief. "What?"

"What?" he repeated, mocking her tone. "Does he know?"

"Richard..." Her cheeks flushed. "I haven't even... I mean, I don't even know what you're—"

"Sure you do."

"How do *you* know?"

What was it? He couldn't explain it. Something about the curve of her nose, or maybe the roundness of her breasts. Her skin was glowing. But it wasn't just that.

The possibility had flitted across his mind the last time he'd seen her, exhausted, weepy, no appetite. He had pushed it away, not wanting to see it. This time, the knowing settled upon him, gentle and solid. Comfortable, like the sturdy warmth of a handmade quilt. He could almost see the tiny life inside her, growing, content, healthy, safe. Loved.

"It's going to work out this time," he said. "Don't be afraid."

Her eyes filled again.

"You're going to be fine." His palm was still pressed against the curve of her abdomen. "This is one lucky kid." He put the mask back over his face and took a few breaths.

Her bottom lip quivered. "Are you mad?"

He gave a gentle laugh, moving the oxygen away again. "I couldn't be happier for you." He took her hand again. "This is what you were meant for. I have someplace else to go."

"I'm scared." She frowned. "And I don't want you to go."

"You've got this. I'll be around," he said, motioning towards the air above them. "I promise."

A nurse walked into the room. "You're awake," she said, surprised.

"Y'all haven't seen the last of me yet."

Natalie stood and took a step back as the nurse looked him over, listening to his chest, checking his blood pressure and temperature.

"Fever's down." She placed the mask back over his face. "Oxygen level is good." She looked at Natalie. "You must be his good luck charm."

"She is," he said, his voice muffled by the mask.

"I'll let the rest of your family know you're awake," she said.

"Thank you."

The nurse left the room.

He pulled the mask down. "I need to rest now," he said, closing his eyes. "Will you stay with me for a while?"

"Yes." She sat in the chair, took both his hands and rested her head next to his on the pillow. "Is this okay?"

He nodded and put the oxygen back on his face. She was here, next to him. For this one moment, everything was okay.

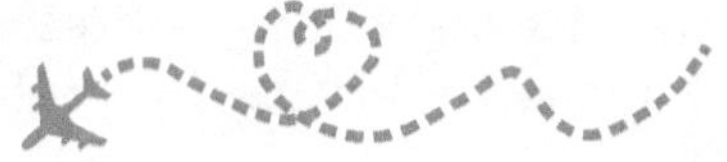

"Hey, Natalie." The hushed voice came from right beside her ear. She must have fallen asleep. She turned her head and looked at Hannah. "Ben's on his way in."

Natalie looked at Richard. He was still sleeping, but his expression was more peaceful.

"Thanks." She straightened up.

"The nurse said he woke up for a little while."

"His fever's down, too." She looked at him. "What time is it?" she asked Hannah, yawning, as Ben walked in the door.

"After five."

"Were you asleep?" Ben asked.

"Yeah," she admitted.

"It's okay," he said. "I think I dozed off too."

"He was snoring in the waiting room." Hannah said with a laugh.

"Melinda asked if we wanted to get dinner together, but I think we both need some sleep. We can come back again tomorrow."

Natalie turned back to look at Richard.

"Let him rest." Ben took her hand.

"I want to say goodbye."

"It's okay," Hannah said. "They're going to wake him for supper, anyhow."

Natalie bent to kiss Richard's forehead, and he stirred and opened his eyes. "Hey," she said. "I've got to go. I'll be back tomorrow morning, okay?"

He took her hand and squeezed it. He shifted his eyes in Hannah's direction and took the oxygen off his face. "Hey, princess."

"You look better, Dad." She bent to kiss his forehead.

Richard looked at Ben. He put his hand out. "Take care of her," he said, his voice a whisper.

Ben hesitated before taking a step towards the bed. He shook Richard's hand with both of his own. "I will, Richard."

"You're a good man, Ben."

"You, too."

Richard looked back at Natalie. "Don't give him any more shit."

"Funny." She rolled her eyes.

"Come here," he said. She bent down until her face was an inch from his. Ben took a step backwards, looking away. "Tell him," he whispered.

"Okay," she whispered back. She brushed his cheek with her lips. "I'll be back tomorrow morning." She squeezed his hand.

She gave Hannah a hug. "See you tomorrow."

"I'll be here."

Ben put his arm around her waist as they walked out of the room. "Thanks," she said.

"For what?"

"For being nice. I know that wasn't easy."

Mike showed up in the hallway with Melinda as they were leaving. "Natalie." He grinned, scooping her up in a big bear hug. "You look good."

"I'm a mess," she said, a fresh batch of tears spilling over. "It's good to see you."

He offered his hand to Ben. "Hi, I'm Mike."

"I'm sorry," Natalie said. "Mike, this is Ben. My husband."

"Ben. I've heard a lot about you. Good to finally meet you." He grinned.

"You too, Mike."

"He's doing better," Melinda said to Natalie.

"Yes."

"That's because of you. Thank you."

Natalie smiled.

"Will you come by the house early tomorrow morning? Mike and his wife will both be there. We'll have coffee and food."

"Is that okay?" she asked Ben. He nodded.

"Around eight? Unless you want to come earlier," Melinda said. "Just give me a call." She put her arms around Natalie, and hugged Ben, too. "Thank you so much for being here."

-52-

The ride back to the hotel was quiet. "Do you want to hit a drive thru?" Ben asked. "What do you want to get?"

"Anything's fine." She stared out the window at the bland suburban landscape.

"Are you okay?"

She looked at him, one eyebrow raised.

"Wrong question. How about this—what kind of milkshake do you want with your cheeseburger?"

She smiled. "Chocolate."

"You got it."

"Let's eat in someplace, that way the hotel room doesn't smell like food all night."

"Whatever you want."

"Thanks, Ben."

"It's no problem."

"No, I mean it. Thanks for being here with me." She put her hand on his knee.

"I'll admit it, I looked over at you sleeping a couple of times and almost turned the car around."

"I wouldn't have blamed you."

He glanced at her. "You didn't have a chance to say goodbye when your Nana died. And I know that was mostly my fault. I may not like the guy, but I wanted you to have a chance this time."

Natalie's lower lip quivered. "Thank you."

After dinner, they went back to the room. Ben looked tired enough to drop. He put his car keys down on the dresser. He took off his t-shirt, sat down on the bed, and kicked off his shoes. Natalie sank into a chair and put her face in her hands.

"You okay?"

"I've been better."

"Come here," he said, standing. He wrapped his arms around her. She buried her face against his bare chest. He kissed the top of her head. She looked up at him. He lowered his lips towards hers.

Natalie put her hands on the back of his neck, pulling him closer. His breath was warm against her lips. He slid her shirt up over her head, unfastening her bra, kissing her shoulders, her neck.

"Is this okay?" he murmured.

"Yes." She unzipped his jeans and pushed him back onto the bed before removing the rest of her own clothes.

She had craved the warmth of Ben's skin against hers for so long. She pressed her body against his, lacing their fingers together, pinning his arms to the bed. Her lips moved against his, wanting to drink him in, engulf him. She moved her lips down his neck, planting soft kisses on his chest, his belly, taking him into her mouth. He gave a soft groan. She kissed her way back up his body, making her way back to his lips. Ben rolled her onto her back, kissing her neck, her breasts. Their bodies joined together, a tangle of lips and hands and legs and warm breath.

She didn't dare to hope this was anything more than his attempt to comfort her, and she didn't care. She surrendered to her senses, savoring the moment, banishing any unwelcome questions that threatened to disrupt it.

Afterwards, he kissed her forehead and pulled away. "I'm going to get a shower." He stood up,

shutting the bathroom door behind him before she could object.

Her eyes stung. He'd never hopped up like that afterwards. Not ever.

He hates me.

She allowed only two tears to fall before taking a breath and forcing them back. She couldn't cry for Ben anymore. At least they still had whatever this was.

She felt a tightening in her lower abdomen. It wasn't painful, but it was uncomfortable. Unsettling. Her mouth went dry. She got up to get some water from the sink.

Looking at her naked body in the mirror, she put her hand on her belly, thinking about what Richard had said to her earlier, at the hospital. His hand on her abdomen, his raspy voice telling her it was going to work out. Those words hadn't stopped echoing in her mind. It was still unimaginable that he was right.

But she knew he was.

She'd suspected it for weeks. She couldn't remember when her last period had been. January, or was it December? She'd always been irregular, skipping several months at a time. She'd given up trying to keep track. But the fatigue, the nausea, all the little things she'd pushed out of her mind, chalked up to stress... she had to admit to herself that she couldn't dismiss the possibility.

She hadn't confirmed it with a test. What was the point? There would be no need to do anything about it. Not really. She would wait for the miscarriage to happen—which it would, she was certain—and keep it to herself. No reason to tell anyone. The loss would hurt less if nobody else knew. No point telling Ben, who was still undecided about their future but would certainly feel obligated to get back together if he found out. And for what? For a pregnancy she would lose, and they would end up right back where they'd been when Nana died. She didn't want that. She wanted him to want her, not the baby.

The baby. She squeezed her eyes shut, pushing that word out of her mind.

Her abdomen tightened again. A mild cramp followed. It felt familiar—too familiar. *No.* Not here, not now. Her heart began to pound. The shower turned off.

She knocked on the bathroom door. "Ben?"

"Come in." She opened the door. Ben stepped out of the shower, dripping wet, wrapping a towel around his waist. His face reflected her worry. "What's wrong?"

"I don't feel so good. I feel like...um...it was probably the cheeseburger, I don't know. Maybe food poisoning. I think we should..." She put her hand on her belly, wincing.

He'd seen that look on her face enough times to throw him into action. "Let's go back to the hospital and get you checked out."

He drove her back to the same hospital where Richard was. She watched him out of the corner of her eye as he drove, wondering what he was thinking. Did he believe her story about food poisoning? Or did he suspect she was hiding something?

He parked the car while she went inside. The waiting room was empty, and she was shown to a room right away.

"I think I'm having a miscarriage," she told the nurse, her voice soft.

"How far along are you?"

She shook her head. "I don't know," she said, feeling like an idiot. "I'm not even a hundred percent sure if I am."

"Pregnant?"

"Yeah."

"One way to find out." The nurse handed her a specimen cup. "The bathroom's right through here." Natalie followed her through the doorway.

Afterwards, she came back to the room and gave the sample to the nurse. She dipped a test strip into the cup and set it down on a paper towel. "Let's get some blood, too," she said as Natalie sat back down on the gurney. Natalie watched as vial after vial of blood flowed into different colored test tubes.

"How soon will you know?"

"I already know." She held up the test strip for Natalie to see. "Positive."

Natalie took a deep breath.

"Are you bleeding?"

"Not yet."

"Having cramps?"

"Yes. My husband and I just, um, we had sex and then afterwards I felt the cramping start."

"When was your last period?"

"I wish I knew," she said. "January, maybe. It's never been regular."

"Why do you think you're miscarrying?"

"It feels like it always does."

"You've miscarried before?"

"Five times."

"I'm so sorry."

She closed her eyes as the tears threatened. She wouldn't cry over this. Not here. "The last time, I lost a lot of blood. I needed a D & C."

"You did the right thing then, coming in." The nurse took a detailed medical history, typing

everything into a computer. She checked Natalie's blood pressure, pulse and temperature.

The ER doctor came in and introduced herself.

"Possible miscarriage," the nurse said.

"How far along are you?" the doctor asked.

"I'm not sure."

"If you are miscarrying, you understand there's not much we can do," the doctor said.

"I know."

"We'll take a look at your blood work and get an ultrasound scan. Okay?"

"Okay."

"Your husband's in the waiting area," the nurse said. "Do you want us to send him in?"

"Oh." *Shit.* "Yes. Thank you."

Ben's face was full of anxiety when he walked in. "Are you okay?"

"I don't know yet," she said. "They did some tests."

She had to tell him what she knew. But she couldn't. Not now, when it was already too late. This would devastate him. She thought of the way his face looked when the last doctor told them to stop trying. How he'd turned away to hide his tears from her.

Ben pulled up a chair. "So now we wait?"

"I guess so."

He turned on a small TV in the corner Natalie hadn't noticed. The distraction was a welcome one.

She had to tell him.

"Ben."

He turned and smiled at her, reaching for her hand. "You okay?"

She lost her nerve. "I feel better." It wasn't a lie. The cramping had stopped. "Maybe we can go."

"We should wait for your test results, just in case, right?"

"I guess so."

A few minutes later, she tried again. "Maybe you should wait outside for me. I'm sure it won't be long."

He squeezed her hand. "It's okay. I'll stay with you."

After what seemed like hours of waiting, a tech came into the room with a sonogram machine. She dimmed the lights, applied some blue gel to Natalie's abdomen, pressed down with the transducer and pointed to the screen.

"There," she said, her pink fingernail tapping the fuzzy image. "Baby looks healthy. Heartbeat's nice and strong. Fluid's a little on the low side of normal, but you're probably a little dehydrated. Look, he's sucking his thumb," she said. "Or she. A little too soon to tell." She turned and smiled at them.

Natalie lay on the gurney, one hand tucked behind her head to prop it up. She glanced at Ben, sitting beside her, silent. He was staring at the image on the screen, his brow furrowed.

"So everything is...okay?" she asked.

"The doctor will look at the scan and double check everything with your blood work, but it looks good to me. Measuring just over fourteen weeks."

She pressed a button and handed Natalie a picture. "Congratulations." She shut off the machine, flipped the light back on and used a towel to wipe the gel off Natalie's belly before stepping out of the room.

Natalie stared at the picture in her trembling hand. She had forgotten how to breathe.

"Ben?"

He didn't reply. She turned her head towards him. He stared at her, his face unreadable.

The nurse walked in with a big white styrofoam cup. "Here's some water for you." She handed it to Natalie. "How are you feeling?"

"A little better, thanks." Natalie sat up.

"No more cramping?"

"No."

"Holler if you need anything. The doctor will be in to talk with you and then we'll get you on your way."

"Thanks." She sucked a long gulp of the icy water through the plastic straw.

Ben sat in the chair, putting his head in his hands. He made a quiet sound halfway between a cough and a sigh. "Natalie."

"Yeah." It came out as a whisper.

"Did you know?" He looked at her face.

Natalie shrugged, looking away. What explanation could she give?

"Why didn't you tell me?" he asked. His tone was gentle.

"I don't know," she whispered, meeting his eyes.

Ben squeezed his eyes shut, stroking the stubble on his chin. He looked exhausted. When was the last time the man had slept? Thursday?

She took another sip of the water. The icy cold numbed her insides. She watched his face, trying to read his thoughts.

"Ben?"

"Yeah," he croaked.

"Are you okay?"

"Ask me later."

The doctor came into the room, followed by the nurse. "Mrs. Kelly." She spoke quickly, looking at the chart. "So, everything looks good with your scan. Baby looks healthy, and all your blood tests came back in the normal range, so we don't think

you're miscarrying. You probably had some minor contractions. Very common after intercourse. A lot of women don't even feel them at this stage of pregnancy. With your history, you definitely did the right thing in getting checked out." The doctor handed her some pamphlets about nutrition and a sample of prenatal vitamins. "I know you're in town visiting family, so I encourage you to follow up with your OB as soon as you get home. In the meantime, rest, lots of fluids, vitamins, and you should be fine. You're into your second trimester, so take a nice deep breath and relax, okay? Everything looks good and the baby is doing just fine. And congratulations to you both." The doctor patted her arm and shook Ben's hand.

"Thank you," Natalie said.

"Thank you, doctor," Ben said as she walked out of the room.

They stared at each other.

"I'll go get dressed." Natalie took her clothes into the bathroom and changed, dropping the hospital gown to the floor. The pain had subsided, and now she felt fine. Dazed, exhausted, but otherwise fine. She put her hand on her abdomen for a second, then snatched it away.

She squeezed her eyes shut. *This is too much. Why now?* The timing couldn't be worse. She and Ben weren't together. He was too afraid to try. Sure, he'd said some nice things to her on this trip, but they were far from working things out. Maybe they never would.

She opened her eyes, looking at her reflection in the mirror. Was it possible that as Richard lay dying in a hospital bed only a few floors above them, her life was finally beginning? The unfairness of it was impossible to bear. She wished for a way to sneak out of the bathroom without Ben seeing. She could go up to the ICU, and...

No, wait. I can't run from this.

I don't want to run from this.

She took a deep breath and put her hand back on her lower abdomen. For a second, she let herself imagine a baby, with chubby cheeks and dimpled hands. If she was certain about anything, it was this: she would be a good mother to this child.

It's going to work out this time.

And if it didn't work out... Well, it would be terrible. But she was strong. She would survive this loss. She would survive without Ben. She had survived everything life had thrown at her so far.

They drove back to the hotel in silence. Natalie clutched the picture in her hand, glancing at it every few seconds. The curve of a forehead, the tiny tip of a nose. It made her heart skip a beat.

"Ben?"

He cleared his throat. "Yeah."

"Talk to me. Please."

"I'm trying to figure out what I want to say." His voice had an edge.

They parked the car and walked into the hotel room. Ben set his car keys on the dresser, sat on the bed, and kicked off his shoes, as he had earlier. This time, he didn't reach for her.

"I'm so tired," he said. "I think we should try and get some sleep." It was after two in the morning.

Natalie sat in the chair opposite him, still sipping water from the styrofoam cup the nurse had given her. "I guess so." She looked at him, watching his face for any hint of emotion.

He squeezed his eyes shut and pinched the bridge of his nose. "Natalie," he said, his voice almost a whisper.

"Uh huh."

"I need you to tell me what the hell is going on."

She looked at him, puzzled. "I don't know what you mean."

"What exactly did we just find out?"

She still couldn't say the words. "Well, they did some tests, and it looks like, um ..." She held up the picture.

"I know what the tests said. But..." He was quiet for a minute.

Natalie waited, thinking of dozens of possible responses, knowing none of them were what Ben wanted to hear. She didn't want to make it worse. "I know you're angry."

"I'm not angry." He took a breath. "Listen. I love you more than anything in this world. You know that, right? I mean, I wouldn't be here if I didn't. That's why I came over to your apartment last night. God, was that only last night?" He ran his hands over his face. "I wanted to tell you I want to be with you. I'm tired of pretending that I don't. I didn't tell you, because everything happened so fast with getting on the road and coming down here. I knew you had other things on your mind. But I should have told you."

He looked at her. He was saying what she had been waiting to hear, but now she couldn't trust it. She waited for the *but* she was sure would come next.

"Some people think it would be crazy for us to get back together, after everything. They'd think it was even crazier for me to come to Atlanta with you, but it made sense to me. Do you know what I'm saying? I listened to those people for too long. I don't care anymore. It doesn't matter what anyone else thinks. I would do anything for you. I would do anything you asked, because it's *you*. I've made

so many mistakes, God knows, there's things I wish I could take back, but the one thing that's never changed is I love you. More than life."

Her eyes filled with tears. "I love you, too. But don't say that because you feel like you have to."

"That's not it." He continued. "They said fourteen weeks. I keep doing the math in my head and that puts us back to the first weekend in February, the night we went to the bar." His words tumbled out in a rush. "Look. I don't know why you didn't tell me. So I have to ask. I mean, I don't want to ask, but you understand why I have to, right? Because I'm pretty sure there's a chance, even if it's a small chance, that—" He hesitated, lowering his voice. "Shit, when did my life become this fucking soap opera?" he said. "The truth is, I'm too scared of the answer."

Oh. She realized where his mind had gone when he'd heard the test results. She got up from her chair and walked to the bed, standing in front of him. "Ben—"

He kept talking, as if he was afraid to stop, afraid of what she would say next. "I don't care if it's mine or not. I mean, I should care. But it's yours, so I'm going to love it no matter what. I'll be there for you. Both of you. I always will." He sniffled, his eyes shining.

Her heart twisted in her chest. "Ben. Listen—"

He gave a short laugh. "I mean, I guess that makes me the biggest stooge on the planet, right? But it doesn't matter. I don't want to live without you. I've tried. I can't. I don't care, and anyway, he's—"

"Stop," she said, putting her finger over his lips. "Ben. Please. Look at me." He looked up at her. "It's yours."

His chin trembled like a little boy's. "How do you know?"

"Because I know." She started to cry. "Please trust me. It's yours." She put his hand on her abdomen, holding it there with both of hers. "There's no chance it isn't. I promise. Okay?"

"It's mine." His eyes filled with tears. "Is this for real? I mean..." His voice broke. He took the picture from her hand and looked at it. "Look at that," he whispered. He traced the outline of his child's face with his fingertip. "Why didn't you tell me?"

She watched him as he gazed at the fuzzy image of his child's face, the corners of his lips curving into a smile.

"Because if it doesn't work out, you won't want me."

"Natalie." He set the photo on the bed and put his hands on her shoulders, looking into her eyes. "I'll always want you."

"Are you sure?"

He kissed her. "I've never been more sure of anything." He stared at her. "Is this really happening? You're pregnant."

"It doesn't feel real." Tears spilled down her cheeks.

He lifted the bottom of her shirt, kissing the spot right below her belly button. "Hey, little baby," he said, laughing and crying at the same time. At the word *baby*, Natalie began sobbing. Ben stood, took her in his arms and wept along with her.

"It's okay," he said. "It's going to be okay."

"You don't know that. It was okay today, but anything could happen. We don't know if—" she began to say. He put his finger on her lips.

"Fourteen weeks. She said it. You're in the second trimester."

Natalie shook her head. "It's not a guarantee. So many things could still go wrong."

"Or everything could go right," he said. "Whatever happens, good or bad, we'll get through it together." He took both her hands in his. "Okay? I want you. I want to be with you. For better or worse. Please." He lifted her hands to his lips. "Please, Nat."

"I'm so sorry, Ben," she said. "I never should have left you. It wasn't fair. It wasn't your fault. I—"

"I forgive you," he interrupted.

"You do?"

"Maybe everything that happened was what needed to happen to get us to where we are right now."

She made a sound halfway between a laugh and a sob. "You really think so?"

"Of course. Nattie, I love you."

"I love you, too."

He put his hand on her belly, smiling. "No matter what." His smile deepened. "Both of you."

-53-

Richard opened his eyes and saw a beautiful young girl standing next to his bed. Her dark hair hung in loose waves on either side of her pretty, pale face. She smiled when she saw his eyes open.

He stared at her, his brow furrowed. "Rosie?" His voice was muffled. He reached toward his face, touching the oxygen mask that covered his nose and mouth.

Her eyes filled with concern. "No, Daddy, it's me. Bella."

He knew that; of course he knew that. Bella had those big brown eyes and freckled cheeks, not Rosie. He moved the oxygen aside. "Bella." He smiled at her, trying to extinguish the fear in her eyes. "I'm sorry. Your old dad must have been dreaming." His back ached. He shifted in the bed.

"Here, let me help you." She straightened his pillows and pushed a button that raised the head of the bed a bit. "Better?"

"Thank you, angel."

She sat in the chair, taking his hand. "Was it a nice dream?"

He nodded. Had it been a dream? His sister Rose had been here, right next to him, waiting for him to wake up. She had whispered something into his ear, he was sure of it. If only he could remember the words.

Hannah walked into the room then, smiling to see him awake. "Hey, Dad." She bent to kiss his forehead.

He moved the mask aside again. "Hey, princess. Where's your mom?"

"She'll be here in a little while. They're having a meeting at the house."

"Who's having a meeting?"

Hannah and Bella looked at each other.

The nurse walked into the room. "Good morning," she said, her voice cheerful. "You look a lot better."

"I feel better, too. Does that mean I can get out of here today?"

"We'll see what the doctor says." She looked him over and checked some of the monitors and tubes connected to him. "Okay, ladies," she said, addressing the girls. "We're going to help your dad get cleaned up and changed. Why don't you go get some breakfast in the cafeteria and give us about forty-five minutes?"

Bella looked at Richard. "Is that okay, Daddy?"

"I'm not going anywhere." He winked at her.

Natalie got a knot in her stomach as Ben parked the car in Melinda's driveway. The house had always intimidated her. She stared out the window, unable to open the car door.

"They must spend a fortune on landscaping," Ben said.

She made an attempt to laugh, but couldn't quite do it. They'd gotten a few hours of sleep, but hers had been fitful, her mind refusing to slow down the pace of her thoughts enough to let her relax.

It wouldn't be long until they needed to be on the road back to Philadelphia, and she didn't want to be here instead of at the hospital with Richard.

"Are you coming inside?"

"I guess so," she said.

"Hey." He took her hand. "We don't have to."

"I know."

Melinda opened the front door as they approached the house. "Good morning." She greeted them each with a hug as they stepped inside.

A brown dog stood next to Melinda, eager to greet them. "Hey, Nora." She bent to pet her. She looked around, thinking she could probably fit her entire apartment in the foyer. She smelled coffee, and her stomach grumbled.

"Come on out to the deck. Everyone else is here." Melinda led them down through the wide hallway towards the rear of the house. As they passed the kitchen, she stopped to pour them each a cup of coffee.

Neil, Mike, and Ruth sat around a large table under an umbrella on the deck. The table was set with a spread of baked goods, pastries, and fruit. Mike and Ruth both stood to hug Natalie before she sat down, and Natalie introduced Ruth to Ben.

When they were seated, Mike asked if he could lead them in a prayer. After he finished, Melinda began to speak.

"We arranged a meeting with the oncologist this morning at ten. I wanted you all with us because I think if we go to Richard as a united front, he'll take what we're saying a little more easily."

"Either that, or he'll think we're ganging up on him," Mike said.

Melinda continued. "You all know this man. He is stubborn as an ox. The more he fixes his mind

on something, the harder it is to get him to see reason. He had it in his head that he was going to make a miraculous recovery and never have to tell any of us just how sick he was. Bless his heart."

Everyone laughed.

"He's well enough to leave the hospital now, but he needs full time care. He can't go back to living on his own at the hotel. Neil and I have decided to invite him to stay here with us and the girls. We'll arrange for a hospital bed and visiting nurses, and I can take time off from work for however long he's with us. Honestly, it wasn't my first choice. We talked about a nursing facility. But Neil thinks he would do better here."

"That's a lot to take on, Melinda," Ruth said. "Are you sure? He could come stay with us. He's always been welcome."

"It's so kind of you to offer, Ruth," Neil said.

"Of course," Ruth replied.

"It is a lot of work," Melinda admitted.

"The invitation stands," Mike said.

"Thank you." Melinda looked at Neil. "I guess we might have to offer it as a second option in case he flat out refuses to come here."

"He won't refuse," Natalie said.

They all turned to look at her. Her cheeks blazed. She'd overstepped. They needed her to be another voice in the chorus when they talked to Richard about coming to stay here, but it was clear they hadn't expected her to express an opinion.

She looked down. "I know you guys don't know me that well, so you don't have to include me in your decision or whatever. But I know the thing Richard loves almost as much as all of you is this house. He still thinks of it as home. He might protest at first because he doesn't want your pity," she said, looking up at Melinda, who laughed. "But I know he'd rather be here than anyplace else."

"She's right," Mike said.

"I agree," Neil said.

"Thank you, Natalie." Melinda smiled at her.

They filed into his room one by one. Melinda, Neil, Mike, Ruth, Natalie, Ben. As everyone said their hellos, Hannah and Bella left to go wait outside, but the room was still packed.

Richard sat in one of the only two chairs in the room. After helping him get washed, they'd gotten him out of bed. Although he'd wobbled a bit, he'd made it a few steps to the chair, free from most of the medical equipment that had been attached to his body. He still needed oxygen, but it was supplied through a tube under his nose rather than the mask. He'd had some food and a cup of coffee. It felt better to be sitting up, though his back still ached. He would have preferred to have clothes on instead of a damned hospital gown.

Ruth settled herself into the empty chair, and Ben suggested that Natalie sit on the bed. So she'd told him. And he'd taken it well. They were going to have a baby. That warmed his old heart. He wished he'd be around to see their dream come true.

"You're looking better, Richard," Neil said, taking the lead.

"I feel okay," Richard said. "Although the way y'all are looking at me is making me a little nervous."

Neil glanced at his wife. "So, your oncologist is on her way."

"I don't know if we can fit one more person in this room," Melinda said.

"I can step out," Ben volunteered.

"You don't have to," Natalie said, taking his hand.

"Good morning." The doctor stepped into the room. Melinda offered a brief introduction of everyone present. "Wow, Richard, you have a big family."

His eyes prickled. "I guess I do." So maybe it wasn't a picture-perfect television family, maybe it was a patchwork of exes and recovering addicts and other characters, but so what? They were all here because of him, in one way or another. These were his people. Even Ben had shook his hand and smiled at him today.

"How are you feeling?"

"Better," he said. "How soon can I get out of here?"

"That's what we're here to talk about." She handed him a folder with papers inside. The words *Hospice and Palliative Care* were printed beneath the hospital's logo.

"We'd like you to come and stay with us at the house, Richard," Neil said. "You can see the girls every day."

"We'll set up a space for you in the den," Melinda added. "You'll have a nurse come each day to check in on you."

"And I'll stop by and visit every day," Mike chimed in.

He was being allowed back home, and it should have made him happy. But he was going home to die.

"I appreciate the offer. But I can go back to the hotel."

"Richard," the doctor said. "You can't stay by yourself."

"I don't want to be a burden."

"You're not a burden, sugar," Ruth said. "You are a gift. Everyone here cares for you. You know that."

Richard looked at each of their faces. Mike, his best friend, his rock, who had stood by him every time he needed him. Ruth, who had shown him more love in the handful of years he'd known her than his own mother had for his whole life. Melinda, who had given birth to his girls and who had loved him when he was at his most unlovable. Who loved him still, in her own way. And Neil, who loved Melinda the way she deserved to be loved.

He looked at Natalie and Ben. They belonged to each other. He could let himself see it now. He could see the guarded joy on Ben's face, now that he knew about the baby. Natalie was beautiful, glowing, even though her eyes were sad every time she glanced his way. He would never forget the way she'd flashed those eyes at him, standing under the tall tree with the little boy's legs dangling above them. She'd grabbed onto his heart and he'd never let go.

He thought about his daughters. They had turned out so well despite having a fuckup like him for a father. Hannah, so smart and kind, about to become an adult and go out into the world. She wanted to be a doctor. She'd told him she decided to go to Penn so she could be close to Natalie. It made his heart happy to think of them looking out for one another. And Bella, his sweet little girl. He wanted to be with them more than anything he'd ever wanted.

"Come home, Richard," Melinda said.

"I'm going to be a pain in your ass."

"You always were." She grinned and shook her head.

Everyone breathed a sigh of relief.

"Okay," the doctor said. "We have some paperwork to fill out, so some of you might want to step out for a bit."

"We can get started on it," Melinda said. "Natalie and Ben have to leave soon, so we'll let them say goodbye." The rest of them filed out of the room.

"I'll give you two a few minutes." Ben kissed the top of Natalie's head. He turned and held out his hand towards Richard, who shook it.

"Thank you for bringing her," Richard said.

"You're welcome."

"And congratulations." He grinned.

Ben looked at his wife, who blushed. "Thank you."

Natalie watched him leave the room.

"Happy looks good on you," he said. "Both of you. I'm glad you told him."

She pulled a sonogram picture out of her purse and handed it to him, smiling, tears in her eyes.

"Look at that," he said, grinning. He handed it back to her.

Her face turned serious. "I don't want to go."

"Come here, baby girl."

She went to him and perched on the arm of the chair, letting him put his arms around her.

"Don't you worry about me. I'm in good hands. The best."

"I know. But still."

"Want to know the worst thing about dying?" he said. "You wind up being the one giving out sympathy to everyone else, instead of the other way around."

She laughed. "That sounds familiar."

He chuckled, holding her tighter. "I never realized before."

"I don't know how to say goodbye."

"Then don't. But go home," he said. "Live your life. Be happy." He put his hand on her belly.

"Thank you for being my safe place to land." She kissed him.

"I was trying to get into your pants from the start," he said with a wicked grin.

Natalie laughed. She pressed her forehead against his. "I'm going to miss you so much."

"I'll always be with you. I promise."

"I love you, Richard."

He kissed her lips. "I love you, too, Natalie. Always."

She gave him one last hug, got up from the chair, and walked towards the doorway. "I'll see you around."

"See you." He waved.

She walked out of the room and leaned against the wall, squeezing her eyes shut, trying to breathe. Out of nowhere, she felt Ben's arms around her.

"I'm here." He held her close.

Melinda and Neil were still at the nurses' station with the doctor and another nurse. Natalie walked over and held up a hand to wave goodbye.

"Excuse me for a minute," Melinda said, standing. She put her arms around Natalie. "I'm so glad you made the trip."

"Me too."

"We have plenty of room at the house if you and Ben want to stay another night." Melinda stood back and looked at them.

"I wish we could. Thank you so much," Natalie said. "For everything."

"No, thank you. Trust me, I couldn't have gotten through to him today without you being there."

"I hope everything goes okay. Please keep in touch with me."

Melinda looked at her, tilting her head to the side. "Are you sure you can't stay?"

Natalie shook her head. "We have to get back."

"Well, you're welcome anytime. I mean it. Even after..." She faltered, blinked her eyes, and gave Natalie a sad smile.

"Thank you." She hugged her again.

-54-

ichard's eyes opened. It took him a moment to identify his surroundings. As it had every time he'd awoken since his arrival, the memory washed over him. He knew where he was. In his den, in the house that was once his home. Was now his home, again. He was going to die here, in this room.

Richard accepted this fact with a sense of peace, unlike the other facts flung at him in recent months. This cozy, wood-paneled room was his sanctuary; his retreat. His *man cave*, although he disliked that term. *Den* had always worked. He'd spent many hours here, working, reading, watching Tennessee football on a Saturday afternoon. Drinking whiskey in the quiet. Sometimes the girls came in to play at his feet while he worked at the desk. It wasn't a bad place in which to spend the remainder of his days.

A few things had changed. The photos, degrees, and artwork that had hung on the walls were now in storage. A new, but smaller, TV was in the corner. But the burgundy paint was the same. The built-in bookshelves were the same. The big leather sofa was the same. It even had the same smell.

His mahogany desk had been pushed against the wall to make room for the rented hospital bed on which he now lay, in track pants and a t-shirt, an oxygen mask on his face. The oxygen compressor

emitted a constant, tedious buzzing sound he tried to tune out.

The pain medications had him disconnected from time. Sometimes he woke up and everything was dark. Sometimes, it seemed like a few minutes later that the sunlight came streaming through the windows and his girls were here, or Mike. The best days were when one of them took him out to the deck and he could sit in the sunshine for a while, or look at the stars.

It was Melinda who was with him most of the time, sitting close by, reading a book or watching TV, helping him change position, giving him juice to drink. He asked her for a shot of whiskey more than once.

"I wish I could, darlin'," she always said, laughter in her eyes.

"It wasn't all bad, was it?" he asked her one day.

"No, it wasn't," she answered. "We had a good life." She kissed his forehead.

He had pain, almost constant, despite the meds. It hurt to breathe. Some days, Rosie came and sat by his side, holding his hand. Sometimes, it was his grandmother. *Come with us*, they said without speaking. *It's time.*

"I'm not ready," he'd say. Hannah's graduation was in a few days. He would hold on until then. He had to.

It was daytime. He wasn't sure of the day. He heard a voice singing. An angel? He opened his eyes.

"There he is." Ruth smiled at him.

He tried to smile.

"We're here, buddy," Mike said. "We're right here, and we love you."

It was dark. Bella held the phone to his ear so Natalie could say goodnight.

"I miss you," she said.

"Miss you too."

Morning again. He couldn't talk much now. He opened his eyes and saw Hannah in her cap and gown. So grown up.

"I love you, Dad." She kissed his cheek.

It was dark. Hannah and Bella came in to kiss him goodnight.

"Where's Mom?" he whispered.

"I'm right here." Melinda took his hand.

"I love you," he said, looking into her eyes. She nodded, blinking back tears.

"We love you too, Daddy," Bella said.

"Go to bed, sweetheart." Melinda kissed her forehead. She turned back to Richard, tears streaming down her face as Bella left the room.

Richard took the oxygen mask off and handed it to Melinda.

"Dad, no," Hannah said.

"It's okay, honey," Melinda said. She put it down and shut off the compressor.

Richard reached for her hand again. She sat on the edge of the bed, looking into his eyes.

"You can go to bed, darlin'," she said to Hannah.

"I want to stay." Hannah put her hand on top of theirs. "I love you, Dad."

"I love you, Richard." Melinda squeezed his hand.

Richard smiled, closing his eyes.

-55-

Natalie awoke early on a Saturday morning. She glanced at the clock. Almost six. Her right arm was asleep. She groaned, rolling from one side to the other, flexing her fingers until the pins and needles subsided. Her hand rested upon her belly, which was beginning to feel a little less soft than it had before.

She felt something then, like a gentle nudging from within, pushing against her hand. Her breath caught. It happened again, with more force this time. "Hey, you," she said. She was rewarded with a soft pummeling sensation. It was the most incredible thing she'd ever felt. She giggled.

"Ben," she said. "Ben, wake up."

"Hey." His voice was sleepy. He rolled towards her.

"You have to feel this." She put his hand on her belly. The nudging happened again.

His face broke into a grin. "Natalie, that's amazing."

"He's really in there. Our baby." It was the first time she had said the word *baby* out loud. Although it was still too early to confirm, she suspected it was a boy.

They hadn't told their families yet. It was still too soon. But they were going to look at houses today. In the city, close to Lisa and George's. Lisa's baby was due in four weeks, a little girl, just as

they'd hoped. Natalie grinned in anticipation of the look on her sister's face when she heard her news.

Ben kissed the back of her neck. She turned onto her back and looked up at him. "I love you," he said, lacing his fingers with hers and laying them flat against her belly. "And I love you." He kissed the spot where they'd felt the kicking.

It's going to work out, she told herself. She steadied her breath as the ever-present anxiety began to rise within her, threatening to ruin the happiness she was beginning to allow herself. Richard had said it was going to work out. She trusted him.

The girls had called her every night since their return from Atlanta. Richard still slept most of the day. He had stopped eating. Only a few sips of water or juice now and then. He was in a lot of pain. Sometimes they put the phone to his ear so Natalie could say goodnight. Last night Hannah said he was awake, and that he'd smiled at the sound of Natalie's voice.

A sudden breeze fluttered the curtains of her open bedroom window and drifted against her face. For a second, she smelled the ocean, and with it the faintest hint of cigarette smoke. She sat up.

"Natalie?" Ben looked at her, concerned. The baby kicked again, echoing his father's worry. "You okay?"

"It's Richard."

Ben's brow furrowed. "What do you mean?"

Her phone began to ring.

Ben's face fell. "No," he whispered.

"Hello?" She kept her voice calm.

"Hi Natalie, it's Neil."

"Hey, Neil." She held her breath.

"I'm so sorry to have to tell you this, but Richard passed away just a little while ago."

Natalie breathed out. Ben took her hand.

"He told us last night he was ready, and he took off his oxygen and just went to sleep. It was peaceful. Melinda and Hannah were with him."

"How are they?"

"They're pretty worn out. And very sad. But he's not suffering anymore."

Natalie didn't say anything.

"He wanted me to tell you something. I'm not sure why, but he said, 'Tell Natalie it's a boy'."

Her eyes burned. "He said that?" She made a sound somewhere in between laughter and sobbing.

Neil laughed. "Yep. Does that mean anything?"

"Yes." Natalie fell apart.

"Neil? Hey, it's Ben." He took the phone from Natalie's hand, putting his arms around her. "It's okay, kid," he whispered. "I'm right here."

SPRING 2007

ulls called to one another as gentle waves rocked the boat, still tied up at the marina as its occupants waited for the last three members of their group. Hannah and Bella stood together, taking turns peering back towards the parking lot to check if the car had arrived yet. They didn't even know what kind of car they were looking for, but they kept checking.

Mike and Neil discussed the Braves, who looked great this spring, while Melinda and Ruth sat talking on the other side of the boat deck. Bella was giving her mother a hard time. It was her first year of high school, her father was gone, and Hannah was away at college. Her grades had tanked and she'd made friends with some older girls Melinda didn't care for. Ruth assured her she was doing the best she could and Bella would be okay. And that she was praying for her. For all of them.

Every head turned when they heard the crunch of tires on the gravel lot. Bella squealed. "They're here!"

Ben exited the driver's side and waved in the direction of the boat. He walked around to the passenger side of the car and opened the rear door.

"My little brother!" Bella said.

"Bella." Hannah rolled her eyes. "You know he's not really our little brother, right?"

"Duh. I'm not an idiot. He's the closest I'll ever get to one, though."

"True." Hannah laughed.

"It's not fair, you get to see him all the time. This is only the second time I'm seeing him."

Bella had flown to Philadelphia with Melinda right before Christmas, when Hannah finished her first semester, to visit Natalie and meet the baby. It was true Hannah had seen him several times, but with her class schedule and work, going to Natalie and Ben's house was a luxury.

Natalie got out of the back seat of the car, carrying the baby in his car seat. Bella rushed to meet her, giving her a hug and then eagerly holding out her hands to take the baby. Natalie smiled, handing over the seat with her son buckled inside.

"Hi, Brendan." She lifted the seat to her face and gave the baby a kiss. She laughed as Brendan grabbed a fistful of her hair and shoved it in his mouth.

"It gets less cute the fifteenth time he does it," his mother said as she and Ben boarded the boat. They had the happy, exhausted look of new parents.

Hugs were exchanged all around as Neil and Melinda untied the boat and prepared the launch. Hannah and Bella took the baby out of his seat and took turns fussing over him, tickling him under the chin to make him laugh. His parents, grateful for the break, sat near the stern of the boat.

Neil navigated south along the narrow inlet, rounding the southern tip of the island and heading toward the open water. The ocean was relatively calm, the sea breezes gentle. The sunshine peeked in and out of the clouds.

"Perfect fishing weather." Melinda looked up at the sky. "Richard would have loved this."

Hannah handed Brendan to his father and stood with her mother, holding her hand. Bella took the other one.

Brendan looked at the water, wide-eyed, as Ben bounced him in his arms. He had his mama's blond curls, his daddy's brown eyes, and a dimple on each chubby cheek. Natalie smiled at the two of them, and Ben leaned over to kiss her. Once they were far enough from the shore, Neil cut the engine and let the boat drift.

"I'd like to begin with a prayer," Mike said. They all gathered around him, in silence, at the stern of the boat. "Let's join hands." He said a prayer of thanks for the day, for each person there, and for the love that united them. "Thank you for my brother, Richard. He was a good man, a complicated man, but most of all he was a father. A friend. A partner. We're grateful for the time we had with him." He paused to draw a breath. "Amen."

Everyone else echoed, "Amen." Ruth sang a verse of *Amazing Grace.*

Hannah brought out the urn. She unscrewed the lid, tears dripping down her cheeks. Each person took a turn tossing a handful of ashes onto the water.

"I can't believe you've been gone a whole year," Natalie whispered as the ashes fell from her hand. "I miss you."

They stood watching as the ashes were slowly swallowed by the sea.

"Dad always wanted to live on the water," Hannah said, tears in her eyes. Ruth hugged her.

When the ashes were no longer visible, Neil started the engine and began piloting back to the marina.

Natalie sat overlooking the stern as she nursed Brendan. Melinda came to sit by her side. "He's just precious, Natalie."

"Thank you," she said, smiling.

"You look so happy. And tired."

"Always." Natalie laughed. "He was miserable on the plane. Plus, he's teething." She looked down at his face. "But I love him so much. It's overwhelming. Sometimes I can't even believe he's mine."

"I remember those days." She glanced at her daughters. "Sometimes, I still feel that way."

Natalie eased Brendan's sleepy mouth off her breast and readjusted her bra. "Would you like to hold him?"

"Could I?" She put out her arms, and Natalie gently placed Brendan into them. Melinda kissed the top of his head before putting it on her shoulder. She patted his back. "It's so much easier when they're tiny," she murmured, inhaling his scent.

"I know Bella's been giving you a hard time." Melinda looked at her, puzzled. "Hannah told me," Natalie explained.

"Right."

"Fourteen is tough for everyone, I think."

"I know. She's making it harder for herself, though."

"I've been talking to her a little bit. She texts me every once in a while, you know."

"I didn't know." Melinda sighed. "She won't talk to me."

"She's a good kid. I think she's going to be okay. Grief is hard."

"Thank you, Natalie. You'll let me know if anything –"

"Of course, Mel."

"I'm glad she has you."

"I'm glad I have her," Natalie said. "And you. Thanks for letting me be part of the family."

Ben came up behind her, wrapping his arms around her and kissing her cheek.

"He's perfect," he said, looking at his son, sleeping in Melinda's arms.

"He is, isn't he?" The depth of love she had for him took her breath away. Life with an infant was hard sometimes, but it was worth it. Nothing else mattered when she looked at his angelic face. Like Ben had said, everything that happened had gotten them to where they were now.

She turned and put her arms around Ben, hugging him close as they approached the shore.

Acknowledgments

Getting this novel from idea to print has been a long and rewarding process.

To Mae Wagner, my constant partner along this writing journey, my collaborator, my encourager, my dear friend: I love you and am grateful for the gift of you every single day.

To Lisa Danford, thank you for creating the B2W group way back when. This book would not exist without you.

Special thanks to my editor and friend Britt Laux for believing in Holding Pattern and helping make it better than I knew it could be. To CL Walters, Willow Ford, and Leisa Greene, thank you for being my first readers and for your invaluable feedback, help, and encouragement. To KC Loesener and Dustin Nelson, thanks for helping this introvert gain some confidence! To the incredible women in my Carpe Diem writing group, I can't say enough about what an honor it is to create alongside you every week.

Thanks to my three favorite humans, Jacob, Evie, and Judah, for putting up with your weird, nerdy mom. And for just being you. Thanks to my mom and dad, for giving me life and putting books in my little hands.

To Matt, my husband, my person, my lobster. Thank you for everything. Always. I love you.

And finally, to Jimmy, who helped me conceive of this story, and who continues to inspire me long after leaving the earth. Thank you for being the whisper in my ear, the devil on my shoulder, the encouraging voice every time I wanted to quit. I miss you.

ABOUT THE AUTHOR

Maggie Friedenberg lives in Philadelphia, PA with her husband and three children. When she's not writing, you can find her advocating for women's health with PCOS Challenge, helping co-host the Rainy Day Collective Podcast, catching up on Star Wars and Marvel shows, or, most likely, curling up with a good book and a cup of coffee. Her short fiction has been published by Indie It Press. This is her first novel.

Visit her website at
www.maggiefriedenberg.com
and follow her on Instagram
@maggiefriedenberg.